DR. FELLOW

Copyright © 2024 by Big Woods Publishing, LLC

Book Cover by Silver Grace, Ever After Cover Design

Edited by: Sadie, dottheiedit.com

All rights reserved. No part of this publication may be reproduced, distributed, or transmitted in any form or by any means, including photocopying, recording, or other electronic or mechanical methods, without the prior written permission of the publisher, except as permitted by U.S. copyright law. For permission requests, contact Big Woods Publishing, LLC.

The story, all names, characters, and incidents portrayed in this production are fictitious. Any similarity to real persons, living or dead, is purely coincidental and not intended by the author.

To all of my nurses—
The degradation kink in this one might hit a little too close to home.

Chapter 1

Walker

I wipe a few excess drops of Sweetwater 420 from my stubble-covered chin as the lively neighborhood bar hums around us. We opted to sit on the patio tonight because the January air is unseasonably warm—and by warm, I mean it's in the low fifties and we're huddled beneath a space heater.

"You might be slower at chugging beer than you are at throwing stitches," I comment, unable to help myself from making the dig.

Beau's gaze narrows on mine as he slowly glugs down the rest of his beer, his overly friendly brown eyes shining with mirth despite the shitty day that we had.

One of our easiest cases was riddled with complications, and instead of using it as a teaching opportunity, I took my frustrations—both personally and professionally—out on him.

But what did the big lunatic do afterward?

He found me in the hallway, clapped me on the back, and reminded me of our plan to get drinks tonight. Sometimes I genuinely wonder if he has a screw loose in his head considering the rest of my interns know better than to even look in my direction when I get like this.

"I'm still faster than the others though." He shoots me a megawatt grin and signals our waiter for another round. "And much better looking too."

I shake my head, concealing a smile—the guy really is talented, even if he's arrogant as hell. Out of the four orthopedic surgery interns who have been following me around since July, Beau is easily my favorite. Not just because he's a goon, but because he's taken the time to get to know me when I didn't deserve it.

Spending upwards of a hundred hours a week with someone for six months forces you to learn a thing or two about each other. I usually try to stick to surface-level pleasantries, but he's taken our professional relationship and thrown it out the window. And as much as I enjoy giving him shit, I really am thankful for his friendship.

"You sure you're down for another round?" I ask, glancing at my phone to check the time. At this point, we've already been here for several hours, and while I have nowhere to be, I'm sure he's sick of my grumpy ass at this point.

"Fuck yeah I'm down," Beau drawls, his southern accent becoming more pronounced as the night wears on. Two frosty glasses and a full pitcher are placed in front of us, and he pours us both fresh beers before taking his and holding it up in a toast. "We're celebrating tonight, dude."

I arch my brow at him because it sure as shit doesn't feel like we should be celebrating anything after my atrocious fuckup in the OR this morning. Sure, everything worked out in the end, but at this point I should be delivering consistent results, not missing something even an intern would have caught. And considering my board exams are only six months away, my mistake doesn't exactly put me in a celebratory mood.

Beau answers my unspoken question, oblivious to my inner turmoil, "I heard you accepted the sports fellowship at University Hospital. Do you have any idea how fucking cool that is?"

My beer starts to turn sour in my stomach as shame floods through me. The University Hospital fellowship would be cool—impressive even—if it hadn't come at such a huge cost.

"Sure do," I comment dryly, letting out a long exhale as I try to rid myself of the emotion lodged in my throat.

"What made you finally give in? You love me so much that you couldn't fathom leaving Atlanta yet?" He runs his fingers through his light-brown waves, clearly amused with himself as he strokes his oversized ego.

"Something like that," I reply, keeping my tone cool and controlled with the hope that he'll drop it.

I close my eyes, savoring the hoppy taste of my beer as the bar buzzes around us. When I open them, Beau is lounging back against his worn, wooden chair, attention glued to the naked ring finger of my left hand.

We both know that he won't say anything about it—he'll happily sit in silence until I bridge the gap and come clean. This isn't our first rodeo, and he's about as stubborn as a prize-winning bull.

I lean forward, resting my forearms on the sticky table between us. "Got anything you want to ask me?" I ask, trying my hardest to make him uncomfortable.

His gaze flicks up to meet mine as he takes a deliberate sip of his beer, allowing the silence to stretch between us just long enough for the question to hang heavy in the air.

He finally shrugs.

"Don't ask. Don't tell. That's the motto I live by these days." His lips curl into a thin line like he's trying to hide a smirk. "Just ask Parker."

I can't help the slight chuckle that escapes me.

While Beau was in med school, he spent a year shadowing Parker, which forced them to become close from sheer proximity. At this point though, Parker might say that they're a little too close, considering Beau is now both living with, and dating, his sister.

"You're such a little shit."

"You calling me small?" he challenges, purposely flexing his massive bicep as he picks up his glass again. "I may be two inches shorter than you, but trust me, I'm big where it counts." He winks at me and tips back his beer to chug it down.

I follow suit, releasing a long, satisfied exhale when I finish. It's a damn good thing neither one of us has to work tomorrow, because at this rate we'll be staggering out of this bar completely wasted.

"You want to talk about it?" Beau asks softly.

His attention drifts back to my naked ring finger. The finger that's been surrounded by a thick gold band for the past five years of my life. The finger that I thought would be surrounded by a thick gold band until the day I died. The finger that has only been bare for a week because even though my wife left me a month ago, I wasn't willing to admit to anyone, let alone myself, that I had failed.

Pathetic.

I force a laugh, more out of exhaustion than amusement, and rake my fingers through my dark, finger-length hair. "It's all good. I've talked about it enough in therapy."

His mouth drops open dramatically. "How could you? I thought I was your go-to therapist."

"Too peppy," I state simply, though that's the farthest thing from the truth.

Because the truth is that Beau was there for me when I finally emerged from the surging whitewater rapids of residency and recognized that my marriage was in trouble last fall. He gave me space to talk through my issues, somehow sensing that I needed a friend even when I didn't want one. Unfortunately, even his admittedly good advice didn't matter in the end. Our relationship was broken beyond repair, and my efforts were too little, too late—Lane had run into the arms of another man who could give her everything I couldn't.

The funny thing is, I don't even blame her for what she did. Throughout residency, it never felt like we were on the same wavelength. While I had an entire life inside the hospital that consumed my every waking moment for years, she had a life in the real world that was just as full—without me in it.

Beau snorts at my critique. "What would you have preferred? If I told you there was no hope at all, and that you shouldn't bother trying?"

"At least you would have been right for once in your life."

"So you took the fellowship," he states, grabbing the half-full pitcher to refill our glasses.

"I took the fellowship," I confirm, my voice hollow.

The statement hangs in the air like a thousand shards of failure prickling my soul. Accepting the year-long sports medicine fellowship was never my original plan. Yeah, it's incredibly prestigious and something I've worked for my entire career. But I was supposed to give it all up for her. I had promised to give it all up for her—to make a sacrifice for once in our relationship and put her first.

So forgive me for not feeling like I have anything to be excited about. The fellowship only reminds me that I'm a failure.

What a thing to celebrate . . .

"Well, it's her loss," Beau declares, clinking his glass against mine with a heavy hand. "She's going to be so pissed when you meet all those famous athletes."

"I think you're probably more jealous than she is," I reply. "She hates sports."

"God," he groans painfully, drawing out the word. "I knew I was right about her. She's Satan's mistress, and I hope she chokes on his fiery ball sack."

I let out a reluctant laugh because he might be a pain in my ass, but the man knows how to lighten up a conversation. "Did you even meet her?"

"No," he confirms, shaking his tipsy head. "But it doesn't matter because she hurt my Walker-boo-boo. She's as good as dead to me."

I can't help the way my lips twitch. Not because I wish my future ex-wife any ill-will, but because I appreciate my friend's blind loyalty—it's refreshing.

"You're lucky I like you. If anyone else called me that, they'd be smacked upside the head."

Beau snorts, staring at the black ink on my left arm. "You know you don't scare me right? I mean, the tattoo sleeve really gives you that don't fuck with me, intimidating vibe. But I know you're just a big softie."

He pauses and pulls out his phone to answer a text. "Plus, this is payback for that stupid-ass 'Buff' nickname of yours. You know it's caught on, and everyone in the OR calls me that now? I swear to God, I'm the butt of every joke with the attendings."

I shrug my shoulders. "You already were the butt of every joke, bud."

Beau's eyes flick to the parking lot, his usual swagger giving way to an almost guilty hesitation. Tracking his gaze, I see Parker Winters making his way through the line of cars toward our table.

Parker and I have known each other for several years because he was a year ahead of me in residency, though he specialized in general surgery rather than orthopedics like myself. I respect him a ton, and have always thought that we were similar, at least in terms of our personalities. But until Beau brought us together last fall, our relationship was strictly professional, filled with case communication or the occasional gripe about some new departmental policy. It's been surprisingly nice getting to know him a little better outside of the hospital these past few months.

I glance back at Beau who grimaces, as if in a silent apology for inviting him to our night out. To be honest though, I don't mind—I could use the distraction. And considering Parker's appearance, something tells me that he could too.

I've never seen him look so disheveled. Typically, Parker is the poster boy for calm, cool, and collected, even when it comes to his life outside of the hospital. But tonight he looks like a completely different person. The expensive, tailored outfits I'm used to seeing have been replaced by a Yale long-sleeve T-shirt and tattered black sweatpants. His dark-brown hair is tousled, like he's run his fingers through it hundreds of times today, and his jaw is covered in at least a week's worth of untamed beard growth. In summary, he looks like shit.

"Sorry," he says, sliding into the open chair beside Beau. "Lap chole took a little longer than expected because some idiot intern nicked an artery. You guys staying a little longer?"

Beau crosses his meaty arms and turns to face his friend. "One, don't hate on the interns. We're trying our best," he argues. A sly smirk forms on his lips like he's about to poke the bear. "Two, we're here for as long as the guest of honor wants. I owe him a fuck ton of alcohol for the extra shit he had to do after your tantrum, *brother*."

He enunciates the last word, causing Parker's mouth to set into a firm line. "What did I tell you about calling me that?"

Unbeknownst to anyone, Beau was dating Parker's sister for a while in secret. I'm still not sure exactly how the details came to light, nor do I really care, but Parker was pissed when he found out. He told the entire department that Beau withheld his type 1 diabetes diagnosis from a pre-employment physical, and claimed that the omission put a patient at risk during a case.

Fortunately, nothing came of Parker's outburst in the end. But because Beau was my intern at the time, it resulted in a ton of paperwork and conversations with administration that I would have rather not had.

Did I think Parker's reaction was warranted? No—it was childish as fuck. But he found me the next day to apologize, and we moved on like adults. It's water under the bridge now.

"What?" Beau muses, his broad chest heaving with suppressed laughter. "You told me if I ever hurt Claire, I'd be dead meat. Well, I happen to like my meat, and so does your sister, which means that I could be your *brother* one day. I'm just stating the facts here."

Parker's stormy blue eyes find mine, searching for an ally.

"Buff," I grunt, giving him a warning glare. "Get your ass up and grab us another pitcher. My glass is empty."

Beau rolls his eyes. Pushing back from the table, he bows exaggeratedly and says, "Yes, sir. Can I get you anything else?"

"A fucking clue," I shoot back.

Parker lets out a strained chuckle as Beau makes his way to the bar.

"Thanks," he murmurs. "Been a rough couple of weeks, and the moron doesn't know when to quit. He really is perfect for my sister."

I get the sense that there's more going on with Parker than a simple frustration over his best friend dating his sister. But I have no idea what it could be because the guy seems to have everything. He's a well-respected junior attending, comes from a fuck ton of money, and is engaged to an incredible woman. From an outside perspective, he won the damn lottery.

"You okay?" I ask hesitantly.

He doesn't strike me as the kind of person who enjoys sharing personal shit, so I wouldn't blame him if he told me to fuck right off. It's what I would do if I were in his shoes. But if the litany of therapy I've been in since December has taught me anything, it's that sometimes it's not good to keep things bottled up.

Parker exhales, shifting his attention to the crowd. I don't push him because I understand his unspoken words all too well, and we sit in comfortable silence as the bar noise drowns out whatever thoughts are ricocheting through his mind.

A few moments later Beau returns, balancing two pitchers and an extra glass in his arms. "Peace offering," he says, setting them down and pouring out three drinks.

Parker looks up to meet his gaze, a faint smile flickering on his lips. "Thanks, *brother*."

Beau's eyes light up and before taking a seat, he claps Parker on the back and says, "Rolls right off the tongue. Doesn't it?"

"Who knows . . . at this rate, you'll probably get married before I do."

Parker's comment feels like it's out of left field because his engagement party was only a few weeks ago, and at the time they seemed incredibly happy. So happy, in fact, that I had to excuse myself from their love bubble because it made me feel physically ill watching them cuddle on the balcony.

All of the amusement on Beau's face fades as he glances at me, and then at Parker. "Hey man, he doesn't mean anything. He's in the past."

Parker winces, staring into his full glass like it's a crystal ball. "Right."

I have no idea what they're talking about so I sip my beer quietly and let them work through their issues.

"What did Cass say?" Beau asks tentatively.

Parker's jaw clenches so hard that it looks like he might crack a tooth. "After she ran out of my office like a coward?" he snorts. "Nothing. We haven't spoken about it since."

"Hmmm." Beau leans back in his chair and crosses his ankle over his knee, just like a damn therapist. Honestly, if he wasn't so talented in the OR, I'd encourage him to go into psychiatry—he clearly enjoys this kind of thing. "Have you talked to Weston?"

Parker's nostrils flare at the name. "Not sure why that's my responsibility."

Beau continues, "I heard he left his fellowship and accepted the open attending position in general surgery."

They must be talking about Weston Southerland. He graduated residency with Parker and moved to Chicago for a trauma surgery fellowship. We got to know each other decently well over the past few years, and I always thought he was a solid guy, maybe a little too cocky for my liking, but we're surgeons—we're all cocky.

"Good for him," Parker sneers, finally taking a long swig of his cold beer. "Bastard gets everything he wants, doesn't he? Including my fiancée. They should just go ride off into the damn sunset together."

"That's out of pocket," Beau argues, his voice tense in a way I've never heard before. "Cass has no intention of doing that, which you would know if you would just fucking talk to her, rather than avoiding the conversation and working your dick off."

"We all work our dicks off," Parker corrects.

"Listen, you have every right to be angry. Hell, I'd be angry too. But holding onto that anger, especially without knowing every side of the story, is only doing more harm than good. There's more to it, I'm sure."

"Oh, you're sure?" Parker scoffs. His tongue momentarily darts across his lower lip as he narrows his eyes in challenge. "Because all I'm sure of, is that a little over a year ago my best friend of almost a decade single-handedly ruined both my surgical career and my relationship in a week. And then, when I finally pulled my shit together, my fiancée had the *audacity* to see him again and keep it from me. That's what I'm *sure* of."

I don't give a damn about petty work rumors and drama, so I doubt I know the full extent of the situation. But when Parker was in his chief year, there was some sort of incident with the research he and Wes were doing. It ultimately cost him his fellowship, which is how he ended up here as a general surgery attending after residency. As for his comment about his relationship, I don't have a clue what he's talking about.

"Cass wouldn't—"

"You know Wes was her first?" Parker interrupts, shooting icy blue daggers at Beau. "First kiss. First fuck. First *love*." He practically spits the last word, tilting his head back to focus on the night sky. "God, I'm so tired of constantly competing with him. What's the fucking point?"

He exhales like he's been holding on to those words for far too long.

Beau glances at me uncertainly, like he's not exactly sure how to respond to his best friend.

I have no skin in the game here, but I've learned a thing or two recently about relationships. If I can help someone avoid the same mistakes that I made, maybe my shitstorm of a life will be worth it.

"The point is that she loves *you*," I start, the words coming out more tersely than I intend. "So she loved someone first? Who cares? She loves *you* now."

Parker's eyes are soft and glassy as they meet mine. I'm not sure why he's listening to me instead of Beau, but I take it as a sign to continue.

"The point is that you have something people spend their entire lives searching for—a true partner. A partner who understands your life and your job in a way that not many people do. A partner who sees you in a way that nobody else does."

That's something I remember vividly from the engagement party—the way Cassidy looked at him. Parker isn't exactly the most likable guy in the world, and she was staring at him with rose-colored lenses on, like he was someone completely different than the person we've all gotten to know.

I don't think he realizes how unconditionally she loves him. And if he doesn't figure it out soon, he's going to end up just like me—alone.

"Listen, I know I'm not the guy to be doling out relationship advice," I offer with a humorless laugh. "But I do know this—the only person you're competing with right now is yourself. And you're never going to win until you get off your pompous ass, and start prioritizing your relationship."

Beau grins at me like a proud brother, but I ignore him and take a sip of my beer.

"Just trust me on this one."

Chapter 2

Morgan

I never thought that I would be interested in living in the burbs, but I'm starting to see the appeal. It's quiet, there's plenty of room for activities, and most importantly, there's running water. I would honestly force my best friend to let me stay another night if I didn't have to see her fiancé, Dr. Demonspawn around the house. Even a single night under Parker Winters's roof while I wait for the plumber to fix the pipes in my Virginia Highlands rental makes me nervous that I'm going to get kidnapped by his underlings and sent to his hellish lair.

"What do you think of Cliterate Cumsluts?" I ask, plopping down onto the brand-new sectional in Cassidy's massive living room.

I recently created a group text for my friends, and I've been waffling on the name of it for days. Cass keeps vetoing all of my suggestions because she hasn't spoken to her fiancé in a week and can't appreciate my brand of humor at the moment. But she knows that she can't reject my ideas forever—I'm impossible to resist.

"Do you have nothing better in your arsenal of alliteration?" Cassidy asks, rolling her hazel eyes as she tangles her bare feet with mine. "That's disgusting."

Her long blonde hair is pulled into a messy bun at the top of her head, a few wispy strands escaping to frame her face. She's wearing an oversized sorority T-shirt and boxers, and I try not to think about who owns the underwear because I'm currently lounging around in a matching outfit myself.

I got the call about the water situation this afternoon while I was at work, and since the plumber couldn't come until tomorrow, Cass offered to let me stay over tonight. I agreed, figuring that I could kill two birds with one stone—spending time with my bestie, and taking a nice hot shower.

"Claire liked the name," I respond defensively. "She said it's perfect because that's what she's turned into recently."

Cassidy's nose wrinkles, and she kicks my shin. "Gross, Morg. Some things are better left unsaid."

Giggling, I start to flick through the movie options on Netflix. Her future sister-in-law never actually said those words, I just wanted to see how she would respond—sometimes you've got to amuse yourself.

While Cass and I have been friends for several years because we work in the same department, I've only known Claire for a few months. But sometimes it feels like I've known her longer because we're so in sync. Honestly, if we weren't almost a foot apart in height, I would think we were twins who were separated at birth.

I was sad she couldn't hang tonight, but apparently she has her first nursing school exam next week and needs to study. I told her that studying is for losers, and the only things worth knowing are the ones that she'll learn in clinical, but she didn't believe me. One day she'll realize that I'm right about everything, just like everyone eventually does.

"What are your thoughts on Margarita Mamas?" I ask, moving my legs out of the strike zone to prop them on the white-washed coffee table which also looks brand new despite the slew of junk covering the surface.

An entire box of Mellow Mushroom pizza has already been stuffed into our mouths. A bottle of red wine is well on its way to being emptied. And we're about an hour away from passing out on the couch. Nights like these with my best friend are truly priceless.

"That group name would make sense if any of us were moms." Cassidy shoots me a concerned glare like she's trying to determine if I am, indeed, a mom.

I roll my eyes because she should know better. I wouldn't be half a bottle of wine deep if I was pregnant... I am a nurse after all. And despite my daily nutritional intake of zero fruits and vegetables, I do have some sense of health promotion.

"Don't give me that look," I state with a pout. "I haven't had sex this entire year. There's absolutely zero chance that I'm pregnant, unless it's with a fictional man's baby."

To be fair, my dry spell is entirely self-imposed—it's not like there haven't been loads of guys blowing up my DMs, but at some point, I got tired of lackluster sex with men who didn't make me feel anything other than bored.

Yeah, I like the attention and it strokes my massive ego, but you can only pretend to come so many times before you start wondering if there's more to life than faking it. At this point, I'm totally fine living alone with my vibrator and one-handed reads because at least I know I'll always be satisfied.

"It's only January fifteenth."

"Exactly. I'm practically celibate," I groan, spitting a strand of hair from my mouth. "Find us something to watch while I fix my damn braid. Not sure how I let you convince me that I'd look good with shoulder-length hair. This is worse than when I had bangs."

I sit up and toss the remote at Cass. She conned me into chopping off my gorgeous chestnut locks last Halloween for a Spice Girls costume, and I've been trying to grow it back ever since. My hair only slightly passed my collarbone, and I'm about at my wits' end of patience. At this point, I either need to overdose on Biotin or pay for extensions because I'm tired of the effort that having short hair requires.

"Anyways," I say as I secure a clear tie at the base of my braid and flop back into my original position, "I know for a fact that I'm not a mother because my New Year's Resolution was to stop hooking up with guys who don't make my kitty purr."

My best friend clamps her lips together to hide her smile. "Interesting."

"What's interesting?"

"Oh you know," she starts, clearly amused by whatever is about to come out of her mouth. "It just looked like Walker was well on his way to doing that the night of my engagement party."

My cheeks flame as I fumble for a lie.

"Not sure what you're talking about," I scoff, though I know exactly what she's talking about.

The way that Walker Chastain looked at me that night was unlike anything I'd ever experienced before. It was like he wanted to devour me. Like he wanted to ruin me. Like he hated everything about me, but at the same time, he couldn't stay away.

And even though it goes against everything I believe in, I couldn't either.

I really can't explain my visceral reaction to him that night because he isn't my usual type. He's a physician, and if there's anything worse than a man who only cares about his own pleasure, it's a man who went to medical school. I have a strict rule to never, ever, look twice at anyone in scrubs, which is probably why I never really noticed him until that night when he was disguised in a tuxedo.

Cass leans forward and takes a sip of her Merlot. "I never thought you'd be into a guy with tats."

Me either.

I've never felt uncertain and nervous around a man in my life, but Walker made me feel that way with a single look. He's broody and quiet—the kind of guy who you have no idea what's going through his head when you look at him because he's so good at controlling his reactions.

And honestly, it isn't even his impenetrable vibe that makes me uneasy when I think back on that night—it's his eyes. Eyes that are a deep, rich brown but completely empty, like they were once sucked free of all of the joy in the world. It made me wonder what had to happen in his life to have eyes like that. Eyes that don't really see.

The weird thing, though, is that despite how much he seemed to be fighting it, it felt like all he saw that night was me.

"First of all," I state, pretending to be disinterested in this conversation despite the way my pulse is racing. "I'm not *into* anyone. Walker is just another name on the long list of men who are obsessed with me. Second of all, he's married, so it wouldn't even matter if I was."

"Is he?" Cass asks, a smug expression on her face.

I roll my eyes. "Yes, dumb dumb. According to Dr. Google."

I may or may not have put my FBI agent cap on the next day because I wanted to understand why in God's name he would walk away from me. It felt like we were playing a game of cat and mouse that we were both enjoying until he suddenly forfeited at the last second, right before he planted a kiss on my lips. He caged me in and then set me free like I wasn't worthy of keeping, which pissed me off until I found his wedding photographer's website from five years ago and everything made sense—the fucker isn't on the market.

While I like to think that I'm adventurous in bed, the one thing I would never do is cross the line with a married man. Part of that is because I'm a Leo, and I refuse to share attention with anyone. The other part is that I'm a child of divorce, so I intimately understand the repercussions of illicit affairs—I have no desire to cause anyone to go through the headache I watched as a kid. Not even for the most gorgeous man in the world . . . which he isn't, but he's definitely close.

"Hmmm," Cassidy muses into the rim of her wine glass. Her eyes are sparkling, like they're dying to tell me something.

"Yes?"

She takes a deep breath to build suspense and then quickly blurts, "Parker told me that Walker is actually getting divorced, and they've been separated since December, and it's supposed to be final soon."

I feel my eyes go wide because there are multiple interesting things about the statement she just made. And while I would love to unpack the part about the surgeon who made my entire body tingle with just a single look, I decide to shift gears on our conversation—this is the first time she's mentioned speaking to her fiancé in a week.

"Oh, Parker told you? Care to update me?" I plaster a fake grin on my face like I'm happy for her when the truth is that the fucker does nothing but piss me off.

I've never felt like he deserved my angelic best friend, and all I can pray for is that she comes to her senses before the wedding. But if she doesn't, I'll pray that there's no prenup. That way she'll take half when she inevitably gets sick of his bullshit.

"Well," Cass says tentatively, setting down her wine glass on a ceramic coaster. "Remind me what the last thing I told you was?"

"That your bitch boy fiancé can't see that you're the best thing to ever happen to him," I answer.

Cassidy didn't say those words, but I'm paraphrasing.

Basically, Parker acted like a petulant child and wouldn't speak to her because his ex-best friend, Weston, came back into town. And yes, it doesn't help that Weston also happens to be Cassidy's high school ex-boyfriend. Or that Cass kept in touch with him behind Parker's back. Even I will admit that it wasn't her best choice. However, I'm going to support her in whatever she does because my loyalty lies with my best friend, not her fiancé.

"Ah," she sighs, looking away for a moment like she doesn't want to tell me anything.

I probably should have phrased my words better and controlled my tone, but sometimes I struggle to hold my tongue.

Sorry that I'm human.

"By the way," I add, trying to draw her back in, "you know that I support you in whatever you do right? If you want to go all 'Goodbye Earl' and wrap Parker's ass in a tarp, I'll be the one next to you giving him the black-eyed peas. And if you want to elope and marry his ass tomorrow, I'll call in to the hospital and

DR. FELLOW   21

personally cover your shifts. I'll be there for you no matter what you decide."

Her expression softens despite the threat in my words. "I know. You're the most loyal person I know, Morg, and I'm sorry I haven't updated you. I've just been terrified that things wouldn't work out, and I didn't want to admit that to anyone, let alone myself."

She takes a deep breath like she's gathering her thoughts before continuing, "I think I just needed to sit with my guilt for a minute because the situation was entirely my fault. Parker asked me not to keep secrets from him, and I went behind his back. Again."

I feel my blood start to boil.

Has he considered why she kept secrets from him?

Maybe it's because he's a goddamn baby who can't handle any truth other than the one that he makes up in his tiny little brain. And maybe if he pulled his head out of his ass and listened to her side of the story, they wouldn't be in this situation at all.

If I were in her shoes, I would've just been honest with the fucker, let him blow up, and then moved on like an adult. But for some reason, Cass walks on eggshells around him. And I hate that for her because she deserves better. She deserves more than a life of treading on thin ice.

"He doesn't—"

"He does," Cass interrupts me in a harsh tone. "He does get to ask that, Morg. And he had every right to react the way that he did."

"So, what?" I ask, throwing my arms in the air dramatically because I clearly can't be tamed when it comes to defending people that I love. "He's just going to ignore you every time you do something he doesn't agree with? Gaslight you into thinking that you're the problem, when really it's him? That's manipulation, Cass, not a beautiful marriage."

She blinks a few times, like she's stunned by what I just said. "Do you really believe that?"

I have to take a second to think about how to respond. I didn't mean to be so honest, but the words just spilled out and now I can't take them back.

"No, I don't," I reply, though it's a half-truth. "I think the two of you will figure your shit out and be totally fine. But I also think that you let him steamroll you just because you want to be together. And sometimes I don't understand why. I mean, I know he's got a big dick and all, but is it really worth it?"

My joke lands and her lips twitch into a small smile, slightly easing the tension between us.

"It's worth it," she teases. "But I understand where you're coming from. When Parker came home from drinks after work yesterday, we hashed it all out. We're in a much better place now."

"Did you?" I arch my brow. "God, please tell me that your ass is okay."

My bestie doesn't share a ton about her sexcapades, but I know for a fact that they do some kinky shit, and I can only imagine the makeup bang-session that occurred after a week of the silent treatment.

"Only slightly sore," she giggles, leaning her head against the back of the couch. "No, we just laid everything on the table and had a long talk about communication. He apologized for walking away without letting me say my piece, and for making me feel like I couldn't tell him about Wes. I apologized for betraying his trust, and for going behind his back. It felt good, and we both acknowledged that we probably should have had that conversation sooner."

"No shit, Sherlock," I reply, offering her a smile in return. "I'm glad you worked through it, though."

"Me too. I promise everything is going to be okay, Morg, and if it's not, I know who to call."

"Damn right you do," I snort, grateful that she's not pissed at me for how candid I was. "So, what's going on with Wes? Is he back in town for good?"

Cass told me a few months ago that Weston was in Atlanta working on some personal stuff, but she was under the impression that it was temporary. So when I ran into him the other day in the ER, I had to do a double take because he was rounding like he was back for good. And while I can't say that I care for some of the bullshit that the entitled prick has done, we've always gotten along well—he's more likable than Parker at least.

"I honestly don't know what's going on. He told me that he left the fellowship back in November, but I had no clue he would come back to Midtown Memorial."

"Hmmm," I muse, taking a sip of my wine. "Have y'all talked recently?"

Cassidy sighs. "He's texted a few times, but I wanted to talk to Parker first."

"And?"

She purses her lips for a moment before replying, "I mean, he isn't happy Wes is back, obviously, or that I want to have a friendship with him. But he also understands now that the love between me and Wes is related to my brother and those shared memories, not anything romantic. Or at least, he should because I spent an hour trying to explain that to him last night."

She pauses, tracing her fingertip along the rim of her glass.

"I think I'm just going to leave things with Wes alone for a while though. At least until we're through the wedding."

I arch my brow at her. "Your mom's okay with that?"

From what Cass has told me, their families are still super close. I know that her mom was making a push to invite Weston and his parents to the wedding because she didn't think Parker would care.

She clearly doesn't know her future son-in-law that well.

"I haven't told her. I'm just kind of ignoring the issue until we have to send out invitations in April."

"Oh yeah," I mutter sarcastically, "because ignoring your problems has worked out so well for you in the past . . ."

Chapter 3

Morgan

What boosts morale in the hospital more than a pizza party? Festive decorations... duh.

Even though my inbox is filled with required training modules, I'm currently running around the unit with my arms full of heart-shaped garland. Valentine's Day is only two weeks away, and I firmly believe that staff satisfaction trumps learning about boring new policies any day of the week. At least that's what I'm going to tell myself when I leave the training to the last minute and have to stay late to finish by the deadline.

As I'm standing on my tiptoes to hang a string of garland, a booming southern voice calls in my direction. I ignore it, stretching my five-foot-two frame taller to attempt to catch the edge of the sign above the ER desk. When I miss the mark for the third time, I let out a frustrated sigh and drop back down to the ground—what's the point of wearing Hokas that add three inches if I still can't reach anything?

"Brute," I say, turning toward the voice that always makes me smile. I wouldn't normally talk to a doctor like this, but Beau and I have always had the best banter—he doesn't take things too seriously, and neither do I. "Make yourself useful and pick me up so that I can reach this damn sign."

The light-brown irises of his eyes glow with amusement. "I pulled a muscle last night, if you know what I mean," he responds cheekily. "Make Walker."

I didn't even notice Walker standing next to us, but it seems like my body certainly did because everything inside me suddenly feels tighter. Taking a quick breath to collect myself, I plaster on all of the confidence I can find and look up at him.

Walker's face is unreadable, all emotion concealed by his olive skin and jet-black facial hair, but his brown-black eyes flicker slightly, like he can't control his response to me.

"Since your intern is apparently incapacitated," I say with a pointed look at Beau, whose smirk is growing wider by the second, "I require your assistance."

"You know I can just reach the sign on my own, don't you?" Walker asks, tone flat as his eyes quickly return to that stony indifference.

We haven't seen each other since Cassidy's engagement party, but I'd be lying if I said his reaction doesn't make a tiny bit of pride swell within me.

He remembers.

And he should—I'm a memorable bitch.

I narrow my eyes. "You wouldn't do it right."

"Yeah, Walker boo-boo, you wouldn't do it right," Beau teases, leaning against the desk casually. His ridiculous cat-covered scrub cap is slightly crooked, and it would be so easy to make a joke to knock him down a few pegs, but I hold my tongue—I'm off my usual game because of Walker.

"You don't do anything right," Walker shoots back, glaring at Beau. "And *you*," he says, turning to face me with annoyance, "are such a little devil. Turn around."

His commanding words ignite something in my core, fanning an inferno of lust that's been dormant for too long.

Spinning around to face the desk, I allow a full grin to bloom on my face.

What can I say? I like to win.

Walker's long fingers wrap around my waist, the same way they did at the condo when he found me in the hallway and pinned me against the wall. This time though, his grip is firmer, like he's pissed that I'm forcing his hand and wants to remind me that he's in charge.

I lean forward slightly when he hoists me into the air, pushing my ass toward his face as I begin to tie the decoration in place. I'm sure the view from down there is great, and hopefully reminds him what he missed out on.

Once I finish hanging the garland, I glance back at him. "Other side."

His gaze lingers on mine for a moment too long before he grunts and sidesteps to allow me to continue with my work. When I'm done, I nod to signal that he can let me down.

Gently, Walker lowers me to the ground. I'm suddenly very aware of every point where his hands touched me, like his grip somehow seared my skin.

"Thanks," I manage to say, trying to regain my composure.

He simply nods and steps back, putting some much-needed distance between us.

Beau snickers beside me. "Seen Claire?"

I roll my eyes, not surprised that's why he actually came over.

Beau has been dating Claire officially for a month now, and he's just as obsessed with her as I am. She's been working on our floor as a nurse extern while she's in school, which basically consists of me ordering her around while I attempt to teach her everything that I know. It's a blast for me, but I'm not sure how fun it'll be for her after an entire semester.

"I sent her to get us lunch," I answer casually as I whip out my phone to check on my friend.

She's been gone for a while now, and my stomach is gurgling like crazy—hospital sushi is calling my name.

"Know when she'll be back?"

My gaze darts up from the screen, met with warm, gold-brown eyes that are impossible to hate but incredibly easy to tease. "Got a hot date in the ortho call room? Who knew bed sheets could be *so* versatile?"

Beau's lovable face flushes as a wide smirk spreads across his lips. "Oh, she told you about that, did she?"

"Very inventive," I respond, placing my phone on the desk so that I can adjust my ponytail. A few wisps have fallen around my eyes, and they're irritating the shit out of me.

"What can I say?" he chuckles heartily. "I'm an innovator."

I shake my head as I pick my phone back up, gluing my eyes to the group messages between my friends. "She said the line in the cafeteria is long, so it'll be a bit."

He groans dramatically, and I have to keep my focus on the screen so that I don't burst out laughing when I add, "She also said you have a tiny cock."

Beau lunges forward to pry the phone out of my hands. "Let me see that shit."

Unable to help myself, I glance over at Walker. The corner of his lip twitches slightly as he watches Beau's dumb face scroll through my messages to find something that doesn't exist.

"What the fuck is Team Daddies?" Beau asks, furrowing his bushy brows.

"It's the group text between me, Claire, and Cass. We talk about romance books and how small your dicks are."

The first part of my statement is true. I finally got the green light from Cass on a group text name because the one trope we all agree on is a single dad romance. There's just nothing sexier than a hot dad who knows how to get down in pound town.

Beau shoots me a salacious smirk. "Mine's bigger than Parker's though, right?"

I roll my eyes, annoyed that I got myself into this situation. "Not from what I heard."

I'm lying through my teeth because the one thing we definitely do not talk about in the group chat is the size of their boyfriends' penises. I'm pretty sure Claire would lose her shit if anything sexual about her brother was shared—those details are unfortunately reserved for me.

Beau blows a raspberry and hands me back my phone. "Well, size doesn't matter when you know how to use it."

"Tell that to my current book boyfriend who has the girth of a soda can."

"That's not even anatomically possible," Walker comments out of nowhere.

Beau and I glance at him and then back at each other before we burst out laughing.

"Obviously," Beau says once he catches his breath. He claps his hand on Walker's shoulder. "But that's what women think they want."

Walker looks genuinely perplexed as his expressionless eyes roam over my frame. "You're so tiny. Even if you wanted to, there's no way you could take a cock that big."

He's assessing me in the most clinical way possible, but my skin still feels like it's boiling under his gaze. It makes me wonder what it would be like if we continued what we started a month ago—if our sizzle would turn into a simmer, or completely boil over.

So when his eyes find mine again, I shoot him a wink and say as seductively as possible, "Oh, Walker, I could take it."

His dark pupils widen momentarily, like my response caught him off guard. "I seriously doubt that."

We probably look ridiculous right now, staring each other down in the middle of the ER, but I couldn't care less. This spark is the thing I've been missing with every other guy—a volt of electricity that makes my body come alive.

"Hmmm," I muse, completely ignoring the fact that Beau is still standing beside us. "Ever heard of the size-gap trope?"

Walker cocks his head like he misheard me.

"You know, when the guy is way bigger than the girl," I add.

I drag my gaze over his looming frame in a way that overtly signals I'm talking about us, because even with my tennis shoes on, he has over a foot on me.

"I got that, but what the fuck is a trope?"

"It's like a theme in romance books," I explain. "For example, this moron is a prime example of the secret relationship trope."

I point to Beau, who groans dramatically. "Oh god, not this shit again."

"What's the problem?" I ask sweetly. "Big, bad Beau can't be bothered to understand what women want?"

"I only have one woman to understand, and I've got that under control, thank you very much."

"Sure you do," I taunt, making a lewd gesture.

Beau shakes his head. "With that, I'm out," he says with a loud exhale. "Morg, I love you, but sometimes you're exhausting."

"Not everyone can keep up, old man," I reply. "Go find your girlfriend and tell her to bring me back some Diet Coke, please. I'll be here educating Walker on my favorite books."

Beau shoots Walker an apologetic glance and mouths the word "*sorry*" before he turns on his heel and scurries away.

I peer up at the handsome, yet intimidating, man still standing next to me. He looks just as exasperated as Beau, but instead of running away, he stays. And that tells me everything I need to know about Walker Chastain. He might not want to be interested in me . . . but he damn well is.

Chapter 4

Walker

"How are you feeling about the holiday today?" the hospital therapist, Dr. Kinkaid, asks.

His thick head of gray hair is bent over his notepad as he reviews our notes from previous sessions. They all probably say something along the lines of:

> **He failed at the one thing the majority of people succeed at. How tragic.**

"What holiday?"

I glance at the massive clock on the wall like it will tell me the date.

It doesn't.

We've done this dog and pony show every week for months, and it always goes the same way. He asks how I'm doing before we dive deep into whatever he wants to discuss, and eventually, we end with small talk.

Apparently, today we're changing things up and going straight for the small talk.

Dr. Kinkaid looks up from his notes with a serious expression. "Valentine's Day."

I groan audibly, not entirely sure why I came this afternoon other than the fact that the appointment was scheduled. This question has nothing to do with therapy, he's just trying to fill the time in order to bill the hospital for services that are no longer necessary.

To be fair, they were necessary at first. When I walked into this office one morning after a night on call, I wasn't really sure how I got here. All I knew was that I had reached the point where I was short-circuiting, and I needed someone to flip the switch to make me run properly again.

And it worked.

We've talked through pretty much everything from my childhood trauma, to my feelings about the divorce. I determined what my non-negotiables were in relationships, how to communicate more effectively, and a whole slew of other coping mechanisms that helped me get my shit together and feel normal again. But at this point, I'm not sure why I'm still here—I'm fine, and this feels like a waste of both of our time.

"I think it's a day for card companies, chocolate makers, and sex shops to sell more of their products to couples who aren't really in love."

"I see," he muses, jotting something down on his pad. "Have you ever enjoyed the holiday? Or do you just feel that way now?"

I wrack my brain, trying to think of a time when I celebrated anything at all.

"I don't do holidays," I state simply, not fully answering his question.

"Why is that?"

A dull throb starts to pulse behind my eye—for someone who provides counseling to healthcare workers, he really is very dense.

"My time isn't my own."

Surgical residency doesn't allow for a life outside of the hospital, let alone time off to enjoy fabricated days that promote consumer spending. Almost every Christmas, Thanksgiving, and Fourth of July for the past four and a half years was spent at work. Then, you have the countless birthdays, baptisms, and date nights that were also missed because of my choice to become an orthopedic surgeon. It all adds up, and sometimes I genuinely question if the personal sacrifices were worth it.

Dr. Kinkaid puts his pen down and looks at me thoughtfully. "You're almost done with your residency, are you not?"

"A few months to go."

He nods and leans forward, staring me straight in the eyes. "And when do you intend to start living your life again, Dr. Chastain?"

The question hits me like an unprotected punch to the gut.

I don't know how to live my life.

I've spent the past thirty-one years in pursuit of one thing—proving everyone wrong. I went to the best college in Georgia for free and graduated top of my class while swimming competitively. I didn't party. I didn't drink. I lost out on what most people consider the best years of their life all for the chance to become a doctor.

Then, when I got to medical school, I kept climbing. I studied nonstop. I networked. I grinded my ass to get accepted into one of the most competitive specialties in the country at my top choice hospital. And when I reached that goal, I did it all over again with residency. I took extra cases. I mentored. I did everything I could to get offered the fellowship of my dreams.

Every waking second of my life has been spent working toward achieving the same goal.

So what do I do once I finally reach it?

I genuinely don't know.

Sure, I still have my fellowship to go, but it's the cushiest year in all of medicine. There's no call requirement, and all you do is absorb everything you can about your specialty. Fellowship is essentially like slamming on the brakes after finishing a five year long NASCAR race—you're a winner because you survived the worst years of your life, but then you look around and realize that there's nobody to party with.

So why would I be excited to live my life again?

I never started living it.

But before I can reply with a smartass comment, my pager goes off.

"Sorry, gotta run," I say, standing from the too-firm couch in a rush.

Dr. Kinkaid removes his glasses, eyeing me with concern. "Same time next week?"

"Uh, sure," I lie, already on the way out of the room.

I won't be coming back.

"Dr. Chastain?"

I glance back at him with my hand on the door, ready to make my escape.

"Happy Valentine's Day. I hope that one day you will allow yourself to celebrate again."

***

On top of the divorce, the past two months have been fucking miserable. In orthopedics, we spend the first half of our chief year on trauma, teaching the interns and taking call. It's supposed to hone our leadership skills and provide us with additional responsibility, though I honestly have no idea if I was a good example at all because the sheer exhaustion of it was miserable.

But I'd still rather be drained, than bored as hell like I am now because we spend the second half of the year on elective time. We basically prepare for our fellowships by scrubbing in on interesting cases, finishing up any research that we were working on, and studying for our board exams at the end of June. In theory, it's supposed to give a nice cushion in between residency and fellowship so that we can tie up any loose ends, but there's one major problem—I don't have any loose ends to tie up.

My research has already been published in a journal. I've been yelled at multiple times for exceeding my hours on elective cases. And there's only so much studying I can do before my eyes start to glaze over. For the first time in my life, my schedule is normal. And while that would be exciting to anyone else, it's my worst nightmare.

Which is why I'm currently running to ER triage to answer Beau's vague page that said:

Need a set of hands in bay 1. Code 8008135.

I have no fucking idea what the numbers mean, but the big idiot probably can't type with his huge fingers.

When I arrive at the trauma bay, I pause and look around. The area is empty, and it doesn't seem like anything has come through, but maybe he mistyped the location?

I decide to do a quick sweep of the floor before heading back to my office. As I pass by triage, I spot Beau leaning over the edge of the circular desk with a goofy smile plastered on his face. He's flirting with his girlfriend, and whatever he said must have been wildly inappropriate because her pale cheeks flush a bright pink, and she lovingly slaps him on the arm.

"Buff," I snap, purposely using the nickname he hates as I walk up behind him. "Where the fuck did the trauma go, and why aren't you there?"

He turns to me, squishing his fluffy eyebrows together. "Huh?"

I blink at him for a moment, the absurdity of the situation momentarily rendering me speechless. My adrenaline had been pumping, fueled by genuine excitement to do my job and finally feel useful. But now the realization hits me—there actually isn't anything to do at all.

"You paged me to triage bay one," I state, unable to help the irritation threading through my tone.

"Why would I page you? You're not even on call anymore. Plus, the new guy is way nicer and doesn't give me stupid-ass nicknames." He smirks, knowing that his comment will piss me off.

It does.

I snag the pager out of my navy scrub pants and flash the message in his smug face. "Who the fuck sent me this, then? A ghost? Because it came from your number."

As he reads the screen, his expression morphs from confusion to realization, and then, annoyingly, to amusement. His hearty laugh echoes through the empty triage area, leaving me standing there feeling like an idiot because I don't understand the joke.

"Code boobies. Damn, that's a good one," Beau manages between breaths. He turns to Claire. "You know anything about this, pretty girl?"

Her icy blue eyes twinkle with delight. "Maybe I do. Maybe I don't."

I tune him out as he replies with some deviant comment about what he plans to do to her tonight as payback.

Out of the corner of my eye, I notice Morgan trying her hardest to stealthily sneak up behind Beau with something clutched in her hand. Since I know for a fact that nurses don't carry pagers, I can only assume that she swiped Beau's and is now attempting to return it while he's distracted. Under normal circumstances, she might go unnoticed and succeed. But I'm here, and whether I like it or not, I notice everything about her.

I notice the way her small dimples kiss the edge of her full lips when she smiles or laughs. I notice the way I make her nervous, how her breath quickens and her skin flushes around her ears when I'm close. But most of all, I notice the way she responds to me—and no matter how hard I try, I can't help but respond back.

Lunging forward, I snag her arm before she can reach Beau's back pocket. "Whatcha got there?"

Her eyes shine mischievously as they meet mine, then drop to my hand tightly wrapped around her forearm, as if she feels what's happening between us just as much as I do. It's almost like a current of energy is flowing from her skin to mine, sparking to life pieces of me I thought were long dead. It happened the night of the New Year's Eve party. It happened two weeks ago when she made me lift her up to hang the damn decorations in the ER. It's happening now, and I want to hate it . . . but I don't.

"I was just returning something," she replies with a sly smile.

Releasing her arm, I hold my hand out for the pager in a bullshit attempt at maintaining some semblance of distance between us. Her gaze sharpens in challenge as she places it in my palm, purposely brushing her fingers against mine, almost like she's baiting me with her touch because she knows that I can't resist her.

Beau grabs his pager and spins to face Morgan. "I can't even be mad. That was fucking hilarious."

She winks at me before turning to bump her knuckles against his massive ones. "You like the message? Some of my best work."

"Hell yeah, I did. What's wrong, Morg?" he asks, frowning down at her with amusement. "Your titties feeling a little lonely today? No Valentine to show them some love?"

My eyes inadvertently drop to her chest.

While it's not the first thing I noticed about her, she really does have a nice rack. They're perky and plump—the kind of tits that most women pay thousands of dollars for. The kind of tits that I have the sudden desire to sink my teeth into.

"I have plenty of Valentines," she jokes, rolling her emerald green eyes. "Just none that are worthy of my time at the moment. Why would I want to see someone again after a pump and dump? It truly baffles me."

"Pump and dump?" I hear myself ask.

Morgan turns her attention to me, her brow cocks like she can't believe that I don't know what she's talking about. "Yeah, you know, when a guy gives you a few mediocre pumps before he blows his load, and then confidently asks if you came."

I grit my teeth, digesting her words.

That was the last thing I was expecting to come out of her mouth, and it sends a surprising prickle of irritation down my spine. Not because she's hooking up with men, but because she isn't being satisfied by them. Because they're using her for instant gratification and not reciprocating. I know I've only slept with one woman in my miserable life, but even I know that sex is a two-way street.

"Yeah, Walker-boo-boo, how could you not know what a pump and dump is?" Beau taunts, clearly intent on getting under my skin today.

I scoff, shooting him a nasty glare. "I'm going to pump and dump in your nasty-ass protein shakes if you keep calling me that."

"What about me, Walker-boo-boo?" Morgan chimes. Her tone is playful, but her expression is defiant. "What are you going to do if I call you that?"

I hear Beau and Claire snicker, but my eyes stay locked on Morgan as a reel of depraved fantasies plays through my mind in answer to her question. She makes me want to tap in to parts of myself that I didn't even know existed until recently. I want to tease her. I want to test her. I want to tie her up and torment her for making me feel this way.

But I don't say any of that. I simply bend low and whisper in her ear, "Oh little devil, you don't want to know what I'd like to do to you."

Chapter 5

Morgan

I think if I had to choose a single alcoholic beverage to enjoy for the rest of my life it would be a margarita—something about them just speaks to my soul. It could be because nine times out of ten, I'm enjoying one with a massive bowl of chips and queso. It could be because of the numerous country songs devoted to the frozen concoction. Or, it could just be because they're freaking delicious. Whatever it is, I'm the happiest version of myself when I'm sipping a marg . . . until my friends start talking about Parker Winters.

"Are you sure you don't just want to call off the wedding?" I ask, my tongue already loose from the extra tequila they put in my beverage at Señor Cuervos. "I mean really, I wouldn't judge you. I'd kick him to the curb for leaving the cap off the toothpaste."

Cassidy glares at me from across the table, and continues to complain to Claire about the frustrations of living with a man. I tune them out, taking a long sip as I peer down at my cleavage.

My titties look awesome tonight, and it's a damn shame that I'm the only one who's going to appreciate them. Even though it's a girls' night, I'm dressed to the nines in a tight, black V-neck sweater and medium-wash jeans. My hair is straight, my brows are plucked, and my face is perfectly made up. Look good, feel good—that's the recipe for a happy life. Well, that, and margaritas like I previously mentioned.

"Well, since you *insist* on marrying Doctor Delightful," I interrupt, waving my hand to force their attention back on me. "Can we please talk about where we're going for the bachelorette? I'm in desperate need of a trip to warmer weather. Whoever said that it was acceptable for it to be twenty degrees at the end of February was seriously sadistic. Shouldn't spring be around the corner?"

Cassidy's wedding is only four months away, and I've been waiting on pins and needles for her to share the plan. My friends have been so busy lately with their boyfriends, work, and school that I've been feeling a little lonely. A drunk girls' weekend is exactly what I need to pick me up.

Claire gives her sister-in-law a hesitant look, tucking a dark curl behind her ear, something she tends to do when she's nervous. Her icy-blue eyes are somewhat glassy after just a single drink, and I know for a fact that one of us is going to have to make sure she gets home safely. I love her to death, but she's the biggest lightweight that I know, and she acts like a baby giraffe when she's had a few too many.

I lean forward to grab a chip and fill the awkward silence between us. "Why is nobody saying anything?"

"We're going to Vegas . . ." Cass replies. Her tone is careful, and it almost sounds like she isn't excited to visit the city that never sleeps.

Or is that New York?

I've never been great at geography.

And I mean, I get her hesitation. She isn't really a dress up and put on a show kind of girl. In the two years that I've known her,

I've seen her in a full face of makeup maybe five times, and all of those were because I forced her into submission, not because she chose it for herself. But even if she were wearing a trash bag with her hair completely unbrushed, she would still be the most gorgeous person I know—both inside and out.

Cassidy's long blonde hair is pulled into a high ponytail, several stray wisps falling around her face haphazardly. Even though she and Claire came straight from work, they look like they walked out of a damn Pinterest board for hot nurses. When I leave the hospital, I have bodily fluids all over me, smell, and could easily be mistaken for a grunge goblin.

Life isn't fair.

"Oh thank God." I release a dramatic breath I didn't realize I was holding. "I was worried you were going to say that you're not having one, or that it's going to be somewhere lame like 30A, or something."

Claire takes a long sip of her margarita, watching me curiously like I'm a ticking time bomb that's about to explode.

I'm honestly not surprised she's keeping her lips locked—she hates confrontation. But Cass usually lives for it, which makes me suddenly very nervous about what's going to come out of my best friend's mouth.

"Nope," Cass answers simply, avoiding my stare. "We're *definitely* going to Vegas."

"God, don't sound so excited," I snort, leaning back against the red leather booth. "So who else is coming? Anyone I know?"

"It's not finalized yet . . ." Cass says, shifting in her seat slightly. "We're going to keep it small, but for sure it will be the three of us and Caroline. She has that weekend off for med school, and promised to be there."

I don't know the youngest Winters sibling very well, but when I introduced myself at the engagement party, she didn't have a whole lot to say and was acting somewhat standoffish. I always try to give people the benefit of the doubt though, so I'm sure I'll come to love her just like her sister. She was probably just having a bad night, and honestly, I would've had a bad night too if I were her—the guy she was talking to looked like a total wet blanket.

"And what weekend would that be, my dear bestie?" I ask, slurping down the remnants of my margarita.

"The first one in April."

My face must be an open book to my thoughts because Cass apologizes, "Sorry—it was the only date that worked for all seven of us. I made sure you were off work, and Claire already handled the hotels, flights, and everything. All you have to do is show up at the airport."

I wasn't really concerned about the logistics or money because I've always been a fly by the seat of my pants kind of woman. If there's a good time to be had, you can bet that I'll be there. Plus, I'm a champion at the airport—TSA has never seen a more efficient traveler.

"Wait, who else did you invite?" I ask, focusing on something else that she said. "You named four of us—me, you, Claire, and Caroline—but you just said seven."

"Yeah, Cass," Claire teases, biting her bottom lip to hold back a fit of giggles. "Who else did you invite?"

I feel like there's some inside joke going on here because the guest list of a bachelorette party shouldn't be that funny. I would assume that the extras are some of her random childhood friends, but I think she kind of lost touch with everyone when her brother died a few years ago. And I know it's definitely not any of our coworkers because she doesn't hang out with people from the hospital other than me, Parker, and his sisters . . .

Cass narrows her eyes on Claire and snarls, "I'm going to kill you."

"No you won't. You love me," Claire sings, making a kissy face with her lips. "Even more than you love my brother."

"It depends on the day, but right now he's winning by a mile."

"Ahem." I snap my fingers, redirecting their focus back to the more important matter at hand. "Care to share who else is coming, Cass? The guest list sounds pretty final to me."

She glances at Claire who just shrugs. "She's going to find out eventually."

With a resigned exhale Cassidy says, "So . . . Parker and the boys might also be coming for a joint trip."

The words catapult through my head like little pinballs of rage threatening to erupt through my skull.

Looking down at my empty glass, I suddenly realize that I'm not drunk enough for this conversation. I press my lips into a thin line as I signal our waiter for another round of drinks, trying my hardest to listen to the angel on my shoulder rather than the devil.

"Joint trip, as in . . . both parties together?" I finally ask, trying to mask the incredulity in my tone.

I hope to God that I'm being punked right now. That a camera crew is going to turn the corner and reveal themselves, and then we can all laugh about this over a round of tequila shots.

"Yep," Cass confirms, looking to Claire for encouragement who just grins, knowing that pandemonium is about to ensue.

This plan has Parker Winters written all over it. The control freak can't let her have this one thing? One single moment of fun before he ruins her life?

I could kill him.

I won't.

But I could.

This is exactly why I refuse to ever walk down the damn aisle—you lose all sense of personal identity the moment you promise your life to someone.

"God," I groan a little too loudly. "Can Parker just let you live for once? I swear, he has the most punchable face of all time."

Cassidy gives me a horrified look, and I suddenly realize that I've gone too far.

"Kidding—I would never punch his pretty-boy face because we all know he would sue me."

I don't know when it happened, but my best friend seems to have lost her spine.

Where is the woman who marched into his office in January to defend Beau? Where is the woman who told him off last year in the middle of the busy ER? Where is the woman who stood her ground when he told her that she should follow his orders?

I'll tell you where—she's kneeling at the feet of a man who sucks the fun out of everything.

"It was actually Beau's idea, not Parker's," Claire chimes in, smirking at me like she knows that I'm holding back. "So don't be too mad."

I take a deep breath to steady my racing pulse. While that insight does make me feel slightly better, it doesn't change the fact that I still have to spend the entire weekend with my archnemesis.

"But you can totally still punch my brother," she continues. "I kicked his ass all of the time when we were kids because we were super into Wrestlemania and liked to pretend that we were WWE fighters. For a surgeon, he has surprisingly horrible reflexes."

Her story pulls me out of my rage spiral, and I let out a reluctant laugh as I glance at Cass. She's shaking her head in resignation like she's outnumbered by the two of us.

And she is.

I'm the President of the Parker Winters Hater Committee, and Claire occasionally votes in my favor.

"Can y'all please just be nice to him?" she pleads, darting her eyes between us. "He tries really hard."

"That's the problem—he tries too hard."

"He lets loose in other ways," Cass argues with a kinky grin.

Claire and I both pretend to gag, knowing exactly what she's talking about.

"Add that to the list of things that give me nightmares, along with this shit show of a weekend in Vegas. Am I allowed to call in sick? Asking for a friend..."

I wouldn't actually miss her bachelorette for the world, but I have to get my jabs in where I can—she knows that I mean well.

"It's going to be the best weekend ever," Claire sings. "All of my favorite people in the land of slot machines and bottomless beverages."

A wild snort reflexively comes out of my mouth. "That's because I'm sure your brute of a boyfriend is coming along. You won't even leave the hotel room."

If I had to make a prediction, our weekend in Vegas will result in the two of them paired up with their men, leaving me and Caroline in the damn dust.

Whoop-de-freakin-doo. I get to hang out with mini-Parker for forty-eight hours straight. All I can do is cross my fingers that she has a little bit of her older sister in her somewhere.

"Beau isn't the only brute going." Cass smiles, pausing for dramatic effect. "He invited Walker too."

Chapter 6

Morgan

The best thing about working as a nurse in the emergency room is that you never know what you're going to get. Some days are tough. Hell, some weeks are tough, but that doesn't make me love my job any less. Sure, I could leave the floor for a cushy nine-to-five in a plastic surgeon's office where I give Botox all day, but where's the fun in that?

Some people might say I'm a glutton for punishment, or that I have masochistic tendencies because the painful parts of my job just hurt so good. But that's what all ER nurses are, in one way or another—depraved, chaos-loving wildcards.

"Can we go?" my patient's teenage son whines to his mom. "Travis asked if I could sleep over."

"Ooo, a sleepover. Do teenage dudes watch movies and gossip too?" Claire quips, her comment lightening the mood and momentarily distracting everyone from my feeble attempt at listening to my patient's abdomen. Realistically, there's no chance I'll hear anything other than gas, but I do my due diligence here just in case.

In retrospect, Claire should have been paired with literally any other coworker of mine today because I have a hard time focusing when she's around. We're like two damn peas in a pod, and while I love having her by my side, I'm starting to get a little nervous about this situation.

When my patient came in, he looked completely fine from the outside. He was walking normally, talking normally, and only had one major complaint—crushing chest pain that ripped through to his back. Now, I recognize to the general population that description might just sound like indigestion, but to an ER nurse, it sounds like a problem. There are certain words that make you move just a little bit quicker, and this gentleman has already used several of them.

As soon as we got him to his room, I asked Claire to go tell Cass that I would need her to watch my patients. While she was gone, I hooked the patient up to telemetry, a device we use to monitor a patient's heart rate and rhythm. Then, I started two lines with the largest gauge needles I could find. Call it nurse's intuition, but something tells me we're going to need them.

"No," the son scoffs at Claire, trying to look cool as he runs his fingers through his dirty blonde hair. "We play Xbox and hang."

His mom glances over at me, as if she's asking permission to allow her son to leave.

"You'll be here for a while," I state simply, not wanting to elaborate until I have more information.

She reaches into her overstuffed purse and grabs a set of house keys, tossing them to her son. "Go on. Just please feed the dog on your walk over, and text me when you get there."

My patient chuckles, his oversized belly rippling with the sound. "Not worried about your dear ol' dad?"

His son rolls his gray eyes, identical in color to his father. "You're fine, Dad. Travis just broke up with his girlfriend. He needs me."

But when he turns to leave the room, he looks back for a moment with a flicker of hesitation on his acne-covered face. "Love you."

After I finish my focused physical assessment, I draw a set of stat labs, inverting the tubes a few times to ensure that the blood doesn't hemolyze before it can be tested.

"Hey, Claire," I state calmly as I stand from the ground. "Can you please walk this to the lab?"

She's been happily talking to the patient and his wife about their plans for the weekend . . . I think. I honestly couldn't tell you because I've been running through a mental checklist of everything I need to do.

While I appreciate her enthusiasm, and love that she's the kind of person who likes to intimately know everyone she meets, I learned long ago that you have to set boundaries if you want to continue doing this job and not have a complete mental breakdown—one day she'll learn that too.

"Walk?" Claire's baby-blue eyes, the same color as my scrubs, meet mine with confusion. "Why can't I just tube it?"

She's referencing the station near the nurses' desk that looks similar to Mission Space at Disney World. It allows us to send things through the hospital in capsules, rather than having to physically bring them somewhere. In theory, it's a more efficient system because you can use it for anything that will fit in the pod, but there are occasions where the samples will get lost in hospital space, for lack of a better analogy. And because these labs need to be run as soon as possible, I can't afford to hope they make it to their destination . . . I need to know they're going to make it.

"Because I asked you to walk them there," I snap. "Ask Cass how to get to the lab if you're not sure, and when you're back, go help her with my other patients."

She looks at me suspiciously but nods. "Aye, aye, Captain."

Once she leaves the room, I recheck my patient's vital signs and excuse myself to go find the doctor on call.

The floor has been bonkers today because of the weather. A few snow flurries in Atlanta means that everyone forgets how to drive and ends up in the emergency room. The overflow and weather would be fine in any other situation, but I have a nagging feeling it's going to be a problem for this patient if my suspicions are correct.

"Did you see what we just got in bay two?" I ask the brunette doctor sitting at the desk in the middle of the ER. She's focused on her computer screen, but I know she's listening, so I continue, "Fourty-eight-year-old male with crushing chest pain radiating to the lower back. Came in with stable vitals. History of smoking and hypertension. I got two sixteen gauges in him, drew labs, and started tele. Couldn't hear shit on physical abdominal exam though."

Her brown eyes go wide at my summary before she looks back down at the screen to open the patient's chart. Technically, I'm supposed to go to the resident first with updates or requests, but I don't bother in this situation. I need someone who isn't fresh out of medical school to put their eyes on this case.

"When did it start?" she asks, quickly scrolling through the patient's information.

She just got back from maternity leave last month, and I'm happy to see her back. I'm sure it's hard for her to work in a male-dominated specialty, but she's a badass and one of the only physicians that I genuinely like. Most ER doctors are weirdos who like to rock climb and use words like *chill* and *dope*. While there's nothing wrong with that, sometimes I just want to shake them and tell them to shut the fuck up.

I lean over the desk to peek at her screen.

"According to the wife, around noon. They were out to lunch when the chest pain started, and he ignored it. But I guess it got worse, and she made him come since they live around the corner."

"Thank God she did." Dr. Averill's concerned eyes flick up to mine momentarily. "Get him to CT. I'll make some calls."

She must be thinking the same thing—a ruptured abdominal aortic aneurysm. Depending on the size and stability of the clot, you can sometimes use a "watch and wait" approach. However, since our patient is already symptomatic, the chance of rupture is pretty high.

I might not believe in marriage, but in cases like this, I can see the benefits—his wife might have saved his life by making him come in today.

"You don't want the lab results first?" I ask, thinking through my next steps. "They should be back soon because I had them run down."

"His ability to tolerate contrast doesn't really matter if he's actively bleeding into his abdomen."

Valid point.

She picks up a phone, presumably to call CT and inform them that I'm on the way. Normally you don't need to go with a patient to imaging—it's a task that can be delegated to a medical assistant—but in situations where a patient is unstable, you have to be physically present in case you have to run a code.

"Alright, Mr. Morningside, let's get you hooked back up to that IV," I say when we make it back to the room after the CT.

Once the scan results come back and confirm the rupture, we'll likely get this guy into surgery to remove the aneurysm and stabilize the bleed. Fortunately, everything has gone smoothly so far, and my nurse radar is starting to calm down. He's not out of the woods yet, but at least we have a plan in motion to save his life.

My patient sways slightly as he stands from the wheelchair. I hold him steady while he takes two heavy steps to the bed. His face has substantially paled in the short time it took me to wheel him back from the scan, and a thin sheen of sweat is now covering his brow despite the ever-present chill of the ER.

The radar starts beeping again.

I grab the blood pressure cuff from the wall once he's settled on the bed and quickly wrap it around his upper arm. We already have a pulse oximeter, a device to check blood oxygenation and heart rate, connected to our central monitoring, and considering no one has run in here, I know he's not in serious trouble . . . yet.

"Everything okay?" his wife asks, watching me intently.

I can tell she's nervous because her hands are clenched tightly in her lap, like the pressure is holding them steady. And I don't blame her—I'm nervous too.

I plaster on a fake smile. "Yep. Standard to get another set of vitals after a scan."

The automatic blood pressure reads 82/56, a value which could be acceptable depending on the circumstances, but in this situation, it makes my stomach flip. I pull my stethoscope out of my scrub pants and check the blood pressure manually. Sometimes our machines act wonky and give inaccurate readings, which is what I'm hoping for.

The manual reading is even worse at 76/52, so I leave the cuff on and restart his fluids at a faster rate. Part of my scope of practice allows me to make certain clinical decisions based on my nursing judgment, fluid rate being one of them. The increased flow should help stabilize his pressure while I go get the doctor.

Looking down at my patient, I explain what's happening as calmly as I can. "Your blood pressure is just a little low, Mr. Morningside. I added more fluids, and I'm gonna grab the doctor to come check you out."

He brushes the sweat-soaked hair off his forehead. "Do you know what's wrong?"

I swallow hard. "We think you have a ruptured clot in your stomach. If that's the case, we'll just go in and surgically remove it. Hopefully, the scan will confirm that soon, but I want the doctor to see you while we wait."

There's no use lying to him. If I've learned anything over the past five years, it's the importance of clear communication with families. Not only does it provide them with updates on the care their loved ones are receiving, but it also helps keep them as calm as possible throughout the chaos. Not everyone has the same level of understanding when it comes to healthcare, so simple details can make all of the difference in the world.

"Will he be okay?" The wife's lower lip is trembling now.

"You're in good hands," I promise, unable to confidently say anything else. "We see this kind of thing all of the time, and we have a great team of doctors who can fix the clot."

I'm telling a partial truth.

I've seen clots before, but I've never personally encountered a ruptured abdominal aortic aneurysm firsthand because cases like this usually get sent to the trauma hospital fifteen minutes away. I also still have no idea if it can even be treated surgically, but I'm making my best educated guess based on the knowledge that I have of other emergencies.

Sometimes being a nurse requires you to speak with unwavering confidence, even when you have absolutely no clue what you're talking about. This is especially true when you're barely taller than five feet and have to assert your competence just to get anyone to take you seriously. If you waffle, even for a second, you immediately lose any credibility you had. And right now, I need all of the trust that I can get because I have a feeling things are about to get bad . . . very bad.

"Be right back," I tell them before stepping out of the room.

"His BP is dropping," I say as soon as Dr. Averill is within earshot, skipping formalities. She's already heading toward me like she somehow knew I needed her. "I increased the fluids, but think you should go in there and update them."

She nods. "I let blood bank know we needed O-neg. Go grab them. I'll meet you back in there."

I pause, confused by her instructions. If she already confirmed the rupture, we should be rushing the patient to the OR, not giving him a transfusion at the bedside. "No surgery?"

The bags under her eyes have somehow deepened in the hour since I last saw her. "Who would do it?"

"I don't know. How about any of the egotistical asshats on call? Surely there's one who wants to get in on this case."

She sighs and starts walking toward the patient's room. "Midtown Memorial doesn't have any vascular surgeons on staff."

I grab her arm, holding her back. "Send him to Grady, then," I demand, hearing my tone sharpening. "Life flight would get him there in less than five minutes."

DR. FELLOW

"You have no idea how much I'd like to do that, but they stopped all flights thirty minutes ago because of th[e ice]."

I can feel my throat closing up as I process her words. I don't like feeling helpless. It's one of the reasons I became a nurse—to help people who are helpless—not to feel that way myself.

My eyes dart around the ER, searching for a solution because it shouldn't be this hard. "Have Blue over there drive him," I plead, pointing at a paramedic whose name is momentarily escaping me. "He's not busy."

My grip on my favorite doctor's arm tightens as she tries to pull away, resignation written on her long face. "There's no bus. All of the ice has everything backed up."

"There's not even any ice left," I argue, feeling my chin wobble in frustration. "People just can't fucking drive."

"Let's go," she says. "We're going to do everything we can."

I've heard that phrase more times than I can count, and I hate it. It's just a platitude that we use to make ourselves feel better when deep down, we already know what the outcome will be—death.

Chapter 7

Morgan

It turns out that the reports of black ice and worsening weather weren't wrong. Over a few hours, the temperature dipped to around twenty degrees, and all of the water that melted this afternoon is now frozen again.

Did the city put salt on the roads? Absolutely not. Because that would require preparation, and if there's one thing Atlanta is good at, it's pretending that winter weather doesn't exist.

Even though my Infiniti QX50 has something called snow mode, I still skid to a stop on the street in front of my rental house. While most of Atlanta is hilly due to its location at the foothills of the Appalachian Mountains, my street is relatively flat. Which is great news, because if it wasn't, I would definitely roll backward on the slick road because I still have no idea how to work the parking brake. And yes, I have had my car for over a year, but automotive care is none of my business.

I nearly slip as I hop out of the driver's seat, and I have to crawl on all fours to make it the remainder of the way to my front door. While that isn't ideal, it beats the hell out of turning back around because of a broken wrist.

My rental was slightly out of my budget, but the second I saw the blue guest house, I knew I had to have it. The space used to be a garage the owner converted, so the ceiling is tall and held up with beautiful wood beams which make the five hundred square feet seem much larger. Sure, it has issues, but the unique style makes up for it one thousand percent.

Unlocking the front door from my knees, I feel the delicious warmth of my apartment wash over me. I love air conditioning and keep my apartment at a brisk sixty-six degrees in the summer, but the thermostat stays locked at seventy in the winter.

What can I say? I'm a southern girl through and through, even though I technically spent the first six months of my life in Connecticut, a fact my little brother loves to remind me of whenever he's in the mood to piss me off. The number of times I've had to yell at him for calling me a Yankee is honestly egregious at this point—we shouldn't fault people for things they have no control over.

Dropping my keys on the hook by the front door, I kick off my Hokas, and make a beeline for the kitchen. I barely had time to eat anything all shift other than a slice of old pizza in the break room, and I feel like I'm on the verge of passing out. While I would love to sit and read my current mafia romance, what I need right now is to shove some mac and cheese into my mouth, take a long shower, and then flop down on my freshly made bed.

Today officially goes down in history as the most draining one of my career, and somehow, I have to get up tomorrow and do it all over again, like none of the emotional trauma ever happened.

I love being a nurse most of the time, but there's nothing that can erase some of the things we witness. We just have to keep going, soldiering on like trauma doesn't fundamentally change us to our core. We don't have time to process our feelings because we force ourselves to keep working until, eventually, everything piles up and explodes after years of ignoring our emotions.

That's the one part of the job that doesn't get easier as time wears on—the death. You just keep adding the names of patients to your subconscious list of losses, thinking of them whenever you can. Sometimes, you even think of them when you don't want to. A song, a specific food, or a familiar scent will trigger a memory, and suddenly, it's like you're face-to-face with a ghost. I recognize that probably doesn't sound healthy, but it's the truth—death sticks with you no matter what.

I spent my first few years in the ER writing in journals to work through my emotions. But at the end of the day, I still felt the losses deep in my core. Nothing could erase them, and I eventually got tired of trying so I constructed a wall of impenetrability around myself.

And that wall has worked for the most part. It worked through the horrors of COVID and the helplessness that came with fighting a virus that nobody knew anything about. It worked through the frustrations of short staffing and feeling like we were failed by our healthcare system. It worked for pretty much everything I've experienced as a nurse over the past several years.

But for some reason, my steel barricade of protection was completely obliterated in a few hours this afternoon. I don't know if it's because I saw so much of my own father in this patient and started feeling guilty because I haven't called him in a while, or if it's because I finally hit the limit on the number of deaths I could experience without allowing myself to process them, but I'm on the verge of a serious breakdown. I can feel the pain swirling in my chest, begging for some sort of release that I'm not quite sure how to let loose.

"You've got to be fucking kidding me," I mutter under my breath as I turn on the kitchen faucet and no water comes out.

I blink back tears of frustration now that mac and cheese is out of the question, opening the refrigerator to search for something to eat. Unfortunately, I usually order takeout or buy shitty cafeteria food at work, so my options are somewhat limited. I try to always keep milk for cereal in situations like this, but I've been working so much overtime that all I see is a pile of Chick-fil-A sauce, six cases of Dr. Pepper Zero, and a bundle of smelly broccoli that needs to be tossed in the garbage.

A responsible adult would keep pizza in the freezer for emergencies, but I only find a half-empty bottle of Tito's. Apparently I'm only here for a good time, not a long time.

At least I won't have a puffy face when I starve to death though, because my ice roller is primed and ready to go. I pull it out and slide the cold stone along my cheekbone as I cross the kitchen.

My final option, the pantry, is more promising, and I discover a few homemade oatmeal raisin cookies from Claire's recent batch. Score. That's two food groups in one—carbs from the oats, and fruit from the raisins. If anything, it's more nutritious than eating the stash of Nerd Clusters I always keep handy.

I decide to warm the cookies in the microwave to trick my body into thinking that it's getting a real meal. Shoving one in my mouth, I slink to the floor of the kitchen and lean my head against the white-washed cabinet.

I have no idea what to do about the water. I feel disgusting and dejected after everything I witnessed at the hospital, and I desperately need to cleanse my body of the day—both physically and mentally. But there's no way in hell that my shower is going to work if my sink doesn't.

In any other situation, I could drive to Claire's condo since it's less than ten minutes from my house. But the ice on the road is horrible, and there's no way I can get there safely. I might be careless with a number of things, including what I put in my body, but my life isn't one of them.

As I'm running through the list of people I know who could possibly live nearby, I remember something Cass told me when we got dinner the other night. It turns out there actually is someone . . . the problem is that I'm not sure reaching out to him is any less dangerous than going back out on the roads.

Chapter 8

Walker

Icy roads mean car wrecks.

Car wrecks mean broken bones.

Broken bones are an orthopedic surgeon's dream.

But when I called to pick up a shift this morning and help with the increased caseload, I got a stern lecture from the chief of surgery. I was so desperate to get out of the house that I even offered to work for free, but that wasn't as well received as I anticipated because apparently, I've already grossly exceeded my reportable hours. He told me that I was on a fine line with the department and if I didn't sit my ass back down, he would put me on leave for a month.

So, all I've done today is pace back and forth while I read my research abstract for the thousandth time, even though I know it like the back of my hand.

I guess this is the point where a normal person would enjoy their time off, maybe watch some television or something. But if there's anything I hate more than quiet, it's laziness.

Beau keeps trying to convince me that I should date again, but I blow him off by saying I don't have any time, even though that's clearly a blatant lie. I have all the time in the world, I just don't know how to be a good partner to someone when medicine is all I've ever prioritized.

I don't feel like getting my heart ripped out again when someone ultimately decides I can't be what they need. So even though I might have time, I don't see the point in spending it with someone when the relationship is going to end the same way that it did the first time around—in divorce.

As I'm pouring myself a glass of bourbon, my phone pings. I have no idea who could be messaging me at nearly nine in the evening—the only people who text me these days are my lawyer, my coworkers, and robot spammers.

> Hey! It's Morgan. Do you have water?

My blood stirs slightly as I read and re-read the message, making sure that I'm not hallucinating. I don't have her number saved, but Beau created a group text for everyone going to Las Vegas, so I bet that's how she got my information.

I should respond with something welcoming, considering I've thought about her nonstop for two months, but there's just something about Morgan that makes me want to get a rise out of her. She's naturally confident and self-assured, but for some reason, I have the ability to make her flustered. And that shouldn't excite me, but it does.

> Morgan who?

My phone immediately pings.

> ...seriously?

I feel the corners of my lips quirk up for the first time in days as I type a response.

> Pretty common name. You need to be more specific.

My eyes remain glued to my phone, wondering what she's going to reply as three dots appear. I kind of hope she doesn't back down—I like her fight.

> You're a dick.

My smile widens as I type out a response, vividly recalling the words she said to me at the hospital the first time I saw her after New Year's Eve.

> What was it that you said?
>
> You can take it.

She presses the thumbs down button on my message which actually makes me laugh. Then, she adds:

> Just because I can doesn't mean that I will.

My fingers fly over the keyboard faster than the logical part of my brain can keep up.

> We'll see about that.

Instantly she shoots back an eye roll emoji.

> Can I please come use your shower?
>
> My pipes are frozen and Cass said you live nearby.

I don't want to be a dick, but it just comes naturally with her, like it's part of our little game.

> I love it when you beg.

She dislikes my message again but doesn't say anything else. When a minute passes without a response, I start to feel guilty and send her my address as a white flag.

I kept the pipes dripping all day, so I have no problem with her coming over to use my shower. And if I'm being honest with myself, I'd prefer it to her ending up at the house of one of those pump-and-dump guys. Even though we haven't seen each other in weeks, that comment about other men has been stuck in my head on a loop. Well, that comment, and a lot of other ones . . .

Twenty minutes later there's a loud pounding at my front door, followed by a few curse words, and another round of pounding.

"Who is it?" I yell as I pad across the living room to the entryway.

"Open the door you imbecile," Morgan calls between knocks. "It's fucking cold."

I crack the door, peering down at her. "What's the magic word?"

"Motherfucker," she mutters under her breath as she meets my gaze. She's still in her light blue scrubs, covered by a thin sweatshirt that can't be very warm, and her eyes are the same color as the sky when a tornado is coming in—bright green and filled with tiny specks of chaos.

I start to close the door even though I don't intend to let her stay outside in the cold. I'm not a monster—I just have this insatiable need to see her give in a little bit.

"Wait—" she blurts, eyes flashing like lightning as she stretches her arm out to keep the door open.

"Yes?" I force my face into a mask of indifference with the hope that my body will direct my mind because I'm suddenly having the urge to pull her into my arms.

I've always been able to easily control my emotions, but Morgan has awakened this gentle beast inside me that feels like it's constantly at war with itself. She makes me want to care for her but challenge her, to soothe her but rattle her, to draw her close but push her away. And I can't seem to figure out which part of me is going to win out, or why these feelings even exist in the first place.

"Please let me in." Morgan winces as she says the words, like they were physically painful to speak.

I bite the inside of my cheek to suppress my smirk as I pretend to consider her request. After a moment, designed more for effect than actual deliberation, I swing the door open.

"Was that so hard?" I ask, stepping aside to let her in.

She sticks out her tongue before brushing past me, a visible shiver running through her as she enters the warmth of my home.

She rubs her hands together and looks around the tiny living room opposite the dining room like she's suddenly unsure of herself.

"Bathroom's that way," I jerk my chin toward the back of the house. There's only one, so she can't miss it. "Towels are in the cabinet under the sink."

She simply swallows and nods, heading down the hallway without another word.

Chapter 9

Morgan

It turns out that Walker only lives a block away from my rental. His place is surrounded by two larger renovations which dwarf his white craftsman-style home. Because of the neighborhood's proximity to Piedmont Park, the property values for the land alone are insane, and investors are beginning to flip the quaint original homes into McMansions that ruin the vibe of the neighborhood.

It's kind of funny, really, that a huge, broody man lives in this tiny two-bedroom house, and it honestly makes me wonder how he ended up here when most residents live in apartments or condos closer to the hospital.

And while I'll never admit this to him, I'm glad I came over. Seeing him after a day like today made me instantly feel better because he may intimidate the hell out of me, but that feeling also reminds me that I'm alive. That I can stop trying so hard and just let go.

So I do . . . just not in front of him.

I drop down to the floor of the porcelain tub, allowing myself to finally process the emotions of the day. The tears begin to stream down my face and mix with the constant cascade of scalding water. At first, they are a release of pent-up frustration about my apartment, but they quickly turn into an emotional extrication of the trauma I witnessed melded together with everything I've held inside for too long.

Because my patient was bleeding out, we hung several units of blood to help with the shock and hopefully control the situation until we could find a way to get the patient to the trauma hospital. The problem, though, wasn't the blood loss. It was the heart. Blood couldn't circulate through the body effectively, so backed up into the lungs and made breathing difficult.

Once the patient's oxygen dropped to dangerous limits, the respiratory team was there to intubate. The tube allowed for some momentary relief, but the damage had already been done. We were losing him, and the only thing I was told that I could do was control the symptoms and provide comfort care.

Obviously, I didn't accept that answer.

I called everyone I could think of to get a second opinion—our charge nurse, another ER doctor, the cardio team. I was so desperate that I even tried calling Parker to see if he would operate, but the jerkoff refused and said something about a specialized set of skills for that procedure. It still makes no sense to me because I feel like all surgeons should know how to control excessive bleeding, but what do I know—I'm just a nurse.

It felt like I was searching for a solution that didn't exist, and the only thing I could do was sit there feeling helpless while I waited for the patient to code. When he finally did, we spent an hour performing CPR with the wife sobbing in our periphery until time of death was called.

There was nothing more that we could do.

I don't know how long I sit in the shower and sob, thinking about how I wish I could have done something for the man today. And how lonely this job can be. And how much I needed this release of emotion.

I cling to my legs, burying my face in my knees as I let it all out, losing sense of everything other than the emotions that I'm finally letting go. I can hear my wailing, but I can't bring myself to care because I'm letting the water wash everything away. The frustration, the guilt, the pain—they all become lighter with each sob until I feel a set of strong hands wrap around my shoulders.

The initial touch sends a jolt of surprise through my body, reorienting me to the fact that I'm not in the safety of my own home—I'm in the shower of a doctor I barely know, driving up his water bill and embarrassing myself.

Instinctively, I yelp and go rigid. Not because he's seeing me naked, but because I've never let anyone see me cry before. I feel vulnerable and humiliated, and it only makes the tears come faster.

But before I can run away, Walker rubs his fingers along my upper arms soothingly. "Shhhh. It's okay, little devil. I've got you."

His voice is soft, a stark contrast to the firmness that he uses with everyone else, and his words send a shudder of longing through me.

I'm not sure how to react because I've always prided myself on being strong, independent, and untouchable—the kind of woman who doesn't need anyone other than herself. But I didn't realize how exhausting it was to be alone until I needed someone tonight. So even though my instincts are telling me to protect myself, I lean back and allow him to pull me against his chest.

Walker wraps me in his arms, shielding my body from the hot water. His fully-clothed body surrounds mine, protecting me both physically and emotionally in a way that feels so at odds with every other interaction that we've had.

Normally there's a tide of lust-filled tension between us, but there's nothing sexual about what's happening right now, and the tenderness in his touch as he strokes my arm with his thumb makes me cry even more. I have no idea how he knew I needed this, or that I was in here making a fool of myself, but somehow he did—somehow he knows me better than I know myself.

"I'm so sorry," I murmur once I finally catch my breath and the tears begin to subside. I shudder, more from embarrassment than from the chill of the water still beating rhythmically on our legs. "I didn't realize—"

Walker cuts me off, his voice raspy, "Don't apologize. I've been here before too." He lets out a half-chuckle that vibrates his chest against my back. "In this exact spot actually."

His admission surprises me, but I don't dare look back at him. It's not that I don't expect him to have feelings, but he seems so impenetrable. So closed off. So . . . tormented. And while it shocks me that he's broken down like this, it shocks me more that he's admitting it.

Every interaction we've had has been filled with flirty banter, with pushing each other back and forth until one of us gives in. It was purely entertainment to me, seeing how far I could go, because I thought he was just like every other doctor I've met—overconfident and obnoxious. But every other doctor I've met wouldn't get into the shower fully clothed to comfort me. And I wouldn't have let them.

Chapter 10

Walker

When Morgan left to find my bathroom, all I could do was pace back and forth by the fireplace. The thud of my heavy steps against the hardwoods echoed the turmoil in my head as I tried to pinpoint the reason for the weight in the pit of my stomach.

Something about the situation felt entirely off. When we're together, it feels like there's a current of electricity that runs between us and surges back and forth as we banter. But tonight, that spark was almost dim, like she wasn't in the mood to play.

We might not know each other well, but I know without a doubt that Morgan is not the kind of woman who folds easily. And once I pulled myself out of my head long enough to recognize that the shower was still running after far too long, a knot of worry tightened in my chest. I knew there had to be more to the story.

I knocked several times before entering the bathroom because I didn't want her to think I was being a pervert or something. But when she didn't answer, the knot turned into a medicine ball of dread, and I opened the door to check on her.

The sounds coming from the shower almost knocked the breath out of me, clawing at my long-dead heart. Because above the noise of the pounding water, came the most gut-wrenching wails that I'd ever heard. Even if I had wanted to stop my body from going to her,

I wouldn't have been able to. That intense draw between us that's been irritatingly present since the night of the party forced me into action. In that moment, her pain was my pain, and I needed to be there for her in a way that felt primal.

The self-assured, feisty woman I haven't been able to stop thinking about was crumbling. And I needed to let her know that she wasn't alone—that she was safe with me.

The water ran cold by the time we finally got out, which was an impressive feat because in the thirty-ish years that I've spent in this house off and on, I don't think that has ever happened. The last thing I wanted to do was let her go from my arms, but her body started to shiver despite the warm steam in the air. I forced myself to untangle our limbs, and gave her some space while I went to change out of my soaked clothes.

"Ahem."

The sound of Morgan clearing her throat startles me as I'm bending over to dry my legs off, and I realize she's probably warning me that she's got a direct line of sight with my bare ass.

A surge of heat creeps up the back of my neck as I wrap a towel around my waist and turn to face her. I try to ignore the way my heart beats wildly as her eyes travel over my body, like she's searching for the right words but also surprised by the view.

"Like what you see?" I joke, breaking the silence between us.

She lets out a small, almost inaudible laugh as she leans against the door frame. The hint of a smirk plays at the corners of her mouth, though her eyes still hold a heaviness that I feel in my soul.

"I've seen worse."

"Be careful there, little devil, I might think you actually like me."

"Well, we can't have that," she replies coyly, reaching up with one hand to brush her wet hair from her shoulder. "You might be net negative for previous infractions, but you do get a point in the like category after tonight. Thank you."

For a moment she hesitates, and I notice a flicker of vulnerability cross her face. She inhales harshly like she's resetting herself, and it's gone in a flash, instantly replaced by her usual impenetrable confidence.

"However, if you tell a fucking soul that this happened, I *will* chop your balls off."

I ignore the threat, instead focusing on her admission that she likes me. I don't know why it feels good—it shouldn't feel so good. I shouldn't care what she thinks about me, but right now it seems like the most important thing in the world, and I can't stop myself from wanting to know if I've been on her mind as much as she's been on mine.

"How do I get more points?"

I cross the room, drawn into her orbit like a lost moon that suddenly found its warming sun. I stop a foot away from her towel-covered body, and the smell of my cedary-bourbon body wash on her skin invades my nose, filling me with an acute sense of longing.

"Did you not hear my threat?" She snorts, crossing her arms defensively. "I swear if you tell anyone that this happened tonight—"

I step closer, resting my fist on the door frame above her head. "I heard it."

My eyes drop to her full chest, and I have to bite the inside of my cheek to stop a groan from escaping my mouth. Her tits are a masterpiece.

Morgan's breath hitches as the air between us shifts. "And?"

I study the remaining drops of water on her shoulders, fighting the sudden urge to bend down and taste her, to rough her up and force those walls that she just put back up to come crashing back down.

"It's not a concern of mine."

She swallows harshly as goosebumps scatter across her flawless olive skin, and I know without a doubt that they're not from the temperature in the air.

"What *is* a concern of yours?"

I drag my attention back to her face. I'm close enough now to notice the smattering of freckles that pepper her button nose, and the slightly darker rim of yellow that surrounds each iris. The color sparks into her pupil like a vibrant explosion on the Fourth of July, and it occurs to me how fitting that is for her. Because Morgan Lovett is a goddamn firework that erupted in the middle of my darkest night, and as much as I've been trying to find solitude in the silence, her booms keep coming louder and louder.

"Getting a higher score," I reply, unable to help myself from telling her the god's honest truth.

She's quiet for a moment, then shakes her head. "God, you ortho bros are so competitive."

When I don't say anything, she lets out a resigned sigh and adds, "Fine. You can start by letting me borrow some clothes so that I don't have to walk home naked. I only have my dirty scrubs with me because I wasn't thinking when I came over. It was a long day."

"I can do that. Not sure I have anything that'll fit you, though."

Morgan's eyes twinkle with amusement as she smirks deviously. "We'll make it fit."

Turning away, I suppress a matching smile and head to my dresser. I dig through the drawers until I find a soft T-shirt and a pair of sweatpants that I wore in high school but never got rid of.

"Here," I offer, handing her the clothes. "Hopefully these work. Bathroom's all yours. Just don't take too long, or I'll have to check on you again."

She rolls her eyes with a practiced defiance that makes my blood stir. "Don't threaten me with a good time."

Once she disappears, I toss on a fresh pair of black sweats and a gray hoodie before making my way to the kitchen. I clearly don't know shit about what women want, but I do know that it's cold as fuck outside and she probably needs something to warm her up on her way home.

Halfway through making her a fresh cup of coffee, I realize that it's after ten in the evening and she'll never sleep if I offer this to her now. Dumping the muddy liquid down the drain, I try to come up with an alternative plan.

I scour the cabinets and eventually find a gift bag of assorted teas that the hospital gave the residents for a morale-building initiative last Christmas. I have about as much understanding of tea as a newborn baby, but I choose the peppermint option because it seems like it would be soothing. Since there are two bags of each, I decide to make myself one as well.

As I'm pouring the hot water into ceramic mugs, I frown. I really should give her a travel container so she doesn't feel obligated to stay, but something stops me—I don't want her to leave. For the first time since I moved back in, I haven't completely loathed being in this house.

"Whatcha doing?"

I turn, trying my hardest not to react to the sight of Morgan in my clothes. But that's really goddamn challenging when they look perfect on her. Even from a distance, I can see the way her nipples pebble beneath the thin cotton of my oversized Braves T-shirt.

My balls start to tingle with obscene desire, and I cough to distract myself. "You like peppermint tea?"

Her thin brows furrow as she pads closer, her feet practically silent on the worn hardwoods. "Do you like blow jobs?"

"Uh—" I stammer, caught off guard.

She shrugs and reaches for the mug I put on the counter. "Thought we were asking each other stupid questions."

For a moment all I can do is stare at her. How can she go from being so vulnerable, to completely closed off at the drop of a hat? It's not like I expect her to cry to me again, but I guess I just didn't think she would immediately revert back to her normal, combative self.

"Alright," I concede, watching as the steam from the tea frames her face in a hazy mist. "I take it that's a yes to the tea, then?"

"I take it that's a yes to the blow jobs, then?" she echos, her tone full of playful mockery.

Jesus—is anything easy with this woman?

I lean back, resting my weight against the kitchen cabinets. "Who doesn't like a blow job?"

Morgan lowers her mug, staring at me as she wets her lips. I doubt that she means the gesture seductively, but it instantly makes me hard as a rock. "Most women don't."

I desperately want to ask if she's one of those women, to banter like we usually do, but I hold myself back. I need to make sure she's okay first.

"Want to talk about what happened tonight?"

Her tongue prods her cheek like she's considering my offer. Letting out a prolonged exhale, she says, "Not particularly."

Even though I was hoping for a different response, I don't push her.

"Sit with me." The words come out more like a command than an offer, but I don't regret that—I can't let her go yet.

Morgan dips her chin in acknowledgment, and I gesture toward the small wooden table a few feet away.

"Sorry about the papers," I say, my tone softening. "I've been using this area to work."

"I really hope this isn't your office," she comments, choosing the chair directly beneath the window.

I take a seat across from her in the only other chair. "Technically I don't have one at the moment. I've been working on converting the guest room, but it's not done yet. Funnily enough, I have pretty much everything done, except for buying a desk."

When I moved back into my childhood home in December, I decided to turn one of the two bedrooms into an office. I figured that it didn't make much sense to have a guest room when I'm never going to have guests, but now I'm wondering if I made the decision too soon.

"So where do you do all of your stupid doctor things, then?"

Unable to help myself, I chuckle.

"At the hospital, you know, where I do my *dumb little* surgeries," I answer, repeating a phrase she once said to me.

The words come back to me like the lyrics of a song I haven't heard in years, though I doubt she even remembers them because she never looked twice at me. I think she views all doctors as an annoyance that she has to tolerate, but whether I wanted to or not,

I've always seen her. Maybe not in the way I do now, but it's hard to forget a woman like Morgan.

"If I'm studying at home," I add, sipping the flavored hot water, "I'll usually just sit here or on the couch."

"I never took you for someone so informal," she says, slowly drawing circles on the rim of her mug with her index finger.

I offer her a teasing smile. "Yeah, the tattoo-covered arm really screams formal, huh?"

Morgan scoffs as her eyes rake over the ink I've had since I was eighteen. "You know what I mean."

"Actually, I don't."

Given the way I grew up, the word formal isn't something I would ever associate with. That's mostly because I barely had the money to buy basic necessities, let alone purchase anything nice for myself. But now that I have more money than I know what to do with, I still don't relate to the word in the slightest.

A flush blooms on her cheeks. "It just seems like you're the kind of guy who likes control and order. You're so . . . serious all of the time."

"And you're not."

Morgan is playful, and passionate, and frustrating—the complete opposite of anything I've ever had, or thought I would want in a woman. And yet, every conversation we have just keeps drawing me in—she's just so damn captivating.

"Not if I can help it." She grins, settling more comfortably into her chair.

I study her. "Why not?"

She hesitates and peers down into her tea like my simple question caught her off guard. She's quiet for a moment before she looks up at me.

"I think it's because the pain and trauma I see at work reminds me that I'm alive. It gives me the perspective to leave the hospital and truly enjoy life. Because I see so much of it end, that if I didn't, everything I witnessed would be a waste."

Her voice breaks on the last word, and I watch her throat work to hold back emotion. Her eyes dart to the window, focusing intently on the street light in front of my house.

Clearly something happened at work that caused her to feel this way, something that pushed her over the edge. I want to reach out and touch her, to let her know that I understand. I might choose to express the sentiment differently in my daily life, but there's no one who can empathize more than me.

"I like that about you by the way . . . it's refreshing."

She glances back at me curiously, like she does't quite believe my admission. "It's very different from you."

"We all process death and trauma differently."

Neither one of us is wrong for the way we handle our life experiences, and I appreciate that she shared this with me when she originally said she wasn't interested in talking.

Morgan sinks her teeth into her plump bottom lip. I can tell she wants to ask me something, but she's holding herself back.

"Yes?"

She fidgets, drawing her legs up almost defensively. "What made you become so serious, then?"

I take a slow sip of the tea, trying to determine how much I should tell her . . . and why I want to tell her anything at all.

"I didn't have much order in my childhood, so I had to create it for myself."

She leans forward to rest her chin on her knees. "What happened?"

"My mom overdosed when I was eighteen, and my dad died a few years before that. Had to grow up fast."

I don't elaborate further, and she doesn't ask.

"I'm sorry," she offers, and even though the words are simple, the sincerity behind them is evident. "That doesn't sound easy."

"It wasn't," I admit, allowing myself a moment of raw honesty. "But it taught me a lot. About resilience. About self-reliance. About creating the kind of life I want, despite the circumstances I was dealt."

I don't know why I'm telling her all of this. I guess I just feel like she's been vulnerable with me tonight, so I can be too.

Morgan nods thoughtfully, the soft glow of the streetlights filtering through the windows and onto her heart-shaped face. "You didn't have any other family?"

"My grandfather, but I saw him maybe once a year until he died last September."

"Why?"

"I think it was a boundaries thing," I explain, recalling the situation as best as I can because it's not something I've thought about in a long time. "He didn't approve of the life my parents were living, and essentially grouped me in with them, even though I was just a kid. I had come to terms with our relationship until all of his assets, including this house, were transferred to me when he died. He had been sitting on a mountain of cash, which really pissed me off since there were times in high school when I didn't know where my next meal was coming from because my parents spent the money on drugs and God knows what else."

She reaches for her mug, her hands gripping the ceramic so tight that her knuckles go white. "I'm sorry but he can rot in hell."

"Don't be sorry," I laugh. "I feel the same way."

Morgan reminds me a lot of Beau with the way that she defends me, blindly giving me her unearned loyalty. I've never had anyone like that in my life until recently, and it makes me feel at ease in a way that I didn't know I needed.

Her lips purse as she studies me. "You don't look like you do."

"Did you not just tell me how good I was at control? Comes from years of practice. Plus, not all of us have the most expressive faces in the world."

"Do not." Her brows furrow argumentatively.

"Do too."

She tries to school her face into indifference, though her eyes still shine with her signature fire. "What am I thinking right now?"

"Hmmm," I murmur, pretending to be stumped by her question. "You're thinking that you like me a little more."

I have no idea if my statement is true, but I'm hoping that it is.

Her expression softens as a genuine smile breaks through. "I can neither confirm, nor deny that accusation," she says, placing her mug on the table. "But I am glad that you told me."

"Me too."

Morgan makes a dramatic yawning sound as she stretches her arms up in the air. "I'm beat. Probably should get going since I've got to work at the ass-crack of dawn."

I feel my lips tilt to the floor, unable to help my disappointment. "No problem."

As I watch her put on her thin sweatshirt and tennis shoes, I'm struck by the sudden urge to stop her. To tell her that I want her to stay, though I can't really explain why.

By the time her hand is on the door to leave, I still haven't come up with a good reason to stop her from leaving.

"Thanks again for tonight," she says quietly. Her mouth opens and closes, like she wants to add more but stops herself. It strikes me as odd because she isn't the kind of person that holds back what she feels. After a moment she adds, "Fingers crossed I make it back in one piece. On my way over earlier, I slipped on some ice and practically surfed down the sidewalk."

A mix of emotions that I have no business feeling begin to run through me. The thought of her going out there this late makes my chest burn with discomfort because I suddenly feel incredibly protective of her. I want her to be safe, but I also surprisingly want to spend more time with her—I shouldn't, but I do.

I feel myself letting out a breath I didn't even realize I was holding. "Stay."

Chapter 11

Morgan

I can't decide what's happening here. Men are simple, pea-brained creatures who only want one thing. But each time Walker gets remotely close to acting on that one thing, he pulls back. He's not actively pursuing me, but he also doesn't want me to leave—his mixed signals are driving me up the wall.

"Stay the night?" I ask, genuinely curious about his intentions. "You know I have a 5:00 a.m. wake-up call, right?"

Walker's face almost looks pained as he watches me from the kitchen, his hands clenching the edge of the counter. "No, Morgan, you're going to call in."

I feel my blood start to boil. "Says who?"

I'm not sure what planet he thinks we're living on, but it can't be this one. He doesn't get to tell me what I'm going to do. There isn't a man in the world who has that pleasure, no matter how thoughtful or vulnerable they are.

Walker pushes himself off the counter and stalks toward me. "It's fucking dangerous out there," he says, stopping a foot away and staring me down with his unreadable, dark eyes. "You shouldn't be driving."

Technically, he does have a point. It would be dangerous to try to go into the hospital tomorrow, and after the shift I had, I was planning to call in and tell them that I need a personal day. But that doesn't mean he has to know that. I don't want him to think that I'm just going to roll over and follow his commands. It's not in my nature.

I square my body with his and cross my arms. "Then I'll walk."

Walker looks at me like I've lost my mind, frustration and concern etched deeply on his face. "Walk? On an icy street at six in the morning? You might be irritating, but I know you're not reckless."

I study him closely, unwilling to back down but also aware of the worry lacing his tone. "Look, I appreciate what you're getting at, but I can take care of myself. I've been handling things on my own for a long time."

"I didn't say you couldn't," he counters, scrubbing his hand over his face and letting out a long breath. "I just want you to be safe."

"I'm not sure why it matters to you . . ." I mutter to myself, though he clearly hears it because his eyes darken.

He lets loose an incredulous laugh. "I don't fucking know why either. Maybe because I enjoy being around you, even though you drive me nuts. Maybe because you need someone tonight, even if you won't admit it. And maybe I need someone too—a friend."

"Friend," I say the word out loud, trying to get its bitter taste out of my mouth. Suddenly everything makes sense—that's why he hasn't made a move. I'm being friend-zoned.

Walker winces almost imperceptibly, like he hates his delineation almost as much as I hate hearing it.

"I like you . . . when you're not being annoying as hell."

I snort. "Wow, such high praise."

"You'll get my praise when you earn it," he shoots back, his voice lowering an octave.

I'm not sure if he meant the statement to be sexy as fuck, but something in my low belly flutters to life. I ignore the sensation and refocus on what he really thinks of me.

"Sure I will, *friend*," I taunt, purposely emphasizing the last word. "So what's the plan, then? Braid each other's hair? Talk about boys? Cuddle in that big bed of yours?"

I recognize that I sound like a raging bitch right now, but that's because I feel like a raging bitch.

He wants me to stay, but he doesn't want to hookup and only has one bed. He says that we're friends, but he looks like he's going to devour me if he steps even a foot closer. He's gentle and respectful, but there's a carnal beast beneath the surface that I sometimes see a flicker of, and I just don't understand why he's fighting it by calling us friends.

"I'll sleep on the couch. You take the master."

I can feel my face twisting in incredulity. "I'm like half your size. I'll take the couch."

His eyes travel down the length of my body in a way that's both disarming and electrifying. "Do you ever do what you're told?"

"Very rarely," I admit, enjoying the way his gaze snags on my lips. "But that's part of the fun."

"For you, maybe. All it does is piss me off."

"Exactly," I tease. "I'll take the bed. Not because you're telling me to, but because I want to hear you admit that I was right tomorrow morning when you wake up with a sore neck from sleeping somewhere that's too small for your big-ass body."

A small, victorious smile tugs at the corner of his lips. "Good girl."

My breath catches in my throat, sure that I heard him wrong. "Walker Chastain," I say, narrowing my eyes on his slightly amused expression. "Did you read the book I recommended to you?"

After I explained tropes to him a few weeks ago, I jokingly suggested that he read my favorite dark romance. While it's possible he happens to have a praise kink, the deliberate way he's staring at me makes me think he used the term on purpose.

"Would that get me another point in the like category?" he asks, taking half a step forward. The smell of his woody cologne floods my senses, rendering me momentarily speechless as my mind races to come up with a witty response.

"Only if you give me a book report."

"Alright." He sticks his tongue in his cheek and goes quiet for a moment, pressing his hand to his mouth like he's thinking hard. "It wasn't bad. I can understand why you read stuff like that."

"Not bad?" I gawk, blinking once. Then another time.

I spew bullshit nonstop, so the fact that Walker was paying close enough attention to not only remember my recommendation, but to read it, is genuinely shocking. And annoyingly endearing because it makes me like him even more.

So yeah, he totally gets another point . . . I'm just not going to tell him that.

"I mean, I can't say I cared for the corrupt mafia surgeon, and a ton of it was factually inaccurate from a medical perspective. You can't remove that many human organs and have the patient survive."

I bark out a laugh. "Of course you would focus on that."

"The other stuff was interesting though," he says, leaning forward almost imperceptibly. He's looming over me now, my back against the door and his broad chest inches from mine. "I learned what an anal hook was."

My heart slams in my chest. "And?"

"Pretty damn hot."

It takes a full minute for me to find my voice because my mind starts swimming with filthy images of us. I swallow harshly to reset and remind myself of what he said earlier.

"Well, it's too bad that we're just *friends* because ass play happens to be my favorite."

This time he's the one caught off guard, except rather than flashing with surprise, his eyes flare with something that looks suspiciously close to arousal.

"Too bad," Walker echoes, holding my gaze for a second longer than is comfortable before he abruptly turns and walks down the hall. "Gonna grab you a sweatshirt for bed."

"Don't worry about it," I call behind him, making one last attempt to rouse the beast within him. "I always sleep naked."

Chapter 12

Walker

I wake up with the most painful boner of my life. Usually a little morning wood isn't a problem because it goes away once I get on with my day, but this one needs immediate attention. I was right in the middle of a dream that involved Morgan riding my cock in reverse while I pulled her cheeks apart and fingered her tight little hole. I've always been an ass man, and the moment she said she was into it also, I knew she could possibly destroy me.

Groaning, I roll onto my back. The last thing I should be thinking about is what gets her off.

It was one thing to open up with her last night, but it's an entirely separate matter to cross the physical boundary that we've been dancing around since the party. That's why I played the friend card—to remind myself of who I am, no matter how intense the pull is between us.

At the engagement party, I nearly gave in to Morgan's temptation and acted on impulse. But I reined myself in at the last moment and walked away, knowing I couldn't be what any woman needs. And ever since then, it's like every time I'm around her, she tries to challenge me on that belief. It's like she sees something in me that I don't, and it takes all of my practiced control to hold back.

But it's really fucking hard to find the strength to resist her when I know she's naked in my bed, probably rubbing her sweet scent all over my cotton sheets.

I open my phone to check the clock.

Five in the morning.

I need to get up and relieve this tension in my body.

Pushing myself to a seated position, I hear a creak and can't decide if it's my neck or the door to my master bedroom. When soft light suddenly floods the hallway, I quickly tuck my throbbing erection into the waistband of my sweats and grab a pillow from the couch, tossing it over my crotch for good measure.

"You're up early," I say casually, watching Morgan walk toward me as she rubs her sleepy eyes.

"Girls gotta work," she replies, not meeting my gaze as she continues into the kitchen to search for her shoes.

My body tenses. "Morgan?"

She stops, innocently peering over at me. "Yes?"

"Did we not go over this last night?" My tone drops an octave, the way it often seems to do around her.

Despite the light from the hallway, it's still dim in the house. I can just make out the corner of her lips curving into a smirk. "Go over what?"

She's going to be the death of me.

I take a deep breath as my heart begins to thunder in my chest. "You were going to call in," I remind her.

Her blatant disregard for her safety is one thing, but it fucking pisses me off how she is pretending like she doesn't remember our conversation—we had an agreement.

"Was I?" she asks sweetly. "Because I actually don't recall promising that."

My mind rapidly turns over our conversation from last night, thinking back on everything that was said. I come to the conclusion that while she is *technically* right and she never verbally agreed to call in, the implication was definitely there.

Morgan starts moving toward the front door, and I find myself on my feet in an instant, physically barricading her from the only exit to my home.

She stops in front of me, lifting her chin in challenge. Her nostrils flare like she's the one that's frustrated here, when really it should be the other way around. All I'm trying to do is keep her safe, and she's hell-bent on putting herself in harm's way.

"What are you going to do, Walker?" she goads, her emerald eyes glimmering with daring ferocity. "Force me to stay? Tie me to your bed? No. You won't do that because you don't have it in you. Now get out of my way. I'm going to work."

I snap, finally freeing the part of me that she's been feeding for months. Reaching out, I wrap one hand around her delicate throat while the other snakes around her waist, pulling her body flush against mine.

"Be very careful, little devil," I rasp in her ear, "I told you that I like you, but I'm about thirty seconds away from treating you like I don't. Are you sure you want to keep pushing me?"

Her chest heaves with heavy, frustrated breaths as my thumb gently presses on her pounding pulse. And though the flame in her eyes flickers in answer to my question, she doesn't immediately respond. Instead, she lets out a forced laugh, like she's taunting me with her irreverence for the situation.

"I've never been more sure of anything in my life," she answers callously, gripping my wrist in her tiny hand. "*Friend*."

It's like she knows exactly what I was trying to do by drawing that line in the sand between us, and she's stomping right on it.

Every boundary I've tried to set with her, every dark impulse that I've tried to hold back is eviscerated in an instant.

I turn my head and capture her mouth with mine. Her lips are soft, pillowy, and fucking perfect as I press hard against them, kissing her like I've never kissed anyone in my life.

Morgan doesn't fight back like I'm expecting. Instead, she leans into me like my kiss is exactly what she's been waiting for. She lets out a desperate moan against my lips that sounds like fucking velvet as it ricochets through my mouth, and I can practically taste her desire as it travels down my throat.

As much as I want to give in to her baiting force, to show her what I've been holding back for months, I'm also a man who delivers on his promises.

She's about to find out what happens when she walks into the lion's den.

Pulling back from her lips, I bend low like I'm about to tackle her petite frame, only instead of taking her to the ground, I shove my shoulder into her waist and stand. My arm wraps around her knees, holding them tightly against my chest as I walk toward the master bedroom at the back of the house.

"Put. Me. Down," she breaths, dramatically beating her fists against my back.

I don't answer, bending slightly so she doesn't hit the frame of the door to my bedroom.

Tossing her on the mattress, I flick on the gold sconce lights that I drilled into the brick behind the bed and turn to dig through the middle drawer of my dark wood dresser.

I've worn a tie maybe ten times in my life—for my parents' funerals, my college and med school graduations, and a few interviews in between. Most of the time I prefer to go with the whole open collar look since it's more casual.

But it turns out I'm suddenly feeling very formal.

I slip two neckties into the pocket of my sweats and spin back around, my eyes falling on the devil in my bedroom. She's leaning back on her forearms and wearing a shit-eating grin. Her cheeks are flushed slightly pink, probably from being held upside down over my shoulder, and all I can think about is how I want to do things to her that will only make that color richer.

"Something funny?" I ask, dipping my knee on the edge of the mattress in warning. She won't be amused in a minute—not when she's stuck writhing beneath me.

"You're so predictable," she says, eyes briefly falling to the bulge between my legs before returning to mine. In the commotion, my erection sprung free from the confines of my waistband and is now pointing directly at her.

"Am I?"

"Mhmmm," she sings, clearly enjoying herself.

"Call out of work," I repeat my instruction from earlier because this might be a game to her, but it it's not one to me.

Her slightly swollen lips purse, a squeaky sound flowing through them like she's considering my order. "I think not."

I crawl on top of her body, caging her beneath me. Her breaths are steady, like she's not at all afraid of this predatory part of me that she purposely unleashed.

She should be.

"Call out," I growl, leaning down to nip at her earlobe.

I can practically hear her pounding pulse beneath my lips as I kiss her jawline—Morgan isn't as in control as she'd like for me to think.

She gasps almost imperceptibly as I hover inches above her lips, unable to mask her desperation for more. Our eyes bore into one another, daring each other for something that we aren't quite willing to give ourselves.

Her eyes narrow. "Make me."

I don't think—I just act. Sliding my arms beneath hers, I drag her body up the sheets so forcefully that her head lightly thuds against the black metal frame. I grip her wrist in one hand and raise it above her head, securing her to the top of the bed with one of my silk ties. She doesn't fight me, though I doubt she could in this situation considering I overpower her substantially in strength and sheer size.

Repeating the process with her other arm, I sit back on my heels and admire my handiwork. The silk isn't tight enough to cut off blood flow, but it doesn't allow for much movement either. While this isn't something I've done before, it does the job like I intend—she won't be going anywhere.

"Good luck getting to work now," I taunt, noticing the way her nipples have pebbled under the thin material of my T-shirt.

I want to reach out to pinch them, to tease her now that she's at my mercy. Instead, I stifle the urge and slowly run my hands along her thighs, enjoying the way she needily squirms beneath my touch.

She lets out a hesitant laugh. "Looking for weapons or something?"

I ignore her joke and dig my fingers into her pockets, pulling her phone out of the right side. My other hand remains on her hip, digging into the crease of her leg possessively.

Opening her phone, I search for the charge nurse's number.

Morgan's face goes pale, all amusement and self-satisfaction instantly dissipating when I press the speaker button and let it ring.

"Who are you calling?" she hisses quietly, tugging at the restraints on her wrists.

I don't respond, holding the device out until an exhausted voice answers, "Midtown Memorial ER, this is Marisa."

The vibrant green eyes beneath me go wide as silence settles on the line. "Hello?" the charge nurse says after a moment.

Finally, Morgan clears her throat and speaks, shifting her attention to the ceiling like she's afraid to look at me. "Sorry girl. Didn't mean to dial your number."

I feel my jaw clench but before I can say anything, the woman on the other end says, "No worries. You have second thoughts and decide to come in? We could always use you, though Lauren and Allanah were able to make it."

I blow out a long, hard breath as the situation registers in my brain.

The little devil baited me.

"Oh good," Morgan replies weakly. "No . . . I think the ice is still bad here, so it wouldn't be safe to drive in."

Her gaze slowly drops to meet mine as her shoulders draw up apologetically.

"Totally understand. GDOT was able to put salt down on most of the surface streets near the hospital, but I doubt they got to the neighborhoods yet. Most of the people who came in live super close. It's a skeleton crew, but we should make it. When are you back?"

"Uh, I think in a few days."

"Nice," the charge nurse responds as someone yells in the background. "Well, I'll let you go. I would say enjoy your snow day, but there's no fucking snow."

Morgan lets out a forced laugh. "Yeah. Sorry again. See you next week."

I end the call, dropping the phone on the bed as I wait for her to say something. All she does is blink up at me with those irresistible, wide eyes, now filled with reluctant uncertainty, like she's expecting me to yell. When I remain silent, her mouth curls into a half-smile.

"You think this is funny?" I finally ask, my voice low and controlled as I try to keep my emotions in check.

Her tongue darts over her bottom lip. "I mean kind of," she says, amusement slowly transforming to guilt. "I knew you'd be upset if I tried to go into work, and I was trying to make a point."

"And what point is that?" I spit.

"That I'm not going to break, or run away, or whatever it is that you think will happen if you touch me. We've been skirting this line for two months, Walker, and every time it feels like you're about to make a move, you pull back. It's confusing as fuck, so I figured if you want to play games, I will too."

"That's what you think?" I ask, feeling my pulse skyrocket. I tug my hand away, worried that I'll bruise her if I keep it on her hip. "That I'm playing a goddamn game here?"

Morgan frowns, her gaze drifting to the wall beside her as she shifts beneath me. "I mean you called me your friend last night and then said it was too bad. That's kind of confusing."

I lurch forward so that my face is inches from hers. "Hey, look at me."

She doesn't listen, because of course she doesn't—nothing is easy with this infuriating woman.

Reaching out, I hook her chin with my thumb and two fingers.

"Look at me," I repeat, waiting for her to follow my instructions. When her eyes finally meet mine, I continue, "I called you my friend because you had a shitty day, and I wanted to take care of you. Because I care about you. Because I told myself that if you were just my friend, I wouldn't cross that line with you physically."

Morgan huffs, blowing hot air onto my hand. "There's nothing physical between us."

My grip on her chin tightens. "That's a fucking lie, and you know it. You know how I know you're lying?"

"How?"

"Because believe it or not, I'm so in tune with you that it's almost painful."

Her eyes roll as a disbelieving laugh escapes her lips. "Sure you are."

"You have no fucking idea," I confess, rubbing my thumb along her jawline. "I hear the way your breath slightly catches when I get close, like I make you nervous, but you're too damn confident to show it. I see the way your body tenses when I look at you, like you're uncomfortable with my attention but not anyone else's. I smell the way your body reacts to my touch, like it's desperate for more even if you won't admit to it. There isn't a thing about you, little devil, that I don't notice."

A whirlwind of emotion swirls in her eyes as I watch her bravado fade. "You do?"

"Every fucking detail," I answer, my voice soft but firm. "It's infuriating, actually, because it means that I can't ignore you, no matter how hard I try. And believe me, I've tried."

Her lips part, but no words come out. Instead, she swallows hard, like she's trying to digest the intensity of my admission.

"Why?" her question slips out, almost inaudible.

"Why what?" I prompt.

"Why would you try to ignore me?"

"Besides the obvious that we work together?" I joke with a soft chuckle, trying to lighten the mood even though our professional relationship is the last thing I'm actually worried about.

I release her chin and sit back on my heels, thinking for a moment before I continue, "Because I'm damaged, Morgan. Because I only officially got divorced two days ago. Because I can't be what you need me to be."

I don't mean to be so honest, but the words just spill out.

I've made peace with my ruined marriage. It killed me that I failed the one person I promised my life to, that I couldn't be enough. But I've gotten over the pain and resigned myself to the reality of who I am—a man who can't love anyone properly. And Morgan deserves so much more than that.

"Are you done?" she asks, looking more assured than she did moments ago.

"Yeah?"

"Good." She nods her head. "First of all, everyone's a little damaged. That doesn't make us bad people—it just means we've experienced life. Nobody gets out unscathed."

Morgan pauses, sucking on her full bottom lip. "Second of all, we can be friends while still giving in to the physical attraction between us."

"I don't—" I start, but she interrupts.

"Listen, I have no desire to be in a relationship. Not now. Not ever. So when you think about it, we're kind of in the same boat here."

"Okay. . ." I trail off, trying to choose my words carefully. "So you want to be physical without a relationship?"

I don't know what I'm struggling to understand about this—she doesn't want anything serious, and I can't give her anything serious.

She laughs and rolls her striking green eyes. "Yes, boomer—it's called being friends with benefits."

"I'm only thirty-one," I correct, shooting her a warning look. "And right now I'm not seeing any of the benefits associated with this friendship."

"Me either." She matches my glare in challenge. "Untie me."

While her innate defiance reignited my arousal, there's not a chance in hell I'm pushing any more boundaries with her today—we should take some time to think about this. I haven't been intimate with anyone other than my ex-wife, and while I have no doubt that I want to explore this with Morgan, she also has a way of bringing out parts of me that I've never tapped into. She isn't a sweet, steady lover like I once had. She's a passion-fuelled flame that burns blindingly bright. But just because I want to make sure I'm ready to feel her fire, doesn't mean that I can't have a tiny bit of fun to make her reconsider testing me earlier.

I press my erection into her center, my tone lowering to a rasp. "You think you deserve to be untied?"

She squirms beneath me, trying to grind against my dick. "Duh."

"Hmm," I muse, looking up at the ties like I'm considering her request. "Only good girls get untied. Do you really think you've been a good girl? Or have you been a filthy little cock tease?"

Her breath catches but she tips her chin up in challenge. "Depends on your definition of good."

I feel my dick pulse with arousal knowing that she's completely at my mercy, that she can't do anything other than take what I'm giving her, and yet she still chooses to bite back. It's like the tension from our everyday banter seamlessly transitioned to our sexual dynamic, and it sends a rich thrill through me—maybe this could work.

"Wrong answer," I tut, slowly scooting down the bed. "Try again. This time with an apology."

Morgan watches me silently, as if she's hedging my bet and doesn't believe that I'll actually leave her tied up.

She's wrong.

If there's one thing I excel at, it's patience. I have no problem spending the time it takes to teach her a lesson, waiting for her to submit to me. I would wait all goddamn day if I had to, and just as the thought crosses my mind that I might have to, she opens her mouth.

"Okay, okay," she relents with a huff, like she's come to some sort of internal decision. "Fine."

I arch my eyebrow, waiting for her to continue.

"I shouldn't have pretended that I was going in to work this morning when I had already called out. I did it to get a rise out of you, and it wasn't nice, especially when you were just looking out for me." She sucks in a breath that sounds almost painful before saying, "I'm sorry."

I want to grin, but I keep my mouth set in a firm line. "So what does that mean, little devil? Were you good, or were you bad?"

Her eyes flare with reflexive fire before they close. "Bad."

Adrenaline shoots through my veins at her submission. I love the way that I had to work for it—how she taunted me before eventually giving in.

"And what happens to bad girls?"

"I don't know."

"Yes you do," I prod. "What happens to bad girls in those books you read?"

The color of Morgan's cheeks deepens to a rich shade of red, like she's somehow embarrassed to say what she's thinking out loud.

I repeat the question, and she finally meets my gaze, her voice quiet as she says, "They get punished."

A dark part of me that I'm beginning to enjoy vibrates with pleasure. "And what do you think an appropriate punishment is here?"

Her legs shuffle, searching for friction because she's just as turned on as I am. But that's not what this is about—this is about us trying something together that's either going to work beautifully, or blow up in our faces. This is about something so much bigger.

"Uh," she mumbles breathily. "You've honestly got me there."

"Well, I think two punishments are in order here."

"Do you?" Morgan mocks, though she doesn't roll her eyes again like I'm expecting.

"I do," I confirm. "First, you're going to beg me to untie you."

"Easy," she answers confidently as her lips kick up into a grin. "Untie me."

I can't help but smile at her directness, her ability to play along while still maintaining her inherent defiance. "Oh, I think you can do better than that."

She sighs dramatically. "My arms are tired from being held up, and I've learned my lesson. I won't do it again. Please untie me, *Sir*."

She says the last word sarcastically but the formality of it makes my cock ache.

"That's a good girl." I wink at her before I begin to move up the bed.

Her eyes follow me hesitantly. "What's the second punishment?"

"The second punishment," I echo, leaning down. I carefully loosen the makeshift restraints, my fingers lightly grazing her skin as I work to remove the silk ties. "Is actually untying you."

Morgan sits up, gently rubbing her wrists. The look she gives me is one of gratitude mixed with slight trepidation. "How is that a punishment?"

I grab her hand, helping her off the bed before I check her skin for marks. There's only a small amount of redness on her wrists, but it should go away quickly. I may not be experienced in bondage, but the physician in me knows that you have to be wary of circulation with stuff like this. I've heard about far too many sexual accidents from colleagues of mine in the ER over the years to not take safety seriously.

"It's a punishment," I finally answer, running my fingers gently up her arms, "because I know that if I slipped my fingers under the waistband of those sweatpants that you're wearing, I'd find your needy pussy soaking wet. It's a punishment because you're desperate for a release that I'm not going to give you."

Goosebumps erupt in the wake of my touch, but she steps back and crosses her arms irritatedly. "You're the worst. Why wouldn't you just spank me or something?"

I huff an exasperated laugh. "Something tells me that wouldn't be an effective punishment for you. It's not supposed to be fun—that's why it's called a punishment," I explain, wrapping my arm around her shoulder. "Come on, I'm walking you home."

Chapter 13

Morgan

"How do you know the lungs are clear?"

I pause my charting and look over at Claire.

She's sitting beside me at the main nursing desk with a pad of paper in her lap, taking notes on everything I say and do. We've had a pretty busy morning so far, and I'm finally able to sit down to catch up now that a few of my patients have transferred out.

"Huh?"

She reaches forward to point at the respiratory assessment section of the chart. "You marked that the lungs were within normal limits."

"Right..."

I have no idea where she's going with her questions. I'm so tired that I can barely think straight.

Her perfectly plucked brows furrow like she's trying to understand a complex calculus equation. "How do you know that they're within normal limits if you didn't use your stethoscope?"

I roll my lips to hide a laugh, and the sound gets stuck in my throat like a suppressed cough. "I just know."

After working in the ER for five years, I can easily tell when someone needs a thorough physical exam and when they don't. This specific patient is a forty-year-old woman who slammed her foot in a car door and came in with multiple fractures. Sure, she's in a shit ton of pain and will definitely need surgery because her bones look like mush, but her respiratory status is totally normal. I don't need to listen to each lobe of her lungs to determine that, nor do I have the time.

"Hmmm." Claire slips her pen between her teeth thoughtfully. "You know they teach us not to do that in school, right? You're supposed to do a full physical assessment on every single patient."

I shoot her a glare before I continue charting. "Go become an ICU nurse, then. You'll get to bitch at me every day about the patient's skin, and my IV in the AC."

If I hear one more complaint from the intensive care unit when I'm giving report for a transfer, I might lose my shit. Who cares what the patient's skin looks like, or what kind of line they have? They're stable and alive thanks to us—that's all that really matters.

"Just saying," she teases, writing something down in her notebook that probably says something along the lines of:

Don't listen to Morgan.

Claire allows me a minute of charting in peace before she asks, "What does NPO mean?"

I take a deep breath, trying to remind myself that she's trying to learn, not be annoying. This is precisely why I always avoid precepting nursing students. Any time they swarm the unit, I'll mysteriously have an urgent patient need that requires me to be absent when the assignments are made. I only agreed with Claire because I love her . . . most days.

"Nothing per oral," I answer, scrolling through the twenty orders that have suddenly appeared on my task log. "Basically they don't want our patient to eat because they're planning on doing surgery in the next few hours."

"What happens if she ate?"

"Depends who's on call." I laugh, remembering a hilarious fight that I witnessed a few years ago between a surgical resident and an anesthesiology attending. "Typically the team weighs the risks and the benefits. With emergencies, you can't really control food intake because the patient needs surgery as soon as possible. You just kind of have to hope they don't aspirate on the table."

Claire's curiosity seems to spark even brighter, her baby-blue eyes lighting up with a mix of fascination and excitement. "I gotta ask Beau about that. You think it's happened to him?"

"Probably not. The ortho cases we see typically aren't emergent," I explain, scrolling through the list of redundant orders that some asshat placed without bothering to look at what's already been done. "Plus, bones aren't exactly part of the ABC's of critical care."

My joke goes right over Claire's head—she doesn't even laugh. She just sits and blinks at me like I'm speaking a different language, though I guess since she's only a few months into school, it probably sounds like I am.

"Ask your brother," I suggest, spinning in my chair to face her. "He's probably got some good stories."

I've been feeling super guilty since our dinner at Señor Cuervos because I let my personal frustration with the trip overtake my loyalty to my best friend. Of course, I wish things were different about their relationship, but it's also just that—their relationship. I'm not the one marrying the fucker. So I've made a resolution to only say nice things about Parker Winters from now on . . . out loud.

"Ew." Claire scrunches her nose at my suggestion. "He would just use his robot doctor voice and lecture me for an hour about something I've somehow done wrong. No thank you."

I hold my tongue so that I don't start gossiping and return my focus to the computer .

"See this one? Type and screen." I hover the mouse over a lab order. "Know what that is?"

Claire studies the order closely. "Not a clue."

As much as she drives me nuts, I'm kind of enjoying teaching. Plus, I could get used to having her do my dirty work while I catch up on things that I need to do. At the very least, I know I'll leave on time tonight because I've got an extra set of hands to help with the menial parts of my job.

"It's for a blood transfusion," I reply, clicking into the patient's chart to show her the results. "A type and screen is a lab test that determines the patient's blood type and screens for any antibodies that could react with donor blood if they have to use it during surgery. I doubt there's going to be a ton of blood loss, but we still need to know the information. Some idiot ordered it again though, because as you can see, it's already been done."

I check the order again and feel my stomach twist when I read the name of the physician who wrote it.

Dr. Walker Chastain.

We haven't spoken since he kicked me out of his house.

Okay . . . kicked out is a dramatic way to put it considering he offered to walk me home like a damn gentleman. But I told him that I was perfectly capable of walking on my own, given the night included absolutely no dicking down.

Who would have thought that a sleepover with bondage and punishment could be entirely non-sexual? Not me.

It's been three days since I saw him, and I haven't heard a peep. Not a measly "*just checking in*" text. Not a "*thinking about you*" text. Not even a classic "*you up?*" text.

Nothing.

Which, quite frankly, is rude and tells me that he has no interest in either part of the label "friends with benefits." And while I am currently on day seventy of my dry streak, I refuse to be the one who texts first. Maybe it's the southern woman in me, or maybe it's my Leo zodiac energy, but I don't consider a man worthy of my time unless he's actively pursuing me, even if this is just a casual situation.

His loss.

I glance up and notice Walker stepping out of the elevator, his brown eyes trained directly on me. My traitorous body reacts—my heart starts hammering so hard that feels like it might fly through my throat, and I'm pretty sure my palms could out sweat a whore in church.

"Hey, Claire," I say quickly, hoping she doesn't notice the change in my tone. "Can you go ask our patient when the last time she ate was? I can't remember."

"Yep. Gotta pee anyway." She puts her notebook down and pops up quickly, completely unaware of my distraction tactic.

I train my eyes on my computer screen, pretending to be engrossed in my work, but I can sense Walker looming over the desk, like he sees right through my charade.

Looking up, I adjust my ponytail casually. "Don't you have any manners, Chastain? You're supposed to buy a girl a drink first before you fuck her in the ass with orders."

His lips don't even twitch which is a damn shame because I'm funny as hell. "Oh? But I thought ass play was your favorite?"

The deadpan delivery of his response leaves me momentarily speechless, as a flush of heat crawls up my neck and betrays my indifference.

"Among other things," I reply smugly, leaning back in my chair to maintain a comfortable distance from him because the closer he gets, the more my brain short circuits. "Is there something I can do for you?"

His gaze softens almost imperceptibly. "Do you have a second?"

"Not when I've got a mile-long task list thanks to *someone*." I give him a pointed look. "You know I'm not doing some of these, right? There's zero indication for another CBC. She's not actively bleeding, and I just ran one an hour ago."

"It's a standard pre-surgical orderset," he counters, scrutinizing my face in a way that feels incredibly disarming.

I return my focus to the chart and begin to dictate what I'm typing for him to hear. "All repeat labs ordered at 1430 not drawn. MD aware and verbalized understanding."

Saving my note, I glance back up at Walker and notice what looks like a flicker of amusement on his hardened face. Maybe? Could be irritation. I genuinely can't read him at all.

It's not that I'm purposely trying to be noncompliant to get under his skin, but sometimes I think physicians blindly order tests without checking to see if they've already been done or if they're needed at all. I once had a doctor order a massive dose of insulin for a patient with normal blood sugar and no history of diabetes. Granted, he was a new resident, and the medication was meant for another patient. But if I hadn't been paying close attention, there could've been serious issues.

If I've learned anything as a nurse, it's that you can't just simply follow every order that comes through, no matter how trivial they may seem. Sure, an additional lab doesn't sound like a big deal, but if my patient didn't have a line, it might mean that I'd have to re-stick her and cause unnecessary discomfort. Plus, each additional test costs money, which is an entirely separate soap box I could hop on.

Doctors never think about how their orders impact patients, so nurses are the ones that have to. We have to question anything that doesn't feel right, and use our power to advocate because while the physicians may be the checks, we're the balances.

"Well, thank God the MD is aware," Walker says, a small smile tugging on his annoyingly perfect lips.

As much as I want to act like I'm callous and unbothered by him, I find myself smiling back. "Damn straight he is. Though you just earned yourself negative points, so you're going to have to try really hard to make up for that."

"I'll come up with something," he promises. His voice is lower than before, intimate almost, and I feel like there's an innuendo there—or at least the sexually starved part of me does. "I just wanted to check in after the other day. Have you had time to think?"

Heat prickles down my spine because I've thought about a lot of things in the past few days. I've thought about how good it felt to have his hands on my body. How natural it was between us. How his dominant touch altered my brain chemistry. But I've also thought about how he's impossible to read. And how he makes me feel needy when he's not around. And how I hate not being confident in where we stand.

"All the time in the world," I reply sarcastically.

He doesn't say anything. His patient gaze remains locked on me like he's waiting for an admission of the dirty details spinning through my head. It's unnerving how he can just stand there, exuding calm amidst my internal storm, but I'm not going to break unless he does.

He's going to work for this.

"Have *you* had time to think?" I ask, throwing his question back at him as I return my focus to the computer screen.

"Yes, Morgan, all of the time in the world."

Unable to help myself, I hear a laugh escape my lips. "Is there an echo in here?"

He leans in closer, not taking my bait. "What are you doing tonight?"

The question catches me off guard, and I glance up reflexively.

Walker's face is less than a foot from mine, and I can't help but think about how handsome he looks. His short facial hair softens the lines of his jaw, making him appear slightly less intimidating, and his coffee-colored eyes are almost milky beneath the fluorescent lights of the ER.

"Got a hot date with a bottle of The Prisoner and an episode of *Summer House*," I answer truthfully, holding my sass back. "You?"

He studies me for a moment before the corner of his lips quirk up ever so slightly. "Sounds like I've got a hot date with a bottle of The Prisoner and an episode of *Summer House*."

Chapter 14

Walker

"Shit," Beau blurts as he attempts his running subcuticular stitch for the third time.

"If you don't know what you're doing, don't fucking do it," I grumble loud enough for everyone in the room to hear me. "The point of this stitch is to leave the patient with less scarring. You know that right?"

The big idiot just chuckles and continues to work, throwing the stitch perfectly this time. He might look ridiculous in his cat-covered scrub cap, but he really is talented. He works well under pressure, doesn't let negative feedback get under his skin, and learns quickly. He's going to be a great surgeon one day, and I'm not just saying that because he's one of my only friends—I really do believe in him.

Sensing that we're almost done, the anesthesiologist looks up from her position at the patient's head. "What's the EBL?"

Beau pauses his work and peers up at me from across the operating table, his eyes searching mine like I'm going to provide him with the right answer.

I don't.

"Uh." He glances over at the table of saturated lap pads, then back at the anesthesiologist. "Let's say a hundred," he replies confidently.

I close my eyes, taking a moment to collect myself before I say something really rude. "Try again."

Estimated blood loss has to be carefully tracked during all surgical cases. Every procedure is going to have some amount of blood loss, and it's important to accurately assess the total so that you can determine if any replacement is needed.

Surgeons, especially those of us in orthopedics, are notorious for underestimating blood loss. I was in a case during my intern year with a seasoned attending who charted a fifty milliliter deficit for a hip replacement. The patient's hemoglobin dropped by four points in his post-surgical labs, a value associated with closer to one thousand milliliters of loss, not fifty. While the patient was stable and didn't require a transfusion, the case was something that stuck in my head so heavily that I focused my residency research on it.

"Three hundred?" Beau guesses again, less sure this time.

"Each one of those soaked sponges holds about a hundred milliliters. Count them, then give me a number based on reality."

He tallies the total silently, then looks up sheepishly. "Five hundred, tops."

"Better." I nod toward the incision, indicating he should continue. "Always overestimate, rather than underestimate. Some guys think the less blood they admit to, the better they are at their jobs. But they're just egotistical dickheads. Being honest with your documentation doesn't make you weak—it makes you safe."

Once he finishes his stitches, he looks to me for approval. I lean in slightly and stare at his work, pretending that I haven't been watching him like a hawk the entire case. During his intern year any procedure we do together is under my license, meaning I'm the one liable if shit hits the fan. I like the guy, but he's got a long way to go before I trust him with my career.

"Looks good."

Despite the surgical mask covering most of his face, I can see the huge, prideful grin that he's sporting. "I may be a brute, but I'm also an artist."

"A struggling artist," I correct, stepping back from the table.

"Even DaVinci started somewhere, right? Just call me Leo."

I start to peel off my gloves, ready to get the fuck out of here because for the first time in a long time, I want to be somewhere other than the hospital. "You have the highest self-confidence of anyone I've ever met."

Beau laughs, following me out of the OR. "You must not have spent much time around Morgan, then. The other night she was hanging out with Claire, and the shit that came out of her mouth was absolutely ludicrous. I'm honestly terrified of Vegas."

"Someone say Vegas?"

Beau goes stiff as a board next to me because Weston Southerland looks up at us from his phone. He's leaning against the wall outside of the adjacent OR with an eager half-smile.

"Yeah. Heading out there in a few weeks, man," I reply casually, nudging Beau to remind him to behave. "Good to see you by the way. How's the attending life treating you?"

Because my schedule has been so light, we haven't run into each other since I heard he was back. I thought someone told me he was only working part time, but it's possible things changed—we get so many fucking emails that it's hard to keep stuff straight.

"Could be worse." Weston laughs half-heartedly and pulls off his navy scrub cap. "Could be a hell of a lot better though."

"We're all living the dream," I reply sarcastically, studying the hollow bags beneath his hazel eyes. I'm sure the workload for a junior attending isn't great, but it's a hell of a lot better than a resident—he shouldn't look so tired.

He runs his fingers through his dirty blond hair and lets out an almost pained exhale. "You boys need an extra? Feels like I haven't left the house, or hospital, in months."

Beau shifts uncomfortably beside me, and I can tell that he's going to say something rude if I don't keep talking.

"It's just a few of us flying out for Parker's bachelor party. Next time though."

Weston's face falls dejectedly. "No of course. Well, y'all have fun. I'll catch you around."

He shoves his hands into the pockets of his scrub pants and nods at me before walking away.

Beau leans in as we start down the hallway again and whispers, "Dude, that was so fucking awkward."

He shudders dramatically before wrapping his meaty arm around my neck. "Anyway, like I was saying, I'm kind of terrified of our trip."

"I don't understand why you didn't just plan a separate bachelor party."

I think Beau felt sorry for me about the divorce and impulsively invited me to go to Vegas a few weeks ago. Even though I like Parker, it's not my style to crash someone else's party, and the words to politely decline his offer were on the tip of my tongue when he mentioned that the girls were going too.

Images of Morgan dancing on a table or going home with a random guy flashed through my head. And since I knew Beau and Parker would be preoccupied with their significant others, I agreed. At the time I justified it with the fact that I felt this carnal urge to take care of her that I couldn't explain. But after the other night, I realized that my reaction was more . . . so much more.

"With what time?" Beau scoffs. "I've been slammed in trauma. The only reason I got to see your pretty face is because you decided to cover for Dr. Owens. Thanks, by the way, he blows a fat one."

I nod, knowing exactly what he means—the guy is a huge douche.

Beau continues, "Plus, Claire already had a dope-ass trip planned for the girls, so it was easier to just mooch off of them."

"Do you even know what we're doing when we get there?"

"She hasn't told me shit," he answers, tapping the button for the elevator. "We'll be fine though. She knows that there will be consequences if she pulls anything ridiculous."

I shake my head because from what I know about Claire, she's going to purposely do something to provoke a reaction. "Who else is going?"

"Besides us?" Beau glances at me as the elevator dings open. We step inside, and he leans against the back wall. "Just their sister, Caroline."

"She's in med school, right?" I ask, vaguely recalling meeting her at the engagement party.

"Yeah, she's literally a mini Parker." He closes his eyes for a moment as the elevator lurches upward. "They look fucking identical. It's creepy."

While I was pretty drunk the night we spoke, his description isn't wrong. You can tell she's much younger than her brother, but I remember thinking that they could almost pass for twins. Hell, even their mannerisms were the same.

"Well, at least we'll have someone responsible to watch Claire and Morgan."

Beau shakes his head as a wry smile tugs at his lips. "Those two are pure chaos when they're together. At least I can attempt to corral Claire with my charm. Morgan is immune to it. I genuinely don't think she can be tamed."

I'm not sure she can either, but I damn well want to try.

***

The post-op notes for the day don't take as long as I expect, so I've got plenty of time to swing by Publix before heading to Morgan's house. She refused to give me her address and said that if I really wanted to find her, I would. Normally, a bullshit game like that would piss me the fuck off, but everything about her just draws me in like a damn magnetic force that's impossible to break away from.

Her rental is situated behind the property owner's main house, and as I walk up the driveway, I find myself surprised. I don't know why I thought she was a woman who would only accept a life of luxury. Maybe it's her confidence or outgoing nature, but a tiny guest cottage isn't remotely what I expected.

The home is painted a pale blue color with white trim around the windows and doors. There's a small porch with a wooden swing hanging from the beams above, and while it's still too early in the spring for new plantings, the front flower beds are well kept.

After knocking, I notice a squirrel stealing seeds from the bird feeder in front of the bay window. As I'm shooing it away, Morgan opens the door wearing nothing but a triumphant expression on her face and a gray T-shirt that stops at her mid-thigh.

"You know the squirrels are eating your bird food?"

"Yes?" She looks at me like I'm crazy for asking the question. "I feed them because they're cute, and they bring me happiness."

Of course she does.

Her eyes narrow on me but glimmer with amusement, like she can't decide whether she's pissed or excited to see me on her front porch. "So who spilled the beans? Was it Claire? She always says that I can't keep a secret, but she's just as bad."

I step inside before she has a chance to close the door on me.

"Actually, it was Beau," I admit, holding up the bottle of wine in my hand as a peace offering. "Don't kill him—he's tired and easily manipulated."

I told Beau that I needed Morgan's address to return her credit card because she dropped it in the ER this morning. That obviously never happened, but because trauma service is busting his balls, he didn't even question it—the man is a living, breathing zombie at the moment.

"God, he's such a dumbass." She takes the bottle from me and closes the door. "A big, loveable, dumbass."

"Can't argue with you there," I reply, sweeping my eyes over her body as she heads for the kitchen.

She must have recently gotten out of the shower because there's a dark spot on the back of her shirt. The hem rides up to just below her ass, exposing her toned thighs as she reaches for two wine glasses. I can't say with certainty, but it doesn't look like she's wearing anything other than the thin cotton.

"Ugh," she sighs, returning to her feet. "It's much more fun to banter with you, though."

I chuckle, watching her uncork the wine bottle. "Don't worry—we have all night. There's still plenty of time for you to work your magic."

Morgan smirks as she pours the wine, her playful green eyes flicking up to meet mine. "All night, huh?"

She hands me a glass and we both pause, silently acknowledging the mutual jolt of sensation. She pulls away quickly and walks across the kitchen toward the open-concept living room.

"Well, come on, then." She flops down on the white leather couch which takes up the majority of the room. "Don't just stand there like a stiff tree. You're the one who wanted to intrude on my evening of bliss, so get your ass over here. It's time to watch the greatest reality show in the history of television."

I bite back a snide comment because watching a trashy show is the last reason I came over here—it was just an excuse.

Morgan grabs the remote, tucking her feet under her as she starts searching for the show. The oversized T-shirt slips slightly to reveal more of her legs, and the casual intimacy of her posture makes the space between us feel even more charged.

I sit beside her and try to distract myself from the way my blood is rushing to my groin by taking in her space for the first time. There's art hanging on the walls, books filling the built-in shelves, and fresh hydrangeas sitting on the glass coffee table in front of us. It's surprisingly homey and doesn't feel like a rental at all, but a place that she curated to her own tastes.

My focus snags on several gold picture frames placed on the white-washed mantle beneath the TV. One in particular catches my eye—Morgan's slightly tanned cheek is smashed against a guy who looks to be around her age, maybe slightly younger. She has the biggest grin on her face, and you can feel the love radiating through the photo.

"Who's that?" I ask, nodding in the direction of the frame. I don't want to appear jealous, but I can hear my tone change as the words come out.

"Calm down, killer. It's my younger brother Jake. That was the day he graduated college."

I release the breath that I didn't know I was holding, and look back at the photo. Now that I can think straight, the resemblance between them actually is striking—they share the same dark-green eyes, olive skin, and wide smile.

"What does he do now?"

An exasperated laugh escapes her lips, and I'm sure if I were to look over at her, she would be staring at the image with pride.

"Other than date every blonde in the state of Alabama? Baseball. He works for a college team as an assistant coach. He never made it big, but he has so much passion for the game that he decided to make a career out of it. I've always admired the way he never let his struggles as a pitcher diminish his love for the sport. Not many people have that kind of resilience."

I glance over at Morgan, realizing now that the logo on her massive T-shirt belongs to a college.

Her gaze follows mine and an answering grin forms on her lips. "Yeah, it's from his team. Makes me feel close to him even if we don't get to see each other much. We're five years apart, so growing up we were sometimes on different wavelengths, but I've always been his biggest supporter."

There's a warmth in her voice that softens the edges of her usually tough demeanor. This woman who acts so unbothered and uninterested in love, clearly cherishes her personal relationships deeply.

"And the others?" I gesture to the frames sitting beside the one of her brother.

She smiles, though it's tight and not as bright as it was before. "My parents. They got divorced when I was in middle school. They both live in different states, but I talk to them occasionally and we see each other once a year or so. I love them to death, but they were always hot and cold growing up, so my brother's been the most consistent thing in my life—I'm lucky to have him."

"He's lucky to have you too," I offer, wondering if her family dynamic is the reason that she's so intent on avoiding relationships. It would make sense, but it also makes my chest feel tight for some reason.

"Oh, I make sure he knows it," she jokes before taking a long sip of wine. "Especially around the holidays when it's just the two of us with their new families... anyways, enough about that. Are you ready to have your mind blown by the absolute dumpster fire that is *Summer House*? This season is honestly the best one in years, so I'm going to need you to zip it because I don't want to miss a second."

As much as I'd love to enjoy a carefree evening with her, we need to talk more about what happened at my house. It's the only thing I've been able to think about for days, and I know that I won't be able to relax until I get this off my chest.

"Mind if we chat first?" I ask. "You said you've had time to think since the other night?"

"Yep," she answers flippantly, shifting her position on the couch. "And?"

She rolls her eyes, placing her wine on the coffee table in front of us. "And what? I had time, but that doesn't mean I needed it. Nothing I said the other day has changed—this was entirely for you."

I guess I never considered that while I might need time to process everything, she might not. But it makes sense because she's more self-assured than anyone I've ever met. Even when she's opening up and showing me her vulnerable side, there's still no wavering in her core confidence.

"I'm sorry," I reply, searching her face. "You're right. It was completely about me."

Her eyes widen like she can't believe what just came out of my mouth. "Hold on."

She flails her body as she searches for something on the couch. When she finds her phone, she holds it up like she's recording. "Say that again."

"Say what again?" I ask, playing along. "It was about me?"

Morgan doesn't reply, arching her brow as if I should know better.

I chuckle and lean forward. "I'm sorry."

A wide grin forms on her lips. "I don't think I've ever heard those words from a dumb doctor. Oh my god, they were just as satisfying as I imagined."

Despite the dig, I find myself matching her expression because she's not wrong—as a physician you're paid to be right, or at least to convince your patients that you're right. Over time, most of us let that go to our head and we have a hard time admitting fault in anything we do, even when it comes to our personal lives. I certainly felt that way until the divorce turned my world upside down and gave me the perspective that I desperately needed.

"Well, it's a good thing you recorded, then," I reply, watching her do something on her phone. "Because I doubt it'll happen again for a long time."

Morgan sets her phone down. "Don't worry, it's not going anywhere. I already sent it to Claire and Cass just in case you accidentally delete it. The caption said '*I've achieved the impossible.*'"

Reaching over, I wrap my hands around her ankles and tug, dragging her body across the couch. She giggles and kicks her legs wildly until I place her feet firmly in my lap, holding her steady. The movement slides the length of her T-shirt up her body, its semi-frayed hem now resting at her waist.

I can't help myself from trailing my eyes up her toned thighs, pinpointing my focus on the thin, red material between her legs. God, it would be so easy to inch my fingers up her soft skin and rip the delicate fabric right off her.

My thumbnail digs into the arch of her left foot. "Did I say you could send a video to them?"

Morgan squeals and tries to squirm away, not expecting the sensation.

"No," she answers once she regains her composure, thick lashes fluttering innocently up at me. "But you didn't say that I couldn't either."

"Would you have listened?" I ask, amused by her playful defiance. I love the way she challenges me, but I crave more from her—I crave her submission.

A sly smirk plays across her wine-stained lips. "For the right incentive."

"I'll keep that in mind next time you misbehave," I murmur, the words low and laden with promise.

There's a quick flash of surprise in her eyes, followed by a slow simmer of arousal that matches my own.

"So you thought about it," she states, studying me curiously.

"I did—you were all I fucking thought about for three days. And no matter how I ran through it, I kept finishing at the same place."

"And where's that?"

"That I can't stay the hell away from you."

The words sound more intense now that they're out in the open. It's like I couldn't quite give into the pull between us until I spoke them out loud—until I told her the honest truth.

"So don't," she says matter-of-factly, flexing her feet in my hands.

I inhale sharply, trying to gather the strength for this conversation even though I'm rock-fucking-hard. But I promised myself that I wouldn't take things any further unless I knew that she'd communicate with me. Every depraved, sadistic thing I've fantasized about requires open discussion and checking in. I don't feel comfortable jumping in until I make sure that we're on the same page.

"We need to talk about some ground rules."

Morgan rolls her eyes playfully. "Doesn't really feel like we're on even ground right now."

In one fluid motion, I snake my arm beneath her back and pull her onto my lap. She laughs, sinking her full body weight onto my crotch as she gets comfortable. Her hands tangle around my neck as if it's the most natural thing in the world, and her eyes study mine, like she's seeing something far deeper than anyone ever has.

"We've never been on even ground, little devil. You've always been the one in control, and you'll always be the one in control."

Chapter 15

Morgan

I'd be lying if I said I wasn't hoping this would happen when Walker knocked on my door this evening. One reason is that he showed up looking like a damn Calvin Klein model in his tight, light-wash jeans and navy crew neck sweater. His short facial hair was freshly trimmed, and he smelled like warm Kentucky bourbon—the kind that tastes amazing, even though it burns on the way down.

The other reason is because ever since he kissed me, I knew I needed more—so much more. I've never been kissed like that—like I was something to be devoured and overtaken. It wasn't a tentative first kiss of lovers, it was a declaration of power. A claim. And it's a kiss I desperately need to experience again.

"Alright," I say, weaving my fingers through his thick hair. "What do you want to talk about? I should warn you though, that I am *not* a very good rule follower."

"You don't say?" he teases, voice low and raspy. "Well, you will be by the time I'm done with you."

Walker's delicious threat shoots a rush of heat directly to my core, fanning the embers of arousal from the pressure of his massive erection beneath me. I'm not anything close to a virgin, but that thing feels like it might just split me in half. And considering how starved I am for sex, I hope to God that it does.

"Rule number one," he murmurs as he leans closer, the warmth of his breath brushing against my ear, "we communicate how we're feeling. If we don't like something, we tell each other. If we want to try something, we tell each other. If we want something to stop, we tell each other. The only way that this is going to work is if we're both open and honest."

"Deal." I nod, having a hard time thinking clearly. His hands were resting innocently on my knees, but they've started to skate along my bare thighs, slowly inching higher. "So now would be a good time to tell you that when I said I'm into ass play, I meant your ass?"

His jaw clenches and something that sounds like a growl comes out of his mouth. "I hope you're joking."

I want to keep fucking around, but he's clearly serious about this conversation so I suppress the urge.

"Yes, Walker, I'm joking." I bite the inside of my cheek to stifle my laugh as I watch the color return to his face.

"Rule number two," he continues, ignoring my comment. "The dynamic we have when we're hooking up only exists in that moment. If I ask something of you, I expect you to do it without talking back. Save the sass for our normal interactions."

I've read enough kinky romance to know what he means by this rule, and I'm curious to see how it will play out. Walker definitely gives off dominant vibes considering he's gigantic, intimidating, and hard to read. But I've never seen myself as someone who submits like a well-trained animal. If he wants this version of me, I'm going to make him earn it.

"Sounds good," I reply, tilting my head to give him better access to my neck. My breath catches when he briefly presses his lips against my skin.

"Rule three—"

"Rule three," I interrupt, growing tired of this conversion. "No more rules. You're overcomplicating this."

Walker pulls back, eyes searching mine for a moment. "You sure about that? Because I can simplify everything down to one rule if this is too much for you."

A slow, wicked grin spreads across his face.

"Oh?" I quirk my brow at him. "And what's that?"

His hands resume their exploration, fingertips tracing up my thighs and shooting prickles of desire to the surface of my skin. "You listen to me."

A loud noise that sounds like a single "*ha*" comes out of my mouth.

The balls on this man . . .

"And what kind of benefits do I get from following that rule?" I ask, rolling my hips to tease him the way he's teasing me.

Walker inhales sharply, eyes narrowing in challenge. "My cock, for one."

"Hmmm," I muse, repeating the movement. "You think that's enough to make me listen?"

His fingers pause and dig into the crease of my hips. A bullet of arousal shoots through me, like he just pressed a pleasure-filled button on my body that I didn't know existed until he discovered it.

"Based on how your needy pussy is grinding against me, I'd say you already know the answer to that question."

I want to tell him that he's right. That even though his erection is contained by his jeans, I can feel that it's not even remotely average. But I just can't help myself from continuing to tease him.

"Even if I admit that you have an impressive dick, which I'm not doing by the way, I still have concerns. I assume that you've only slept with, what, one woman in your life? There's no way you even know how to use that thing."

Walker's near-black eyes don't flicker with emotion—he just stares at me, silently blinking for far too long. The only hint that he even heard me is the ripple of his jaw, like he's trying hard to hold himself back.

"You think I don't know how to use my fat cock?" he growls, voice deep and gritty. "You think I don't know *exactly* how to hit that spot deep inside your pussy that no man has ever *quite* reached? That I won't give you everything you need, and more?"

The intensity in his gaze makes my pulse thunder in my ears, reminding me of his natural dominance that I've been callously testing the limits of.

I swallow harshly, trying to push down the inexplicable unease coursing through my veins. Not because I'm scared, but because I believe every word that just came out of his mouth.

He leans in again, panting gruff, shallow breaths in my ear as his grip tightens on my hips. "My cock is going to wreck you, little devil. It's going to tear you apart, inch by fucking inch. And that pain? It's going to feel so goddamn good that you'll get on your knees and beg for more."

His threat sends a sharp pang of lust directly to my low belly, and I have to take several steadying breaths to regain my composure. I pull back and search his hooded eyes, finding no indication that he's joking.

"Are you going to make me?" I taunt, biting back a smirk because I just can't help myself.

"No," he snarls, not even the slightest bit amused. "That's not how this is going to work. You're going to give in because you want to, without any sort of fight or pushback. The dynamic in our friendship is very different from what's about to happen, and I need to know that you're okay with it."

He's right—there's nothing vanilla about what's been simmering between us. This isn't two of the unlikeliest of friends getting naked and fucking, it's way more. I knew at the engagement party that if Walker and I ever got to this point, it would be different from every other hookup I've had. That it would be a complete test of my limits and my boundaries. Which is why I don't hesitate for a second before I respond to him.

"Yes, Sir."

His eyes flare with either pride or lust, as he lifts me off his lap in a swift motion and plants me on my feet in front of him.

"Get your ass to your room," he grunts, gaze snagging on my half-parted lips. "And while we're in there, make sure you remember rule two."

I don't want to listen, but my body has other ideas because my feet begin moving on their own accord, padding across the worn hardwood floors. Halfway across the kitchen, I finally remember my backbone and pause, glancing back at him.

"What was rule two again?" I ask sweetly, knowing what I'm about to say will drive the final nail in my coffin. "The one that says you like a finger in your butt?"

Before I even have a chance to let loose a giggle, Walker stands and crosses the room in two long strides, crowding me against the kitchen island. Our size difference was less overwhelming when we were on the couch, but now that he's towering over me, that slight unease creeps back into my brain. He could break me so easily if he wanted to, and despite what I might admit to everyone else, I would happily let him.

His hand gently tilts my chin up to look at him, his touch surprisingly tender despite the brutal pressure of his hips forcing my back into the butcher-block countertop. It's like he's telling me that he's about to be rough with me, yet there's nothing but security and trust between us.

"I wonder," he muses, his thumb lightly brushing across my upturned lower lip, "if you'll have this much fun when I fuck the fight out of this bratty little mouth. You think you'll be smiling then? When I own those filthy lips and watch them wrap around my thick cock?"

The intensity in his tone sends another thrill through me, and I lean into his touch despite the depravity of his words. I had no idea he had this in him, but I guess the old saying is true—the quietest ones are always the kinkiest.

"Probably," I challenge, though the word comes out much more like a question than I intend.

Walker's smile is slow and deliberate, like a predator sizing up its prey, and the way his gaze darkens makes a warm heat settle between my thighs. His hand shifts from my chin to the back of my neck, fingers curling into my hair possessively.

"Good." He leans in, and his lips barely brush against mine, the contact so light it's torturous. "Because that's exactly what I intend to do."

His words don't scare me in the least—they excite me. There's something about this side of Walker, this commanding presence that he hides under his usually stoic exterior, that ignites something naturally submissive within me. Like I respect him a little more knowing that he's about to follow through with his promise.

He pulls back and his eyes scan my face like he's searching for any sign of doubt or fear. Finding none, he nods, satisfied with my reaction. "Let's go."

He gestures his chin toward my bedroom door at the other side of the kitchen.

I turn, feeling his eyes on me as I walk. When I reach my room, I pause and lean against the closed door, waiting for him.

He strides toward me with measured steps, stopping close enough that I can feel the heat radiating from his body.

"I know you have a hard time listening, little devil, but if you've heard anything at all that I've said tonight, it's that you are actually the one in control here. You can stop this at any time. Consent between us is always fluid."

"Got it. Don't worry though, if there's one thing you can count on, it's that I'll always use these filthy lips to tell you what I want. That was rule number one, no?"

"Something like that." A hint of relief flickers across his face before it hardens again. "So you can listen. You just choose not to."

I shrug my shoulders. "When what you're saying is important."

"What I say is always important," he comments, his voice dropping to a huskier tone. "But tonight, I'm going to need you to listen to everything. Can you do that for me?"

I nod, my playfulness quickly shifting into something more serious, more eager.

"Good girl," he coos, gesturing toward the bed. "Let's see how this goes."

Chapter 16

Walker

Morgan's bedroom is nothing like I'm expecting. While her entire life resembles chaos from the outside, her personal space is incredibly tidy and inviting. Her white wooden bed is freshly made and covered in a sage green duvet cover that's nearly identical to the shade of her eyes. An ivory wool rug covers the majority of the floor, completely free of dirt or scuffs. Even the cream throw pillows are organized, sitting in a line like she took deliberate care with them.

I softly close the door behind us. "Stop right there."

To my surprise, she follows my instructions without so much as a peep, instantly pausing in the open area in front of her bed and spinning to face me. Her eyes have dulled slightly, her blown pupils calming the colorful storm that normally rages. The bedside lamps behind her shine a dim light, illuminating her soft features in a way that makes it difficult to look away.

I step closer and push the sleeves of my crew neck up my forearms.

"Are you familiar with the traffic lights?" I ask the question with confidence, but I only learned about them from research that I did recently.

Morgan smirks like she wants to reply with a sassy retort but holds her tongue. "I am."

After I finished the book that Morgan recommended, I got curious and started reading about kink—everything from scholarly articles to firsthand experiences in the community. It was either that or sit around the house and twiddle my thumbs, so I figured I might as well educate myself.

My sex life in the past was incredibly vanilla for two reasons—my ex-wife was never interested in anything else, and there isn't a ton of time for kink exploration when you're working over a hundred hours a week. But when I thought more about it, I realized that some of my earliest fantasies involved hardcore BDSM, among other things. I think that's partially because I never felt like I was in control of my own life, so being in control sexually was always arousing to me. But it's also just fucking hot knowing that you have your partner's full submission, something Morgan and I are quickly veering toward.

I tried to consider why I wanted to try this with her, but all I could come up with was that it just feels natural. Sure, outside of the bedroom we battle and banter like the best of them, but there was something about the way she responded to me the other day that made me wonder if this could work—if she wanted to be tamed by someone who deserved her submission.

I know that it's entirely possible that neither one of us will like this dynamic because I've never explored this side of myself, and I sincerely doubt that Morgan has either. But while it could completely blow up in our faces, it also could work beautifully.

"Explain them to me," I state, circling her slowly.

"Red to stop. Yellow to slow down. Green to keep going." Her voice is steady as her eyes track my movement.

"Good. And just so we're clear, those colors apply at any point, for any reason. And when I ask for a color, I'm expecting you to respond accordingly. If you need a minute, I'm going to pause until you can answer."

She nods. "Understood."

"Let's take it slow tonight and see how it goes. But here's what I'm interested in—I want to test how well you can listen. And if you even like listening, for that matter." I wink at her and earn a small smirk in return. "So any time you speak to me within this room, I'd like you to respond with 'Sir' at the end. Can you do that?"

"Yes, Sir."

"Good girl," I reply as I pause behind her. "Did you like being tied up the other day?"

Even though I can't see her expression, I notice her posture stiffen slightly. Either the question caught her off guard, or she wasn't a fan.

"Yes, Sir," she answers, her response a little breathy.

I step forward, crowding her from behind as I let her answer simmer in my mind. Her body naturally presses against mine, making my cock swell uncomfortably because all I want to do is ease the fucking ache with her soft pussy.

My fingers move to the hem of her T-shirt, gently toying with the soft cotton. "Let's get this off of you."

As my hands begin to lift her shirt, Morgan's breathing hitches. I pause and steady my hands at her hips. I doubt this is an issue, but I want to make sure that the change in her breath is one of arousal and not fear or something. I know reading her will get easier, but I'm trying to be overly cautious since this is new for both of us.

"Color?" I ask.

"Green," she confirms quickly. "I promise I'll tell you if I want you to stop. You don't have to keep checking in. Please keep going."

I swat at her exposed bottom, finding the meaty part of her flesh with my palm. "Sir," I correct, gently rubbing the sting away.

"Please keep going, *Sir*."

I slide the soft cotton off her body and toss it haphazardly on the floor. My hands snake around her, gently kneading her heavy tits before tracing the outline of her pebbled nipples. Her body softens beneath my touch, almost molding into mine as I tease the darkened skin, not quite touching the tight buds.

"Please," she whimpers, twisting in my arms.

I pause, swatting the underside of her breast slightly harder than I did her ass. "Please, what?" I ask, returning my fingers to their previous spot.

She sighs, shifting her weight like there's something uncomfortable between her legs. "Please play with my nipples, Sir."

Since she's learning, I honor her request and tweak her hardened buds, rolling them between my fingers. She moans in response, arching her back and pushing her chest into my hand like she's begging for more.

"So sensitive," I murmur into her ear, sliding her hair behind her shoulders to expose her neck. "I don't think that's going to be good for you down the road."

Her breath shudders, and I wonder if it's because of my threat or because my lips just grazed her ear.

"Do you have any toys, little devil? Anything I can use to torment you tonight?"

"Just a vibrator, Sir."

I nibble on the thin skin of her neck, considering her response. While I have no doubt that a vibrator could be useful, I was hoping for something along the lines of nipple clamps.

"Put your hands behind your back," I rasp in her ear.

Morgan immediately complies, and I adjust her positioning so that her arms are bent at a ninety-degree angle. Because of the way they're situated above her waist, if I want to spank her or play with her ass, I've got plenty of space.

My fingers quickly move to unbuckle my belt, sliding it through the loops so fast that you can hear the leather sing against the denim of my jeans.

I wrap the belt around her overlapping forearms several times, making sure that it's not too tight before I cinch it together.

"How's that feel?"

"Good, Sir."

I step back, raking my eyes over her body. I've always noticed her figure. It's impossible to ignore when her hospital scrubs show off her perfect hourglass shape, but seeing her on display for only me is an entirely different experience—it's captivating.

Morgan Lovett is every man's wet dream. She's athletic and strong, but the lines of her body are soft and supple. Her thighs are curvy, yet muscular, and her ass . . . fuck. I haven't gotten a good look at it until now, but it's round and cushiony, practically begging to be worshiped by me.

I come to a stop in front of her and tip her chin up to meet my gaze. She had her eyes averted, and while that might be a traditional symbol of submission, I'm quickly realizing that I want to watch everything she does. I want to see her eyes, her face, everything the moment that she decides to give herself to me.

"Tell me," I say, running my thumb along her plump lower lip. "Are you one of *those* women who hates sucking cock?"

The question has been on my mind for days, ever since she casually mentioned it, and my dick flexes painfully against my zipper like it's begging for the answer to be no.

Morgan snorts as her lips curve into a sly smile. "What do you think?"

I must make a disapproving expression because she quickly adds, "Sir."

"I think that you need to answer my question," I state simply, choosing not to spank her for the missed title.

"I don't hate anything I'm good at, Sir," she replies smoothly, her confidence unwavering.

My mouth clamps together to hide the amusement threatening to break through.

"Is that so?" I press, curious how far she'll let me go. "How about when I'm the one in control? When I'm gripping the back of your head and forcing my cock so far down your throat that you gag. Still think you'll be good at it then?"

"I don't think. I know," she answers, smiling sweetly. "Sir."

My hand falls to her upper arm, and I guide her to the wooden bench at the end of the bed. Because of our size difference, I doubt she can take me in her mouth while she's on her knees. But if I'm sitting with her between my legs, it might give her a better angle.

Lowering myself to the bench, I pull her into position, my grip on her arm still firm. "Get on your knees, little devil. Let's see how well you can take a cock in that bratty little mouth."

Morgan nods subtly, not breaking eye contact with me as she slowly sinks to the floor and awaits my next instruction. She looks so goddamn beautiful with her full tits pushed forward because of the way her hands are bound behind her back. Unable to help myself, I reach out and tweak her nipples between my fingers at the same time.

Her eyes widen, and her mouth drops open as a quiet moan escapes her lips. She shifts on her knees, like she's desperately searching for friction that isn't there. I want more than anything to swipe my fingers between her legs, to tease a release of pleasure from her, but I hold myself back. First I want to test how wet she gets from sucking my cock.

Releasing her nipples with a final pinch, I reach into my pocket and pull out my car keys. She looks at me curiously and bites her bottom lip like she's trying hard not to say anything snarky.

"I'm going to put these in your right hand," I explain, holding up the keys. "Shake them if it gets to be too much, and I'll stop to check in."

Her eyes roll but she replies, "Yes, Sir."

Leaning forward, I pinch her cheeks between two fingers harshly. "Do you have something you'd like to say?"

She shakes her head as much as she can. "No, Sir."

I study her carefully for a moment before I release her face and reach around to place the keys in her hand.

"Show me." I hear the tone of my voice go from controlled to reluctant, but I ignore it as I sit back to watch her.

The keys begin to clang together as she jiggles them.

I nod, indicating that she should stop before I add, "If you *ever* roll your eyes about a safe word, we won't do this again. I'm taking away your ability to speak and move, so I need to know that you have a way to communicate with me if you need to. You can be a brat about everything else, Morgan, but your safety, and my safety, isn't a damn joke."

I use her name to indicate how serious I am about this.

Her expression sobers as she absorbs the gravity of my words. "Understood, Sir," she says quietly, the earlier flippancy gone from her tone.

I want to continue but it's not out of lust anymore, it's out of frustration. I can feel a familiar rage vibrating through my veins, and I know that if we keep going, this isn't going to be enjoyable for either one of us.

"Red," I state firmly, looking down at the ground because I can't meet her gaze knowing that I'll see disappointment there. I stand swiftly from the bench and begin to undo my belt, unraveling the soft leather from her arms.

"I'm sorry, Sir," Morgan says, looking up at me with a storm of emotion in her eyes.

"Walker," I correct, pulling her to her feet and into my arms. "We're done with that for a while."

I rest my chin on her head, taking a moment to cool off.

While my research on kink was definitely eye opening and made me excited to experiment with her, the biggest thing I learned was that the two most important elements of kink are communication and trust. We already have the trust down, but I'm not venturing into something deeper unless we're able to communicate effectively. Even if this is a purely physical arrangement between friends, I still need to know that we're on the same page. And right now, I'm worried that we aren't.

Morgan's breathing is steady and soothing against my chest, quickly calming my racing pulse. I want to keep holding her. To let her know that I'm still interested in whatever is happening between us. That my intentions haven't changed. But I need a second to get my thoughts together.

"We need to talk more about this," I murmur. "Let's finish that bottle of wine in bed."

Chapter 17

Morgan

While Walker went to grab our wine glasses, I tossed my T-shirt back on. Before snuggling beneath my duvet, I swung by my attached bathroom to make sure I didn't look completely disheveled.

My hair was still wet when he showed up tonight, and I was waiting for it to air dry a bit before I used the Dyson that Claire made me buy last week. Even though it's expensive as hell, it makes my life so much easier because my hair is still at the length where it's a nightmare to style. Unfortunately, I don't have time for a full blow out at the moment so I toss it into a single braid and move on. It's not like Walker and I are going to hook up tonight, and he's already seen me at my worst... multiple times, in fact.

"I swear if you spill that shit in my bed, I will ruin your life," I warn as he walks into my room holding two very full wine glasses. He must have emptied the remainder of the bottle because the red liquid is sloshing dangerously close to the rim with each step that he takes.

Walker reaches out and hands me my glass. "You already have ruined my life, little devil."

My heart flutters with his use of my nickname, like things are normal between us again. I feel like he only calls me Morgan when

I'm in trouble, or something serious is going on, so I'm glad that he's not too upset after everything that happened tonight.

"Cheers to that," I reply, unable to help my grin.

Walker places his glass on my nightstand and begins to unbutton his jeans, swiftly dropping them to the floor. I almost choke on my wine as I watch him step out of the denim to reveal fitted gray briefs that hug his lean thighs.

"Sorry, uh, didn't you say you wanted to talk?" I mumble like a damn idiot, though I can't bring myself to look away from him as he moves to take off his shirt.

He pauses, narrowing his gaze in a terrifyingly intimidating way. "I do. But I'm not fucking getting into bed wearing jeans and a sweater. I sleep hot."

There are very few things in my life that have ever left me speechless, but Walker Chastain inviting himself to stay overnight is now at the top of that list. Not only was it the opposite of what I expected after our uncomfortable incident, but I've truthfully never had a man sleep in my bed before. Sure, I've gone home with plenty of guys and stayed the night, but my bedroom is my sanctuary—I've never once considered sharing it with anyone.

I gawk at him in muted awe as he tosses his clothes on the floor and climbs into bed beside me, pulling my duvet cover over his lap like he's done it a million times before.

He releases a long exhale as he leans back against one of my oversized shams. Neither one of us says anything for a moment which he must find odd because he turns his head to me and asks, "What?"

I blink rapidly a few times, trying to gain control of my sex-scrambled brain. "You do realize this is super distracting, don't you?"

Not only is his massive body overtaking the entirety of my queen-size bed, but his tattooed arm is practically resting against mine. My eyes study the intricate artwork on his skin, tracking the design as I try to make out anything distinctive other than waves and non-specific flower petals. It surprises me because I feel like tattoos are usually unique and personal, but Walker's looks like he asked for the most generic design possible.

"I distract you?"

I nod, pursing my lips as I try to work out some sort of witty response but come up with nothing.

He just chuckles and reaches for his glass. "Now you know how it feels."

An exaggerated sigh comes from my mouth as I shift in the bed to face him more directly. "Kind of irritating."

"You're telling me," he says, gaze locking on me as he takes a sip of his wine.

"I'm surprised you're still here," I blurt, eyes going wide as soon as the words leave my mouth.

So much for playing it cool.

"Why's that?" His brow arches in genuine curiosity.

"Uh . . . last time you stopped things between us physically, you left to go think. So I guess I just expected you to do that again."

Walker nods, rolling his lips thoughtfully. "Did that upset you?"

"Kind of," I admit, though I'm not sure why. "Other than thinking that you were missing out, I felt like you weren't interested."

"I get that," he pauses, like he's searching for the right words. "I hope you don't believe that anymore. I didn't know how to process what was happening with us and wanted to make sure that I was ready before we got too deep."

"But this is just sex," I argue, not entirely sure why it's such an issue. We're just two bodies that are giving mutual pleasure to each other—it doesn't have to be that complicated.

"Right." His jaw clenches as his expression becomes more difficult to read. "Well regardless, I didn't want to do anything that would push you away. There, uh, aren't many people I like being around. And your annoying ass is one of the few."

"My ass is incredible," I counter with wink, trying to lighten the mood. "You should know that. You smacked it hard enough tonight."

His lips twitch before returning to a firm line as his eyes rake across my body. "Did you like it when I did that?"

I feel myself shifting beneath his disarming gaze. "Yeah. The whole thing was hot."

It felt like I could turn my brain off and listen to his commands, which isn't something I tend to do in any other aspect of my life. I have a strong personality, often naturally overtaking social and professional situations to become the loudest person in the room. Nobody has ever been able to tame that part of me, nor have they really tried. And that wasn't something I thought I might want until I met Walker.

"Good to know," he says, dragging his eyes back to mine. "I did too."

I bite the inside of my cheek as if it will stop the blush I can feel painting my face. "So why did you stop?"

It felt like both of us were enjoying ourselves, but Walker used his safeword before we could even get to the good stuff. I'd be lying if I said I wasn't confused and left feeling like I did something wrong.

His eyes soften. "Because I couldn't snap out of the frustration I was feeling, and it wouldn't have been good for either one of us to keep going. I knew that we needed to have a genuine talk about this."

His tattooed arm wraps around me, pulling me in close to his chest. For some reason I look down into my wine glass, unable to hold his searing gaze as he continues, "That's why safewords exist, Morgan. To give us both power in the experience. It frustrated me that you weren't taking it seriously, and honestly, it scared me a little. While I think I can read you pretty damn well, I don't feel entirely confident proceeding if we're not on the same page, especially because I've never done this before."

"Really? You haven't?" I ask, staring at the vein bulging in his forearm as it rests in my lap.

"Not formally, at least," he admits. "Not like what we just did."

I feel my nose wrinkle. It surprises me that Walker hasn't explored this type of dynamic before. I mean, neither have I, but he was just . . . so good at it. It felt like the most natural thing in the world, and not something that we were forcing at all.

"So why do you want to try it now? Does something about me just scream submissive? It's because I'm short, right?"

He lets out an exasperated laugh and shakes his head.

"It's not because you're short. Though logistically we might have to modify some things," he says, his voice warm with amusement. "It's more about the energy you give off. You're strong, assertive, and you don't back down. That's incredibly attractive, and in a way, it actually does give off submissive to me—not because it's comfortable for you, but because it's uncomfortable and you have to make the active choice to submit."

He sets his glass down on the nightstand. "But to answer your question about why I wanted to try this with you, I don't know. Maybe it's because you made me read that kinky book, and it made me think about what I like. Maybe it's something I've always wanted to try but never had the right person to explore with. The only way that I can describe it is that the dynamic between us just felt right."

"It felt right to me too." I squirm out of his arms to also place my glass down. "But I also kind of want to hookup normally too, if that's okay. I kept hoping you would kiss me tonight, but that never happened."

In answer, he leans in and dusts his lips against mine. It's wildly different from our first kiss—softer and more attentive, as if he's trying to show me that he can give me both. The strokes of his tongue against my lips are slow and silky, like he's asking permission before pushing forward. I part my mouth in invitation, moaning as he dives deeper.

Before I can flick my tongue to meet his, he pulls back. His hooded eyes lock on my lips like he's trying to hold himself back. "Had to right that wrong before we kept talking."

My heart throbs hard in my chest, desperate for more.

"Thank you, *Sir*." I emphasize the term, hoping that it will entice him to keep going.

He laughs. "Let's keep that to when we're in the mood for something more formal," he says, leaning back against the pillow and pulling me with him.

I pout my lower lip, reaching out to trace the sculpted muscles of his forearm. "What? You don't like it, *Sir*?"

I know I'm taunting him, but I don't know if he would give in otherwise. He seems to always tense when I use that word though, like it triggers a Pavlovian response within him, so it's worth a shot.

Walker swallows harshly as his attention drops to my touch. "Are you trying to brat right now because you want me to keep kissing you?"

Damn. Sometimes I really think he can read my mind.

"Is it working?" I ask, focusing on tracing the lines of his design with my fingers. Even though it's generic looking, it really is beautiful—not too dark or overpowering on his olive skin. I know that I don't know anything about tattoos, but this one looks like it was done by a true artist.

"You might be more convincing if you moved that hand to my cock."

My eyes drop to the duvet covering the lower half of his body as I trail my fingers down his forearm. I pull back the feathery fabric, exposing the fitted boxer briefs that bunch on his upper thighs. Thin dark hair peppers his skin, and I run my fingers through it before I settle my hand between his legs.

I have no idea how large he is when he's fully erect, but I sincerely doubt he's anywhere close because his cock still feels slightly spongy as I curl my fingers around his shaft. A shudder of desire runs straight down my spine as I slowly rub his impressive length, feeling it grow beneath my touch.

"That better?" I purr, enjoying the sound of his sharp inhale as I stroke him over the thin cotton fabric.

Walker flexes his dick in my hand. "Don't let go," he growls, tilting my chin toward him.

Our eyes meet briefly, and we share a moment of wild agreement before pressing forward and crashing our lips together. He takes the lead, once again kissing me like he's never kissed me before. It's not born of frustration, like our first kiss was. And it's not an apology, like the kiss that he gave me moments ago. This kiss is pure passion and lust—the culmination of months of mutual pining.

His tongue flicks over my upper lip, not yet exploring inside my mouth. I whimper into his throat, suddenly desperate for more than a kiss because the teasing stroke makes my core clench, and all I can think about is what it would feel like between my legs. Instinctively, my grip on his cock tightens as his tongue finally dives deeper before quickly retreating again.

His teeth nip my bottom lip as he pulls back. "You distracted me from the rest of our conversation."

I pant, running my tongue along the area he bit as arousal pulses through me. I want the controlled dominant who earns my submission, but I also want this rough, messy side of him that he keeps locked in a cage.

"It's not my fault you have trouble focusing," I reply sweetly, trying to catch my breath. "They make meds for that, you know."

Walker's nostrils flare as his hand threads through my braid, roughly tugging the hair at the nape of my neck. "I wouldn't have trouble focusing if your bratty mouth was occupied with my cock, would I?"

"Hmmm." I smirk, ignoring the delicious tingle of pain as I gently stroke the length of his now fully erect penis. "But what will my hand do?"

"It's going to wrap around the base and warm the length of my cock that you can't fit down that pretty little throat. And then you're going to stay nice and still, while you listen to me like a good slut."

Desire burns through me and if I wasn't already wet, I definitely am now.

He tugs me down to his lap, my face inches from his monster cock. But instead of keeping his hand on my neck and forcing me lower, he releases his grip on my braid, like he wants me to take him willingly.

I sit back on my knees, digging my fingers into the fabric of his briefs to draw them over his waist. His hips lift as I pull the cotton down his thighs, allowing his erection to spring free from its confines. A bead of precum glistens on the tip of the swollen head, pointed right at me because of the slight bend in his shaft.

I feel myself swallow as I assess what I'm working with. I'm no carpenter but that thing is way more than six inches, and I'm suddenly regretting my previous statements that I could take him.

But I wasn't raised to be a quitter, so I channel my inner porn star and wrap my fingers around him. My tongue flicks out, swirling around his soft tip as I taste his arousal—it's sweeter than I expect, and even though I know he told me to simply swallow him down, I can't help myself from taking more, so I flatten my tongue and slowly lick the length of his shaft.

Walker hisses and roughly swats at my exposed ass. "Did I ask for a blow job?"

I lift my head slightly, peering up at him through my lashes. "Trust me, this isn't anywhere close to how I give a blow job."

His sinful eyes blow wide with arousal as he harshly kneads the skin that he just spanked, worsening the sting of the blow. I take a deep breath and wrap my lips around his glistening tip, lowering myself onto his shaft and breathing through my nose.

This isn't an uncomfortable position because I'm essentially kneeling next to him, but I have to focus on my breathing so that

I don't freak out and choke. He can't just want me to stay still, can he? It's not like I'm stimulating him at all—the only thing that's happening is that I'm being gagged by his cock. If I stay here for more than a few minutes, there's a one hundred percent chance that I'm going to start drooling all over his lap.

I try opening my throat as much as possible, but I only make it halfway before realizing the only way I can take him fully in my mouth is if I somehow learn the art of sword swallowing.

"Right there," he groans once my lips reach my fingers, the combination covering his whole shaft. "Don't fucking move an inch. Hold me in your mouth like my good little fucktoy."

I shift, feeling the ache between my legs escalate to a throb. When we were in our scene earlier, he was praising me. But now, his words have turned filthy and degrading in a way that sounds wrong but feels so right. If any other man spoke to me like this, I would clock him. But Walker isn't any man—he's a magician who hypnotizes me with his dominance into someone who loves being degraded.

His fingers start to draw circles on my ass, tracing the crease that he spanked. The touch is soothing and almost puts me into a trancelike state, while his other hand gently threads through my braid, not holding me in place like last time, but almost caressing the sensitive skin of my scalp.

My body relaxes instinctively, giving into the feeling of helplessness, though my mind knows that I'm still in full control—if I needed to pull away for any reason, his hold wouldn't stop me.

"Finally some peace and quiet," he sighs, clearly trying to provoke me. "I should have filled that sassy mouth with my cock a while ago."

My core tightens, making my entire body feel tense with need.

"Put your free hand on my thigh. I'm going to finish our conversation. If I ask you a question, I want you to squeeze my leg once for yes and twice for no."

If I wasn't in a near meditative state, I would bite back with something like, "*why shove your cock in my mouth when you want to talk to me?*" but I restrain myself. Instead, I follow his command and place my right hand on his skin.

"Atta girl," he coos, continuing to rub my bare ass. I don't think the touch is meant to be erotic, but his fingers are veering dangerously close to my pussy, and I can feel my body building.

"Before you rudely distracted me," he starts, trailing his hand down my inner thigh. "We were talking about what happened earlier tonight. I think if we're going to only play with more formal dynamics occasionally, there should be a word or phrase to indicate that we're both in the mood for it. Does that sound like something you're interested in?"

I squeeze his thigh once to indicate yes.

While I loved everything about what happened earlier, I also feel like it was incredibly intense and somewhat clinical. I like to think I'm kinky, but that type of power exchange isn't something I could do all of the time—I'm just not wired like that.

"How about something simple like, 'Do you want to go play?'"

I repeat the single squeeze on his leg, appreciating his respect for my boundaries and willingness to make this work between us.

If you had asked me last week if he had this side to him, I would have looked at you like you were insane. Walker struck me as a hot, but grumpy, doctor who I enjoyed messing with because he happened to be friends with my friends, not someone who I might actually enjoy being around and trust so quickly.

"Before we try it again, we're going to have a discussion on what we want to experiment with and what's completely off the table. For example, putting *anything* near my butt is a hard limit for me. Do you understand?"

I try to laugh around his cock but it comes out as a gurgle because of the spit building up in my mouth.

His fingers dig into my thong and snap it against my skin. The sensation is more arousing than punishing, and I briefly consider continuing to misbehave so that I can experience it again. Instead, I simply give him a single squeeze with the hope that he'll reward me for my active listening skills later.

Walker returns his focus to my inner thighs as he traces fiery lines across my skin. "After a scene, I want us to talk about what we liked and didn't like. This should be pleasurable for each of us. And if it ever isn't, we need to have a serious discussion."

I squeeze once.

"When we play, I want you to address me formally like you did tonight."

I squeeze again in acknowledgment, feeling my lips quirk as his cock hardens further.

"If you misbehave in a scene, you're going to be punished. Unlike that book you had me read, I won't punish you by spanking you. It won't be anything that you enjoy because the point is to learn from the behavior. Do you understand?"

I squeeze his leg as my mind mulls over what punishments he could possibly come up with that aren't pleasurable. Pretty much everything he does to me is enjoyable. I can't think of anything that would be bad enough to make me rethink testing him, except maybe not doing anything at all.

His fingers dance up my leg, cupping my right ass cheek.

"Hmmm. Let's see what else I can ask you while you're completely at my mercy," he muses, kneading the flesh possessively. "What are your thoughts on cockwarming? Are you liking it?"

A gush of arousal flows from me in response to his question, and I hear him snicker like he knows. His hand moves from my ass to the band of my thong again, tugging it through my pussy. I hum around his cock in pleasure as the fabric rubs against my clit, creating the friction I've been desperately craving.

"I asked you a question," he growls as he snaps the elastic band of my panties against my back. "Are you enjoying warming my thick cock in your mouth until I decide to give you more?"

The quick sting makes my core muscles pull tight and I squeeze his leg once, harder than the other times.

"I'll take that as an enthusiastic yes," he chuckles, running his hand up my spine and taking the hem of my shirt with him.

Cold air prickles my skin and my body arches into his warm touch as a moan escapes my lips, desperate for more. The sound releases a stream of saliva from my mouth, sliding over my hand and coating his length. It's sticky and messy, like the tip of his cock resting in the back of my throat created a new type of fluid from my body.

He adjusts my shirt so that the fabric bunches at my shoulders, and my breasts suddenly feel heavier now that they're exposed.

"Do you actually sleep naked?" he asks. His voice is breathy and less controlled as his fingers slowly trace their way down my back, one vertebrae at a time.

I squeeze a single time, wondering if he's thinking about the night that I slept in his bed. While I was taunting him, I wasn't lying when I said that. I only put the shirt on tonight because I thought all we would do it talk—clearly I was wrong.

Walker lets out a satisfied hiss in response, and I can feel his abs clench as his hand moves down my left leg. Once he reaches the crease of my knee, he draws a line to the inside of my thigh and pauses halfway up to gently pinch the skin.

I flinch, not expecting the pain which quickly gives way to a pulse of pleasure. A garbled sound comes from my throat as he continues higher, his finger outlining the seam of my panties along the center of my pussy.

His grip on my braid tightens, the skin of my scalp prickling in delicious contrast to the sensation building between my legs.

"Look at what a filthy little cockwhore you are," he praises, sliding the fabric of my thong to the side. "Your needy cunt is drooling even more than your lips, little devil. It's dripping down your legs, begging to be used just like that bratty mouth of yours."

I don't doubt what he's saying one bit. The throb of desire in my core is almost painful, and I'd do just about anything to have some relief.

"Think we should give this pretty little pussy what it's craving?" His voice is low and raspy as he drags a single finger through my slit, not quite giving me what I need.

My body shudders with desperation, trying to sink onto his teasing digit for more. He quickly removes it and before I can groan in frustration, I hear the distinctive smack of his hand. Only this time, the pain doesn't erupt on my ass—it starts in my clit and explodes through my core.

I whine around his shaft, trying to process the opposing sensations of bliss and agony. The tension at the base of my spine is at an all time high, and even though the smack was jarring, it didn't really hurt—it brought me dangerously close to that edge I've been chasing all night.

"I think you liked that correction a little too much," Walker chides, returning his fingers to my entrance. "Are you going to answer my question? Or do you want to see what I can come up with next? I'll warn you—it might not feel as good."

Like a trained dog, my fingers squeeze his thigh once. I hope he understands that my response is to his earlier question, not baiting him for more punishment exploration.

I've always been aroused by blow jobs, but this is so much more. It's both mental and physical, a glorious test of submission and patience—two things I'm notoriously horrible at. But clearly I love a challenge because my body is climbing faster than ever before, and I'm slightly terrified of what's going to happen once he finally gives me what I need.

"Atta girl," he purrs, slipping the tips of two fingers inside my pussy. "Make sure you keep those lips wrapped nice and tight around me. My cock is going to plug your screams the first time you come for me."

His fingers slide deep into my sex, opening me up for him. It feels like an itch that's finally being scratched, and I can feel myself clench around him as he slowly pumps in and out, testing to see how well I take the initial intrusion.

I nearly choke on my moan when he scissors his fingers, sweeping them along my inner walls. But he twists his wrist and continues pumping, his thumb brushing and teasing my clit. I tighten my lips around his cock, trying to suck him down even though my head remains in place. Having him fill my mouth is oddly comforting, like it's taking the pressure away from the orgasm I'm rapidly approaching.

He must notice because a pained sound comes from above me.

"Fuckkkk," he groans, fisting my hair. "That tight little pussy wants to come so bad. Go on, then. Give it to me. Come with my fat cock in your mouth."

As soon as his fingers curl against that sensitive inner wall that I've never been able to quite hit myself, I'm done. I fly over the edge of my orgasm, trying to scream through it while my body pulses in pleasure. My hand on Walker's cock must tighten as I ride out the waves of ecstasy because I hazily notice him tense beneath me.

His fingers continue to work me as I come down from the high, not letting up in the slightest. I try to wiggle away because I feel too sensitive to be able to tolerate more stimulation.

Walker growls. "Give me one more. Soak my hand with your cunt like you were born to be my cockwhore."

His fingers slide out of me and move to my clit while his thumb presses against my tight hole. My body tenses, naturally resisting the intrusion despite how much I crave it. But the blissful focus on my clit quickly distracts me, coaxing my body toward orgasm once again as the tip of his thumb slips into my ass.

I feel my legs start to shake beneath me as the pleasure builds so fast that I worry I might combust.

"That's it," he praises gruffly. "Look at how that tight hole accepts my finger. I think one day I'm going to have you warm my cock with your perfect little asshole instead of your bratty mouth."

I know it's not a question but I squeeze his thigh in response.

When I told Walker that I like ass play, I meant in the colloquial sense of the phrase. I enjoy when it's slapped or grabbed... maybe the occasional finger if things get really kinky during a random hookup, but I've never actually done any exploration more than that. It's not because I'm not interested—there's definitely always been a curiosity—but I never had anyone I trusted enough to experiment with.

Until now.

"Fuckkk, I'm about to blow. Show me you can take it, little devil. Hold my hot cum in your mouth until I tell you to swallow."

My eyes close as his thumb presses fully into my puckered hole, his fingers coaxing me over the edge. I slam into the brick wall of my orgasm as his thick cock swells and spurts warm liquid along the back of my throat. He grunts as I ease up slightly, lifting my head so that he can fill me up.

Walker tugs on my braid, pulling me off him so abruptly that I struggle to keep all of his cum in my mouth. A mix of fluids begins to drip down my chin, and I feel my eyes widen with embarrassment as he holds me steady, staring at my partially open mouth with rapt fascination.

His fingers slide from my neck to my face, gathering his wet release and smearing it along my lower lip. "My little cum slut looks so pretty with her lips painted. Go ahead and swallow me down now."

I feel my chest flutter, wanting to please him for some ridiculous reason. Leaning forward, I close my lips around his fingers and follow his command, keeping my eyes trained on his.

Walker's eyes glow with salacious pride. "I think you're the best friend I've ever had."

Chapter 18

Walker

"Dr. Chastain. Please come in," the hospital therapist says. He removes his waspy reading glasses and methodically places them in his lap. "I have to say, I wasn't expecting to see you again."

Me either, buddy.

I hesitate at the door frame, suddenly wondering if this is just a big fucking mistake. I've been at a surgical conference in Orlando for the past week, and I thought that my weird-ass feelings would go away with the distraction of presenting my research. Spoiler alert—they didn't.

Taking a deep, resigned breath, I enter the office and shut the door behind me. The click of the handle in the lock seems to echo in the too-quiet space, making me even more uncomfortable.

Dr. Kinkaid offers me a warm smile, gesturing toward the firm couch I'm well acquainted with.

"Yeah, sorry about that," I reply, settling onto the lime colored fabric that looks like it's seen better days. "I felt like we had worked everything out."

He nods, his expression understanding. "It's perfectly normal to think you've resolved issues, only to find layers that you haven't fully addressed."

"That's not it," I state, glancing at the windowsill. "Nothing we talked about has changed."

My eyes land on a much healthier version of a plant that sits in Morgan's kitchen. Hers looks like it's on death's door, in desperate need of water, food, or attention of some kind. The thought makes an uncomfortable tightness settle in the depths of my chest.

Why does everything make me think of her?

"What is it, then?"

His question hangs in the air as I try to verbalize the shit swarming through my head. I scrub my hand over my face, returning my focus to him.

"Do you think there's something wrong with me?" I ask. The words are out of my mouth before I can take them back, so I continue, "I mean, I know you see a lot of fucked up shit. But how much worse off am I than everyone else?"

He offers me a warm laugh. "You're not any worse off than the rest of us."

When I don't say anything, his bushy gray eyebrows furrow. "In what context do you mean?"

I want to yell out, "*everything*," but I don't because that's not what this is about. This is about the ability to connect with people and keep them in my life, something I clearly fail at spectacularly considering I'm a divorced thirty-something with no family and only two friends. Well, three now . . . I guess.

I explained my friendship with Beau as him being a deranged country boy who drank one too many Budweisers and decided to latch onto me. Parker, honestly, I'm still not even sure he thinks we're friends. I was shocked when Beau told me that I was invited to the bachelor party. And even though it was probably only a pity

invite, my friendship with him at least ma'
since we're similar in a lot of ways.

It's Morgan's attachment to me that's throwing ~~
been texting back and forth for the past week while I'v~
Florida. And each time I reply to her, I keep waiting for the o~
shoe to drop. I expect her to ignore my boring messages, or forget about me, or something... but she doesn't. And I don't understand why.

"Relationships, I guess," I answer simply.

Dr. Kinkaid picks up his pen and places it between his teeth thoughtfully. "Is this about the divorce? I haven't seen you since it was finalized. Are you struggling with the finality of the marriage?"

"No." I hear myself scoff, but I'm not trying to be an asshole. It's just instinct when I think of my now ex-wife. "I made peace with that worthless relationship a while ago."

I'm sure to some people it would be concerning that I got over a ten-year relationship so quickly, but the truth is that our marriage simply fizzled out over time. It was probably over years ago, we just never verbalized it. Sure, I always had hope that things would get better once my residency was over, but when I found out about the extent of her betrayal, processing the loss became a lot easier. We all have non-negotiables in relationships, and unfortunately, I learned mine the hard way.

"There are no worthless relationships, only worthless perceptions of those relationships." He gives me a pointed look and leans forward in his chair like he wants me to hear his words better. "With all pain comes perspective. You might not see it, but you have grown substantially in the few months that I've known you. I very seriously doubt that your growth would have happened without your failed marriage."

swallow, knowing that he's right. But sometimes it's easier to sink into the darkness than to search for the silver lining.

"Yep. Well, this isn't about her anymore," I find myself saying, needing to get this off my chest. "It's someone new."

His expression shifts to one of curiosity, but he doesn't say anything. He does that annoying thing Beau does and remains silent, waiting for me to share more.

"A new friend," I add, knowing that the words on their own are a blatant lie. They were a lie when I assigned them to her that night in my house, and they're a lie now.

"And you want to know if you can have a successful relationship with this friend?"

I feel my body tense. "She's maddening—a tiny tornado of constant frustration that destroys my peace."

A smirk forms on his thin lips. "Does she now?"

"Well, she did at first," I answer honestly, thinking back to how I felt each time I saw her after New Years. "Now . . . I'm not sure."

"You like that she destroys your peace." The words come out as a statement, rather than a question, like he's reaching into the cloudiest parts of my psyche and pulling out the truth.

I nod, shifting uncomfortably on the couch. "More than I expected."

I don't know what I'm thinking. Morgan made it clear that she wasn't interested in anything more than a physical friendship with me, and I made it clear that I couldn't be anything more with her. The problem is that over the past week, I've found myself wondering if I could . . .

"Why is that distressing to you?" he asks, his voice gentle.

I shrug as memories of my life flash through my mind like a depressing movie reel, reminding me that I have no business feeling this way. "I'm not exactly the poster boy for how to have a healthy relationship."

When I think about it, I didn't have a single healthy relationship until I met Beau. After everything happened with my parents, I thought the only person I needed in my life was Lane. I clung to her like a lifeline, and she became the only thing I had in my life outside of medicine. It's not that I didn't want friends, I just didn't value them because I didn't think I needed anyone else other than her. But it turns out that's a great way to have your whole world come crashing down in an instant.

"I disagree," Dr. Kinkaid offers, leaning back thoughtfully. "You've been dealt some tough cards in life, Walker. Far more than most people. But you took those hands, and created something valuable. You were with your ex-wife for a long time. There was no lack of love, no abuse, nothing that would concern me about your ability to form true attachments. And the marriage ended because of nothing you did."

"That's not true," I counter, suddenly feeling guilty. "I should have been a better husband."

In the moments of forced silence, I've spent my time thinking about what I could have done differently in my marriage. While there were a ton of things I had no control over because of the nature of residency, I could have made it clear that she was still important to me—that her sacrifice was just as important as my own.

Dr. Kinkaid furrows his brow, studying me intensely. "We all can be better in something, whether it's health, wealth, love, or even friendships. Life is a game of constant self-improvement and growth. You've taken a terrible life event and learned from it—that's the definition of growth."

Silence settles between us as I try to absorb his words.

"I guess I'm just worried that it's going to happen again," I say after a while.

A sly grin forms on his face as he nods in understanding. "Ah, yes. But what if it doesn't?"

Chapter 19

Morgan

There was a time in my life when I lived for the chaos of the emergency room—the way you never know if you're going to have a day that resembles Disneyland or a dumpster fire. Until recently, I truly believed that the best shifts were the ones that went up in flames because it's when I would feel like I was the best nurse.

But something inside of me fundamentally shifted after my aneurysm case. It's not like I haven't witnessed some traumatic shit in my time on the floor—that's simply the nature of the job, but this was different. Maybe it was the straw that broke the camel's back after years of carrying the weight of death, or maybe it was the fact that I've never felt wholly helpless in a situation before, but for the first time in my career, I've dreaded coming to work.

I thought that after a few days, I would get over it, but I can't shake this uneasy feeling every time I clock in. If I didn't deeply love all of my coworkers, I would call out of work for the next month and use the time off to reset my perspective. But I have a guilty conscience and don't want to leave them short-staffed, so I've been dragging my ass here whether I like it or not.

Unfortunately, today leaned more dumpster fire than Disneyland though, because the nursing home decided that they wanted to take a field trip to our ER this afternoon. If I have to do

CPR on another ninety-eight-year-old grandmother, I might just burn the whole hospital down. For the love of all things that are holy, do not resuscitate orders exist for a reason. People should use them.

As I'm walking out of the hospital and bopping to Taylor Swift's new album, Siri announces that I have a call coming in from Claire Winters.

"What's up, slut," I answer, completely forgetting that I'm still within earshot of people as I wait for the parking garage elevator. Fortunately, they are also exhausted healthcare workers with potty mouths, so none of them even bat an eye.

"Do you have a second to talk? Find Friends notified me that one of my Sims had finally left the hospital, so I figured it was okay to call."

I laugh and decide to take the stairs. "Who else do you have on there?"

"Just you, Cass, Caroline, and Beau," she answers. "Doctor Dickhead won't agree to let me add him. He thinks it's an invasion of privacy, or something, which is shocking given his control issues. I don't know, I stopped listening when he started talking about life before cell phones and the internet like he remembers it. The dumbass was born in 1992."

Don't say it.

Don't say it.

Don't say it.

"Do you think when God made him, he forgot to add anything good?"

Oops—I said it.

Claire giggles, knowing we're on the same page about her brother. It's a love-hate relationship.

DR. FELLOW 167

"Wait," I add, considering what she just said. "Cass didn't work today. She shouldn't be at the hospital."

Usually, my bestie and I work the same shifts, but I picked up overtime at the last minute with the hope that I could put some cash toward breaking my lease. Though, based on what I know about Claire's tastes, the more likely scenario is that I'll be using all of the extra money on our Vegas trip.

"Oh yeah," she says casually, "Cass is the only one at home, but I couldn't call her since I had an idea for the bachelorette party."

I let out a nervous breath as I reach my car because Claire scares me when she has ideas. Not that they aren't always amazing, just that I know whatever she comes up with is going to be over the top.

I hop behind the wheel, transferring the call to Bluetooth before I respond. "I think you mean *joint* bachelor and bachelorette party, thanks to benevolent Beau."

"Awww," she sings into the phone. "I love that nickname. He is pretty benevolent, isn't he? Especially in bed."

I roll my eyes. I can just picture Beau checking in every five seconds to make sure the sex is good for her, which is the absolute last thing I want in a lover. I want a man who takes what he wants from me, not a man who worships the ground that I walk on.

Snooze.

"There's someone for everyone," I say flatly, rubbing my tired eyes as I pull out of the parking deck.

My brain desperately wants to shut off and watch reality television until I fall asleep, but my body is on high alert because Walker got back from his lame-ass conference today and asked me to come over after my shift. We haven't seen each other since he stayed over, but we've been texting nonstop.

Something crinkles on the phone line, and I hear a faint, "Sit, Frosty," before Claire's voice returns to normal volume. "Sorry, Beau and I are trying to teach him tricks. He's already learned how to fetch because he's my smart kitty."

I stop at the light outside of the hospital, leaning over the center console to pull a handful of Nerd Clusters from the party-size bag that resides in my passenger seat. "Y'all are insane."

"God, our baby boy has such a big brain," she coos excitedly. "Wait, can you just come over on your way home? He's getting so big, and I know he misses his auntie Morgie."

"Uh—"

I hesitate, trying to come up with an excuse so that I don't have to tell her that I'm going to Walker's house after I shower. I'm not ashamed of the fact that we're fuck buddies, but I just know that she's going to freak out and make it a huge deal. I can literally hear her squealing about how we're all just one big happy family, and that's not what this is.

This is just sex.

Actually, it's not even sex because we haven't gotten that far yet. After I held his dick in my mouth like an oversized pacifier, he stayed the night and took over my bed with his big-ass body. But I didn't have the balls to tell him to get out, nor did I have the heart—especially not when he passed out and unconsciously wrapped his arm around me like he had been doing it his entire life.

"I can't tonight," I tell her, hoping she'll drop the idea.

"Boo, you're no fun," Claire whines dramatically. "Okay, but we do need to talk. Will Cass kill me if I reserved a table for all of us at the Hurricane Heatwave show? I know we joked about sexy, dancing men, but we may or may not officially be VIPs."

Absolutely unhinged images of our weekend flash through my head, quickly vanquished by a car horn behind me indicating that the light has changed.

"Cass should be fine," I reply distractedly, stepping on the gas, "but Doctor Dingleberry will definitely not be pleased."

Claire cackles on the other end of the phone, and I can hear her struggling to catch her breath. "I'm obsessed with you. Will you please marry me?"

"Back at you babe. And if I believed in marriage, you'd be the first person on my list."

"Not true," she counters. "It would for sure be one of your kinky-ass book boyfriends."

She's not wrong—there's just something about a fictional man that hits different. They're broody, hot as hell, and have the filthiest mouths known to man. If I could find one in real life, I *might* be convinced to think about holy matrimony.

"Speaking of book boyfriends . . . did you see the rec I sent to Team Daddies? The plot was average, but the spice was insane. I had over two hundred highlights on my Kindle."

Nobody responded to the reverse harem recommendation that I sent yesterday, though Caroline did like it which automatically makes her my new favorite person. I feel like behind her posh princess exterior, she's a total freak in the sheets—my goal for Vegas is to get her drunk and break that icy shell of hers.

Claire scoffs into the speaker. "I'll never understand why you picked that group text name. All you send are unhinged dark romances where the female main character sobs when they're having sex."

I roll my eyes because she and Cassidy are on a rom-com kick right now. And listen, I get it—everyone loves rom-coms. But you just can't get the right level of kink with that type of book. One of my favorite things about reading is that I learn new things about myself, and the only thing I learn from reading a book with a cartoon cover is that I suddenly have the urge to vomit.

"First of all, they're happy tears," I argue as I come to another stoplight on Peachtree. "You would know, if you actually read them. Second of all, Cass vetoed all of my other suggestions."

"Even Happy Hour Hoes?"

"Yeah, apparently she doesn't have a degradation kink," I joke, tossing more of the greatest candy known to man in my mouth. "It made me sad because that's truly award-winning alliteration."

"So you chose Team Daddies? Why not Puck Bunnies, or something?"

She's referencing hockey romance, a phase we all went through a few months ago. The genre has been innovating a ton recently, and several authors have figured out how to get super spicy while mixing in dark themes. Rom-com writers need to take notes.

"You can't dislike a single dad," I argue, feeling myself about to step onto my soap box. "It's just science."

"What if he's a dick and blond?"

Oof.

"Hmmm—" I have to pause and think about how to respond to that one.

The entire book community hates blond men for some reason. It's never been an ick of mine because I imagine all of them to look like Chad Michael Murray, and you're going to tell me that you hate the teenage heartthrob of the 2000s? There's no way.

"Redemption arcs are a major pillar of modern literature," I answer confidently, using my stern older sister voice. "Without them, we wouldn't have character growth, and you'd be bored."

I pause, taking a sip of my Monster Zero to wash down the baby Nerds stuck to my tongue.

"Also, I genuinely believe that blond men are fucking hot."

"You think all men are hot," she teases.

"I don't discriminate," I say, though my mind flicks to Walker. I've definitely been discriminating against other men by only thinking about him for months. Changing the subject, I ask, "So, how much money do I need to set aside for Vegas? I'm kind of scared."

Claire mentioned that she took care of booking everything since it was so last minute, but she's been uncharacteristically silent about our specific plans. For all I know, I might be maxing out my credit cards to pay for this trip. Which, I'm totally down for because I don't have the best financial habits, but I just need a few weeks to mentally prepare for the destruction of my bank account.

"None, silly, unless you want to go to the casino or something. There's a few hours of free time on the schedule each day."

A wave of relief washes through me, followed by trepidation as the light turns green. "Schedule? Care to share, my precious?"

Claire might seem like the kind of person who goes with the flow, but she is a Winters, after all. Every member of that family has a genetic mutation for lack of chill—I wouldn't be surprised if each aspect of the trip is mapped out down to the minute.

"Nope." Her voice bubbles with excitement. "It's a surprise. Well, other than the stripper show I just told you about. But I'm zipping my lips on everything else."

I sigh, considering how to get the information out of her. It's not that I think she is doing a bad job planning the trip, but Cass isn't the most ostentatious person, and I want to make sure Claire doesn't get carried away. The engagement party she planned over New Year's Eve turned into a huge black-tie affair complete with catering from one of Atlanta's most expensive restaurants, when I'm pretty sure Cass would have been happier with a barbecue.

"Do I need to call Beau for answers?" I threaten, turning onto my street. "He might think he's a big tough guy, but I know how to play him like a damn fiddle."

She giggles. "He doesn't know anything. It's driving him crazy because he thinks that as the best man, he should be included in everything. Trust me, he's been using some very interesting interrogation techniques. But I've held firm."

I smile as I picture their conversation. Claire and Beau are two peas in a pod who playfully poke at each other any chance they can get. It's adorable really, and if I believed in romantic love, they would be the couple that I use as my inspiration.

"You're a true warrior."

"I told him that since he invited himself to my party, he's a guest, not a host."

"Cassidy's party," I correct.

"You know what I mean."

"Okay, well please just promise me one thing," I say as I pull up to my house. "That none of your surprises involve a wedding chapel."

Chapter 20

Walker

I didn't get out of the hospital until mid-afternoon, which was not at all what I intended. Being away for a week obliterated my carefully curated schedule. From basic household chores, to studying for my board exams, I feel like I'm behind in all aspects of my life. And despite rushing around for the past few hours to get caught up, I'm glad I stopped to talk to Dr. Kinkaid after dropping off the conference supplies—I hate to admit it, but therapy works.

As I'm pulling fresh sheets out of the dryer, my phone pings with a text from Morgan.

> Just got home and hopping in the shower.
>
> Be over soon.

She worked today and even though I had no reason to stop by the ER before heading home, I couldn't help myself—I wanted to see her. It must have been a busy day though, because I only caught a glimpse of her rolling a crash cart through the hallway, looking irritated and miserable. I type back a response, hoping a little bit of teasing will turn her day around.

A text bounces back almost instantly, making the corner of my lips quirk up.

> Don't worry.
>
> Two hours max.

I quickly remake my bed and then respond to her message as I walk into my recently finished office.

> I hope you're joking.

Three blue dots pop up, then disappear quickly as her reply comes through.

> Am I?

My lips press into a firm line.

> There are going to be consequences if you take two hours to get your ass over here.

Almost immediately, she starts typing.

> In that case . . .

> See you in four hours. ;)

I read the message several times and shake my head before tossing my phone on the new ebony wood desk I just had delivered.

My finished office is masculine and sexy, with dark floor-to-ceiling bookshelves lining three walls, and a cowhide rug covering the hardwoods. While the space isn't huge, I was able to fit a Chesterfield loveseat and bar cart against the open wall. I never would have imagined that I would enjoy interior design, but this project has kept me company over the past few months, and I'm genuinely proud of the results, especially the false bookshelf I installed which opens to a walk-in closet.

Pouring a glass of whiskey, I sink into the leather couch for the first time. It's surprisingly comfortable, and if Morgan wasn't coming over tonight, I probably wouldn't move—I honestly still might not move depending on how long it takes for her to get over here.

Needing something to pass the time, I open one of the books she texted me about this week. Now that she knows I'll indulge her recommendations, she won't shut up about them. When I got back to the hotel after the conference one night, I opened my phone to a list of required reading that was almost as long as the screen.

And what did I do?

Ordered all of them immediately.

Hey, I needed something to fill my empty shelves—even if they will definitely be hidden at the top where nobody can see them.

I know she was surprised that I finished the first book, but I've always been an avid reader. I'll read pretty much anything that takes me to a different world, especially because my world growing up was one that warranted escaping from. Unfortunately, now that my board exams are looming on the horizon, I'm not sure how much time I'll have to escape anything other than my orthopedic surgery textbooks. But that's a problem for tomorrow—today I'm making the conscious choice to put something other than my career first, knowing that it'll make her happy. Maybe my therapist is right—I have grown.

As I'm diving into chapter four of a book that seems like it's about some sort of post-apocalyptic world, my phone pings with another text from Morgan.

> On my way!
>
> I've got a surprise for you.

A few seconds later an image of a silver hook comes through. It's nearly twice the size of her hand, with a small ball on the end that looks like a marble.

Before I can respond to her message, I get another text.

> Hope you have lube.
>
> It might feel weird at first, but I know you'll like it.

I feel my jaw clench even though I know she's doing this on purpose.

> You're not as funny as you think you are.

Her response comes through instantly.

> I'm not joking.

> RIP to your asshole.

I should have known it wouldn't be a quiet evening with her.

> Morgan.

I hope she reads my message with a warning tone because that's exactly how it's intended.

> Uh, oh. You only call me that when I'm in trouble.

My lips twitch again as I type back a reply.

> You are in trouble.

Right on cue, she presses the dislike button on my text.

> I'm quaking in my shoes.
>
> (at your front door)

By the time I reach her, my heart feels like it's going to pound its way through my chest. She knows exactly how to get a reaction out of me, and I can't decide if that's a good thing or a terrifying one. I take a steadying breath before opening the door to let her in.

Morgan's shiny brown hair is pulled back into a ponytail, dark wisps framing her amused face. My eyes travel down the length of her body, taking in the skin-tight black leggings that show off her juicy ass. A matching top clings to her torso, pushing her tits so high that it looks like they might spill out of the stretchy material.

"You look nice," she says, slowly drawing her eyes over my body the same way I am.

"Better than the tux?"

I can tell that she likes my fitted black T-shirt by the way her gaze snags on my arms, though I doubt there's anything she loves more than the monkey suit.

"Nothing's better than the tux," she answers predictably. "Not even your gray sweats."

"I hate to break it to you, but I won't be in a tux again until the wedding in June."

Her lips quirk into a smirk. "Role play isn't one of your kinks? Not interested in pretending to be a sick billionaire with me as your slutty nurse?"

"You already are my slutty nurse."

Her smile transforms into a grin as we stand in the door frame, locked in a silent battle of restraint. A hailstorm of emotion is pounding into me, conflicting desires fighting for my attention. I want to ravish her, to punish her, to cherish her—and I can't decide what I should do first.

"I missed you, little devil," I admit, stepping aside to let her in. As soon as she's through the door, I pull her into my arms and bury my nose into her hair. She smells like the beach, warm and refreshing after a long day, and I have a hard time wanting to let her go.

"Of course you did," she teases, dropping her purse to the floor. Her face shines with delight as she asks, "How did the conference go? Did you big-dick them so hard?"

Even though we've been texting back and forth all week, we didn't talk about work once. At first, I was kind of pissed that she didn't ask about it, but then I got my shit together and realized that it means she sees me as more than a physician. And as someone who has always felt like they were nothing more than their job, it was surprisingly freeing.

I step forward, crowding Morgan's petite body against the front door. Her back hits the painted white wood, and I reach out to cup her face in my hand. "I'm gonna big-dick you so hard."

The delicate column of her throat works as her emerald eyes flare with desire. "Oh, you want to play?"

Her words make my cock swell painfully in my jeans, like it knows exactly what the phrase means before my brain can catch up. And as much as I want to continue exploring our formal dynamic, I want something else more.

"Not tonight," I answer truthfully, stroking the soft line of her jaw with my thumb. "Tonight I want to hear you scream my name the first time I bottom out in that juicy cunt."

Chapter 21

Morgan

My legs wrap around Walker's bare torso like a koala as he walks us through the hallway. We started making out against the door like a couple of sex-crazed teenagers, both of us removing our tops before he picked me up in his muscular arms and headed for his bedroom. His firm lips remain pressed against mine, kissing me sensually, like he's reminding me just how much he missed me. It makes my heart flutter in a weird way, but I ignore the feeling and focus instead on the delicious clench of my core each time his tongue flicks over my lower lip. The man knows how to use his mouth, that's for sure.

Instead of tossing me on his bed, he gently sets me down on the edge of the mattress. The light in the room is dimmed, casting dark shadows across his handsome face as he drops to his knees in front of me.

His fingers dip into the waistband of my leggings, pulling the fabric over my hips and down my body. Dark, lust-filled eyes land on my bare sex as his tongue darts out over his lower lip, like he needs a taste. His hands grab my ankles and aggressively pull my legs apart, forcing me off balance and onto my elbows.

"Such a filthy little whore," he rasps, running his hands up the inside of my calves. "You didn't wear any panties because you wanted me to have easy access to this greedy cunt. You wanted me to eat you raw, didn't you, little devil?"

My core clenches, confirming that the degradation kink that I suspected I had is definitely there. This friends with benefits thing may have more benefits than I originally thought—you could never ask a random hookup to talk to you like this. Well you could, but they would probably look at you like you're clinically insane.

And honestly, I just might be.

But when Walker and I talked about things that we were interested in with our arrangement, he didn't look at me like I was. He just smirked and said that he wasn't surprised.

"Answer me," he growls, pinching the thin skin on my thighs.

Damn him and his sadism—I'm starting to like it.

"Yes," I whisper breathily, watching him drop to eye level with my exposed center as his hands push me open even further.

He leans in and blows cool air on my clit. I flinch instinctively and try to close my legs, but his fingers dig into my thighs, keeping me open for his torment.

"No, no, no," he tuts, nipping at the skin of my right hip. "You don't get to hide this pussy from me. We might be nothing more than friends, but in my bed, your body is mine."

I shudder beneath him, the sting of his bite rubbed away with gentle flicks of his tongue as he heads south again. He alternates between kissing and nibbling along the crease of my leg, stopping just before he gets to my entrance.

Walker looks up, eyes flashing darker. "Tell me."

I'm panting slow, shallow breaths, desperate for him to keep going. "What?"

"That you're mine. Tell me, and I'll feast on this needy pussy until you're seeing stars."

I don't even think before I answer. Right now I'll be whatever he wants me to be.

"I'm yours."

Pride swells in his lust-filled gaze as he lowers his mouth and peppers short kisses along my swollen lips. His tongue flicks into me before tasting the length of my pussy and landing on my sensitive bundle of nerves.

My eyes roll to the back of my head and I collapse to the bed, my arms giving out beneath me. Heat prickles down my spine as he pauses, his tongue holding my clit hostage. The scratchiness of his beard teases the sensitive skin of my inner thighs, and I feel so needy that I don't think I can wait—I need to come now. I writhe beneath him, trying to get some friction to push me over that blissful edge, but he pulls back with a sound similar to a growl.

"Try that again, and you won't come," he warns, releasing my leg to slap my clit.

Why is that so damn hot?

"Walker, please," I cry out.

His lips curl into a salacious grin as his thumbs move to trace the outside of my pussy. "Did you just scream my name?"

I pant and narrow my eyes in challenge. "It was a request."

"Hmm," he muses, sinking two fingers inside me, "let's see what we can do about that, then."

I close my mouth, trying to stifle the desperate noises coming from my throat as he returns his expert tongue to my sex and begins to trace circles around my clit. His free hand snakes beneath my ass, trapping me between his face and his grasp as he tugs my body closer.

My legs start to quiver, and I have to dig my fingers into the bedspread to anchor my body. I can feel the force of my orgasm about to crash through me like an avalanche, sweeping away a week's worth of pent-up tension.

His fingers hook inside of me, though they don't sweep in the direction of my G-spot, they curve in the opposite direction. At the same time, another finger presses on my tight hole, causing my body to burst in pleasure.

"Fuck, Walker, fuck!" I scream, arching my back as a delicious release zaps through me.

His lips circle my clit and roughly suction my swollen center as I'm coming down from my high. I reach down to pull him away—does he not know that he just did the Lord's work? He can stop now.

His fingers start pumping in and out of me while he maintains pressure on my other hole. If he keeps this up, I'm going to come again.

"I can't," I sigh defeatedly, knowing that no amount of begging is going to stop him.

It's not that I don't want him to keep going, because his expert touch feels incredible. But I've never come in quick succession like this before, and I have no idea what's going to happen. Even when I'm hanging with my vibrators, I give myself a little bit of recovery time—this isn't even enough time to catch my breath.

His answering snarl ricochets through my core, amplifying the sensation to a nearly unbearable level. Without warning, his teeth graze my clit and an almost animalistic sound comes from my lips as the line between my first orgasm and the next one blurs, shattering me into a thousand pieces of overstimulated glass.

I have no idea how long I lie on the bed trying to catch my breath. By the time my heart finally steadies, I lift my heavy head to find Walker planting soft kisses along my hips. His eyes flick to mine, gleaming with wild arousal as he crawls over my exhausted body.

"I'm not done with you yet, little devil. Not even close."

Chapter 22

Walker

I've questioned my sanity for a while when it came to Morgan, but now the truth has become impossible to ignore—I'm obsessed. Watching her come undone beneath my fucking tongue, seeing the way she responds to the simplest touch, the filthiest words, it all has me craving more.

"You must have really missed me, huh?" I ask breathily, trailing kisses up her soft stomach. "Your tight little pussy came so fast on my face. My filthy girl was needy for it. God, you just couldn't help it, could you?"

When she doesn't reply, I lightly pinch her perky nipples. "Answer me."

Morgan's head whips up, her green eyes narrowing like she's about to argue. "Has anyone ever told you that you're very demanding?"

I bite back a smirk and squeeze her tits harder. "Has anyone ever told you that you're a brat?"

"Once or twice."

I tweak her nipples a final time before releasing them, licking soothing circles around the puckered buds—I can't wait to torment them because she's so sensitive to stimulation here.

I push her tits together, squeezing them in my hands as I pull back to look at her. She looks so fucking beautiful like this, splayed out on the bed beneath me, skin flushed from the orgasms I just gave her.

"You ached for my fingers. For my tongue." I bend down, pressing my forehead to hers. "I wonder if there's something else you were aching for."

A coy grin forms on her lips. "I wonder."

"And what might that be?"

"Hmmmm," she muses, biting her bottom lip as she pretends to consider my question. "Your fat cock."

Fuck yeah, she was.

I give her a soft kiss before I stand, my fingers reaching for my belt. I unbuckle the metal and pull it through the loops in one swift motion, keeping my eyes glued to her perfect body. Morgan watches me raptly as I unbutton my jeans, pushing the denim down my legs before I step out of them, leaving me naked—she wasn't the only one going commando tonight.

"You have two options." I step forward, slowly stroking my hard cock. It pulses in my hand, happy to be let out of its confines. "Option number one. I can fuck you the way I've wanted to from the moment you first rolled those eyes at me—rough and punishing."

My grip on the head of my shaft tightens because just the thought of taking her like that is enough to make me come. I want to mark her. To degrade her. To own her.

"Option two. I can fuck you the way you deserve—nice and steady, the way I would for a *friend*."

The last word comes out with a spit because I'm starting to fucking hate it.

"Let's get one thing straight." Morgan pushes herself up on her elbows, the post-orgasmic glow draining from her face. Her eyes narrow into slits, like she's a copperhead that's about to strike my jugular. "I'm the only one who determines what I *deserve*."

I cock my head, trying to hide my amusement because I love her damn fire. "And that is?"

"For you to fuck me like I've never been fucked in my life."

I suck in a harsh, satisfied breath. She doesn't want me to worship her body the way a doting lover would—she wants me to break her wild spirit. To make it messy. To split her apart.

"Be careful," I warn as adrenaline rushes through me, desperate to give her what we both want. "That might be more than you can handle."

Her lips curve with amusement. "I can take it."

My arm wraps around the small of her back, flipping her onto all fours beneath me like a rag doll. I slide my fingers through her sopping wet pussy, still dripping with her slick arousal. She has the tightest little cunt, and while I seriously doubt her promise, because she was gripping my two fingers like a vice when she rode my face, we're damn sure going to try. I slip them back inside, pumping her several times to make sure she's ready.

She doesn't flinch at the addition of a third finger, and I work her cunt mercilessly, feeling the precum leak out of the tip of my cock as it rests in waiting against her hip.

Sliding my fingers out of her greedy pussy, I slap her juicy ass with her arousal. She moans, dropping her head to the mattress in frustration.

"Something wrong, little devil? Feeling a little empty?" I taunt as I cross the room to grab a condom.

When we talked through our arrangement the morning before I left for the conference, I told Morgan that I had been STD tested after my divorce, just in case, and she let me know that she was also clear and on birth control.

I have no problem going bare, and would probably prefer it if I'm being honest, but she's the one who insisted on using condoms. I'm not entirely sure why, because it almost feels transactional and cold, but I ignore the disappointed feeling in my chest as I grip my cock in my hand and roll the latex down my shaft.

I give myself a few quick pumps as I watch her skate her legs back and forth.

"My fingers just weren't enough for you, were they?" I grab her hip in my free hand and dig my fingers into the skin at the crease of her thigh, anchoring my body to hers.

"No," she whimpers as I inch forward, dragging my erection through her swollen lips.

"No," I echo, pausing when the head of my cock brushes her clit. "You've been aching to have me fill you up, haven't you?"

When she doesn't answer, I pinch her leg hard. I've found that I like her to respond verbally because it allows me to check in without ruining the mood.

"Fuck," she answers shakily. "Yes. Please."

I slide back through her cunt, notching my tip at her warm entrance. A gush of arousal leaks down her legs and it takes all of my self-control not to slam my entire length into her.

"Walker," she pleads, trying to push her hips back onto me.

I pull back, not letting her control what's happening here.

"Beg for it," I reply, settling at her entrance again. "Beg for it like a desperate cockwhore, and maybe I'll let you have it. That's what you are, right? My personal cockwhore?"

Morgan lifts her head and twists to look at me over her shoulder. There's desperation in her eyes and a grimace on her lips like it's physically painful to wait for me. "God, yes. Fill me up. Fuck me like you wanted to the night of the engagement party."

My cock pulses, remembering exactly what I wanted to do to her that night. The carnal pull between us was so strong that if I hadn't pulled my shit together at the last minute, I would have forced her into the goddamn bathroom and ripped her apart.

"You want me to fill you up?" I rasp, releasing her hip to slip my fingers through her ponytail. I wrap her hair around my hand and tug, wrenching her neck back. "Then hold on tight because I'm about to destroy every inch of your pussy with my fat cock."

My hips tilt forward, inching my tip inside her tight heat. A beautiful whimper escapes her lips as I press deeper, amazed by the way her body is stretching for me—it's like she was made to take my cock.

Her pussy tightens once I'm halfway in, making me pause to groan in pleasure. I reach around with my free hand and slowly stroke her clit, trying to get her to open up for me.

"Something wrong?" I taunt, tugging hard on her hair. Her back arches, pushing her deeper onto my length. "Is my cock too big? Hmmm? But I thought you could take it?"

A desperate sound somewhere between a moan and scream, comes from her lips as I pull her against me, seating myself fully inside her cunt. I pause, allowing her to adjust to my size before I start pounding into her. But before I can move again, her pussy clamps down on my cock, squeezing me with her inner walls.

"Did you just fucking come on my cock?"

Morgan squeals when I pinch her clit, looking for a response. "Yes," she cries, her legs trembling beneath me. "Sorry. Fuck. You're just so big."

"You just can't stop coming, can you? Your body knows that you're mine so it instantly explodes, doesn't it?"

She's taking me so well, her tight pussy stretching around me as I hold still and allow her pulsing muscles to relax after the orgasm.

"Give me another one," I growl, finally feeling her cunt relax. "Be a good little cockwhore and soak my balls in your cum."

I pull out and ram back in, sinking deeper than ever before. I tug her arms behind her back, holding them still with one hand as I draw her to her knees. Her back is flush against my chest and I lean in, dragging my teeth against her shoulder. My fingers circle her clit the way that I've learned she likes it, consistently massaging the sensitive nerves right at their base. Each repetition makes her pussy grip me a little tighter.

"Oh fuck, I'm gonna come again," she pants, dropping her head to my shoulder as her entire body shakes.

I want to stay like this, to keep my dick buried deep inside of her. But I promised that I would fuck her like I wanted to that night, and if anything, I'm a man of my word.

"That's it. Let go for me, little devil," I grunt, sliding out of her slick heat almost completely before I plunge back inside.

Morgan cries out as she adjusts to the deeper angle, completely at my mercy while I use her for my own release. My cock hammers into her, driving rough, punishing pumps into her swollen pussy until I feel her spasm around me, screaming my name just like I told her to.

Unable to hold off any longer, I fall over the edge with her, groaning as my balls tighten and my orgasm rips through me. I hold her tight as every bit of my pleasure is wrung from my body, suddenly aware of one thing without a doubt—I need more.

Chapter 23

Morgan

Is it bad to be thankful divorce exists? Don't get me wrong, I know that it sucks and ruins lives, but it's just the way that I've always felt. Both my mom and my dad are way happier now than they would be if they were still married. They're also far more emotionally stable, so that's definitely something to be thankful for.

I'm also thankful to Walker's ex-wife for letting him go because this is by far the best sex of my life. My statement that he had no idea how to use his gigantic cock was absolutely ludicrous and unfounded. Especially because it now seems like every time we take a trip to pound town, he's trying to prove to me that he's more than capable of wielding that thing.

Which he is.

Terrifyingly so.

And not only that, but the man seems to have the stamina of an energizer bunny. In the past two weeks, he's given me more orgasms than all of my past hookups combined. By the time he even thinks about coming, I've already had at least two of my own, sometimes more depending on how much time we have. We just can't seem to get enough of each other, like our bodies have this insatiable itch that's never quite scratched.

Unfortunately, I doubt that itch is going to be scratched this weekend because Claire has put all seven of us in the same hotel room. We just made it to reception at our bougie Las Vegas hotel and they handed us each a key for the same penthouse. I mean technically there are four separate bedrooms, but still, there's no way I'm waltzing into Walker's room with my nosy best friends in the same place. I'm horny, but not that horny.

When we make it to the top floor, Claire is practically vibrating with excitement. She hasn't told anyone the plan, but based on the matching velour sweatsuits for the girls, and the flight which included all of us in first class, I have no doubt it's going to be over the top.

"Get ready for the best weekend of our lives," Claire beams, jumping up and down when the personal butler opens the white marble door to the penthouse.

As the chairman of the Me First Movement, I shoot past everyone and take in the new digs. The suite is five times the size of my rental and looks more like something out of a luxury travel magazine than the location of a rowdy bachelor-bachelorette party. There's a full bar to one side, plush sofas in the middle, and what appears to be a game room equipped with a pool table to the other.

"Holy shit," I breathe out, taking in the best part of the entire suite—a panoramic view of the Las Vegas strip.

"You think it's okay?" Claire asks, following behind me. "They didn't have the biggest penthouse available, so you and Caroline are sharing a room. But there are two beds, don't worry."

I glance back at Beau. He's looking at me with the same incredulous expression, and I know without a doubt that he has the same thought—Claire is absolutely insane.

"Oh, well if the biggest penthouse isn't available, I don't want it," Walker deadpans, pushing his sleeves up his corded forearms.

Damn him and his delicious tattoos, they're more distracting than the shimmering crystal chandelier hanging above me from the forty-foot ceiling.

Beau tosses his meaty arm around Walker's shoulder, pulling him toward the game room. "I'm gonna kick your ass in pool."

"No!" Claire yells. "You're going to stay right here and help me decorate until I say you can go play."

Beau grumbles something under his breath which makes Walker's lips twitch.

"Maybe Beau and Walker should share a room instead," she jokes, joining me at the window.

"Seriously though," she continues, nudging me with her elbow, "is this okay? Your face is kind of making me nervous right now. I can totally ask Walker to take the pullout if you want your own room."

Her question is so ridiculous that I can't help but laugh. Sometimes she's so out of touch with reality, and I love her to death for that. This is the nicest place I've ever stayed, and probably will ever stay. Even if I had to share a room with the devil incarnate himself, Parker Winters, I wouldn't complain.

"It's perfect, Claire," I promise, glancing over to the boys who are arguing over pool sticks. "Let's put these assholes to work. I doubt Caroline can entertain them for much longer."

The youngest Winters sibling was tasked with distracting Parker and Cassidy at the hotel bar while we got everything ready in the suite. In a city known for its entertainment, I would think keeping the two guests of honor busy would be easy, but I sat next to Caroline on the plane, and she seemed almost depressed. Her headphones were on for the entire flight, and I could tell that the last thing she wanted to do was talk. I've resolved to make her a cocktail while we're getting ready for dinner because if anyone can get her to open up, it's me.

"Where do you want this one?" the bellman asks, wheeling an oversized suitcase that looks to be part of Claire's matching ten-piece set through the double doors.

She squeals. "Right there, please. Those are the decorations."

Considering how much money she spent on the reservation, I have no clue why she didn't just pay someone to decorate, but I bite my tongue—it's Claire's world and we're just living in it.

***

"Okay, but like would you be DNR or full code?" I ask Caroline as I'm lining her eyelid with lash glue.

We've spent the past thirty minutes doing our makeup together in the opulent bathroom, and I have to admit, I think she's way cooler than I initially pegged her to be. She really is a mix of her siblings—she has the serious, unapproachability of her brother from the outside, but once you talk to her, she's soft and curious, just like her sister.

"Considering the success rate of resuscitation is less than twenty percent for perfectly healthy people, just let me die. I've lived a good life. I don't want to go out with cracked ribs."

I laugh, trying to hold my hand steady while the fake eyelash sets. "I totally agree and would like to officially petition you to become an ER doctor so that we can work together one day."

She blinks a few times, testing my work. "I have no idea what I want to do. Right now it's just lectures and nonstop studying. I'm honestly glad I could even get away for the weekend."

Standing from the velvet vanity stool, she walks to the mirror with the poise of a runway model to inspect her finished makeup. I've been fully dressed for a while, but Caroline seems to be waffling on what to wear because she's still in a plush towel. I would offer to let her borrow something, but she's legitimately six feet tall, and I think all of my dresses would look more like shirts on her.

I try to mind my business and search my travel case for my Dior lip stain, but out of the corner of my eye I see her open her phone. Her high cheekbones seem to sag as she reads a text, her throat swallowing harshly.

I don't have the best vision because I refuse to wear my glasses, but my eyes catch on several choice words in the ridiculously long message—words that I would never even think to say to someone else.

"Everything okay?" I ask, trying to act casual as my attention snaps back to the mirror.

Don't be suspicious.

Caroline sighs and locks her phone, plastering a fake smile onto her face. "Just my boyfriend."

"Oooooo," I tease excitedly, though I feel my pulse pound because if a man ever called me a whore in a non-sexual way, I would lose my shit. I don't know who her boyfriend is, but he just became public enemy number one. "Do tell. Please say he's not a doctor . . . no offense."

She huffs a fake laugh. "Barely—he's a radiology resident at UH."

The old me would commensurate with her and recite the old adage of the four Ps, but that would just be hypocritical given my situationship with Walker. So I just grimace and say, "Want me to key his car?"

Her head cocks like she's not sure if I'm serious, but her smile grows more genuine. "I can see why Claire likes you."

"I'm small, but I'm mighty," I reply, giving her a look that hopefully conveys that I am, indeed, very serious.

She might not be *my* sister, but she's important to someone I love, which automatically makes her important to me. I suddenly feel incredibly protective of her, like I want to take her under my wing and give her the best possible weekend so that she forgets about her asshole boyfriend.

"Let's go," I add, grabbing her hand in mine. "We're gonna get you dressed, take a million sexy pictures before dinner for the spank bank, and then *accidentally* airdrop them to hot guys this weekend. Because what's the number one rule of Team Daddies?"

Caroline's midnight-blue eyes swirl with suppressed amusement under the crystal chandelier above her head. "What?"

"Do it for the plot."

***

One hour, and one hundred iPhone pictures of the girls later, the entire crew gathered at the massive marble dining table in our penthouse as a private chef served us a six-course meal. Rather than gawking, I decided to embrace my rich girl era and pretend like I belong here.

More caviar? Obviously.

Bottomless Dom Perignon? Keep pouring, baby.

This is the kind of life I could get used to.

Even though we still have no idea what the plan is, Claire gave us guidance on what to pack each day. Tonight all of the girls were required to wear short black dresses while Cass wore white. I have no idea what she told the guys but they're dressed almost identically, all wearing dark slacks and a white button down. If someone had their drunk goggles on, we might be mistaken for a group of dominoes.

"You're part of the dead parents club too, right?" Claire asks as we finish off the dessert course.

The question almost makes me spit out my Baked Alaska, and I look up from my plate to see her staring directly at Walker. She's already super tipsy from the champagne that's been flowing all evening—if there's one thing Claire Winters can't handle other than social cues, it's her alcohol.

Caroline's ocean-blue eyes widen in horror. She looks to her brother for backup, but he's deep in conversation with Beau and Cassidy across the table.

"You can't just ask people that," she scolds, tucking her straightened dark hair behind her ear like she's uncomfortable.

"What?" Claire shrugs her shoulders. "It's not rude if it's true."

Walker's lips twitch with amusement. "And how do you know it's true?"

She giggles and narrows her eyes on me. "*Someone* spilled the beans."

I shoot daggers at her, feeling a nervous flush creep over my cheeks.

I know I said that I love my friend, but I'm very close to wringing her long, skinny neck.

She was complaining about being an orphan tonight, so I casually mentioned that she should talk to Walker about it, not thinking anything of it. But now I immediately recognize my mistake and am further validated in my decision not to tell her about our little arrangement—she would be incorrigible.

"Did they now?" Walker asks from my periphery, his tone husky and low. "So you've been talking about me, little devil?"

I swallow, glancing over at him briefly. "Only the worst things."

His laugh rumbles through my body and settles directly between my legs, causing me to shift in my velvet chair.

"Ahem." I signal the rest of the group because I need something to distract me from Walker's unrelenting focus. "Claire was just about to tell us what the plan for the weekend is."

The diversion works like a charm because Claire perks up, waving off our conversation with an airy flick of her hand, her tipsy smile wide. She's been itching to divulge the full schedule all day, but insisted that we wait until after dinner for some reason.

"Right," she exclaims, nearly knocking over her flute of champagne. "I figured tonight everyone could decide between a chill evening in, or the hotel casino since tomorrow is a packed day. Starting at eight, we have breakfast in our suite followed by a group exercise class at nine. We need to release all of the toxins before the afternoon pool party."

I glance over at Cass to gauge her reaction to the plan. She's sitting on her fiancé's lap, looking incredibly content as he rubs her back—I honestly don't know if she's even listening.

"After the pool," Claire continues, leaning forward like she's sharing a secret, even though she's addressing the whole group. Her wild curls sweep over her face, partially obscuring the massive grin on her face. "We have pizza being delivered for dinner to help us sober up while we get ready for a special VIP show at nine. Then we're just going to bar hop and see where the night takes us."

"Hell yeah," Beau whoops, draining the rest of his champagne in one glug. "I hope it takes us to pound town."

Lines of tension bracket Parker's mouth, and he looks like he's debating wringing his friend's neck. "I'm going to take you to pound town if you keep talking about the shit you do with my sister."

"Which sister?" Beau winks, deciding to dig his grave a little deeper.

"Not Carol. She has a boyfriend. Don't you baby sister?"

Claire must have conspired with Beau to get under everyone's skin tonight because they're making their way around the table at a rapid-fire pace.

Caroline's porcelain face turns even more pale. "Claire. Stop."

"What?" she laughs, innocently looking at her sister. "It's not like brother dearest will care. Your boy toy doesn't even work at our hospital."

Claire must not know what's going on with her sister because there's no way that she would bring him up if she did. They bicker and have their issues, but she would never support a toxic relationship like that.

"Speaking of toys," I pipe up, changing the subject and looking at my best friend. "I left a few early wedding presents on your bed. Just wait until you get home to use them, please. Our room is right next door."

Cassidy's cheeks flush as I wink at her, and I hear Claire pretend to gag from across the table.

"I'm suddenly feeling a little tired." Cass lets out a teasing yawn and kisses Parker on the cheek. "Want to head to bed early?"

"Oh my god, gross," Claire groans, pushing back her chair so aggressively that it almost topples over. "Well, I'm going to the casino. Maybe I'll win some earplugs."

Parker rolls his eyes but there's a reluctant smile tugging at his lips, the love he has for his sister overshadowing her never-ending teasing.

Beau grins as he stands and wraps his girlfriend in his beefy arms. "I'm going wherever you go, pretty girl."

I finally gather the nerves to peek at Walker, curious about his plans now that the group is dispersing. He's been silently watching like a bystander, and I wonder if he's had enough of our antics for the day. I wouldn't blame him—we can be a lot, and I already forced him to explore the strip before we got ready for dinner.

"You wanna go?" I ask quietly.

His dark eyes flare with something unreadable, boring into me like a knife. "That depends."

I shift, suddenly feeling like we're the only two people in the room. He has a way of doing that—capturing my focus so that all I see is him.

"Depends on what?"

He leans in, his voice so low that only I can hear it. "What are my odds of getting lucky?"

A dangerous prickle of arousal creeps down my spine. "I'd put all of my money on it."

Chapter 24

Walker

Morgan is bent over the roulette table, eyes sparkling with excitement as she cheers for the wheel to land on red. I've never gambled in my life because it's a ridiculous waste of money and incredibly frivolous, but as I watch her laugh and jump when her color hits, I begin to understand the appeal. Though to be honest, I would understand the appeal of anything that made her this happy.

The rest of the group left a while ago, but she was on a winning streak, and I couldn't bring myself to leave her alone. Multiple guys have already come up to the table to hit on her, and I don't know if she's politely declining simply because I'm hovering like a damn bodyguard, or because she really isn't interested, but I don't intend to find out.

All I can picture is her coming home early tomorrow morning after staying in a stranger's hotel room, and the thought makes me feel twitchy. I wouldn't blame her because the number of times we've both thrown out the word friend is egregious, but I'm very quickly beginning to feel like something has to change after this weekend.

We're not just friends anymore, and we both know it.

"Walkie come on," Morgan pouts, leaning over the table as she slides her winning chips closer. "Help me make a bet. You're allowed to have fun, you know."

I slip my arm around her waist. "I am having fun."

And it's the truth—I can't remember a time when I've had more fun than tonight, and it's all because of the person with me. Morgan has such a giddy joy and enthusiasm for life, that it's impossible to not enjoy every moment with her.

"Well, I would have more fun if you participated." She eyes me like she's trying to be intimidating.

She's not—but it's cute as hell.

I sip my water casually, trying to act unaffected by her tornado of energy. She's glowing under the fluorescent casino lights, her chestnut hair in loose curls that slide over her bare shoulder each time she gets excited and flails her body around.

"What do I get out of participating?"

"Bragging rights, obviously. Though I doubt you can do better than me. I'm up five hundred bucks."

"You're right. I can't," I confirm, not interested in gambling whatsoever. "And we should keep it that way if you want to break that rental lease, don't you think?"

In the past two weeks, I've been over to her place several times to fix various issues. It might be a nice place, but the landlords are pieces of shit and don't address anything in a timely fashion. She's mentioned trying to move, but the lease she signed is ridiculous and requires her to pay over six grand to back out of it. And she won't be getting out of there any sooner by losing all of her money on a game of chance.

"Such a spoilsport," she mutters under her breath, stretching her arms above her head with a small yawn. "Okay, but let's make a side bet, just you and me."

I sigh. "Fine, but you're only putting in the minimum."

Tables in Vegas have a set amount that you have to play for each bet, usually ranging from ten dollars to upwards of thousands. The one we're sitting at is currently asking for twenty-five bucks a spin, and the entire night Morgan has been betting on colors, so the odds are essentially fifty-fifty to win or lose. I have no idea how she's been choosing the correct color each time, but my intuition says that it's best to stop while she's ahead.

"Fine," she echoes, narrowing her gaze on mine. "If it lands on black, you win. We head back to the penthouse and go to bed."

I wait for her to continue, knowing there's more to this based on the glimmer in her eyes.

Her mouth curves into a wild grin as she adds, "If it lands on red again, I win."

"And what, exactly, am I agreeing to if you win?"

She draws her bottom lip between her teeth. "That we'll go play."

***

"Shhhh," Morgan whispers, tiptoeing toward my room.

She looks like she's going on some sort of bear hunt, swiveling her head back and forth dramatically in search of predators. I have no idea what she thinks we're going to encounter—it's well past midnight and the penthouse is silent when we got back. Our friends are definitely asleep, but even if they aren't, who gives a shit? I'm sure they would be proud that we're hooking up.

"You're the one making noise," I reply quietly, swatting at her plump ass as she pauses to open my door.

Morgan yelps and turns, giving me an evil look. We were making out the entire elevator ride up from the casino, and my cock is throbbing painfully in my slacks, begging for some relief. While she ended up losing the bet and we won't be going into a formal scene, that doesn't mean I'm not going to fuck her silly. Her tits have been taunting me all night in that low-cut dress, and all I've been able to think about is marking them with my teeth.

She stumbles into my room, not because she's drunk, but because she's wearing ridiculously tall heels that she can barely walk in. Scooping her into my arms, I close the door behind us with the heel of my loafer.

I set Morgan down in front of the floor-to-ceiling windows, wrapping her in my arms as we take a moment to admire the shimmering lights of the Las Vegas Strip that are illuminating my dark room. It truly is the entertainment capital of the world, and even from floors above, I can feel the energy of the city—it's intoxicating, but still not as intoxicating as the woman pressed against me.

"Did you have fun tonight?"

"Of course," she sighs, nuzzling into my chest like it's the most natural thing in the world.

It makes me feel a deep sense of longing for more between us. I don't just want to be her friend. Or her lover. I want to also be her partner. I want to give her everything that I could never give someone in the past . . . I know I can give her everything.

"You look stunning," I murmur into her hair, telling her what's been on my mind all night.

She inhales sharply, stiffening in my arms. "That's not what this is."

Her words cut deep even though I should have known that they were coming. I can feel my pulse escalating as frustration swirls inside my chest. "Why don't you tell me what *this* is, then."

She spins, staring up at me like she can't decide whether she should say what she wants to say. Her hands reach up to my neck, searing my skin as she begins to unbutton my shirt.

"This is fucking," she replies, popping the first button open.

She reaches for the second, keeping her eyes glued to mine with rageful defiance. "This is pleasure."

Pop.

"A transaction."

Pop.

"An arrangement."

Pop.

My jaw clenches harder with each button she opens, and I'm fairly certain my molars are going to crack if I don't do something. I reach out and grab her wrists to stop her from continuing to rub salt in the wound, pushing her hard against the glass window.

Morgan might say that we're all of those things, but I refuse to accept that she believes it. Not when I saw the way she watched me when women tried to hit on me at the casino bar. Not when I felt the way her body relaxed when I held her in the shower. Not when I heard that she talked about me when I wasn't around.

We both know she's full of shit.

Leaning down, I bracket both hands around her head. "Sure it is."

I don't know who moves first, but our lips collide in a rough kiss of pure passion, each of us trying to prove a point that the other is refusing to understand.

Her tongue presses into mine, fighting for a dominance that I let her take. Her fingers dig into the collar of my shirt, pulling it down my shoulders. I reach forward and tweak her nipples through the sheer bodice of her tight, black dress. She shudders beneath me, always so sensitive to stimulation there.

Part of me wants to spend all night teasing her, but I stop myself. I let go of her perfect tits and shrug out of my shirt as she moans into my mouth at the loss of contact.

I give her my back and walk toward the freshly made king bed on the other side of the room, trying to get a grip on the tornado of emotion pounding in my chest. Even when she's pissing me off, I can't get enough of her—I can't stop myself from giving in to her.

I take a seat on the mattress and slowly remove my black leather belt. She's still leaning against the window, her chest heaving from our kiss.

"Go ahead, then," I growl, unbuttoning my pants as my eyes narrow on her body. "Use me. Take out my fucking cock and ride me."

If Morgan wants to label this as transactional, that's exactly what it'll be.

She hesitates briefly before moving, like she isn't quite sure that she believes the words coming out of my mouth. Every time we've hooked up, I've been the one in control in one way or another—even when she's sucking my cock, I'm still guiding her head and setting the pace the way that I prefer. But if she wants me tonight, she's going to fucking use me.

As she walks over, I pull my wallet out of my pants and remove the single condom I brought for the weekend. I had no idea what the sleeping arrangements were going to be since no details were shared, but I packed one just in case.

Morgan stops between my legs and drags her small hands over my shoulders. Her eyes briefly run over my tattooed arm before she snaps her focus back to me. A tentative smirk forms on her red lips as she flattens her palms on my pecs and pushes.

I fall back onto the bed, lacing my fingers together behind my head. She reaches for my zipper, drawing out the process longer than necessary. Her eyes widen when my cock springs free from my briefs, like she forgot what I was packing. Good—I intend to remind her after I let her have her fun.

I have to bite the inside of my cheek as she rolls the length of the condom down my painfully hard length. My balls instantly draw up, desperate for release when her fingers wrap around my shaft and pump several times.

She shimmies out of her panties and crawls on top of me. Her perfect tits naturally push together with the movement, and I'm trying my hardest to school my face into indifference despite the telltale throb of my cock beneath her.

The heat of her pussy hovers inches above me, testing my restraint. She thinks that I'm going to give in, pull her onto my cock, and take what I need. But I didn't get where I am today without an exorbitant amount of patience. Nothing can make me falter when I've set my mind to something, not even her tantalizingly tight cunt.

She rolls her hips, rubbing her slick arousal along my length. She's soaking wet, and all it would take is a quick movement to be buried deep inside of her.

Her green eyes flutter closed as she finally notches the crown at her entrance, slowly sinking herself onto my length. She sucks in a pained breath as her body stretches around me, trying to take me to the hilt. This would be the time to reach out and rub her clit, relaxing her through it since this position is deep, but I'm trying to make a point here.

"What's wrong, little devil?" I taunt, watching her wince as she sinks lower, still not even halfway. "You can't take my cock? Not quite the same when you're the one on top, is it? You want me to take over?"

Her eyes fly open, daggers shooting right into my soul. She adjusts herself so that she's perpendicular to my body, rather than bent above it. She hitches up the hem of her dress to make room for her fingers to slip between her legs.

She takes me deeper, though her pussy fights with every delicious inch, like it knows that what I can give her is better. When she's finally seated, she gives me a prideful glare that I want to slap right off her smug little face.

All of the blood in my body rushes to my cock as she starts to ride me, just like I told her to. One hand continues to rub her clit as the other reaches up to toy with her nipple over the fabric of her dress. She throws her head back, exposing her delicate throat that doesn't even have a flush to it.

I have to admit, she puts on one hell of a show. If I didn't know her body intimately well, I'd assume she was getting close to climax solely from the sexy song coming out of her mouth. They're needy little whimpers that echo into the quiet expanse of the hotel room, putting a bandage on the truth—that she's desperate for more.

"Beg for it," I say, tone low and controlled as my hands finally run up her bare thighs.

Morgan slows her rhythm, her plump lips opening and closing like she can't decide if she should give in. "What?"

"You heard me." I dig my fingers into the meaty spot at the crease of her thighs that drives her wild. "Beg for me to take over."

"How did you—"

I use my grip on her hips to pull her lower onto my cock, a wild sound of pleasure escaping those pretty lips as her inner walls flutter around me, finally satiated. I tug the front of her dress, forcing her to fall forward. Her hands catch on either side of my head, her face millimeters from mine.

"Beg. For. It," I repeat, spitting every word as I stare into her wide eyes. "Because once I get on top, I'm not going easy on you. You'll feel me so deep inside that tight cunt that you'll gasp for air. And every time you open that bratty mouth, you'll be so breathless that you can't even speak the word *friend*."

"Ugh." Morgan winces like she's just taken some sort of nasty medicine. "Fine. I want you to take control. God, I fucking need to come so bad. Please take control."

Pride swells in my chest, knowing how much she didn't want to submit but chose to anyway. I pull her closer, pressing my lips to hers in a hungry kiss as I flip us so that I'm on top. My hands slide over her chest, ripping the thin fabric of her dress down the middle to finally expose her flawless tits.

She gasps beneath me when I start moving inside her, her fingers holding onto my shoulders for dear life as I slide halfway out and then push deep inside. I trail dangerous nibbles along her jaw, my hands finding her perky nipples and tugging hard. She screams a little too loud, given our friends are right next door, and a rush of her arousal coats my cock as I pull out again.

My mouth replaces my fingers on her tits, sucking and tormenting her sensitive buds. One hand snakes under her head, threading through her messy hair, and I tug her head back, forcing her lips to part so that I can push three fingers down her throat.

"Suck, little devil. Gag yourself on my fingers while your slutty pussy comes all over my fat cock."

Morgan's lips close around my fingers, following my instructions like she was born to be mine. I tighten my grip on her scalp, using her hair for leverage as I hammer back into her, thrusting hard.

"That's right," I growl against her skin, feeling her pussy start to flutter. "That's my good little whore. You're about to come all over my cock, aren't you? Come for me. Show me how much you need me."

My teeth graze her nipple, finally sending her over the edge. A muffled moan ricochets through her throat as her core spasms around my shaft. I grunt, her tight grip on my cock spurring my orgasm and forcing me to erupt in pleasure. But the way her fingernails painfully dig into the skin of my shoulders as she rides out her release reminds me of one thing—she needs more too, even if she won't admit it.

Chapter 25

Morgan

"I'm already sore as fuck," Beau whines, taking a sip from his footlong strawberry daiquiri as we sit on the edge of the massive hotel pool. "That shit was hard."

My body is way more sore from the pounding Walker gave me last night than the pole dancing class the group took this morning. But I keep that to myself. Nobody was the wiser when I snuck back to my room at two in the morning after the delicious hell he put me through, and there's no reason that they need to know.

"I'm not surprised. You're looking pretty small these days, Buff," Walker deadpans, knowing it'll piss off the most muscular friend in the group.

Walker is sucking down a piña colada the same size as Beau's, though I can't tell if it's affecting him because he's so damn hard to read. He could be blackout drunk or stone-cold sober, and I would have no idea either way because he's acting completely normal.

It's infuriating.

Actually . . . what's more infuriating is the fact that he's barely given me a sideways glance all day. Every time I say something, he ignores it like he wasn't balls deep inside of me hours ago. And I know it's not because I don't look hot as fuck—I'm wearing a black bandeau that barely covers my tits, paired with the cheekiest bottoms that I own. He should be salivating over me, not bromancing with his friend.

"I may be small, but at least I'm not soft," Beau counters, reaching across me to pat Walker's chest. "When was the last time you lifted, bro? I can barely see your abs under there."

Walker laughs and then replies, "I may have a soft body, but I've got a hard dick."

Okay, maybe he is drunk—that was actually funny.

When they start discussing who their favorite porn star is, I decide that I've officially had enough of this boys club conversation and leave to go hang with the girls by the VIP bar.

"Where's Parker?" I ask Cass, wrapping my arms around my best friend from behind.

I don't actually care where her fiancé is, but I'm trying to make pleasant conversation. Things have felt slightly off between us ever since I trash talked him at the Mexican restaurant, and I want to get back on track—our friendship is more important than my opinion of her future husband.

Cass tips her head back against my shoulder. "He had a quick work thing to take care of, so he ran up to the room. I'm sure he'll be back soon."

I plop my ass on the cool metal barstool next to her. "Whatcha drinking?"

She's holding some sort of orange slushie that smells like Everclear, and I'm suddenly feeling far too sober compared to the rest of the group.

"Jetfuel."

My eyes go wide as a core memory unlocks in my brain. "Like from Flip Flops?"

"Mhmmm," she murmurs as she leans in and sucks down the sugary alcohol through a long pink straw. "But it tastes drunker."

Flip Flops is a bar in midtown that we visited once, but never returned to again. Not because it wasn't a good time, but because we both got plastered from a drink just like this. I don't know why I thought it was exclusive to that particular establishment, but now that I know it's not, I immediately order one.

"You excited for the wedding?" I ask, stealing a sip of her drink while I wait for the bartender to bring my own.

Cass reaches up to toy with the string of her white swimsuit top. "I'm excited to be married," she answers slowly, her gaze flickering in the direction of the hotel. "But not the actual wedding."

I shift in my seat, not expecting her answer. "Why? You're going to be the most beautiful bride, Cass, and it's going to be the best day ever."

She's getting married on a rooftop downtown that has incredible views of the Atlanta skyline—it even has a helipad on top so you can have the most outrageous exit ever. She hired a DJ so that we can request practically any song in existence, and dinner includes a buffet with a mac and cheese bar. I literally wouldn't change a thing if I were her.

The sunlight reflects on her massive engagement ring as she takes another sip of her Jetfuel. "I know, I know. It's just . . . planning has been so stressful. My mom is refusing to take no for an answer on the Southerlands, and I'm just so over it."

Her shiny hazel eyes flick up to the straw ceiling of the tiki bar like she's trying to hold back tears. "I just wish Carter were here. He would always mediate. I miss him so much."

I love my brother more than anything in the world and can't even begin to imagine the pain she feels from losing hers. But I know if I hug her, she'll definitely start crying, so I make a joke instead.

"You could get married tonight," I suggest with a smile. "Elope in Vegas with all of your besties."

Cassidy laughs, the tension in her shoulders visibly relaxing.

"You know, that doesn't sound like the worst idea you've ever had." She wipes at the corner of her eye. "Can you imagine the look on my mom's face if I actually did that?"

The bartender slides my drink across the counter, and I take a grateful gulp, feeling the potent mix hit my system instantly. "You'd beat out Claire for the most dramatic plot twist of the year."

She rolls her eyes and clinks her glass against mine. "Always a nominee, never a winner. Could this finally be my time to shine?"

"You always shine, babe."

"Did I hear my name?" Claire slurs, brushing her wild curls from her face as she looks over at us. She's been chatting with her sister about pharmacology, which is just about the lamest discussion I can imagine having at a Las Vegas pool party.

I lean over the bar, already feeling tipsy from the few sips I've taken. "Yeah. Cass demoted you from maid of honor, so I had to step up. Sorry."

Claire's bright-blue eyes go wide in disbelief as she stares at her future sister-in-law. Before she can open her mouth, her gaze flicks to mine and her expression shifts—clearly I can't say anything with a straight face.

"You're the worst, Morg," she chides, throwing her plastic straw at me. "I actually believed you for a second."

I won't lie, I was a little bit jealous when I found out that Claire was going to be maid of honor instead of me, especially since Cass isn't having anyone else in the bridal party. But I also understand why she made the decision—I haven't exactly been the most supportive friend with regard to their relationship.

I hop off the bar stool and pull Claire into a hug, my face smashing into her chest. "You love me, though. This has already been such a fun weekend, and you're the best maid of honor ever."

"Damn right I am," she giggles, wrapping her arms around me. "Now come pee with me. I've been holding it for like an hour, and I'm about to burst."

***

On our way back from the bathroom, I stop by the cabana. I know there are a bunch of sunscreen nonbelievers out there, but I intend to look twenty-six for the rest of my life so I refuse to take any chances by not reapplying.

As I'm dancing around like a monkey, trying to figure out how to get the sunscreen on my upper back, a voice that I occasionally hear in my nightmares comes out of nowhere.

"Want some help?"

My chest tightens. "Uh, nope. I've got it."

I continue contorting my body at an awkward angle as I spray myself, refusing to make direct eye contact with my best friend's fiancé.

"You're missing like half your back."

No shit, Sherlock.

My body starts to feel twitchy as I pause and slowly turn to face Parker Winters. He's wearing a black Atlanta Falcons jersey over red swim trunks, looking far more . . . normal than I've ever seen him. Dare I say that he looks attractive? That is, if you're into men that also moonlight as demons.

"Thank you, Doctor Doubtfire," I mutter, loud enough for him to hear.

"Good one." I hear him chuckle as I turn to put the bottle back in my bag. "Can we talk?"

I glance around for a distraction but everyone else is now in the pool, leaving me cornered with the devil incarnate. I need to remember to always travel with a buddy—it's basic safety.

Eventually, I nod and gesture to the beige sofa beneath the cabana. The sooner we get this conversation over with, the sooner I can get back to pretending that he doesn't exist. I sit down, making sure to leave plenty of space between us because the last thing I want is for this to feel like a cozy chat.

Parker follows, awkwardly studying the sleek pool deck before meeting my gaze with his irritatingly gorgeous blue eyes.

"Look, Cass told me not to make this a big deal," he starts, letting out a heavy sigh. "But I know it's been weighing on her, and she would never say anything to you directly, so I'm stepping in."

My stomach lurches as I wait for him to spit out whatever it is that he has to say, and I pick at the dry skin on my cuticles, trying to keep my hands busy. I've had this habit ever since I was a kid, and uncomfortable situations just make it worse.

"She's worried that you don't want us to get married."

I swallow hard. If she brought it up to Parker, it's clearly been bothering her. It's not like I hadn't considered the impact of my words, but hearing the truth out loud makes my heart hurt. I've been acting like an asshole, and she doesn't deserve that—she deserves a better friend.

"Listen, I just want her to be happy," I finally say as I look over at Cass, thinking about how much joy she's brought into my life. "If you do that, and she wants to deal with your irritating ass for her entire life, I'm not going to stand in the way."

Parker cracks a smile. "Well, she deals with your irritating ass too. Must be something she's into."

I don't laugh, but my lips quirk ever so slightly against my will.

His face becomes solemn as he follows my gaze. "You know I love her more than anything, don't you? I love her more than our bad days. I love her more than any fight or obstacle that'll come between us. There's nothing in this world that I love more than her."

His words make my brain feel fuzzy because I can tell he means them. But that doesn't erase how he's treated her—how I've had to be there to pick up the pieces when he wasn't.

"I'm sure you do—"

"She's taken the very worst pieces of me and transformed them into something better. I've grown into a better man, friend, doctor, all because of her."

"And what have you done for her?"

The words come out before I can stop them, but now that they've been said, I don't regret them—I've been wondering for a long time.

Parker shifts as he stares at his fiancée with a wistful look on his face. "It's not what I *have* done for her, because I'll be the first one to admit that it's not enough. But it's what I *will* do for her."

He turns to me, his voice softening with sincerity. "I'll cherish her, the way that she cherishes me. I'll be her rock, the way that she's been my rock. I'll be everything to her, the way that she's everything to me. And I know she knows that, but I need you to know it too."

The tension in my shoulders eases slightly. Maybe I've been too harsh, too quick to judge based on snippets and moments of frustration. Maybe, just maybe, Parker Winters isn't the devil I've painted him out to be in my head.

"Good," I say after a pause. "Because she's the best of us. She deserves that and so much more."

Chapter 26

Walker

There's a zero percent chance that I wake up tomorrow without a hangover, but I can't bring myself to care. It feels good to let loose, even if Beau keeps trying to pimp me out to every group of females at this damn pool party.

"What's the wildest thing you've ever seen at the hospital?" a raven-haired girl with fake tits asks, batting her also-fake eyelashes at me.

If I wasn't already feeling my liquor, I would audibly groan and walk away because that's the absolute worst question you can ask someone who works in healthcare. It's not like the shit we see most days in ortho is even as traumatizing as other specialties. But we all have that one story that comes to mind—the story that haunts us, and will continue to haunt us, for the rest of our lives.

Usually, I make up something about a professional athlete, but I'm still in a foul mood after last night so I answer honestly.

"A college kid was on Lake Lanier with his friends and backed his boat into a telephone pole. Most of them died instantly from the live wire, but he survived. They flew him to the trauma hospital where I was on rotation, and we had to amputate all of his limbs. He would have done fine, but his electrical burns were so bad that he was permanently disfigured and in a fuck ton of pain, so he ended up killing himself a few weeks later."

I don't add the fact that I can still see his face and the screams of his family. I'm drunk and irritated, but I still know when I've gone too far... which it appears that I have because fake tits face goes white, and she excuses herself to go get a drink.

This type of thing is exactly why people in healthcare tend to end up together. You don't have to pretend like you're living a glamorous life because you both understand the realities of the job. Even when I was married, I never felt like I could be completely honest with my wife about work. Especially because the few times that I tried, she didn't seem to fully comprehend the emotional and physical turmoil that it takes to witness the things that we do, so I eventually got tired of trying.

Beau looks over at me with an appalled expression, but I just shrug and slurp down the final sips of my drink.

"Bro, that was dark." He shakes his head as he watches the woman retreat into the crowd. "It's like you never want to get laid again."

"I wasn't going to fuck her anyway. She was plastered."

I don't tell him that I have no interest in hooking up with anyone other than Morgan, even though I haven't been acting like it today. Each time I glance at her, my heart feels like it's being ripped open because we're on two different sides of a game of tug of war—I want more, and she's never going to give it to me. I doubt she even cares that women have been coming up to me right and left this afternoon, vying for my attention, or that the only place I want to put that attention is on her.

"Still." Beau furrows his brow, like he's worried about me. "You know that's not how you flirt, right? Come here, we're going to practice."

Before I can protest, he pulls me into a headlock and drags me over to his girlfriend and Morgan. I try to escape his hold, but the fucker is strong and determined to piss me off.

"How many Sharpies do you think *you* could fit in your ass, big boy?" Claire giggles from her seat at the edge of the pool.

The fuck? What kind of greeting is that?

These two are a match made in heaven.

Beau's hearty laugh shakes his arm around my neck. "Not as many as I could fit in yours. Especially not after that—"

Claire squeals and slings her body into the water, covering his mouth before he can finish his thought.

I wriggle free from his grasp right before they start making out, not eager to inadvertently become part of a threesome with my friends.

Morgan watches them make out with a disgusted grimace on her face. "You guys are insufferable."

She looks so fucking good, it's painful. And now that I'm less than a foot away from her with no one to distract me, there's no way I could even try to keep ignoring her.

With our friends occupied, I give in to the pull between us. Leaning in, I lower my voice. "Hate to break it to you, but so are you, little devil."

Her green eyes flicker with surprise but remain glued on Beau and Claire. "Am I now? Well, it's a good thing you've avoided me all day, then. None of the girls you've been flirting with looked *insufferable.*"

Warmth spreads through my chest—she's jealous. "I'm surprised you care. What is it that you said last night? That this is a transaction? Didn't know paying attention to you was part of the fee."

I know I'm goading her—that for the first time ever, I'm giving her a taste of her own medicine. But if I've learned anything about Morgan over the past few months, it's that she isn't going to admit to anything that makes her feel vulnerable. And there's nothing more vulnerable to a fiercely independent woman than commitment.

Her throat works as she drops her focus to the empty drink clutched in her hands. "Maybe we need to revisit the terms to something more exclusive."

I glance to make sure that our friends are still distracted before I take her chin between my fingers, directing her attention back to me. "Maybe we do."

For a moment, she's silent. Her hooded eyes search mine like they're trying to read my thoughts, but I'm not going to step in. I'm going to let her tell me what she's ready for. Because whatever it is, I'm ready too.

"Uh oh," Claire sings right as Morgan is about to open her mouth. "Morgs, are you in trouble with Walkie-talkie?"

We both freeze, and the look in her eyes tells me that we'll continue this discussion later.

"He's the one in trouble," she jokes, pulling out of my grasp. "Especially now that he has a new nickname."

Beau snickers, wiping his mouth with the back of his hand. "So I take it the flirting went well?"

Chapter 27

Morgan

"Rock me mama like the wind and the rain, rock me mama like a southbound train," I belt under the spotlight at the karaoke bar, turning to Beau who pulls his microphone to his lips with his signature country-boy grin.

"Heyyyyy, mama rock me," we sing together, our harmony completely off-key.

We take a bow as the crowd cheers around us, probably more out of gratitude that we're getting off the stage than in praise for our ridiculous "Wagon Wheel" performance.

"Crushed it." I hop on Beau's back as he weaves us through the sea of people in search of our friends. I have to hang on with one arm while the other holds my Revolve mini dress over my ass, trying to refrain from flashing any strangers tonight.

"That was iconic, but I'm pretty sure they thought you were the bride and groom. And I'm not gonna lie, it made me a little jealous," Claire says once we reach our table, her red lips falling into a dramatic frown.

She's right—on our walk back, several people commented that we made a cute couple. Which—gross—zero percent of me is attracted to that meathead. But it's also entirely her fault because for some ungodly reason, she made us all wear white tonight.

Apparently, Cass mentioned that she wanted to do a black and white theme this weekend, so Claire took that to mean we wear black one night and white the next. If she had just consulted with me, instead of keeping everything secret until the last minute, she would've known that idea was ridiculous.

Beau softly drops me to the ground before wrapping his massive arms around his girlfriend. "Hey, pretty girl. Wanna go dance?"

Claire beams up at him and nods, her earlier pout vanishing in an instant. Before I can even sit down, they disappear onto the crowded dance floor.

"So who was the better duo? Me and Cass, or Me and Beau?" I ask the table.

Parker and Walker are engaged in a serious conversation about board exams, completely oblivious to my question, so I flick my eyes to my best friend and smile sheepishly.

"Obviously you know I love you, but I think Beau and I were the crowd favorites. 'Since U Been Gone' just didn't hit the same way it does in the basement of GJ's."

Our local bar features a live karaoke band on the weekends, and we've been known to light up the room with a duet of the iconic song by Kelly Clarkson. It's always a hit, and the first time we screamed the lyrics, I lost my voice for two days after—now it's kind of our tradition.

"That's okay." Cass laughs, adjusting her gold glitter sash that has BRIDE written across the front. "I received enough applause for a lifetime earlier."

"Hell yeah, you did. Hottest bride and groom that Hurricane Heatwave has ever seen."

Her cheeks flush bright pink, likely thinking back on the moment when the entire crowd at the male strip show was on their feet, screaming for her and Parker while they got a dual lap dance.

I'm sure if they had been sober, it might have gone very differently. But in their tipsy state, they were both having a blast. Parker even broke into a full smile at one point, which I hope means the stick has officially been pulled out of his ass for good.

I look down at my empty glass. "I need a refill."

Cass nods in agreement, her hazel eyes scanning the busy bar and landing on an opening in the corner.

Getting to my feet, I peek at my tits to make sure they're contained before I grab my best friend's hand and lead us through the chaos.

"Two vodka sodas, please," I yell across the sticky bar before turning to Cass.

A massive wave of affection washes over me—she's truly glowing tonight, with her blonde hair in loose curls and a full face of makeup done by Claire. I can't help but picture her on her wedding day, and after my conversation with Parker, I'm genuinely excited about their marriage for the first time.

I reach out to put my hands on her shoulders, steadying myself as I suddenly feel all of the liquor from the day catch up with me. "I love you."

She smiles softly down at me. "I love you too."

"No, you don't understand." My chin wobbles as guilt hits me hard. "You mean so much to me, and I feel horrible for being such a bitch about Parker. I was the worst. And I'm sorry. And I hope you forgive me. Please forgive me . . ."

I lurch forward, squeezing her waist as hard as I possibly can. It's not the most eloquent apology I've ever given in my life—blame it on the alcohol—but I mean it with my whole heart. Cass is like a sister to me, and it would kill me to have done something that ruined our friendship.

"Of course I forgive you, Morg, but I'm going to kill Parker," she scoffs, rolling her eyes as she pulls back from our hug. "He said something, didn't he?"

I blink up at her, trying to keep a straight face as I remind myself that I don't have to tell everyone everything. "Nope."

She chuckles. "You really are the worst liar."

"Okay, but don't be mad at him. I'm glad he did—he's off my shit list. For now."

Cass arches her brow suspiciously, but she doesn't say anything else because fresh drinks are pushed toward us. We both take our glasses and hold them up in a toast. "Well, cheers to that."

"And cheers to being the hottest bitches ever," I add, slinging back my drink in one long chug.

As I'm goading Cass into finishing her vodka soda, Beau comes up to us. Sweat beads on his wide forehead, and he looks exhausted as he holds Claire to his chest protectively. She's clinging onto him with a sloppy smile on her lips, her eyes halfway closed.

"Gonna take her back," he says, understanding the looks on our faces without us having to ask. "Fell on her ass during 'You Belong With Me' and almost took two people out with her."

"Baby giraffe," I state lovingly, referencing the drunk alter ego we gave Claire a few months ago.

He looks down at his girlfriend with adoration. "Baby giraffe."

"Can you please check on Caroline before you go to bed?" Cass asks, finally finished with her drink.

The youngest Winters sibling started puking her guts up in the pool bathroom, so Cass and Parker took her back early while the rest of us enjoyed the party this afternoon. She was still curled around the toilet in our room when it came time to head to the show. I offered to stay with her, but she insisted that she had learned her lesson with sugary drinks and that I should go on without her.

Beau nods with a small laugh as he shifts to better support Claire's weight.

"Yeah, of course. I'll make sure she's still breathing and not swimming in the toilet bowl." He brushes a stray curl away from Claire's face as she mutters something indecipherable, but probably affectionate, in her semi-conscious state.

Cassidy gives him a grateful look. "Thanks—let us know if she needs anything, okay?"

"Will do," he replies, starting toward the exit. "Hey, y'all coming back soon? Or planning on staying out for a while longer?"

I glance at Cass since this is her night.

"We're definitely staying," she says confidently, grinning at me.

"Don't do anything I wouldn't do," Beau calls over his shoulder.

A pair of lemon drop shots appear next to us, and I narrow my eyes on the bartender. She looks overworked, her dark hair slicked back with a mixture of sweat and product.

"From the guy next to you." She gestures her head to the man beside me.

I step back and quickly assess the stranger. He's the definition of a finance guy with a trust fund. In another life, I would have totally made out with him because he's a solid six-five and has sparkling blue eyes. His friends are of a similar caliber, probably all hoping to get lucky tonight by buying women twenty dollar shots.

"You didn't poison these, did you?" I ask suspiciously, taking the shots off the bar and sniffing them. "I'm small, but I can still kick your ass."

"I don't doubt it," he smiles genuinely, the dimples of his clean-shaven cheeks popping.

I smile back before handing one to Cass. We tap the shots together, tossing them back with practiced ease.

"So, what's the occasion?" I ask, setting my empty glass on the bar with a loud clink.

"Just out with the boys." He gestures toward his group. They're loudly cheering on a friend who's chugging a pitcher of beer like he's a frat bro in college. "Saw you two having a good time, and thought I'd add to it. No strings attached."

The man introduces himself as Alex, and we shoot the shit for a while before his buddies drag him away. Surprisingly, he pulls out of their grasp briefly to jog back over and hand me his business card, asking that I call him.

I take it with a laugh, appreciating his effort.

Turning to Cass, I look down and read out loud. "Alexander Cooke, VP at Crosswood Capital Bank. New York, New York."

I give myself a pat on the back because my initial assessment of him was spot on.

"You gonna call him?" Cass asks, handing me another drink.

I shrug, taking a sip of an incredibly strong margarita as I scan the crowd. The bar has gotten substantially busier as the night has worn on, but we somehow still have a line of sight with our table. Walker's dark gaze finds mine, his eyes narrowing in agitation—either he's tired of being here, or he just witnessed what happened.

"Want to tell me why Walker is staring at you like you've done something wrong?"

I squint at him, trying to decipher the expression on his unreadable face. His arms are crossed, and his posture is rigid. But there's a flicker of a dare in his eyes, like he's challenging me to keep it up and see what happens.

Turning back to Cass, I shake my head slightly. "I guess he didn't appreciate the attention from Mr. Finance Bro."

"Interesting." She narrows her eyes on me curiously. "And what about the four P's?"

"Uh." I pause, trying to remember the first part of the nursing acronym. I'm pretty drunk, and I have no fucking clue why she's asking me about this right now. "Pain, potty—"

"Physicians, Morg," she corrects, looking at me like I'm the biggest idiot in the world. "You refuse to date anyone whose job title starts with the letter P, remember?"

Oh . . . that.

First of all, everyone has hard rules that we swear to follow until we meet someone who makes us want to break them—it's called growth.

Second of all, Cass should be happy that I'm joining her stupid doctor dating club. She's been teasing me about Walker since the engagement party, so the fact that she appears shocked right now is bizarre. If I'm so easy to read, how the hell could she not read this?

"We're not dating," I state simply, though earlier today I almost said that I would just to get him to stop talking to other women at the pool party. "We're just friends."

Cass gives me an amused glare, waiting for more.

"That hookup," I add.

She sips her drink with a smirk.

"Exclusively."

Her smirk transforms into a smile, and I roll my eyes.

Fine—if she wants me to admit something to her that I only just admitted to myself, I need more shots.

I wave for another round, needing to brace myself for what's turned into a much deeper conversation than I anticipated. The bartender quickly sets down two more lemon drops, and I grab one, tossing it back before Cass can even reach for hers.

"I think I really like him," I admit, watching my best friend wince as the liquor goes down. "It's disgusting. And I hate it. And I've tried to stop, but he's just . . . he's just really patient."

While everyone was getting ready for the evening, Walker and I had a talk. I still have no idea what, specifically, I want. But today I realized that I know *who* I want—and it's him.

Cass puts her glass down on the bar, her expression softening. "You want more."

It's not a question—it's a statement that I wholeheartedly agree with.

"I want more," I echo.

"More what?" Parker interrupts, wrapping his arms around his fiancée. The second button on his white shirt is undone, peeping a smattering of chest hair that Cass leans into.

"Yeah. What do you want more of?" Walker asks as he comes up behind me. His huge hands thread around my hips, pulling me against him so close that I can feel his hard cock pressed against my lower back.

I gulp and glance hesitantly at Cass. She winks at me before responding, "More fun. Wanna go to another bar?"

Parker kisses her neck affectionately. "Anything you want, sweetheart."

The last thing I remember from the night is my best friend drunkenly running down a random street in Las Vegas and belting out "Can't Help Falling In Love" by Elvis Presley.

Chapter 28

Walker

I groan, throwing a pillow over my face as the pounding pain in my head hits an all-time high. Maybe if I shut my eyes again and try to fall back asleep, the pulsating torture will magically go away.

But the second I do, the pounding gets worse . . . and louder.

Why the fuck is it getting louder?

"Can you go get it?"

Rolling toward the muffled voice, I say a small prayer that it's not a random chick next to me. The last person that I remember talking to was Morgan, but she refused to sleep here the first night, so it's entirely possible that I've got a stranger in my bed . . .

When I finally open my eyes again, the room blurs into a bright haze. Squinting, I focus on the figure huddled beneath the silken sheets next to me. It's Morgan, unmistakably—I'd know those stubby fingers shielding her eyes anywhere. But she must be just as bad off as I am because she's grumbling about something incoherently.

"What?" I manage to croak out, my throat dry as fuck.

She sighs, peeling her fingers apart to peek through the slit between them. "Please go get the door. I think I'm dying."

That explains the pounding.

I push myself into a sitting position, immediately regretting the quick movement when the room begins to spin.

Jesus Christ—are hangovers worse in your thirties? My skull feels like it has been split open with a blunt axe.

I brace myself with one hand on the nightstand, waiting for the dizziness to pass before I swing my legs off the bed. The cold floor is a minor shock to my system, but it helps anchor my body slightly as I stand.

Morgan groans again, yanking the pillow over her head. "Hurry, please."

I shuffle across the room, each step feeling like a monumental task. By the time I crack open the door, I'm ready to sell my soul for a glass of water and a lifetime supply of aspirin.

"You look like you got run over by a bus," Beau greets me with a level of cheer that's far too aggressive for my current state. Dressed in only gray sweatpants and tennis shoes, he looks like he's been up and active for hours.

Fucker.

I reach for the door, ready to close it on his chipper face, but he sticks his foot out to stop me.

"Oh no you don't."

I lean against the wooden frame for support, blinking at him through the crack.

"Is there something you want?" I grumble. "Because if not, you can fuck right off."

"Claire sent me to find Morg," he explains, brown eyes attempting to see into the room behind me. "Do you know where she is?"

His grin broadens like he already knows the answer to his question, and if I had the strength, I would kick him in the nuts for being a shit-stirrer.

"I'm sure she's fine wherever she is," I snap back, not in the mood to entertain his buffoonery.

"Easy, killer," he chuckles, dismissing my irritation with a carefree shrug. "Well, breakfast is ready in the kitchen for everyone. It's almost eleven, and we've gotta head out by two."

My stomach twists, either from nausea, or the realization that I've never slept this late in my life. What time did we even get back last night?

"Thanks. I'll be out in a few."

Beau nods, clapping me on the shoulder in a way that's probably meant to be encouraging, but feels more like a punishment to my aching body. "You need anything? A big ol' hug? Some water? A condom?"

Gritting my teeth, I mutter a goodbye and shut the door before he can throw another jab. Leaning back against it, I take a deep breath and try to gather the energy to move back across the room.

"I'm never drinking again," Morgan whines into her hands. She's managed to sit up, her body drowning in my white dress shirt from last night.

The sight of her in my clothes sends an unexpected rush of arousal through me, despite the rest of my body screaming that I'm at death's door.

Echoing her sentiment, I grab two water bottles from the wet bar and hand one to her before unscrewing the cap of mine to take a deep gulp.

Returning to bed, I settle against the headboard and let out a long sigh like I'm trying to expel the demons from within. Morgan slips her hand over my thigh, conveying a silent thank you with a squeeze. Despite our misery, there's nowhere else I'd rather be—just the two of us in our peaceful bubble, postponing reality a bit longer.

"Your phone pinged while you were talking to the brute."

A smirk tugs at my lips. "You heard that, did you?"

"It was only a matter of time." She leans her head against my arm. "I'm honestly surprised it took him so long to catch on. Though, I guess nobody ever called him bright Beau."

A full-blown smile forms on my lips, the dull throb of my hangover replaced by pure satisfaction. Even after our conversation yesterday, I was prepared for her to fight tooth and nail to keep what's happening between us quiet, especially with our friends. But I wasn't prepared for this—for her to finally give in to me. And definitely not for the way it makes my heart feel.

Leaning down, I plant a kiss on the top of her head as another loud ping rings through the air.

"Probably the group text," I comment, though I reach for my phone with a trace of suspicion.

I silenced that thread weeks ago to focus on my board exams, distracted by relentless notifications from the girls about the trip, so realistically, there's no way that it could be the group text.

Unlocking my phone, I notice that I have a voicemail and three texts from a random phone number with a strange area code. Where the fuck is 702 from? The only area codes I know are 678, 404, and 770—all Atlanta-based numbers.

Even though I'm sure it's spam, curiosity wins out, and I open the messages.

> Congratulations newlyweds!

> Thank you for visiting the Burning Love Wedding Chapel. Please remember to pick up your marriage certificate prior to leaving town. If you are unable to stop by, they will be mailed to the address on record in 6-8 weeks.

Both texts were sent at two-thirty this morning, followed by a singular message that just came through.

> Did you have a five-star experience? Leave us a review online and receive ten percent off memorabilia.

Heat prickles down my spine, my heart slamming into my chest as I read, and reread, the words. Without listening to the voicemail, I delete it. If I have to hear the words out loud, I might actually vomit.

This can't be happening—it has to be some bullshit practical joke that our friends thought would be funny. And it would be *marginally* funny if there weren't several hours last night that are completely black when I try to recount them.

But there's no fucking way we would get married . . .

Morgan only just agreed to something more exclusive over slices of pizza after the pool party. I highly doubt that she meant exclusive by order of law, especially when she's told me multiple times that she has no interest in marriage. And hell, neither do I—it's the absolute last thing I want to try again.

Right?

Right.

So why is there a small flicker of hope in my pounding brain that this is real?

"Who was it?"

I just blink, then close my eyes again as my mind tries to break through the fog of my hangover to grasp the gravity of the situation.

How the fuck am I going to tell her?

Before I have a chance to figure it out, I feel my phone being pulled from my hand.

"What the . . . you're joking," Morgan stammers. Her fingers tremble as she scrolls through the messages, likely retracing my earlier thought process. "This is a joke, right?"

I don't have an answer to her question, so I reach out. My hand finds her thigh, mirroring her comforting gesture from before. Even if this is the biggest shit show of all time, I want her to know that I'm here—she's not alone in this.

After a minute, she looks up at me, green eyes darkening like the sky before an incoming summer storm.

"We wouldn't . . . would we?"

My head shakes shamefully. I know how she feels—the absurdity of the situation is overwhelming. The fragments of the previous night that I can recall are still blurry snippets of laughter, dancing, and too many drinks that mesh into one indistinct memory.

"I don't know, Morg. I really don't," I start, trying to keep my voice steady despite the throbbing in my head and whirlwind of my emotions. "We were drunk. Very drunk. And I don't remember anything after the club."

When we left the ridiculous stripper show, we spent a while at a karaoke bar where I drank a vodka with RedBull to gear up for the rest of the night. I remember thinking I should slow down after maintaining a solid buzz all day, but clearly I didn't listen.

"I don't either . . . wait."

Her eyes widen with sudden inspiration, and she quickly navigates to the photos app on my phone. Most of my pictures are surgery related, but Morgan did steal my phone a few times last night since she left hers back in the room, worried she'd lose it—maybe she's onto something.

"Anything?"

All I notice are images of our friend group, drinks, and random city lights—nothing that remotely resembles a wedding chapel. But I let her do her thing because she's probably better at this than I am.

Her lips curl into a thin line as she locks the screen, like it'll magically erase the truth. "Nope."

"Maybe it wasn't us?" I suggest, watching her lean over the side of the bed.

I instinctively rub her back, thinking she's about to throw up because her skin feels clammy under my hand. But then she sits up, rummaging through her beaded clutch frantically. Her body stiffens as she pulls out two plastic blue rings, the cheap kind that you'd find in a gumball machine.

"It was us."

Before I can say anything, Claire comes barreling through the door at top speed.

"I fucking knew it," she screeches, launching herself head first into the mattress. She quickly turns to face us, propping her chin on her hands as she wags her feet in the air. "Morgan and Walkie, sitting in a tree, K-I-S-S-I-N-G."

Beau follows, slowly trodding across the marble floor with an apologetic look on his face. "She's very persuasive."

Morgan groans beside me, shifting her weight so that she can bury her head in her knees as Claire begins to rattle off every reason she thought we were hooking up.

Beau stops at the corner of the bed, staring at me with concern. "You okay, bud?" His bushy eyebrows draw together as he assesses me more like a physician than a friend. "You look a little pale."

"First comes love, then comes marriage," Claire sings with a giggle, glancing up at Morgan, who slowly lifts her head as if it's made of lead.

I shoot Beau a look that I hope communicates my growing irritation, silently threatening what I might say to his girlfriend if she keeps this up. He catches the warning, his expression softening as he guides Claire to sit by him on the bed's edge. He pulls her into his oversized arms and murmurs something in her ear that makes her lips curl into a silent smirk.

"Can you call Cassidy and Parker in here, please?" I don't want to elaborate further until we have more information. I have no idea how late they stayed out with us, but the last thing I remember is being with them at the karaoke bar. Maybe they'll say something to jog our memories.

Beau frowns but doesn't question me. He simply raises his voice to call to our friends through the open door, his eyes narrowing on me suspiciously.

I stroke my thumb along Morgan's thigh as we wait for our friends in uneasy silence.

Parker shuffles in first, massaging the back of his neck, followed closely by his fiancée. They're both still wearing their pajamas and look just as rough as we do.

Great.

"What's up?" Parker asks, glancing between the four of us piled on the bed. His midnight-blue eyes settle on mine cautiously, as if he's expecting me to be the one who brings him up to speed.

"Do you, uh, remember last night?"

"Which part?" He chuckles, wrapping his arm around Cass affectionately. "The part where we kicked your asses at jello shot pong? Or anything after that? Because my memories get kind of hazy from there."

Jello shot pong?

What the—

I hear Morgan swallow audibly, before she asks, "Anything else? Anything at all?"

Though her question is directed at Parker, her eyes plead with her best friend for answers.

Cassidy wrinkles her nose, darting her attention between us. "Why? What happened?"

Morgan takes a deep breath and glances at me in permission. I nod somberly.

"Walker got a few messages this morning from the Burning Love Wedding Chapel . . ." Her voice trails off, weighted with uncertainty.

Cassidy's hazel eyes blow wide, and even Parker who is typically unflappable, blinks in surprise.

"Wait, what?" he sputters, looking from Morgan to me, then back again.

"Yep," I confirm, my voice flat. "According to them, we got married last night."

"You guys didn't seem that drunk at the neon bar, but I guess I wasn't the best judge of character because I blacked out after that." Parker rubs his forehead, then looks over at his fiancée for some assistance.

She winces. "Everything after the show is a blur for me, and I have absolutely no idea what neon bar he's talking about . . . are you guys sure?"

Morgan looks down at the plastic rings that she's been fiddling with. "Unfortunately."

The room falls silent momentarily before Beau glances at Parker with a sly grin. "Well, you did say you might not be the first member of the friend group to walk down the aisle."

CHAPTER 29

WALKER

Three days after Vegas

I'm reading the same chapter on rotator cuff injuries for what must be the tenth time when my phone pings with a text from Morgan. I'd be lying if I said that I haven't been on pins and needles since we got back from the trip, waiting for her to reach out. It's been killing me to give her the space that she asked for when I drove us home from the airport, and concentrating on anything other than my anxiety has been nearly impossible.

> Alright - I've figured everything out.

I smile reading her message because I can picture her saying those words—it makes me miss her even more than I already do.

> I'm all ears, little devil.

She starts typing, and her fingers must have flown over the keyboard at lightning speed because her response comes through quickly.

> Annulment seems like way too much work.
>
> We'll have to get a divorce once the papers come through.
>
> Sound good?

A tsunami of disappointment slams into me, cracking open my chest and washing away my excitement. I have to read the message several times to make sure that I'm not seeing things, before pressing the lock button on my phone.

I stand and walk to the bar in the corner of my office, pouring myself a generous glass of bourbon. I slam it back without even thinking, savoring the burn as the smoky liquid slides down my throat.

Morgan and I have been seeing each other for a little over a month now, and we only made the decision to dive into something more exclusive several days ago. It shouldn't surprise me that this is what she wants. So why does it hurt worse than the day I received divorce papers from my first marriage?

I pour myself another drink and walk over to the bookshelves, eyeing the section of Morgan's recommendations that I displayed in front of my desk. Initially, I told myself that I would hide them, but when the books came in the mail, all I wanted to do was place them front and center because they reminded me of her—of how she swirled into my life and swept me away.

Getting married again wasn't on the table for me. And with any other person, I'd immediately sign the papers and move on with my life. But with Morgan, I know without a doubt that I can be a good husband to her—I can show her that our love story can end the way it does in the books she reads.

This isn't the exact path I would have chosen for us, but it's the one I know will end happily ever after . . . eventually.

So I sit back down behind my desk and open my phone, knowing without a doubt that my response to my wife is going to piss her off.

> I'm not signing divorce papers.

Two weeks after Vegas

While patience isn't a common characteristic of an orthopedic surgeon, it's something I thrive at—just ask any of my interns from the fall. I'll stand in silence as I watch them make a mistake and only interject when it's necessary. I'm comfortable giving them time to learn and figure out the correct course of action without intervening because I feel like growth is more meaningful when it comes from inside.

And that's exactly how I'm approaching this situation with Morgan. I'm giving her the time and space to come to the same realization I did after the trip—we belong together.

Were there moments when I waffled on staying married? Sure.

It's only natural when you fail at something to have doubts about attempting it again. But those doubts were fleeting and dissipated as soon as I settled back into my normal life.

I know that Morgan will get there too, it might just take her a little longer. And I'm happy to wait until she does.

Three weeks after Vegas

> I'll serve as your personal sex slave for the weekend if you divorce me.

This is the first time Morgan has resorted to offering sexual favors in exchange for divorce. Admittedly, it would be convincing if I were the kind of man who thought only with his cock, especially because she knows that this is a fantasy of mine.

> Tell me more.

I have zero intention of giving in, but I'm curious how far I can get her to go before she gets irritated and resorts to her dramatics. She thinks I'm stubborn, but she's right there with me.

> Whatever you want to do to me within our negotiated limits is on the table for a straight 48 hours, Sir.

I love how she thinks that calling me "Sir" is going to make me agree to her terms. Sure, my cock just jumped in my scrubs as

I imagined what we could do with that amount of unrestricted playtime, but it's going to happen one day regardless—I just have to be patient.

> I don't think you could behave for that long, little devil.

She immediately responds.

> We could find out.
>
> If you would divorce me.

I smile, missing her to death but also confident in my response.

> I'm sure we'll find out regardless.
>
> You're stuck with me.

Chapter 30

Morgan

"Morg."

I ignore Cassidy, rereading my most recent text chain with Walker.

> Remember when we agreed to something more exclusive?

> I meant hooking up with other people.

> Not marriage.

> Must have missed the memo.

> Now that you have it, you should divorce me.

> No.

> Please divorce me.

> Not happening.
>
> But I love the manners, little devil.

> You're the worst husband ever.
>
> DIVORCE ME!!!!!

> Nothing I haven't heard before.
>
> The answer is still no.

There are over fifty iterations of this exact conversation with my "husband" over the past month. Sometimes I offer sexual favors in exchange for a divorce. Sometimes I send depressing paragraph-long pleas, hoping he'll take pity on me. And sometimes I simply resort to pictures of my middle finger.

Unfortunately, nothing has been successful with the most stubborn man on planet Earth.

"Morg," Cassidy repeats, finally getting my attention.

I look up at my best friend. She's leaning over the tall triage desk, looking irritated.

"Yes?"

Her hazel eyes soften. "Are you okay?"

I should be the one asking her that because she looks like she's been through the ringer, and it's only nine in the morning.

"Are *you* okay?" I echo, taking in the mystery liquid staining the front of her scrubs and the disheveled nature of her ponytail.

"You know what I mean."

I take a slow, steady breath to ensure that I don't say anything I'll regret. Being a filterless queen is one of my best character traits, but great power comes with great responsibility, and I have to be careful when I'm speaking to people I really care about.

But that's really hard at the moment because Cass is on my last nerve. She's been constantly checking in about my relationship status and won't leave me alone. Sure, I might be legally wed, but nothing in my life has changed since Las Vegas other than the fact that I'm officially celibate again. It's kind of funny, actually, because I'm pretty sure marriage is supposed to go the opposite way—with all of the life-altering sex happening after your vows, not before. But until Walker agrees to end things with me under the eyes of the law, there's no damn way he's getting back in my pants. Regardless of how much I miss him.

"I'm dandy, Cass," I reply, stretching my arms above my head casually. "Just like I was when you asked me yesterday, and the day before that, and the day before that. What my blackout-self did in Las Vegas is none of my sober-self's business."

Her voice lowers in concern. "Have you talked to Walker yet?"

I yawn to signify my indifference, though inside, my feelings are anything but calm. Other than the daily spats on our marital status, Walker has left me completely alone. Which, to be fair, I did ask him to do as soon as we got back from the trip so that I could process the situation. But I don't know . . . I expected him to try harder, I guess.

"What can I say? The three D's get us all eventually."

She looks at me like I have two heads, so I clarify. "Divorce, death, and disability."

"Morgan." She lets out a resigned sigh. "Is that really what you want?"

"What I want," I reply, though my conviction waivers slightly, "is for this to have never happened."

After Vegas, it only took me a few days to come to the conclusion that divorce was the logical answer. Yes, I recognize that a very small subset of the population gets their own happily ever after, but life doesn't usually end like it does in the romance novels. There will always be fights, or lies, or lackluster apologies. And I don't want that for the rest of my life.

I want what Walker and I have now—or what we had—just without the title of husband and wife. Because from everything I've seen, marriage is just a confirmed sentence for heartbreak.

And that's not just anecdotal. If you view it statistically, more marriages end in despair than in blissful happiness. Just look at my parents—they've both been remarried several times. Hell, look at Walker—he married his high school sweetheart, and she left him for another man. So regardless of how our relationship, or whatever you'd call it, was going, we need to nip this in the bud before one of us gets really hurt.

"But it did happen," Cassidy reminds me. "And you need to have an actual conversation with him."

"Do I though?" I lean back in my chair and cross my arms. "It's really not a big deal, I promise."

The problem is—apparently it is a big deal in the eyes of the law. From the little research that I did before I frustratedly threw my phone across the room, not only do you both need to agree to the divorce, but you also need the physical marriage certificate. And since we meet neither criteria . . . we're in big, fat, accidentally married limbo.

"You're impossible sometimes," she hisses, slamming her hands down on the desk so aggressively that the unit secretary looks over to make sure everything is okay.

I keep telling my friends that Walker and I will figure everything out once the paperwork comes through next month, but none of them seem to understand my reaction. Cass thinks I'm in denial, clearly. Claire is delusional and wants us to stay married. And Caroline, well, Caroline doesn't say anything because she's busy as fuck.

The reality of the situation is that it doesn't matter what they think because this isn't their stupid problem—it's mine. And this problem is making me mad as hell. I'm mad that I finally gave in to Walker and let myself be happy. But I'm even more upset that I went and destroyed that happiness with the one thing that always fails—marriage.

Cass lowers her voice. "I can't believe you're just going to let what the two of you have end without a single word."

My throat thickens against my will, and I swallow to loosen up the ball of emotion that's trying to choke me.

"We exchange words every day," I correct. She's seen screenshots of the messages, so she knows exactly what I'm talking about. "And they've gotten us nowhere because he won't agree to what I want."

"Do you even know why he isn't interested in getting divorced?"

I roll my eyes as far back as they'll allow. "Because he's a physician, and refuses to admit that he made a mistake. Because he enjoys controlling me. Because he's stubborn. I don't know, Cass, the possibilities are endless."

Honestly, I just assumed it was because he was intent on pissing me off. That's our bit—opposing forces that each push as hard as we can until one of us breaks. I guess theoretically there could be more to his reluctance, but again, that would require us to have an actual conversation. And that's something I refuse to initiate, because if he's not going to give, neither am I.

Cassidy pinches the bridge of her nose in frustration, letting out a long sigh. "Both of you are being stubborn in this situation. Hell, both of you have been stubborn this entire time because you've just been dancing around the truth for months."

I bark out a harsh laugh that's completely void of humor. "What truth?"

"That you're obsessed with each other, idiot. But you're too proud to admit it, and Walker's too . . . Walker's afraid to lose you."

I scoff. "Yeah, right."

I ignore her criticism of my own emotional capacity and focus on my "other half." If he's so damn afraid of losing me, why hasn't he tried saying anything more to me than no for the past few weeks? Why hasn't he tried showing up at my door? Why hasn't he made me feel like he wants to keep me?

"I wish you could see what I've seen for months, Morg. Walker looks at you like you're the sun. Like he knows he shouldn't be staring because you're only going to burn him, but he just can't help himself." Her tone softens again. "I know without a doubt that he doesn't want to lose you."

I purse my lips, trying to come up with an argument. But I can't. Because in the deepest parts of my heart, I know what she's saying is true. And if I really think about it hard, I don't want to lose him either.

***

"Morg," our charge nurse Marisa calls to me from across the triage waiting area. "Can you take Kat's patients for a few hours?"

I frown, slowly looking up from my phone because that's the absolute last thing I want to do. Kat is great and all, but she's a new grad and her patients are always a shit show. Even if I take them for two hours, there's no doubt in my mind that I'm going to be running around the entire time.

"Do I have to?" I whine, locking my phone and placing it on the cluttered desk. "I'm a little busy here."

I'm actually not busy at all because triage has been uncharacteristically quiet. So quiet that the only thing on my mind for the past few hours has been composing and deleting the same text to Walker over and over again. Each message contains some variation of the phrase "*Can we talk*," but I just can't bring myself to press send.

Marisa pulls her shoulder-length bleached hair up into a ponytail as she enters the circular triage desk. "I'm up to my ass in modules, girl. Gotta finish them by tomorrow, or there's going to be a nasty-gram in my inbox. You'd think I could get a moment of peace after my honeymoon, but apparently that's too much to ask."

I totally forgot she was out for two weeks because she got married, but now the sun-kissed skin makes more sense. Honestly, the more that I look at her, the more I notice that she's glowing.

Is that what a happy marriage does to you? I wouldn't know.

"Where's she going?" I ask, logging off the computer before I stand to give up my coveted position.

"ACLS recertification," she states, swapping places with me. "It was the only time she could do it. Her assignment isn't bad, I promise, and it shouldn't even take that long. Two hours max."

Yeah right.

It's already four in the afternoon, and I doubt she's going to rush back after the two hour advanced cardiac life support class. If it were me, I'd take as long as possible before returning to this circus of chaos too.

"You okay?" Marisa asks when I don't say anything back, her eyes narrowing on me like she's worried. "I've been trying to assign you to triage every shift like you wanted. Has it been helping?"

After my patient died during the ice storm, I discreetly asked to be put back here whenever possible. I was already working triage occasionally because it's an assignment that's typically reserved for more senior nurses, and since we've lost a ton of staff in the past two years, I am now part of that category.

And to be fair, the change has helped me feel somewhat better. I've been able to dissociate from my patients again because my main job is to delegate and plan, similar to the job of a charge nurse. I determine which patients are seen first based on their clinical symptoms, and the only direct patient care that I provide is limited to drawing labs or giving fluids.

While I like the somewhat removed aspect of triage, I'm still struggling to maintain a positive attitude. It's like I can't get out of this negative brain fog, and each shift only makes it worse. Some mornings I'll sit in silence until the very last moment and only get out of the car when I'm a minute away from clocking in late.

It's wild because I used to crave the hospital. I would pick up every extra shift that I could because I loved it. But now I feel like I'm just trying to make it through the simplest of days. Nursing was something that I was proud of, but now it's something I loathe, and I don't know how to snap out of this funk. The only thing I do know, is that I need to do something soon. Because if I don't, I'm going to burn out like the rest of the damn workforce.

"It's all good, M," I lie, grabbing my stethoscope and a blank piece of paper from the desk. "A few hours on the floor isn't going to kill me."

Fortunately, our charge nurse wasn't lying and the patients I took over really aren't bad—one is pending discharge, and the other three are stable, or waiting to transfer to another floor. Unfortunately, right after I finished taking report from Kat, I had to help Cass and another coworker run an unsuccessful code in bay two for thirty minutes.

As I'm leaving the bay, I notice one of my patient's family members standing outside of their door. She's staring at me with a snarky expression while she taps her Dr. Scholls-covered foot on the tile floor impatiently.

"Nurse," she calls as I'm washing the death off my hands. "Nurse, I've been calling for fifteen minutes because I need ice for my water."

I take a breath, searching for patience that doesn't come. Because in what world is ice more important than saving someone's life?

Walking over to the Karen, I calmly state, "My name is Morgan. I told you that earlier when I introduced myself and wrote my information on the whiteboard. I'm a nurse, but I am also a human being with a name."

Normally I would just take her callout with a smile on my face, but she caught me less than five minutes after listening to a mother's gut-wrenching sobs as the doctor pronounced time of death on her teenage son. And yes, I recognize that this woman has no idea what I just witnessed. She's probably just stressed and taking it out on me. But I simply cannot find empathy for her right now—my cup is empty.

She scrunches up her overly made-up face like she's about to bite back.

"I was in another patient's room," I state calmly, interrupting her before she says something that will really set me off. "Give me a moment, and I'll go get your ice. Do you need anything else?"

She says no and turns to go back inside the room. Under her breath, she mutters, "Lazy-ass nurses don't want to work anymore."

My teeth grind against each other, biting back the words that I really want to say as I walk to get her precious bag of ice.

People want to know why nurses are leaving the bedside and causing a healthcare staffing crisis? This is a prime example.

We witness traumatic events on a daily basis that most of the general population can never begin to understand. And that's okay, because it's what we signed up for. We signed up to advocate for our patients, to treat them with dignity, and to safely care for them like they're our own family members.

What we didn't sign up for is the verbal abuse, the degradation, the dehumanization of our feelings that also occurs. We didn't sign up to be chastised if we take a moment for ourselves after simply doing our jobs. We didn't sign up for a lot of it, but we try our hardest to rise above it.

One of the core tenets of nursing is compassion, but over time it becomes increasingly challenging to have compassion for people who do not also have compassion for us. And when you couple these daily experiences with other ongoing frustrations like unsafe staffing ratios, increases in expectations without increases in pay, and lack of support or recognition from administration, I don't blame anyone for leaving. There are some days when I feel like I have my foot out the door too.

On my way back with the ice, the call bell starts going off in another one of the rooms that I'm covering. I hope that Kat isn't expecting me to chart for her because I haven't had a second to breathe, let alone log into the computer and update anything.

"How can I help you?" I ask, popping my head into the room of her patient scheduled for discharge.

Our ER is set up like a square, with all of the patient rooms and trauma bays located on the perimeter. There's a massive circular desk sitting smack dab in the middle of the room which allows us to help each other when call lights go off. For some reason, however, we have a single patient room that's tucked around the corner, away from the sight of everyone else. Because of its quiet location on the hallway of physician offices, we typically put patients in there who are actively dying. Sometimes, though, night shift admits people to the room when they run out of space, which clearly was the case with this patient overnight.

"I need to get the fuck out of here," the patient states, pacing barefoot back and forth. "Get me out of here."

On instinct, I turn off the call light so the beeping stops. "Social work is trying to get you set up with an outpatient facility. Shouldn't be more than an hour."

This particular patient is a twenty-seven-year-old male who came in early this morning for an STD test. While they ran that lab, they also took a standard drug panel and found that he was positive for meth. And the closer I get to him, it doesn't surprise me—he's tall, but I doubt he weighs more than a hundred and fifty pounds soaking wet.

Apparently, the night shift nurse found him trying to give himself a bath with hand sanitizer and had to administer a sedative because he was tweaking from being awake too long. I didn't have a chance to peek my head into the room before I got pulled into the code, but when I got report, I was told that he was finally calm after sleeping for a few hours.

Calm my ass.

This man is irritable as hell. His blue eyes briefly meet mine, moving faster than normal as they shoot around the room.

"Can I give you something to help you relax while we wait on orders?" I suggest, keeping my tone soothing as I walk over to the computer on the wall. Even though I haven't had a chance to look at the medication record, I'm sure there's an order available for comfort while we wait on the transfer details.

"Fuck no. Get me the fuck out of here," he says, voice rising substantially. "What are you even doing?"

"I'm Morgan, your nurse," I remind him gently as I log into his chart. "You called me because you wanted to be discharged."

He begins to pace again before getting in my face and screaming, "So discharge me, bitch!"

I swallow down my sadness. He's too young to have this life, and if he leaves without getting into a treatment center, I'm worried he'll end up dead.

"Let me check with social work again," I offer, hoping to give him some reassurance. "If they aren't ready, you can always go against medical advice, but I'd really like for you to stay."

As I turn to exit the room, he grabs my arm, his grip surprisingly strong. "You want me to stay? Shut the fuck up, you dumb cunt. I'm going to fucking kill you."

My heart slams into my throat. This isn't the first time a patient has gotten physical with me, or even threatened me for that matter, but it is the first time I've felt genuine fear. Not because I think I'm in real danger, but because I'm entirely alone in this situation.

Normally we room patients who are withdrawing from drugs front and center in case a situation like this arises. Any other day, there would already be a slew of people in this room to help me, and the patient would be restrained.

"Take your hands off of me," I state calmly, attempting to de-escalate the situation. I might be short, but I like to think my nurse voice is stern. "You can walk out of here right now, but you need to take your hands off me."

I glance at the wall, trying to determine how far I am from the emergency button. Unfortunately, it's all of the way across the room, and I can't get to it without making it obvious to the patient.

"Look, I understand that you're scared and frustrated," I say, keeping my voice steady as I feel his grip tighten. "But I'm here to help you, not to keep you here against your will. Like I said, you're free to leave. But I need you to let go of me so that we can walk to the desk together, and have you sign a form."

His nails dig into my skin painfully, eyes wide as they quickly dart around the room like he's searching for an escape.

I continue speaking, trying to keep his focus on the reality of the situation and away from the confusion clouding his mind. "It's my job to make sure you're safe, and that includes helping find support when you leave us. But like I said, we don't have to do that. You can go."

Slowly, I feel his grip loosening as my words seem to reach the rational part of him that's still accessible beneath the drug's influence. But before I can pull free, his fingers tighten again, and he starts dragging me across the room toward the door. Everything begins to blur as I hear the patient threaten me again, followed by a familiar, stern voice coming from the hallway.

"Take your fucking hands off my wife."

Chapter 31

Walker

I don't have a ton of professional experience with patients who are impaired by things other than anesthesia, but one look at the guy who has his beady claws wrapped around Morgan's arm, and I know he's on something. That fact alone should influence me to follow protocol, call security, and verbally de-escalate the situation while we wait for help. But he's assaulting my wife, and every ounce of patience in my body flies out of the window the second I see her terrified face.

Before the patient can respond to my threat, adrenaline courses through me, and I find myself lunging forward and tackling him to the hard ground in a single motion. Fortunately, he releases Morgan on his way down, and she's able to get to the wall and press the emergency button. I swing my leg over the patient's back, pinning his lower half as I work to wrangle his flailing arms.

"We need some help in here," I call for good measure, hoping someone will get off their ass and do their damn job.

I lean into the patient who is muttering irrational threats as he struggles beneath my body.

"Touch my wife again," I warn, feeling something animalistic unlock deep inside of me, "and it'll be the last thing that you ever do."

After what feels like an eternity, though it can't be more than a few seconds, footsteps echo through the hallway. An off-duty police officer steps in and takes my place to restrain the patient, securing him in handcuffs. I stand and ignore the questions that are being hurdled my way to crouch beside Morgan.

She's curled up in a tight ball against the wall, the same way she was the night I found her on my shower floor. Her green eyes are wide when they meet mine, their usual contagious spark clouded by the aftermath of fear.

I reach out and brush a stray hair out of her eyes. She might not want to be my wife, but a title changes nothing when it comes to how I feel about her.

"Can I see your arm?"

The world evaporates around me. All I can hear are the shaky breaths coming out of her mouth as she calms herself down. All I can see is the quiver of her bottom lip as she holds off tears. All I can think is how I need to keep her safe.

She nods slowly, extending the affected arm toward me. My eyes scan her injury, noting the nail marks so deep they drew blood and the mottled red of the skin where he held her.

I hope the fucker pays for this.

I'll make sure the fucker pays for this.

But first I need to get her out of here.

"Just a few scratches. I'll clean it, and you'll be fine," I state, drawing my attention back to her. "Let's get you off this floor."

I reach out my hands and she takes them, pausing before she stands. "I'll clean it. Don't act like you understand wound care."

The corner of her mouth kicks up, and I can't help but smile back—I missed her. God, I fucking missed her, and she scared the shit out of me for a second there.

"Believe it or not, little devil, I am a surgeon. Basic first aid is within my wheelhouse."

She rolls her pretty eyes at me but allows me to pull her to her feet. "So is being a pain in my ass."

I wrap my arm around her waist and guide her out of the room. "The feeling is mutual, I promise."

She's steady and completely fine to walk on her own, but I don't want to let her out of my grasp until I have to. Even as we field questions from various staff members, I find myself standing beside her and rubbing my thumb along her lower back—I want her to know I'm not going anywhere.

After speaking with what feels like everyone employed by the hospital, I step away for a moment to pull the charge nurse aside. It's nearly six in the evening, so Morgan technically has another hour of work, but there's no way in hell she should go back to the floor today—she needs a break and a breather. I don't get any pushback at my suggestion, and after we quickly clean out the scratches, I find myself leading her toward one of my favorite places in the hospital.

We walk in silence, climbing several flights of stairs and weaving through dated corridors until we make it to a nondescript door on the sixth floor. I enter the code that I've come to know by heart and gesture for her to go first. She looks hesitant, so I take her hand and lead us across the slender all-glass walkway that hangs above the main hospital lobby.

I stop when we reach the middle, squeezing her hand to get her attention because her gaze is focused exactly where I expect it to be—on the unobstructed view of a cotton candy sunset blanketing our city.

She turns toward me, the warm pinks of the sky combining with the natural green of her eyes to make them appear almost mauve. I feel my heart leap in my chest as those beautiful colors imprint themselves in my soul, a precious memory to look back on for the rest of my life despite the shit show we just experienced.

"You're . . ." I start, trying to find the right words.

How do I explain the tornado of emotion in my mind? Or everything I've thought about for the past month while I gave her space? Hell, how do I tell her everything I've felt since the moment I allowed myself to truly see her? I have so much to say, but the only thing that comes out of my mouth is trivial compared to the rest of it.

"Glowing."

She lets out a disbelieving exhale. "Yeah, right. I've never felt more disgusting in my life. I can't wait to get home and shower. And after today, it's going to clock in at a solid two hours, probably more if I don't run out of hot water."

I chuckle, unable to look away from the way the evening rays illuminate her face like the sun is only shining on her. "Let me know if you need someone to check on you."

Her cheeks flush, her gaze returning to the expansive windows in front of us. "What is this place?"

"It's a walkway the custodial staff uses to change the flags that hang over the lobby. During my second year of residency, I got to know one of them because she always cleaned the on-call room. Not personally, or anything, just head nods and smiles for months on end. Somehow in those brief interactions, she was able to tell the difference between a typical bad day and a really terrible one. One night, after hours of getting my shit kicked in, she brought me up here, gave me the code, and then left me alone."

My lips tug upward at the memory. "I don't know how to explain it, but a weight instantly lifted off my shoulders. Something about being stories above everyone and watching them experience their own struggles gave me the perspective I needed when I was bogged down in the trenches. I still come up every so often to reset."

"When was the last time you were up here?"

I don't hesitate at all when I answer, "The day after Vegas."

Only, a few hours alone on this walkway didn't give me the reset I was searching for because it turns out that a reset wasn't what I truly needed after the trip. What I needed was to allow myself to feel the one thing that I'd never experienced my entire life—peace.

I've tried to pinpoint why—I even went to my therapist last week to see if he had any insight. But ultimately, I concluded that the reason doesn't matter. What matters is that Morgan and I fit together in a way that only happens once in a lifetime. And a month later, despite her constant barrage of divorce requests, that overwhelming sense of peacefulness hasn't subsided.

And while there's no way in hell I'm letting her go, I'm also not going to push her into anything. She asked for space, so I've been giving her space. I've been waiting until she came to see me because I knew she would when she was ready. And just because she hasn't yet, doesn't mean anything has changed between us, it just means that I have to be more patient. I'm going to give her as long as she needs to come to the same conclusion that I did—our marriage wasn't an accident at all—it was fate.

Morgan's throat works as something that looks like guilt washes over her face. "Oh, right."

That's the last thing I want her to be feeling, especially after everything she's been through today. I squeeze her hand gently. "Come on. Let's watch the sunset."

Sinking to the floor of the walkway, I guide her down beside me. Her eyes briefly flicker with nervousness as the platform shakes from our movement, but she relaxes after positioning herself between my legs. My arms wrap around her body and hold her close as we settle into silence, watching the sun scatter a beautiful array of colors along the Atlanta skyline.

"Thanks," she murmurs after a while. "For helping me with the patient."

I nuzzle my head into her hair, inhaling my favorite scent in the world. "Don't thank me. That's what friends are for."

The word doesn't taste bitter coming off my tongue like it has in the past, probably because it's not said out of jealousy or spite for the designation—I'm calling her my friend because I truly mean it.

Over the course of a few months, Morgan Lovett has worn many titles in my mind. She's been my crush, my tormenter, my lover, and most recently my wife, but none of those titles hold a candle to what she's truly become—my best friend.

I've been trying to avoid thinking about how everything could have ended differently today—if I hadn't been walking past the room on the way to a consult for Beau, if I had been even a minute later, if the patient had used the pocket knife they found on his person—my world could have flipped in the blink of an eye. Because I don't know when it happened, and I'll never know why it happened, but Morgan has become everything to me.

Chapter 32

Morgan

We sat in our own little bubble on the sky bridge for far too long, alternating between slow conversation and comfortable silence. Just like that first night I broke down at his house, Walker didn't force me to talk about what happened today. He just held me in his arms and gave me all of the time I needed to reset in his secret spot.

And it worked . . . though I think that's more due to him, than anything else. I almost forgot what it's like to be around him—the constant crackle of energy flowing between us, the spark that makes even the darkest grays transform into beautiful color.

Walker told me he has something to give me before I head home, so we're currently stopping by the ortho call room on the way out.

I feel myself frown as we enter the small, windowless space.

I can't believe that my friends hookup in here.

There's nothing sexy about a twin-size bed and fluorescent lighting—not even if the man you're with makes you feel all tingly inside.

"Did you get me a present?" I ask, trying to peek past Walker's massive body. He's standing at his locker, searching for something.

"No."

I jump into the air, getting a quick glimpse of a blue bag and a stack of neatly organized books. "Did you make me something?"

"No."

This time I launch myself onto his back, wrapping my legs around his torso so that I can peer over his shoulder.

"Blue Nerd Clusters!" I scream into his ear, reaching out with grabby hands.

Walker mutters something rude that I don't hear because I've secured the goods and already jumped down from my mount. Plopping onto the desk in the corner, I shove a handful of my favorite candy into my mouth, the stress of the day instantly washing away the moment the sugary gummies hit my tongue.

"Best husband ever," I say with a full mouth. "Did you get these for me? Or are you a connoisseur too?"

He grabs something else from his locker and closes the door. "Pretty sure you called me the worst husband less than twelve hours ago."

He settles into the desk chair across from me, leaning back to study me.

"You're net zero today," I explain, closing the bag because I'm suddenly hungry for something other than candy. "It's a sliding scale, not that I would expect you to understand how those work as an ortho bro."

Walker's lips quirk a millimeter but quickly return to his traditional flat-lined scowl. His chin is resting in his hand, thumb rubbing his neatly trimmed facial hair as his eyes narrow on me like I'm in trouble. His expression is giving me flashbacks to dominant Walker, and I suddenly take back everything I said about hooking up in call rooms—you've got to do what you've got to do.

"Interesting," he muses, attention dropping to my lips in the most shameless way.

My skin prickles under his scrutiny, but I keep pushing him. "It would be more interesting if you got a positive score for once. But until you agree to divorce me, that won't be happening."

I don't know why I say that—seeing Walker today changed everything. His physical presence alone might have been enough to make me rethink my stance on our relationship, but after what he did for me, I'm beginning to wonder where the harm in trying is.

I mean, maybe marriage could work between us. And if it doesn't, we'll just get divorced like everyone else. Plus, it was super hot hearing him call me his wife earlier—I definitely wouldn't hate hearing that again.

Walker's dark eyes flicker with something unreadable before he speaks. "If you would give me a compelling argument on why I should divorce you, I'd do it. I'd sign the papers as soon as they came in. But you haven't. All you've done is beg for something that you don't even know if you want. Because if you knew why you wanted to end this marriage, you would have already told me."

He scoots closer, his legs caging me in.

"So go ahead, Morgan. Tell me why you want this to end. Why you don't even want to try." He leans in, his face inches from mine. "I'm all fucking ears."

My traitorous mouth opens and closes, unable to find words for the first time in my life.

This is my chance. All I've done for the past month is come up with positive arguments for divorce, reasons why I should ignore the intense magnetism between us, and think clearly. I created an entire list that was well crafted, backed by logic, and most importantly—factually accurate. So why does my mind go completely blank when I look at the man across from me?

"No?" Walker taunts, reaching out to place something in the front pocket of my scrubs. "Well, until then, here's a key to my house . . . wife."

The metal poetically settles above my heart, weighing me down with more than I can fight right now. I don't have the strength to fight my stupid feelings, my stupid reasons, any of this.

So I don't.

I don't fight when my fingers fist the fabric of his navy scrub top and tug him closer. I don't fight when his lips curl into a self-satisfied smile as our mouths collide. I don't fight when my brain magically forgets all of my core beliefs about long-term relationships, and how I promised I wouldn't touch him until he agreed to my terms—I simply give in.

Our first—sober—kiss as husband and wife is explosive. It's passionate. It's the closest thing I've felt to wildfire. But most importantly, it's a physical reminder of why I haven't let go. Of why I've been avoiding this conversation. Of the one thing I've been afraid of but know now beyond a shadow of a doubt.

That Walker Chastain is my twin flame—he's the other half of my soul. The one who has simultaneously ignited and tamed my furious blaze. He's what I've been running from, but he's also what I need more than air. We've always belonged to each other, and no matter how much I try to fight it, we always will.

So I guess Cass was right. Walker might look at me like I'm the sun, but it's only because he knows I'm the one person who won't blind him. And I think I finally understand why I don't want to—because I think I might love him.

So that's how I kiss him. I kiss him with everything I have, winding my fingers through his hair to pull him closer. Our tongues flick against each other, and I savor his taste as his large hands move beneath my thighs, squeezing my flesh aggressively as he lifts me off the desk.

I wrap my legs around his waist as he walks us across the room while we feverishly claim each other. I whimper into his throat as my back slams against the wooden door of the call room, his hips pressing into me as he reaches down to lock us in.

I can feel the slick heat of my arousal surge through me as his hands possessively knead my ass, a groan of matching desire coming from his lips. He turns and crosses the small room to lower us to the twin bed, never once pulling back from our kiss.

My feet dig into his hips, and I arch my back to feel him as close as possible. I slide my fingers from his hair, over his harsh jawline, and down his sides to reach for the hem of his top, yanking it free from his waistband.

His hard cock teases my sex briefly, taunting me with nostalgic pleasure as he adjusts his body and pulls one arm free from beneath me. He sinks heavily against me, pressing his chest against mine so snugly that I can't break even an inch of contact between our bodies.

"Remind me," I rasp against his lips, raking my fingertips up his spine toward his broad shoulders.

Before I can explain what I mean, Walker's chin dips in understanding, and he begins planting feverish kisses along my jaw. A sliver of pain pricks my skin, forcing a surprised yelp from my swollen lips, followed by a satisfied sigh as his steady tongue soothes the sting away. I throw my head back, nearly breathless as

I give him the access that he needs to mark me, to claim me, to remind me, just like I asked.

A primal desire ignites deep within my soul, firing through my body until I feel the insatiable need to mark him too. My nails drag harshly across his back, clawing into his sweaty skin as my hips attempt to grind into him, desperate for more.

In answer, Walker's fingers drag up my arm and settle on my exposed neck, digging gently into the curve of my jaw as his mouth moves to my earlobe.

"Remind you of what?" he growls into my ear, his hot breath caressing the flames of my desire as a shudder pulses through me at his delicious possession. "Remind you that you want to be collared?"

His strong fingers press into the exact spot where my pulse hammers in my throat, eliciting a greedy whimper from my lips.

"Remind you that you belong to me?"

His teeth sink into my earlobe, and my core clenches hard with the controlled pain, nails digging into his skin in response.

"There are so many things I'm dying to remind you of, little devil. So many ways I'm desperate to own you, but not until you admit that you want this. That you're mine."

He licks the length of my jaw, placing a rough kiss on my forehead before he sits back on his heels and releases me from his hold. His hooded eyes search my face, waiting for a response.

My chest heaves under the weight of his gaze.

"I want this," I whisper, the lack of his physical touch suddenly feeling painful. "I'm yours."

His jaw clenches, and I can tell he's warring with himself on whether he should believe me.

I don't blame him given my desperate pleas for freedom and the conversation we had only moments ago, but I'll give him what I can—the truth.

"I want this, Walker," I repeat, my tone earnest. "I need this. And I need you."

I hope he knows how much the words mean to me. The last thing I ever wanted in life was to need a man—to need anyone. But somehow, I've come to need Walker. And finally admitting that is freeing.

He nods, reaching down to brush his thumb over my lower lip. "I need you too," he says, dark eyes flickering with lust.

His thumb holds my lip down as his first two fingers sink into my mouth, pressing hard against my tongue. A wave of desire washes through me as I close my mouth around him, letting him take control. His fingertips practically slide to the back of my throat, and I feel my eyes go wide, trying hard not to gag when he holds them in place.

He leans in, pressing his forehead to mine as he stares at me like he's peering directly into my soul. "I need you in more ways than you could ever know. In more ways than you *will* ever know. But right now, I need to fuck you like you're the last thing that I need."

A shudder of physical approval rips through me, and I reach up to squeeze his tattooed forearm once, hoping he remembers our nonverbal signal for yes.

His pupils flare in understanding and he sits back again, dipping his fingers into the waistband of my scrubs. I plant my heels on the bed, arching my hips into the air so he can pull the fabric over my ass, his touch much more gentle than I'm expecting.

I can feel my obvious arousal coating my inner thighs as he slides my pants and white cotton thong halfway to my knees. I drop my hips back to the mattress, tugging my lips between my teeth as I focus on the bulge between his legs, knowing exactly what I'm about to see—my husband's perfect cock.

Walker works his way out of his pants enough to let his erection spring free, a glistening pearl of liquid coating his thick tip. I want more than anything to lick it off, to remember how every inch of his body tastes, but that's not what this is about—this is about claiming each other after fighting it for so long.

"No condom," I mumble breathily as my heart beats wildly in my chest. "Let me feel all of you."

Even though I've been on birth control for over ten years, I've never not used protection with a man before. But this isn't just any man—it's my husband. And despite the ridiculously cliché fact that we're about to have sex in a call room, I have an overwhelming urge to experience this with him right now.

His expression turns feral, gaze landing on my slick center as he looms over me.

"You need me to fill this pussy up?" he grunts, grabbing my ankles to plant my feet flat against his solid chest. "My wife needs me to coat her cunt in my hot cum like a greedy little cock whore, doesn't she?"

My dripping sex clenches, completely exposed to him as he wraps one hand around both of my ankles to hold them in place. His cock hangs low between his thighs, and he gives himself a quick stroke before leaning forward to trace his swollen tip through my slit.

"God, I do," I confirm on a long exhale, fisting the sheets beneath me as he finally positions himself at my warm entrance. "I totally do."

A ripple of pleasure races up my spine as he impales me with his monster cock, my body instantly remembering how to accept his size. When he bottoms out, I shudder, feeling him deeper than ever before in this position. He pauses briefly, nostrils flaring and jaw hanging slack as he lets me adjust.

This is unlike anything I've ever felt before, and not just because the angle allows for penetration of my internal organs. I can feel the heat of his girthy length pressing against my inner walls, molding us together like we're one singular body. It's intimate and the most intense sensation I've experienced, not only sexually but emotionally.

I know Walker feels the same thing because his dark eyes heat as he says, "I do too."

The double meaning behind his words doesn't go unnoticed, but I'm too overstimulated at the moment to think about it. I feel tight and tingly everywhere, my orgasm embarrassingly close after a single thrust.

Is this what it's like to be a man?

I go a month without sex and suddenly I'm a one-pump chump.

His grip on my ankles tightens as he slowly drags his cock out of me. The slight curve of his shaft combined with the angle of the position transforms the burn of my arousal into an intense pressure in my low belly.

I gasp, feeling my eyes go wide as he slams back into me, delivering on his promise to fuck me like he doesn't need me. I meet each one of his punishing thrusts, rubbing my clit against his pubic bone in search of more friction as I chase my own pleasure.

Walker's hands drop to my hips for leverage as he increases his frantic pace. His fingers dig into the sensitive skin at the crease of my thighs, and it feels like a bomb of pleasure has been dropped.

"I'm gonna—" I warn with a whimper, unable to finish my thought because a powerful orgasm detonates through me.

Fire combusts in my core, spreading an inferno of heat to every cell in my body as my pussy clenches around him. Through the dull roar in my ears, I can hear Walker grunt out something unintelligible as he thrusts a final time, emptying himself into me.

My blurred vision finally focuses on his face, and I take in the sharp features of the man who has been nothing but patient with me. He's breathing heavily, staring down at me like I'm his entire world. And surprisingly, that doesn't scare me—because in a few short months, that's what he's become to me too.

Chapter 33

Walker

I smile as I read Morgan's message, tugging on a pair of black jeans and buttoning them. She's been bombarding my phone, trying to figure out where I'm taking her on our first official date.

> Can you please just tell me what we're doing tonight?

I respond the same way that I've responded all day, immune to her cute little antics.

> No.

Sitting on the edge of my bed, I slide on a pair of Adidas sneakers that I've had for years but never get to wear.

> Just a general idea so that I know how to dress.

Again, I type out my usual response before standing to grab a basic white T-shirt out of my drawer.

> No.

I peek in the mirror, not entirely loathing the look of myself for the first time in a while. None of that has anything to do with my actual appearance, and everything to do with the woman who challenges me every damn day.

> Fine, I'm showing up naked then.

I take that back—she challenges me every second of the day. I quickly reply, sliding my phone into my back pocket before walking to the front of the house to find my black button-up jacket.

> I wouldn't do that if I were you.

My ass vibrates as I reach the front door, and I ignore it for a moment while I grab something from the kitchen. When I open the message, I can't stop the laugh that escapes me.

> So we're not going to a nude party?
>
> I was really hoping to get kinky.

Oh, we're going to get kinky alright . . . but not until later. The first half of tonight is reserved for showing my wife that being married isn't the worst thing in the world, like she's been led to believe for her entire life. I reply to her message and walk out the door.

> You're a damn handful.

Another text comes through that makes me briefly consider adjusting our plans for the evening.

> I might be a handful, but so are my tits.
>
> So it cancels it out.

A picture follows her message—she's topless, a white lace bra holding up her full breasts as she leans into a mirror to put makeup on, her lips pursed out sensually. I type back a response, trying my hardest to ignore the uncomfortable tightening in my pants.

> I'll be over in five.
>
> I'm wearing jeans, FYI.

I find myself smiling as I drive to her house, reflecting on how different our text thread looked just a week ago. It was filled with desperate pleas to end our marriage, not the jokes and flirty messages we exchange now. Since our breakthrough in the hospital, she hasn't once mentioned divorce. To be fair, she also hasn't talked about staying married, but progress is progress, and I'll take what she's giving me. It feels like things have settled back to the way that they were before, and that's all I can ask for.

Pulling up to the blue guest house, I park my car and head for the front door. Even though Morgan has stayed over at my place every night this week, she hasn't said anything about moving out of this shit hole. Just yesterday, a family of roof rats made their way into the air conditioning ducts, and she nearly had a mental breakdown because it turns out that her biggest fear is being eaten alive by a rodent clawing at her stomach.

I told her she needs to stop reading those mafia books, which resulted in her shooting me a daggered glare and telling me to go fuck myself.

Lesson learned—never tell a woman what to read.

Morgan swings open the front door before I'm even halfway up the sidewalk. Her chestnut hair is down, and she's wearing a pair of holey jeans paired with a tight black top that hugs her hourglass figure. A massive smile spreads across her face as her eyes focus on the flower arrangement in my hands.

"Whatcha got there?"

"Aiming to improve my score on the husband scale," I reply with a matching smile.

While her points system has become a fun game between us, bringing her flowers has nothing to do with that. I did it because I want her to know that even when we're not together, I'm still thinking about her. That she's important to me. That I'm making an effort.

Her face lights up as she exits the house with a skip. "How did you know I liked hydrangeas?"

"Were you not listening when I said that there isn't a thing I don't notice about you? They were on your coffee table the first time I came over."

She hums and takes the arrangement from my hands. "Most of the time I tune you out, if I'm being honest."

"Go put them inside." I shake my head, swatting her behind as she turns back to the house. "We're late."

She lets out a playful yelp, shooting me a mock glare over her shoulder. "Careful, or you might lose those points you just earned."

I chuckle, watching her disappear and praying that she hurries. I spent a few hours at the hospital this afternoon because I had a couple of meetings, and unfortunately, the last one with our department chair went a little longer than expected, so we're already slightly behind schedule.

"Ready?" she asks, running down the steps a moment later.

"Ready."

I reach for her hand, and she nuzzles into me as we head to the car together.

While I drive, she chats about her day, filling me in on everything from the rodent situation, to the most recent book she's reading. I already told her that I would help her break her lease, and made it clear that she's more than welcome to stay with me if she decides that's the route that she wants to go. But I doubt she'll take me up on it since she's frustratingly independent, but the offer stands. The offer will always stand.

"And then," she continues, tossing her feet up on the dashboard. "The main character put a knife in her ass, handle first obviously, and fucked her. He had little stab wounds all over his pelvis."

I shake my head, keeping my eyes on the road. "I really hope people don't read that and experiment in real life."

"Me too, because we would totally know what happened if they came in for stitches," she giggles, pulling out her phone as we approach a red light. "Oh my god, speaking of that. Look at this X-ray from the other day. You'll never guess what this dude had in his ass."

I glance over, holding my tongue on the blatant HIPAA violation. "You know, most couples talk about their plans for the weekend, not scans of shit that people stick inside themselves."

Her eyes sparkle with delight. "We're not most couples, Walkie."

The light turns green, and I refocus on the road, but her words linger in my mind. She's right—we're not most couples. Our relationship has always been unconventional, but it's what makes us work so well together. The banter, the dark humor, the way we understand each other's worlds—it's ours.

As we pull into the strip mall parking lot, I park and turn off the engine. "You still haven't told me what was in the X-ray."

She unbuckles her seatbelt, looking over at me with a smile. "A flashlight. I'm not even kidding. And guess what the best part was?"

"What?"

"It was still on when we removed it."

I shake my head. "Gives new meaning to the term fleshlight."

Morgan's smile turns into a grin as she erupts into a fit of uncontrolled laughter, and I can't help but watch her, feeling a sense of pure contentment wash through me.

For so long, my entire world felt colorless and clinical. I was simply trying to get through life, focused on each new professional goal as the years wore on. But suddenly it feels like none of that matters. Because with Morgan, everything feels brighter, like daybreak has finally come after a long night.

"Who would've guessed that Walker Chastain had jokes," she teases, wiping a tear off her cheek. "You're just full of surprises, aren't you?"

I let out a single laugh, leaning over the center console to press a kiss on her forehead. "Ready for another one?"

***

When I was trying to determine where to take Morgan on our first date, I knew without a doubt that I wanted to go to a bookstore. She talks about reading nonstop, and it's something we bonded over, so it just seemed like a better fit than going to a movie or some other bullshit.

I was expecting to have to visit a chain, but a quick internet search helped me find this spot—Blind Love Books, a west side bookstore that specializes in romance. Their website said that they weren't opening for another week, but I reached out to the owners, and they agreed to let us stop by tonight while they stocked the shelves.

Morgan freaked out when she realized where we were. Apparently, she's been following them on social media for months and was planning on visiting once it opened to the public.

She spent an hour gushing over her favorite authors, making suggestions for merchandise, and darting from shelf to shelf like a kid on Christmas morning. Her reaction was worth every bit of effort that went into planning, along with every charge racked up on my credit card. She was glowing, especially when she realized that several exclusive editions were available. I have no idea why that matters to her, but if it makes her smile, I'll buy her all of the exclusive editions in the world—she deserves it.

Since the west side has exploded over the past few years, there are a ton of new restaurants, bars, and shopping in the area, so after we finished at the bookstore, I had planned to take her to a popular Mexican spot. I know she loves margaritas, and I figured we could grab a bite to eat before we headed home. But while we were walking to the car to set her armful of purchases down, she batted her thick lashes and asked if we could change our plans.

My girl wasn't hungry anymore—she wanted to go home and play.

As we're driving down 14th Street on the way back to my place, my phone rings. I glance at the screen and wince when I read the caller ID. It's seven in the evening, and I'm not on call. There's absolutely no reason I should be speaking to the hospital unless there is a serious problem.

"This is Dr. Chastain," I answer, putting the phone on speaker so that I can keep one hand on the wheel and the other on Morgan's thigh.

A raspy voice that I immediately recognize as my mentor, Dr. Weaver, asks, "Ever seen a rotationplasty?"

Morgan shifts in her seat beside me, her ears suddenly perking up.

"Uh," I hesitate, thrown off by the question. "No, not in person."

A rotationplasty is a relatively new surgery. It's commonly performed for patients with osteosarcoma, a rare bone cancer, but it can be done in other cases too. You remove the malignant bone, only instead of amputating the entire limb, you transform the ankle into the knee joint. I know how to do it in theory, but I've never seen one. This type of surgery typically goes to

University Hospital since it's more of an academic institution. The only reason our hospital would ever get a case like that is if the patient personally knew one of our physicians.

My mentor's voice crackles through the speaker like he's holding the phone too close to his face. "Well, you're in luck because I've got one in the morning, and I'd like you to assist."

The offer hits me straight in the gut, almost knocking the breath out of my lungs. Getting to assist on a case like this is something I've only ever dreamt of. While it's possible that I'll see one during my fellowship, it's more likely that I won't—UH has only done two in the past five years.

My mind races, torn between the excitement of being involved in such a rare procedure, and the plans I made earlier with my wife. The offer is tempting as hell, and nearly impossible to refuse, but the team that Morgan's brother coaches for is in town for a playoff game. When she told me that she was going to attend, I asked if I could tag along too.

I glance over at her, searching for any sign of disappointment, but instead find curiosity and support in her eyes.

I know without a doubt what I need to do.

"Sorry, Dr. Weaver," I reply, the words tasting sweet as they come from my mouth. "I've already got something important planned for tomorrow."

He scoffs. "You're sure you can't reschedule? This isn't something you see every day."

"I'm sure. But if you need an extra set of hands, bring Buffington in. He's got more potential than I ever did."

His disappointment is palpable through the phone, but he masks it with a professional tone. "Alright—thanks for the recommendation."

"No problem. Good luck tomorrow." I feel a weight lift off my chest as I end the call and stop at the light near Piedmont Park.

People are still out and enjoying the spring weather despite the sun setting an hour ago. A middle-aged man and his partner are walking across the street, completely outside of the crosswalk when traffic thins. Normally I'd scowl and think about all of the potential injuries they could sustain, but for some reason, all I think about is how content they look . . . and how content I feel.

"What's a rotationplasty?" Morgan asks softly, like she understands the gravity of what I just did. "Sounds much more important than a college baseball game."

I squeeze her thigh. "Nothing is more important."

She rolls her eyes, though I can see a blush paint her cheeks beneath the city lights. When we start moving again, she discreetly whips out her phone to search for details on the surgery.

"Are you crazy?" I can feel her staring at me, probably scrunching her cute little nose up in disbelief, but I don't dare look.

"I've never felt more sane in my life," I reply, letting out a humorless laugh. "We're going to the game tomorrow. I'm going to meet your brother. And you're going to let me."

"But it's your career . . ."

I pause before answering, trying to adequately summarize the thoughts that have been swarming through my mind for weeks.

"No, Morgan," I reply, glancing over at her briefly so that she can understand the significance of my words. "It's our career."

Chapter 34

Morgan

Walker and I have had sex almost every night since we made up, ranging from rough and primal, to soft and tender. But none of those moments remotely come close to beating this, because what's happening right now is another level of intimacy. This is about trust and vulnerability. Exploration and communication. It's sexy and beautiful, but it's also challenging and rigid. It ties everything we feel for each other into one perfectly kinky bow.

There are so many emotions and sensations associated with kink that it can be hard to focus on just one singular thing. But if I had to choose something to pinpoint, it would be love. Because even though Walker has me strung up in his office, standing on the balls of my feet with a hook in my ass and clamps on my nipples, he's watching me like a hawk. There's sinful lust swimming in the pools of his eyes, but there's also intense adoration shimmering through the surface.

"Give me a color," he asks, glancing up at me from his textbook-covered desk. He's been pretending to "study" with his bare feet kicked up for the past ten minutes, but I know without a doubt that there's no way he's focusing right now. How could he?

"Green, Sir," I reply despite the ache in my calves.

When we got back from our date, he asked me to go to his office, undress, and wait for him in a kneeling position facing the wall. While I knew exactly what he wanted because we've discussed expectations if we use a more formal dynamic, I couldn't help myself from waiting for him in his desk chair. Technically, I *was* naked, kneeling, and facing the wall, but he didn't seem to find as much humor in it as I did when he entered the room.

I had to bite back my smirk when he told me to try again, his tone dry and harsh in the most delicious way. When I eventually followed his instructions, he bent down and told me that there would be consequences for my "*silly little deviance.*"

And he wasn't lying.

After making me wait far too long while he went to get something from his closet, he wrapped a soft rope around my wrists and tossed it over a bolt in the ceiling so that my arms were raised in a prayer-like position. He instructed me to stand, pressed his body against my back, and reached around me to place two clamps on my nipples.

I let out a moan, feeling my core clench with needy arousal as I wondered what the purpose of the rope was. It didn't take long to figure it out though, because as soon as he tugged on it to raise my arms higher, an intense pain burst through my nipples.

He held the rope taught while he teased my body to the edge of orgasm. Eventually, he slid his fingers from my pussy to my ass and pushed one into the tight hole as he continued to torment me until I was begging for more.

In a quick exchange, he replaced his thick finger with something cold and metal around the same size. He let whatever he had just inserted sit comfortably inside me, murmuring praises at how well I was taking it. At first, I thought he had put a small plug in my ass, preparing me for some back door fun later on, but then the metal started to pull at my hips, like I was being lifted in the air.

I tried to turn and see what was happening, but Walker spanked me hard in correction. The movement pushed the device further inside my back entrance, shooting ripples of desire through me despite the unusual sensation.

I shifted on my feet, trying to lower my arms from their strained position and alleviate the ache in my nipples. But as soon as relief came, an intense tension coming from the metal inside my ass demanded my attention, forcing me to return to the original position.

A whimper came out of my mouth at the realization that I was stuck—the hook in my ass was connected to the clamps on my nipples. I needed to find my balance or one end of my body would be stuck in erotic hell.

As Walker worked to tie the contraption off, he leaned in again and asked if I was ready for the punishment. I wasn't sure what he was talking about, nor could I really concentrate because all of my attention was focused on staying as still as possible to keep the tension in equilibrium.

But then, he lowered to a squat behind me, nipped at my inner thigh, and had me lift my heels off the ground so that I was standing halfway between my tip-toes and the floor. Once satisfied, he trailed his fingers up the backs of my legs and instructed me not to drop down to the ground. He made another quick adjustment to the rope before he stepped back and ordered me to face him.

Instinctively, my heels dropped to the ground as I pivoted in his direction. The shift caused the ache in my nipples to transform into a spasm of pain, and I spewed a stream of curse words at him.

I quickly righted my position, standing as tall as I could on the balls of my feet to ease the pull on both ends of the rope.

I shot Walker a dirty look through the wisps of hair that had fallen over my eyes, hoping he knew what I thought of this particular punishment. The predicament of the rope between my ass and clamps was incredibly arousing because I had to find a balance, or risk delicious pain. But the addition of the stress position was almost cruel and left me wondering how long I could last.

He watched me struggle for a moment before he reminded me of my safeword and turned on his heel to walk away. Lounging back in his chair, he turned on the lamp at the corner of the desk and schooled his focus to his work.

I could feel the arousal dripping down my leg as I shifted, trying to get comfortable as my calves grew tired. Who knew kink could be such a workout?

When Walker finally checks in, he seems pleased. He closes his book and stacks items on his desk with deliberate slowness. I feel my body relax despite the tension in my legs, knowing that he's had enough punishment and is ready to finish our play.

Standing from his desk, he crosses the small room. He stops inches from my face, his body towering over me with pure dominance. My eyes drop to his dark jeans, noticing the distinctive bulge between his legs that tells me he's just as into this as I am.

He reaches out to redirect my attention, his rugged, heady scent washing over me as he brushes my sweaty hair from my face. "Are you ready to continue?"

I close my eyes and lean into his touch, wanting to feel more of him. "Yes, Sir."

"Good girl."

My core clenches with his words, surprised by how much I like the praise when normally his filthy degradation gets me off. But this scene isn't about rough sex or name calling, it's about freely given submission—it's about experimenting together, pleasing each other, and finding mutual enjoyment from a new dynamic.

Walker drops his hand from my face and moves it to the slick area between my legs. He easily slides his fingers through my pussy and slips two inside of me, resting them against my inner wall. I adjust my feet, hoping for some additional friction, but the slight movement shifts the strain of the rope on the hook and forces a whimper from my lips.

"I can feel your pussy clenching around my fingers, trying its hardest to come for me," he says quietly, breath hot against my ear. "Is that what you're hoping for?"

His thumb grazes my clit and a shudder of arousal pulses through my core from the slight touch.

"Yes, Sir. I want to come, Sir."

A deep growl of satisfaction rolls through his throat. "I'll tell you what. You let me play with you a little longer, and I'll let you come. How does that sound?"

I swallow harshly, not sure how much more playing I can take. "Good, Sir."

Walker steps back, slipping his fingers out of me so abruptly that I have to focus on keeping my body steady, and not the empty ache from the loss of his touch. He moves out of my view without another word, leaving me wondering how long he'll keep me strung up and needy.

God, I hope it's not long.

A moment later, he returns with a black riding crop and stops in front of me. Other than spanking me with his palm occasionally during sex—something I definitely enjoy—we haven't explored any other impact play. I draw my eyes over the instrument, noticing the triangular tip at the end.

He caresses the metal length of the crop with his hand, his biceps practically bulging out of his fitted T-shirt. Holding his palm out, he smacks the tip against his skin a few times. The sound of the crop as it swooshes through the air is intimidating, but with each blow, he doesn't even flinch.

If I had to guess, I'd assume he has a high pain tolerance given the ink smattering his left arm, but the sting can't be that bad if he doesn't react at all . . . right?

Desire races through me as he touches the leather tip of the crop to the base of my neck, dragging it along my collarbone. He presses it into my skin, flattening the head against my shoulder and rubbing it down my arm in a gentle caress. Repeating the process on my other side, I feel myself arching into it, like the toy is an extension of him in some way.

He glides the cool metal up my neck and to my cheek, before pulling back and tracing my bottom lip with the rough edge of the tip.

His eyes fall to my mouth. "Kiss it. Run those pretty lips and tongue along my crop before I use it to kiss your soft skin."

I meet his dark, lust-filled gaze as I press my lips to the toy, darting my tongue over the short length to wet the leather. His pupils dilate when I move to take the entire thing in my mouth, soaking it in my saliva before I release it with a slight pop. A distinctive sense of pride runs through me as his lips quirk into a smirk, praising me once again before he continues.

People always rag on submissives for being weak, or timid, or powerless. But the truth is, I can't think of a time in my life when

I've felt more powerful. I could stop this at any time, make him question his carnal desires, and shame him for his kinks, but I'm making the conscious choice to give myself to him for our own mutual pleasure—I can't think of anything more empowering.

Walker trails the tip of the crop down my body, benevolently avoiding my clamped nipples. He slides it over my belly, and I widen my stance while trying to avoid the tug of the hook on my ass from the movement. The leather strokes the length of my inner thighs, all of the nerves singing with desperation beneath its gentle caress.

Once he reaches the crease of my thigh, he slowly slides the flat side through my slit, stopping right above my clit. I feel my core clench in anticipation of him swatting the sensitive bud, but he doesn't. He just holds it firmly against my pussy, watching me with hooded eyes like he enjoys the way I squirm.

I wince when he finally pulls back, my body tensing as I prepare for a blow that never comes. Instead, he lifts the tip to his nose, inhales deeply, and lets out a raspy groan like he's savoring the smell of my arousal.

He drops the crop to his palm again, giving it another testing swat before he positions himself beside me. His body feels like a solid wall of muscle as he presses against me, grabbing my hip with one hand to hold me in place while he drags the crop from the top of my ass to the back of my knees.

Walker strokes my skin like he's defining the area that he's about to mark, and I focus on my breathing, each heavy exhale reminding me of the delicious pinch of the clamps.

Finally, he settles the crop against the meaty part of my ass, holding it steady as he tightens his hold on my hip.

"You're in quite the predicament, little devil. Strung up in my office and forced to decide between the pull from the hook in your ass, or the clamps on your nipples," he rasps breathily, his erection pressing into my side. "I'm going to use my crop on you now. If I were you, I'd stay as still as possible and take every blow like a good girl. Show me how much you like the pain, and I'll reward you with pleasure."

I only nod, bracing myself for the sting.

He strikes my flesh so softly at first that I barely feel it, and then repeats the same tender kisses every few seconds as I adjust to the sensation. Once he's marked the entirety of my ass, he doubles the force of the blows. This time I hear the distinctive sound of the crop through the air, but the feeling is still tolerable.

Despite the slight pain, the tension in my body fades into a deeply relaxed state, just like it did the night I held his cock in my throat. I take slow, soothing breaths as the pace of his crop escalates, now coming every second and with more force. The hum of arousal in my core is at an all-time high, not nearing orgasm but simply existing in a state of pleasurable pain. It's intoxicating, and I almost miss the moment Walker stops his whipping.

He drops the crop to the floor and shifts his body to wrap me in his arms. A wave of warmth washes over me with his embrace, and I tilt my neck to allow my head to fall against his chest. He murmurs praises into my hair, telling me that he's so proud of me, that I did well, that I deserve to come.

I close my eyes with a prolonged sigh as his fingers skim my pussy and slip between the slickness to circle my clit. Almost immediately, the exquisite tension returns, the freight train of my impending orgasm racing toward me. My legs start to quake, both from the exhaustion of holding myself up on the balls of my feet and from the torment of release on the horizon.

Walker immediately picks up on it, slowing his movements.

"No," I beg, my eyes finding his. "Don't stop, Sir."

His brow knits, trying to understand. "Give me a color."

I wrack my brain, not wanting this to stop but also fully aware that I can't come like this.

"Yellow, Sir," I whimper.

His free hand gently reaches down to slide my sweat-covered hair off my neck. "Tell me what you need."

"I need . . . I need to come so bad but I'm going to fall."

My legs are far too close to giving out, and if that happens, my nipples are going to rip right off my body.

Realization floods his face, and he quickly snakes his arm around my low belly to secure me against his hard body. The strain of the clamps and hook is still present, but I know without a doubt that he won't drop me.

"Better," I confirm, offering him a small smile. "Keep going, Sir."

I know it sounds ridiculous to use the formal phrase at this point, but I like it. It helps me differentiate between this dynamic and everything else we do, solidifying us into this space with a single word.

Walker's eyes flicker with arousal as his fingers begin to tease my sensitive bundle of nerves, building me back up as I race toward my release.

He tilts his hips forward, grinding his cock against me, and the shift pulls my arms higher, tugging on my nipples just enough to make me wince.

"I want you to come for me, little devil. Let that pain from those clamps push you over the edge of pleasure."

His permission is all that my body needs to let go. I crash over the edge just like he commanded, my core spasming and searching for something to connect with. My inner muscles clench around the hook as the strongest orgasm I've ever experienced shatters through me. My legs definitely give out, but Walker holds me in place, murmuring praises as he rubs me through the exquisite high.

When I finally come out of my euphoric fog, I feel jostling behind me. The rope connected to the hook in the ceiling slackens, allowing me to lower my sore arms from their raised position. I finally settle to my heels, the ache of my calves easing substantially now that I'm on the ground.

I turn to face Walker, holding my hands out so that he can release me from the rope secured around my wrists.

The harsh lines of his mouth tip up, an amused smirk forming on his lips. "Oh no. I'm not done with you yet. Kneel."

I blink at him for a moment, confused but too placated by my orgasm to question his request. Sinking to my knees, I feel the hook jostle inside my tight hole, reminding me that I'm still very much in submissive territory.

Walker grabs something from his desk drawer before lowering his body in front of me so that we're at eye level. It's funny that I once questioned how he felt about me because the look in his eyes now is exactly the same one that he had the night of the engagement party—yearning.

I don't look down at what's in his hands, instead choosing to focus on the man in front of me.

"Once I put this gag in your mouth, you're going to need to use your nonverbal safeword. Do you remember what it is?"

We've used squeezes before, but that only works if I'm touching him. So instead, I shake my head back and forth twice, holding his gaze.

"Good girl," he praises, voice low and soft. "Open up for me."

My eyes flutter closed as I follow his command, body tingling with contentment. Something slides along my tongue but it stops before I feel like I have to choke. A soft leather panel similar to a muzzle covers the lower half of my face, and though they're not being held open like a traditional gag, my lips instinctively wrap around the rubber.

I breathe through my nose as he secures it behind my head, pulling tight so the gag presses deeper into my mouth. As best as I can, I run my tongue along the toy, trying to work out what is.

"It's a cock gag," Walker says, answering my non-verbal question. His fingers tug on the rope attached to the hook, jostling the metal deeper into my ass as he secures it to something. "Figured I would keep your mouth occupied while I fuck that tight little pussy on my desk."

He pulls on the back of the strap, forcing me to arch my neck to avoid choking on the rubber. My eyes fly open, trying to determine what's happening even though I know that he's still behind me, and I won't be able to see a damn thing. Drool starts to collect in my mouth, and I groan with frustration when I realize that I can't swallow. My lips tighten around the dildo to keep the saliva in as Walker appears in front of me, the end of the rope in his fist.

His foot kicks out, jerking on the chain between my breasts. I'd almost forgotten about the clamps, but his movement sends a sharp sting down my spine and directly to my clit. I suck harder on the gag to silence my whimper, keeping my eyes glued to him.

"You know," he muses, wrapping the rope around his hand several times. "I think I'd actually like to go for a walk before I fuck you. What do you think?"

My mouth must drop open slightly because I feel a distinct wetness run down my chin. His dark eyes follow the trail of drool, blowing wide with arousal.

His tone transforms from soft to mocking. "I think you'd like that, wouldn't you, little devil?"

I don't answer because that's not what he wants. I just blink up at him through my lashes, wondering what the hell he's planning.

He shows me instead of telling me, the muscles in his tattooed forearm rippling as he yanks on the rope. It sends the hook deeper and presses into some inherently pleasurable area that I've never tapped into. I shift on my heels, trying to alleviate the ache building between my legs again.

"Let's walk to my desk," he commands, drawing his gaze over my naked body.

I move to stand but he tugs on the rope again, jerking me back to the ground.

"No, no," he tuts, lips in a harsh line. "I'm going to walk. You're going to crawl in front of me, leashed to the hook in your ass like the good little sub you are."

I nod to indicate my understanding, his words turning the tingle in my body to a full-blown sizzle. In any other situation, this would be humiliating. But with this man, it's hotter than hell. I shift my body to the desk, leaning forward so my weight rests on my hands and knees.

Walker instructs me to keep my head up, but I must not do it to his liking because he tightens his grip on the rope, simultaneously adjusting the position of my head and the strain of the hook. The arch of my neck forces my jaw open and a waterfall of saliva spills onto the cowhide rug beneath me.

"Crawl for me, little devil. Show me how that stuffed ass and soaked pussy look while your gagged mouth drools all over my floor."

My body pulses with need as I follow his orders, sliding my still-bound wrists forward. My legs trudge behind, trying to work in tandem so that the strain on the rope doesn't get too tight.

When I make it to the corner of the desk, I sit back on my heels and wait, thankful to give my knees some rest. The majority of the room might be covered in a rug, but there are still hardwoods beneath that make crawling surprisingly painful.

Walker tugs on the hook, lurching my body backward so that I'm sitting on my ass. I stare up at him, noticing the ripple of tension in his jaw and the riding crop in his other hand.

When the hell did he pick that thing up?

"Did I tell you to stop?" he growls.

I try to mutter the words "No, Sir" around the gag, but that only causes more drool to pour from my lower lip. My legs right themselves, sliding beneath me to return my body to a crawling position.

"Let's do another lap around the room. This time, you only stop when I tell you to."

My chin dips in acknowledgment before I turn my head and focus on the floor in front of me. I'm half expecting him to swat me with the crop, but the delicious sting never comes, so I lurch forward at a quicker pace now that I've adjusted to the tension of the rope.

When I'm halfway around the room, I stop to shift the gag with my tongue so the spit pooling in the back of my throat can escape through the corner of my mouth. As if he was waiting for me to fail, Walker immediately pulls on his makeshift leash to reorient my head and the tension of the hook. I grunt in frustration as I start to move again, earning me a harsh swat to my exposed ass.

"Got something to say?" he taunts, voice grating like sandpaper through the air.

I don't reply, remaining focused on my end goal as I begin to move again. Walker kisses my skin with the occasional light swat of the crop, like he only just remembered that he was carrying the toy. A torrent of arousal slides down my thighs despite the overwhelming exhaustion overtaking my body. My jaw aches, my legs ache, my pussy aches, and yet somehow I still need more.

Once the requested full circle of the room is complete, I hesitate because he's not telling me to stop like he said he would. I slow my crawl, attempting to crane my neck and glance back at him.

"I think you have one more lap in you," he comments, amusement in his tone. "Keep going for me. The last one is always the best one."

At this point, I'm starting to wonder if my husband has unlocked a new kink because this is a different level of humiliation, even for him.

I attempt to pick up my pace, determined to get through this as quickly as possible, but the rope pulls tighter each time I try, forcing me to crawl . . . well . . . at a crawl.

When I make it to the first corner, the immediate need to come ripples through me, jerking me to a stop. I clench my thighs together to avoid my impending orgasm as I try to figure out where the urge is coming from. It feels like my body is vibrating from the inside out, a steady hiss of pleasure rolling through my entire lower half.

A hard smack lands on my ass, reorienting me to the situation. "Keep going."

I don't move, whipping my head in Walker's direction as another sting kisses the skin of my other cheek.

"I must have forgotten to tell you that the hook vibrates."

He looks like he's enjoying himself at my expense, and if I wasn't gagged, I would break protocol to stick my tongue out at him.

"Keep going," he repeats, tone dropping lower. "Oh, and little devil? There *will* be consequences if you come without permission."

I grit my teeth around the rubber dildo so hard I'm sure they'll leave puncture marks, summoning the strength to move my body forward. Each second that passes sends me higher into ecstasy, and I focus everything I have on staving off my release.

As soon as I round the final corner and think I'm in the clear, the vibrations intensify—because of course they do—creating an intense pressure in my pussy. I can't help the moan of pleasure that escapes my lips, giving away the fact that despite the humiliation, I'm enjoying the hell out of this.

"Atta girl," Walker coos when I finally reach his desk. "You did so well. You can stop now."

He pulls me to my feet, peering down at me with nothing but satisfaction in his eyes. The pad of his thumb brushes the drool from my chin, gently rubbing it down my neck like he's painting me. I lean into him, forgetting my impending orgasm as he pulls me into his arms.

"You think you can take a little more?" he murmurs against my hair, pressing his erection into my belly. "Because all I can think about is fucking you on this desk. Making you come on my cock while your ass clenches around that metal hook."

I nod into his chest because I might be full in other ways, but my pussy has been aching for him all night.

Walker helps me onto the desk, positioning me on my hands and knees again. His palm presses into my upper back, guiding me into a modified child's pose. The clamps rub against the wooden desktop, intensifying the sensation in my nipples as I settle into place.

"Look at my wife," he drawls to himself, trailing his fingers down my spine and over the sensitive areas he marked with the crop. "Dripping wet for my cock after taking my torment so well. How the hell did I get so lucky?"

My heart claws at my chest, more from emotion than arousal as he squeezes the crease of my ass and slips his fingers into me. I've asked myself that exact question multiple times this week because the truth is that I feel the same way—only we don't need luck because what Walker and I have could beat all of the odds.

Chapter 35

Walker

Morning light streams through a crack in my blackout curtains, illuminating Morgan's face as she shifts in my arms and mutters something unintelligible. I have no idea if she knows this, but she talks in her sleep. I've been listening to her mumble complete nonsense for the past few minutes, and it makes me wonder what she's dreaming about because the words "limoncello" and "pool boy" just came out of her mouth in close succession.

My arm went numb beneath her head a while ago, but I can't bring myself to move it—she just looks so angelic and peaceful. And after everything I put her through last night, she deserves all of the rest that she needs.

After I fucked her on my desk until we both came, I picked her up and carried her to the bathroom. I intended to draw her a bath and let her relax, but she asked if I would get in with her, just like the night of the ice storm. And just like that night, I held her in my arms until the water turned cold, fully content.

As I'm mentally going through my to-do list for the weekend, Morgan stirs and slowly opens her eyes.

She blinks rapidly, pupils dilating and contracting as they finally focus on my face. "You're up?"

I shift, wiping the drool-crusted hair from her face. "I've been up for a while, listening to you dream about . . . Italy?"

"Close." Her lips tilt into a sleepy smile. "A billionaire boyfriend named Lorenzo."

I scowl. "Oh, so your real-life boyfriend isn't enough?"

"Real-life husband," she corrects, running her fingers along my arm that's draped over her bare stomach. "Though, I'd be happy to also find a real-life boyfriend if you want. You know what they say, sharing is caring."

My fingers pinch her side, making her squeal and squirm. When she finally settles I ask, "How does your ass feel?"

I was hoping that we would've had a chance to talk more about the scene last night, but most of our time in the tub was spent in comfortable silence, and she passed out immediately after we climbed into bed.

She tilts her head toward me, brow cocked with amusement. "Why? Thinking about spanking it?"

I let out a soft laugh. "If you keep talking about sharing, I might. But I wanted to check in after last night. How are you feeling about what we did?"

The entire scene I kept my attention on her, reading her body language and breathy little sounds to ensure that I didn't push anything too far. It seemed like she was enjoying herself, and she even voiced a few things that she liked about it briefly in the tub, but her opinion could be different now—I hope it isn't, but it could be.

"I feel like you might have a humiliation kink," she replies, shooting me a teasing wink.

When I don't react, she adds, "It was honestly more intense than I was expecting. Not in a bad way, just in a surprising way.

I think whenever we do that again, we need to make sure nothing is planned after, or I won't survive."

I swallow hesitantly before asking, "So you want to do it again?"

"Duh." She grins at me like the little devil that she is. "Yeah it was intense, but it was also hot as fuck."

I smile and press a silky kiss to her lips, feeling a sense of contentment that's hard to describe. "I agree."

Her fingers lazily trail up my arm, tracing the lines of ink covering my skin.

"You do that a lot," I comment, watching her eyes follow her feathery touch like the tattoos are a book she's trying to read.

Morgan furrows her brow, studying the ropelike design on the top of my forearm. "I don't understand them."

"You don't understand my tattoos?"

She nods slowly. "Yeah, don't get me wrong, I like them. It's just that usually people get meaningful things inked on their skin, and yours just look like a bunch of random shapes and shading."

"And?"

Her lower lip draws between her teeth as she finally turns to face me, a curious expression on her face. "Why?"

I hesitate for a moment as a feeling of uneasiness washes over me. It would be so easy to reply with a snarky comment about how I thought they looked badass when I turned eighteen, but she doesn't deserve that—she deserves to know the truth. And I want to tell her.

"Remember how I told you that my parents died when I was a teenager?"

"Yeah . . ."

"My dad and I were in a pretty bad car accident when I was fifteen." I flop onto my back and let out a pained breath because it's been a long-ass time, but the words still hurt. "He died on impact, but I was thrown from the car despite wearing a seatbelt."

I study the crown molding above my head, recounting the memory vividly even after sixteen years. Morgan threads her fingers through mine, squeezing my hand as I work up the strength to continue.

"Both of my parents were addicts who struggled with sobriety off and on for years. I was walking on eggshells for my entire childhood and never wanted to do anything that set them off. So when my dad told me to get in the car with him, I listened, even though I knew he was high."

I swallow and close my eyes, the image of him hanging upside down in our beat-up SUV flooding back with vivid clarity. An ambulance showed up a few minutes later, declared him dead on arrival, and rushed me to the hospital.

"Mom died a few years later," I add, blinking away the memories. "Overdosed the night after I left for college."

Saying everything out loud sounds a lot worse than it feels. Sure, it's hard to talk about, but I worked through my shit years ago. And while I would have loved a different childhood, it made me into the person I am today.

"So, uh, yeah," I pause, trying to remember the point of this story other than pity. "The wound from the accident was pretty nasty, and the doctors at Grady did the best they could, but I ended up with a big-ass scar that ran down my forearm. As soon as I could afford it, I got a tattoo to cover it up. I didn't give a fuck what it was—pretty sure I just told them to do the entire arm and handed them a wad of cash."

Morgan nuzzles into my side, pressing her cheek against my chest. "I'm sorry that you went through that. And I'm even more sorry that I asked."

"I'm glad you did," I reply, stroking the back of her hand with my thumb as I meet her gaze. Her emerald eyes have turned glossy, like she's fighting back tears. "And I'm glad it happened because I probably wouldn't be a doctor otherwise."

I didn't make the connection until much later, but the experience actually solidified my interest in medicine. The team that worked on me was thorough, comforting, and incredibly talented. If it hadn't been for them, I would have a fuck ton of debt because my parents didn't have health insurance. The vascular surgeon spoke with social work to ensure that the surgeries were pro bono, and I left the hospital without a single bill.

"For what it's worth, I'm glad you're a doctor."

I plant a kiss on her forehead. "I'm glad I'm a doctor, too. Because it means that I met you."

Silence settles between us as I think back on the past five months.

When my wife left me, I resigned myself to a life without love because I assumed that I couldn't be a good surgeon and a good husband at the same time. I figured there was a reason the divorce rate in residency was so high, after all. But it turns out that the problem wasn't my career specifically—it was a lack of perspective, both from myself and my partner.

The hospital is a unique microcosm that you can really only understand from the inside. The doctors, the nurses, the technicians, we all spend more time with each other than we do with our own families. We laugh together, we cry together, we grow together, and we fall apart together. And because of the rawness of human emotion that we experience in our careers, it doesn't take long to form bonds with our coworkers that rival any other relationship in our lives—bonds that are foraged in mutual suffering, enlightenment, and deep acceptance.

Oftentimes, when we try to live our normal lives outside of our jobs, it can be challenging to feel understood. And the more that I think about it, that mutual lack of perspective is what ended up becoming the biggest detriment to my first marriage. I lacked the perspective to understand how alone Lane felt when I was working hundred-hour weeks, and she lacked the perspective to understand how alone I felt after those hundred-hour weeks. Neither one of us was wrong, and while it was fucked up that she had an affair, I understand now that it was because she was lonely—we were both lonely.

Having a career in medicine can sometimes feel like you're living two different lives—one at work and one at home. But with Morgan, those lives have merged effortlessly into something beautifully whole. Something that I never want to let go of.

"Actually, I do have one tattoo that means something," I murmur after a while, my voice barely above a whisper.

I promised myself that I wasn't going to show her until it felt right, but now seems like just as good of a time as any—I want her to know how much she means to me.

Her ears perk up, and she lifts her head. "Please tell me it's not a Creed song. I didn't realize how obsessed you were until I opened your phone to play music in Vegas and saw that your username was in the top zero point one percent of listeners . . ."

"It's not a Creed song," I confirm with a soft laugh. "See if you can find it."

Shifting my body, I turn to face her again and hold out my arm so that my palm is raised to the ceiling.

She mutters something snarky about how she's already seen my tattoos a million times, but her stubbornly curious gaze travels along my skin, trying to confirm that she hasn't missed anything. When she reaches the inner part of my upper arm, her face pales.

"Hang on. What's—" Her voice crawls to a stop, like she's had the wind knocked out of her.

"I got it after Vegas," I explain, the amusement from her shock warring with the sudden rush of emotion that just slammed into my chest. "It's the Tasmanian Devil."

Morgan swallows and touches the fresh ink. Her fingers trace over the animated character swirling around in a tornado that appears to be coming out of a wound in my skin. Because of its location, you wouldn't know the tattoo was there unless I called attention to it, so I'm not surprised that she didn't notice it yet. But now that she has, I don't think she'll ever unsee it again.

"But why?" she asks quietly, keeping her eyes glued to the permanent art like it will answer the question for her.

"Because you swirled into my life like a little devil—unpredictable, powerful, and intoxicating. You swept me away, and I haven't wanted to be back on my feet ever since." I reach out to cup her face, directing her attention to me. "I wanted to carry you with me, regardless of what happened with us in the end. Even if you decided you didn't want me, I knew that you'd always have me."

Her bottom lip wobbles. "You're serious?"

I nod, swallowing down my own emotion. "You have my heart, little devil, and you'll have my heart until the day that I die. I love you."

The words are everything I can offer her, and yet somehow not enough, because what I feel for Morgan is so much more than love. She's the most important thing in my life, and she will continue to be the most important thing in my life until I die.

The raw emotion that crosses her face tells me that she feels the same way, and even though I don't expect her to say anything, she whispers, "I love you too."

My fingers tip her chin, angling her face so that I can capture her mouth. Our kiss is all-consuming, filled with passion, vulnerability, and pure understanding. It's a kiss that I never thought I'd experience, but one that I feel so goddamn lucky to have.

She pulls back, her reddened lips quirking into a humored smirk. "I hate to burst your bubble, but you know that tattoo isn't on your heart, right?"

I bark out a laugh, not expecting her comment. "It's not? Guess I should just cover it up, then."

She starts to protest, her eyes widening in alarm, but I cut her off. "Relax—it's here to stay. However, if you had paid attention in anatomy class, you would understand the significance of the location."

"Listen, C's get degrees."

I roll my eyes and gently adjust her arm to better illustrate my point.

"The basilic vein," I explain, tracing a finger up her smooth skin, "is located on the medial side of the arm. It's the preferred location for PICC lines because of its size and close proximity to the surface."

"Okay . . ." she says, drawing out the word like she's unsure where this is going.

"It also has a direct line to the heart."

Morgan snorts, her smirk transforming to a wicked grin. "And here I thought you ortho bros only knew about bones."

Chapter 36

Walker

"I still can't believe you skipped the rotationplasty," Beau says for the tenth time today, twisting his oversized body toward me in the ortho lounge.

I shoot him a glare, beginning to regret my decision to study here. Board exams are less than a month away at the end of June. And while I feel prepared, I also don't need to be interrupted every five minutes by the boasting of an intern, no matter how much I happen to like him.

He doesn't catch on, continuing his soliloquy. "I mean, I appreciate you giving me the call-up to the big leagues. But damn. It was the coolest thing I've ever seen. You missed out."

"There will always be more surgeries," I comment, providing the same response that I've given to all of my other coworkers who said the same thing.

"Not like this one," he retorts, drumming his fingers excitedly on his knee. "You essentially said no to going to the moon. Or Mount Everest. Or the Titanic."

"These days I don't think anyone wants to go to the Titanic."

I sigh and close my book because he clearly has no plans of letting this go. We haven't seen each other in weeks because he's been on his surgical ICU rotation and busy as fuck. I can tell he's been busting at the seams to give me the play-by-play of the case.

Beau laughs and reaches for his protein shake. "True. But you get the point."

"I don't actually."

If he's trying to equate the surgery I turned down, to a once-in-a-lifetime experience, he's not going to convince me, no matter what he says. He could tell me that the patient magically grew their legs back, and I still wouldn't care. The only thing that's once in a lifetime is being married to Morgan.

"Just that it must have been a hard decision."

"Truthfully, it was the easiest decision I've ever made." I turn in my chair to face him. "And one day it will be for you too."

Beau takes a sip, letting out a dismissive sound after he swallows. "Nah, I'd give my left nut to be able to do that again."

I understand where he's coming from because for so long, surgery was the most important thing in my life. If there was another case, I would take it. If there was another patient, I would see them. The entire length of my residency, there wasn't a single thing I would say no to because I thought giving in would make me weak or less of a surgeon.

But the reality of the situation is that the hospital will give you lots of things, but it will take even more. It will provide you with education, growth, and a career to be proud of. But it will also demand that you trade those things for your time, your money, your friendships, and your family—until you're left with no life outside of the thing that didn't actually give you that much at all. Because at the end of the day, your career isn't going to be there for you when you're celebrating at the peaks of the mountains, and it's definitely not going to be there for you when you're in the depths of the valleys—people will be.

"Let's say you had important plans with Claire that day," I say, trying to impart some wisdom on my friend so that he can learn from my mistakes. "Would you have taken the case then?"

"Obviously," he scoffs, not hesitating for a second. "She would understand."

"What if she didn't?"

Beau knits his furry brows as he considers my question.

"I'd make it up to her later," he finally replies with a lewd wink.

His answer doesn't surprise me—we see it all of the time with physicians, particularly residents. Surgery is this bright, shiny, Disneyland full of possibilities. We all succumb to its allure at first, drawn in by our egos and drive to succeed. But the number of us who end up bitter and alone is astounding, and the last thing that I want is for Beau to fall into the same trap I did.

"You love Claire, and you're planning to marry her one day," I state, knowing the answer but trying to provide context for the point I want to make.

He leans back in his chair, crossing his arms as a bashful splash of color forms on his tan cheeks. "Yeah, assuming Parker doesn't kill me before I can make it happen."

"Then you need to understand something," I say solemnly. "Marriage is a constant race to the back of the line."

He looks at me like I'm speaking a different language.

"Inherently, humans are selfish. We put our needs and our desires first, always striving for more, even after we achieve our goals. But what you have to understand, is that in a marriage you can't do that. Well . . . you can, but it won't end well."

I suck in a heavy breath, letting it out slowly.

"Your spouse should automatically become the most important thing in your life—more important than any surgery, case, or career achievement. They're not going to ask you to choose, and you're not always going to have a choice. But when you do, choose them."

"Look at you, Walker-boo-boo," Beau coos, goofily grinning at me. "You've turned into a big-ass mush. Morgan did this to you, didn't she?"

I fight a smile but eventually give in to his charm and try one on. "She did."

When the reality of what happened in Vegas set in, I made a vow to myself that I would do everything I could to be a better husband than I was the first time around. The most important way that I could think of to do that was to put my wife first. And while a career in medicine is inherently going to require personal sacrifice, you can set boundaries and still reach the peak.

I knew Morgan wouldn't ask me to skip the case, but there wasn't a chance in hell I was going to miss our plans. I was going to honor my commitment to her, regardless of the professional repercussions. And I'm so glad that I did because it was worth every ounce of the sacrifice.

"Well, speaking of marriage," Beau says casually. "You ready for Parker's wedding this weekend? I bought cigars for the rooftop reception—we're gonna look bougie as fuck."

"Actually, I need to talk to you about that . . ."

***

I sling my backpack over my shoulder, leaving Beau to sulk in the lounge because he's on call tonight. As I'm starting down the hallway, I spot a familiar face headed in the opposite direction.

"Wes," I call out, grabbing his attention.

Weston stops, his look of surprise quickly shifting to a fake half-smile. "Hey, bud. Long time, no see. How's ortho?"

The last time I ran into him, I got the sense that something was off, but I couldn't put my finger on what it was. Today, it's even more evident—he looks defeated.

"People break bones, we fix them," I say with a chuckle, trying to lighten his mood. "You're full time now, I hear?"

"Yeah, I initially had to take care of a few things, but officially transitioned to full time last month," he answers with a shrug, his tone flat.

I don't press him on the details because he clearly isn't interested in sharing. But I also understand the importance of having people in your corner, and right now he looks like he needs a friend.

"Hey, want to grab a drink sometime?"

Truthfully, I don't have a ton of time given everything on my plate at the moment, but for some reason, I'm worried about him.

Weston used to be this larger-than-life guy who everyone in the department wanted to be around. He didn't take anything too seriously and in a specialty of people who are nothing but serious, he was a breath of fresh air. But now he looks just like the rest of us—dejected, jaded, and exhausted.

His hazel eyes flicker with interest. "Tonight? I've, uh, got something I need to take care of but I could probably meet you around nine?"

"Tonight works," I reply, surprised that he took me up on the offer since we've never been close. "Let me just send a quick text to Morgan to let her know the plan."

He nods and leans against the wall as I start to type. "I heard about what happened in Vegas."

I pause, looking up at him curiously. "Did you?"

I haven't told anyone at work about our marriage, and there's no way in hell that Beau or Parker said anything. Which only leaves one person...

"Morgan gave me a brief rundown the other day," he confirms. "I walked into her patient's room for an emergent appy consult while Parker's sister was teasing her about her new wedding band."

I smile as I picture her wearing the ring I bought her a few weeks ago. It isn't much—just a silicone band that she can wear at the hospital and not feel guilty if she loses it.

"It's been a wild few months."

"I can only imagine," he says with an amused exhale, his expression slightly less grim than it was a few minutes ago. "Well, you've got a good one."

I certainly do.

Chapter 37

Morgan

I've been asking Cass to send me her wedding details for weeks—simple things like where to be, and when to be there—only to be pacified with blanket statements and bizarre distractions. She's been acting more like a bridechilla than a bridezilla, and it's throwing me off.

According to her, last night was a *"family only"* rehearsal dinner. But when I stalked Cass and Claire on social media, both of them were uncharacteristically silent. Not a story, not a post, not even a tagged picture. Nothing.

Normally I would've done more sleuthing, but like every night for the past few weeks, I stayed over at Walker's house. He distracted me with his tongue until the last thing on my mind was my best friend's lack of information. And while I can't complain, because my body is deliciously satisfied from a night of intense playtime, I feel like I'm officially behind schedule—whatever that schedule is.

When I begged Cass for more information yesterday, the only text I got back made me want to pull my hair out.

> Today - Rehearsal + Dinner. (Family only. Don't try and crash it lol)

> Tomorrow - Report to the venue at Noon for lunch. Hair + Makeup after. Bring a dress and shoes. Nothing else.

I sent a screenshot to Claire to ask if she had any additional information, but she just responded with a slew of shrugging emojis.

I feel like I'm way more stressed about this than anyone else. I've been in a handful of college friends' weddings, and they were all way more chaotic. I mean, I get that I'm not the maid of honor, but there should definitely be . . . more.

"Have you seen my curling iron?" I yell into the hallway before throwing open the bathroom cabinets to frantically search for my getting-ready supplies.

"Aren't you having your hair and makeup done this afternoon?"

Oh, right.

I walk into the bedroom wearing one of his T-shirts. "What did Beau tell you? Are you staying at the venue when you drop me off? Or are y'all going somewhere else?"

Walker is shirtless and leaning against his metal headboard as he furiously types something on his phone

"Uh, not sure yet," he answers distractedly, keeping his eyes glued to the screen.

What the hell is happening? Usually, I have his undivided attention any time I speak.

I swear today is starting to feel like the twilight zone.

"Okay . . ." I mutter, deciding to shoot off a text to Team Daddies.

> What time does Walker have to be with the guys?
>
> He seems to know nothing.
>
> Typical man.

Technically, he isn't in the wedding either since Cass and Parker only chose a best man and maid of honor, but the guys are supposed to meet up and *"get ready"* together. I would imagine that includes drinking, talking about boring doctor things, and combing their hair five minutes before the ceremony starts, but what if there's more? What if they have to pick something up at the last minute?

Claire responds to my message with a picture of her holding a bottle of champagne.

Claire:
> Walkie-talkie has his signals crossed hehehe.

> Have you already had a mimosa?
>
> Wait for me!!!!!

Caroline:
> No—she's just as annoying when she's sober.

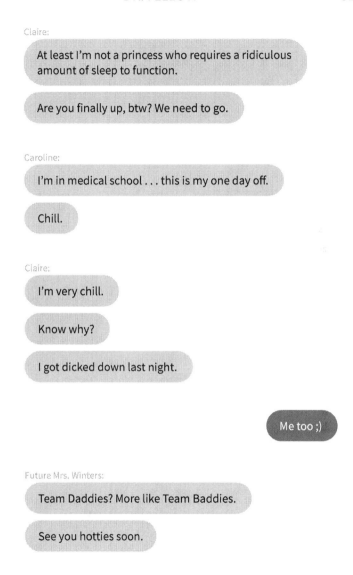

Claire:
At least I'm not a princess who requires a ridiculous amount of sleep to function.

Are you finally up, btw? We need to go.

Caroline:
I'm in medical school ... this is my one day off.

Chill.

Claire:
I'm very chill.

Know why?

I got dicked down last night.

Me too ;)

Future Mrs. Winters:
Team Daddies? More like Team Baddies.

See you hotties soon.

I laugh and press the like button on Cassidy's message before tossing my phone on the bed. I might not have any additional information on the plan for the day, but I know without a doubt that it's going to be one to remember.

***

"What kind of wedding dress do you think she's gonna wear? I feel like it's got to be classic, but I could see her in something sexy since she has the hottest bod. It's honestly a toss-up."

My skin feels like it's vibrating with energy, all of the atoms inside me swirling a little faster with excitement. The only reason I haven't completely jumped through the roof is because Walker has his arm around me, physically grounding my body as we ride the elevator up to the venue.

"You'll know in a few hours, I'm sure," he replies calmly, adjusting my ten-year-old Vera Bradley duffel bag on his shoulder.

I sigh, wishing the damn elevator would climb faster. It feels like it's ascending the forty stories of the building at a glacial pace, and all I want is to get to the top so that I can hug my bestie on her big day.

Walker took his sweet time getting out of the door this morning, promising that we were on schedule when we definitely weren't. For some ridiculous reason, he took the longest shower known to man and acted like it wasn't a big deal. By the time he was finally ready, we were cutting it so close that I threatened to drive myself. But then he whipped out his dominant voice and insisted that he give me a ride.

I was powerless to refuse him—I'm just a girl, after all.

I did, however, shoot Cass a text when we pulled up ten minutes late to blame his ass. I love him, but I'm definitely going to throw him under the bus when he deserves it.

"I bet it's a mix of both," I continue, hearing my foot tap on the black tile floor.

Walker's thumb soothingly strokes my bare shoulder. "Patience, little devil."

Fortunately, I don't have to search for patience because the elevator pings, and I launch myself through the doors in search of my favorite bride.

I only make it a few steps before I pause in my tracks, jaw dropping as I look around. The venue is even more beautiful than it appears online—sleek opulence surrounded by thirty-foot windows that overlook the downtown Atlanta skyline.

Even though the wedding isn't for several more hours, everything appears to be set up already, from the photo booth to the dinner tables. Unable to help myself, I reach out to touch a beautiful floral arrangement near the elevator, a classic assortment of white hydrangeas and other flowers spilling out of a massive metal goblet.

"Cass," I yell, weaving around the white linen tables covered in fresh greenery. "Where's the getting ready room?"

When nobody responds, I swivel my head around to try and spy their belongings. She never replied to my text, so it's possible that I made it before her, but it's already twelve-thirty. . . we're late.

"Hello?" I call into the empty space, hoping someone is around who can direct me.

Walker appears behind me. "Beau told me he was on the patio. Maybe they're outside."

"That's why they pay you the big bucks." I wink at him before speeding toward the doors, thankful I wore tennis shoes and an athletic dress because I have the zoomies.

On the way over, Walker told me that the guys were meeting at the venue before driving to GJ's for lunch. While it doesn't make any sense because the bar is in the opposite direction of downtown, I didn't question him—as long as they're ready for the wedding, I could care less what they do all day.

I make it outside, searching for my friends. The outdoor space is almost the same size as the interior. There's a roped-off area with rows of black metal chairs facing a huge floral arch, and two bars that appear to be fully stocked despite the lack of bartenders. It looks like someone set everything up and then abandoned ship.

Weird.

"Cass?" I call, feeling like this is a game of hide and seek that I'm losing.

"Up here."

Her voice cuts through the perfect June air, and I do my best to follow it. I swear it sounded like she was above me, but that can't be right. We're on the rooftop . . .

"Cass?"

"Morg," she replies, her voice louder now.

I take it back. This isn't hide and seek—this is Marco Polo.

"Where the hell are you?"

"Take the stairs."

I find the stairs, taking them two at a time. When I reach the top, I throw open the door and take a tentative step onto the painted pavement.

I totally forgot that this place had a helipad.

"What's going on?" I ask, blinking several times at my friend.

She's sitting on the concrete with her legs crossed, hair up in a ponytail like she doesn't have a care in the world. Parker, Beau, Caroline, and Claire are with her, their bodies forming a semi-circle with an unopened bottle of champagne between them.

I swear to god if the next game is duck, duck, goose I'm going to lose it . . .

"Why aren't you getting ready?" I direct the question at the group but keep my focus on Cassidy.

When I don't receive an answer, my eyes shift over each of them, trying to understand what's happening here. They just stare back at me with various shades of amusement on their faces—even Parker Winters has a smirk on his lips.

Am I in the upside down?

I redirect my attention to Cass. "Do you not believe in superstition? Pretty sure the bride and groom aren't supposed to see each other on their wedding day."

I know that I'm not one to do things traditionally, as evidenced by my surprise wedding in Vegas, but Cassidy definitely is. She should be in the bridal suite getting her hair and makeup done, not sitting beside her future husband on a helipad.

"That's because it's not our wedding day."

She has a huge grin on her face and is watching me intently like she's waiting for my reaction.

"Fuck. Did you . . . call it off?"

I don't know why that's the first thing that comes to my head, but I instantly regret the words as soon as they come out of my mouth. I shouldn't have even put the thought into the universe.

This time it's Parker who speaks. "We didn't call it off."

The gentleness in his tone makes me relax.

"Okay . . ."

I hear Beau and Claire shush each other like they can't contain themselves. They look like they're about to burst, giggling like hungry hyenas at dinner time.

My eyes return to Cass.

"It's not our wedding day," she says, taking a dramatic pause after the repetitive statement. "It's yours."

Sorry.

What?

My face must project my confusion because she points at something behind me, indicating that I should turn around.

I follow her instructions, my heart pounding in my throat as my gaze lands on Walker. He's on a single knee, looking up at me from only a few inches below my eye level with pure satisfaction on his face. His hands reach for mine, and I take them, thankful for something to keep me steady because I'm suddenly feeling shaky.

"Will you marry me today, for real?"

Everything around us blurs into my periphery, and I feel my head shake. "What do you mean? We're already married."

Walker smiles up at me, squeezing my fingers to reorient me to the situation. "Just say yes, little devil. Marry me today."

I'm not entirely sure how I reply because everything goes fuzzy, but the next thing I hear is the pop of a champagne bottle behind us. Walker's hands surround my face as he crushes his lips against mine, kissing me slowly and deliberately as our friends cheer in the background. When he finally pulls back, I have to blink a few times to confirm that I'm not in a dream.

"How did—"

The words barely leave my mouth before Walker spins me to face our friends. His arms wrap around my body, pulling me close as they rush over.

"Sorry for being so weird," Cass gushes as she glances back at Parker. "This entire thing was too stressful, and I've always thought the lake house would be the perfect wedding venue, so we decided that we would get married up there, just the two of us. When Walker found out, he worked with Parker to replan the day since everything was already paid for."

I tilt my head up to my husband, my words coming out croaky. "You did?"

He nods. "You deserve it."

My throat is thick with emotion when my eyes return to Cass. One day I'll let her know how grateful I am, and how much this means to me. But right now, all I can manage is a weak, "I love you."

"I love you more . . . Bride."

Chapter 38

Morgan

It turns out that the boys actually did have something to do this afternoon, because as soon as we finished the champagne on the helipad, they left us to run errands. I'm not sure where the others are going, but Walker told me he had to pick up a few special guests from the airport. I still have no idea how they pulled this surprise together, but it honestly couldn't have been more perfect.

"How pissed was your mom," I ask Cass as I blink in the mirror.

My makeup is full glam and not understated in the least, which is funny because it's the opposite of what my best friend would have done with this makeup artist. I've got fake lashes, shimmery shadow, and so much bronzer covering my face that I look like I just arrived home from a beach vacation.

I love it.

"She's got a huge case going on right now, so she got over it because now she doesn't have to take off work."

I smack my gloss-covered lips, turning my head to check out the intricate low bun that my hair is pulled into. Floral pearl pins accent the design, and the stylist left a few short wisps out to frame my face. I can't believe this only took her an hour—the thing is a work of art.

"Well, selfishly I'm glad you decided to elope because being a bride is way more fun than I expected."

We've spent the past three hours relaxing in the spacious bridal suite while listening to '90s country hits and getting pampered. Claire bought us all matching silk robes with feather trim to lounge around in, and if I had known this was what having a wedding could be like, I might have thought about it more seriously.

"Ready to see your dress?" Cassidy's hazel eyes swirl with delight as they meet mine in the mirror.

I nod with a nervous grin and strip down.

Because Cass is the only one who knows anything about the gown, she shoos Claire and Caroline out of the room so that I can make a grand entrance. The photographer wanted to capture the genuine reactions of my friends, and I'm crossing my fingers that this thing fits; otherwise, the only reaction I'll be getting is one of horror as I walk down the aisle in the pale pink maxi I had originally planned to wear today.

From what I could determine before the fabric was pulled over my head, the wedding dress is made of a shimmery satin that feels expensive because it's super heavy. This is definitely not a last-minute dress that they ordered from a discount shop—it's a high-quality designer gown. I shove my arms through the off-the-shoulder sleeves, sucking in my belly as Cass slides the hidden zipper all the way up the corseted bodice. Stepping into four-inch white heels to complete the look, I take a deep breath and turn to face the floor-length mirror.

My lip quivers as I take in the entire ensemble. I've never really paid much attention to wedding dresses, but if I had to choose one, this is nearly identical to what I would pick.

The gown is perfectly tailored to my body, like the designer had all of my measurements and custom made it for me. The neckline is strapless and pushes up my breasts just enough to make me feel sexy. At my waist, the fabric flares out with a high slit that shows off my legs, which look like they're a mile long thanks to the heels.

Emotion balls up in my throat because I feel so damn beautiful—I feel like a bride.

"How?" I whisper, blinking up at the ceiling to stop the tears.

Cass comes up behind me, holding my shoulders as she peers at us in the mirror with a smile. "Walker."

My brows furrow. "What do you mean?"

"He took your measurements when you were asleep to make sure they were perfect."

"Of course he did," I laugh, shaking my head. "I think the man might be developing a somno kink."

My mind starts replaying the time that he woke me up with his hand between my legs, gently rubbing me until I was on the verge of orgasm at six in the morning.

"Wait—" I snap, interrupting my thoughts. "How did you get the dress so quickly? We only made the decision to stay married, like, a month ago."

I'm pretty sure a wedding dress takes months to make. I guess in theory they could have purchased it off the rack and paid to have it altered, but even that takes time . . .

Cass winks and squeezes my shoulders. "Turns out that money talks, and we happen to know someone with a black AMEX."

I turn to face her, letting out an amused exhale. "Claire does love spending money, doesn't she?"

"It was actually Parker."

Out of everything that has almost made me cry today, those four words send me over the edge. Guilt sits heavy in my stomach as the tears start to fall, painting little tracks of amnesty down my cheeks. I don't know if he did this as penance to prove his character to me, or if it was out of the goodness of his heart, but it seems that Parker Winters isn't the villain I thought he was... he might just be the hero.

Cass grabs a tissue and hands it to me.

"I'm sorry," I sniffle, trying to contain my waterworks. "I was such a shitty friend, and I don't deserve you. I don't deserve this."

There isn't an ounce of anger, irritation, or resentment on her face. All I see is the pure love of a friend who knew that my heart was in the right place and didn't let my words impact our relationship.

She pulls me in for a hug, telling me that I shouldn't apologize and that she loves me over and over again until a knock sounds on the door.

I peek in the mirror to check my makeup, silently thanking the engineers who invented waterproof mascara because my face still looks flawless. Nobody would ever know that I had crocodile tears streaming down my face a second ago.

Nobody except... Walker?

"What happened? Are you okay?" He glares at Cass as he walks toward me in his perfectly tailored tuxedo.

I laugh, not even bothering to cover his eyes as they rake over my wedding dress. We've never done anything traditionally, so why start now?

"Down boy," I tease, shooting Cass an apologetic glance before returning my focus to my husband. "They're happy tears, I promise."

Walker lets out an audible exhale, but the worry from his stubble-covered face doesn't dissipate. He leans in and quietly says, "I intend to tell you just how incredible you look, but give me a second."

Turning to Cass, he asks, "Do you mind giving us a few minutes? Parker is outside the door and wants to speak to you as well."

"Um." She sticks her tongue in her cheek and furrows her brow. "Okay? Did something happen?"

Walker says no, but his somber expression tells a different story.

Once we're alone, we settle on the baby-blue velvet settee across the room, my body draped over his. I lean my head against his chest carefully, not wanting to get any of the ten layers of foundation on his crisp, white shirt.

"Caroline and Claire are going to be so pissed that you ruined the dress reveal," I offer, trying to diffuse his mood.

"*I'm* pissed that I ruined the dress reveal," he grumbles, tilting my chin to meet his gaze. "You look stunning, and this isn't how I wanted it to happen. Trust me."

"How did you want it to happen?"

A wistful smile forms on his lips. "With me holding back tears while you walked down the aisle."

"Yeah, right. You don't cry," I argue, trying to imagine him blubbering like those wedding videos you see on social media.

He laughs and takes my hands in his, intertwining our fingers and placing them in my lap. "You make me feel a lot of things for the first time, little devil."

A surge of emotion flows through me as he squeezes my hand affectionately. Walker may be a broody, serious man on the outside, but he has this side to him that's open and pliant, like he's soft for only me. But right now it's like he's warring with two versions of himself. The one that he's let me see over the past few months, and the one that he's had to adapt from a life of disappointment.

"What happened?" I ask quietly, looking away because I can't bring myself to face him when the other shoe drops.

I can hear his hard and obvious swallow. "Remember how Beau needed to get an extra cummerbund from Parker's house because he lost his?"

"Yeah?" I reply, feeling the tension in my shoulders ease.

This is about the formal dress code?

Beau could come to the wedding wearing sweatpants and his cat-covered scrub cap for all I care—it's really not that big of a deal.

"When he got there, he found something on the doorstep of the house . . ."

I pull back to meet his dark-brown eyes. "I didn't shit on Parker's doorstep, I promise. In January, I totally would have. But we've come around."

"I'm glad to hear that." His jaw is still tight but he lets out a laugh. "But the package on the doorstep was actually filled with documents."

"Okay . . ."

"Legal marriage documents from Nevada," he adds.

My lips tilt to the floor as I try to understand. "Why would we use Parker and Cassidy's address? I barely even know my own address."

Walker drags his gaze over my body with a pained expression, like it's the last time he's ever going to see me. When he finally focuses again, he stares for what feels like an eternity before saying, "Because we didn't actually get married that night. They did."

I can feel all of the blood drain from my face as my heart tumbles to my feet.

That can't be right.

The text messages were sent to Walker's phone number—not Parker's. Why would the venue send them to him if we weren't the ones to get married?

"Are you sure?" I challenge, not wanting him to be right. "I could totally see drunk me thinking that it would be funny to put their names down on the certificate instead of ours."

He wets his lips before responding, "We called the chapel this afternoon to confirm. They keep detailed notes on each ceremony for this specific reason, and according to them, Parker and Cassidy's phones were dead so I gave them my number instead. They left a voicemail to explain, but I deleted it the next morning like a dumbass."

I guess that makes sense as to why Walker's phone was the only one with pictures on it. When I scrolled through them the morning after, the only image that would remotely indicate a wedding took place was so blurry that you couldn't tell who was in it. And since Claire insisted we all wear white, I automatically assumed I was the one in the photo.

Clearly, I was wrong.

"So—" I pause, trying to work out what this means for us.

If Parker and Cass are the ones who got married in Vegas, that means Walker and I aren't really married. And if we aren't really married, what are we doing here today? My mind feels like it's going a million miles a minute, staring down multiple dimensions of possibilities like a tesseract.

Before I can get the next words out of my mouth, Walker speaks, "We have about an hour until guests arrive so you can take some time to think. I'll handle it either way, but I need to know what you want to do."

"Well, what do you want to do?" I ask, searching his face for a hint and finding nothing.

I know without a doubt that Walker loves me. He's made it abundantly evident over the past month in everything he does. From the way he started reading books that he knew were important to me, to the way he got a tattoo to remind himself of me, his feelings have never been more clear.

But that also doesn't mean he wants to be married again if he doesn't have to be. Sure, he was confident and annoyingly rigid in his stance after Vegas, but what if that never happened? Would we still be here?

He squeezes my hand firmly. "This isn't about me. Our relationship has always been about you, and it will always be about you. I'm not going to let my choice affect yours. If you want to get married, we'll get married. If you want to call it off, we'll call it off. Whatever you want, is what I want. And whatever you need, is what I need."

I chew on my lip, pretending to mull it over even though this is the easiest decision I've ever made.

I've always been told that marriage is the hardest thing you'll do in your life. That it will take from you, challenge you, and frustrate you. That there are no true happy endings. But if I'm being honest with myself, this past month hasn't been the hardest of my life; it's been the easiest, and I think that has a lot more to do with who my husband is, than the actual institution of marriage itself.

When I first got to know Walker, I thought he was an enigma—someone who was closed off, hard to read, and incredibly frustrating. But I've learned that his character actually boils down to a singular trait—determination.

Determination to build himself a better life.

Determination to learn from his mistakes.

And determination to make our relationship work, regardless of a title.

He's shown me that love and submission not only go hand in hand, but they go both ways. And considering I've spent my entire life putting myself first, I think it's about time that I change that. Because there's no one I'd rather submit to than Walker.

So when the words leave my mouth, they feel comforting and exciting, like I'm opening the first chapter of my favorite book I've ever read.

"I want to marry you."

Chapter 39

Walker

"Damn dude," Beau says, clapping me on the back as I wait behind a glass door for the guests to take their seats. "You clean up nice."

I sigh, sweeping my eyes over my friend's ensemble. "I'd say the same thing but your pink cummerbund looks ridiculous."

Considering Parker has a massive wardrobe, I'm genuinely shocked that he doesn't own several sets of traditional tuxedo accessories. Or maybe he does, and Beau just chose the most obnoxious one in the closet . . .

"You know what they say," he drawls, giving me an asinine smirk. "You can't say cummerbund without saying cum."

My lips purse. "I sincerely hope your jizz isn't that color."

"Wanna find out?"

I glare at him, not the least bit amused by his games.

My body feels itchy and off-kilter, like I'm coming down with a bug. I reach up to adjust my collar, trying to relieve some of the tightness in my neck, but it doesn't help.

In the past, I would have made fun of guys who couldn't control their emotions on their wedding day, but now I completely understand. Because even though Morgan and I have spent the past two months believing that we were married, that doesn't change the significance of this moment. Today we're making a conscious decision to choose each other for the rest of our lives. We're growing from our separate pasts, and building a future full of mutual promises. It's powerful and the significance of the moment isn't lost on me . . . or my body.

"Ready?" the young wedding coordinator asks.

She's fresh out of college but smart as a whip. She's been working with Parker and me to make a few changes to the original plan, and I can honestly say that I've never been more thankful to someone for taking control. We didn't know what the hell we were doing, despite my having done this once before.

When Parker and Cassidy decided they wanted to elope, he reached out to me to see if I wanted to hijack their wedding before canceling the vendors. Even though it was only a few days after Morgan and I had reconciled, I knew without a doubt that I would take him up on his offer. Because the timing was so last minute, we kept the guest list relatively small—some of her local friends, our coworkers, and her family. I probably won't know half of the people here because Cassidy handled the invitations, but if they're important to my wife, they're important to me.

"Ready," I confirm, giving the coordinator a curt nod.

The soft, classical music of Ludovico Einaudi does nothing to steel my nerves as I start to walk down the aisle covered in white rose petals. I'm so keyed up that all of the guests grinning at me appear faceless, my mind lost in a tunnel of emotion.

I turn at the front and dip my chin to Parker and his sisters in the first row, silently thanking them for everything. I never expected them to become my friends, nor would I have imagined they would become my family. And I don't think I'll ever be able to express the gratitude I feel to them for welcoming me into their lives.

Beau walks Cassidy down the aisle next, his prideful smile forcing me to swallow back the raw emotion collecting at the back of my throat. Without him, I wouldn't be here today, marrying the woman of my dreams. I've taught him how to be a surgeon, but he's taught me so much more—about seeing the good in people, keeping life fun, and most importantly about true friendship. I love the big lunatic.

He moves to stand beside me, whispering something in my ear that I don't hear because the music changes. An instrumental version of "Accidentally in Love" starts playing, and the guests stand for the bride.

For my bride.

As soon as the doors open and I see her, all of the emotion that I've been holding back finally breaks free. My hand flies to my face to stop a sob, my head shaking in disbelief because it suddenly hits me . . . I finally have something to celebrate.

Beau's reassuring hand lands on my shoulder as I look down at my shoes to try and pull myself together. I can feel the tears sliding down my cheeks, but there's no way in hell I can stop them at this point.

I force air into my lungs and find the strength to lift my head. Cassidy offers me a hazel-eyed wink of encouragement before I turn to face my girl.

She's glowing with calm confidence as she holds her brother's arm, a wide grin plastered on her flawless face. My heart feels like it's going to explode as they join me, feeling overwhelmingly lucky that she's mine.

I used to think that Morgan was a tornado of chaos. She swirled into my life and tormented me with her inescapable pull. She made me question everything I thought I knew about my future, and forced me to feel when I was hell-bent on never trying again.

But now I know that she's so much more.

She's my second chance.

She's my greatest gamble.

She's my little devil.

But she's also my loving angel.

"Who gives this woman to this man?" the officiant asks, his voice booming over the outdoor speakers.

When nobody answers, Morgan elbows her brother in the side. She asked him to walk her down the aisle because they've always had a stronger relationship than her parents, but maybe we should have done a quick rehearsal prior to the real thing.

"Uh," he responds with a hesitant cough. "I guess I do."

The audience laughs as he moves to take a seat next to his parents.

Morgan doesn't know this, but when we went to his baseball game, I asked him for her hand in marriage. I know how much he means to her, so it just felt right. She had already told him about our Vegas wedding, and while he was shocked, he couldn't have been more supportive of a traditional ceremony. He handled everything with their family and moved hell and high water to be here today. And I couldn't be more thankful because the joy on her face when they walked in this afternoon almost brought me to my knees.

It's a joy that I can't wait to witness for the rest of my life.

The officiant begins with several generic remarks on love before he informs us that we should hold hands because it's time to proceed with the declaration of intent.

I reach out and intertwine my fingers with hers as the officiant holds the microphone up for me to repeat the traditional wedding vows. "I, Walker, take you, Morgan, to be my lawfully wedded wife. To have and to hold. From this day forward. For better or for worse. For richer or poorer. In sickness and in health. 'Til death do us part."

"Thank you, Walker," the officiant says, nodding his head before he looks at the audience. "I believe you have something else you'd like to add?"

Morgan cocks a brow at me, her nose wrinkling with curiosity. I squeeze her hands, stepping closer because these words aren't for anyone else, they're just for her.

Reaching into the breast pocket of my tux, I take out the additional promises I wrote this morning while she was getting ready, and I read them.

Being a surgeon is work.
Work that I've done for
the entirety of my adult life.
Work that I took an oath to put before
anything—to love more than anything.
But today, our vows overtake that oath.
Because today I vow that the most important
work I ever do will be the work that is done
within our marriage.

It's short and simple, but it's significant—I would give it all up for her, and I want her to know that.

Her emerald eyes dance in the sun as she smiles and leans in close. "Guess this means I finally have to move in with you, huh?"

I smile back at her. "Guess so."

She steps back and looks at the officiant to signal that she's ready to say her own vows. But I barely hear her speak because all I can think about is how she's about to be my wife for real this time.

When the news about the marriage certificate broke, I wasn't sure how she would react. Of course, I knew that she loved me, but she was abundantly clear that she never intended to get married. I prepared myself for the possibility that when she was no longer bound by law to be my wife, she wouldn't be interested in me.

But her response shocked me in the very best way, just like the words that come out of her mouth after she finishes her vows.

"I actually have something to say too," she adds, looking at the officiant.

The crowd laughs as he nods in permission.

"Why am I not surprised," I tease, shaking my head in amusement as she steps forward. "You always have something to say."

Morgan rolls her eyes and reaches into her dress pocket to pull out a piece of paper with chicken scratch writing on it. "I wrote them just in case."

I've always heard that you're not supposed to
keep score in a relationship.
But every time you look at me,
I feel like I've won.
I've always heard that marriage is hard.
But with you, it has only felt easy.
I've always heard that soulmates exist.
But I never believed it
until you opened my eyes.
Because you always have been, and you
always will be, so much more than my friend.

Chapter 40

Morgan

As a self-identifying nature hater, the absolute last place I wanted to go on my honeymoon was anywhere near the woods. My ideal destination was something along the lines of an over-the-water bungalow in Bora Bora, not a tiny cabin in Blue Ridge without access to basic amenities like Wi-Fi. That being said, the past two days have been some of the most relaxing that I've had in a while. And I think Walker can say the same thing because he hasn't once mentioned work, his to-do list, or anything related to life outside of our mountainside bubble.

The knotty pine cabin he inherited from his grandfather is small, with a main living area that includes a small kitchen, a two-person dining set, and a leather couch in front of a gorgeous stone hearth. The only bedroom is a loft that's barely big enough for a king-size platform bed, though we've not been doing a ton of sleeping because we've spent a good portion of this trip naked in some form or another. And after this crazy month, an all-you-can-kink buffet is exactly what the doctor ordered.

Once we were officially married, I broke my lease and moved into Walker's house. There were a few moments when I thought he was going to lose it during the process, like when I procrastinated packing until an hour before the movers were supposed to come and started frantically tossing things into boxes.

But I married the most patient man on the planet, so he simply let out an exasperated breath and got to work.

Other than helping me unpack, Walker spent the month locked in his office as he studied for his board exams. It's the main reason we postponed the honeymoon—well, that, and because I already used my vacation days from calling out too much.

As soon as he finished his boards, we got our asses in gear and drove up to the mountains because we only had a four-day period between the exam and the start of his fellowship. The morning after we got here, at the ass crack of dawn, Beau and Claire called to tell him that he passed. At first, I thought they were in trouble because all we could hear were unintelligible screams and wild noises from their line, but they eventually got themselves together to deliver the news.

While Walker was happy about the exam results, I honestly think their call meant more to him than the actual certification. He's mentioned numerous times this weekend that he can't believe they were stalking the website for him. But I can—because that's what you do for the people you love.

We're currently curled up on the floor by the hearth, recounting our favorite parts of our wedding. The low tonight is in the sixties, so while we don't need the fire to stay warm, I asked Walker to turn it on—sometimes you have to live life for the vibes.

"Did you like the first dance song?" My husband's brown eyes reflect the glowing flames as he smiles down at me in his lap.

"How did you even know I liked Trace Adkins?"

"Beau gave me a few country artists, and I listened to their music until I found one that fit."

"And he says I can't keep a secret." I laugh and roll my eyes. "Your choice was perfect."

I never realized how sentimental Walker was, but it's quickly becoming one of my favorite things about him. When the song "Timing is Everything" started playing for our first dance, I was shocked because it's one of my all-time favorites, and I hadn't heard it in a while. But as we lazily danced in the middle of the floor, the meaning of the lyrics really hit home.

Love has the power to hurt us or heal us. But the timing has to be right for either one of those things to happen. And fortunately for us, it was.

"You wouldn't have preferred 'Hooked on a Feeling'?" he asks with an evil grin as his gaze lingers on my breasts.

I bite my lip to hide my amusement, though I hear my breath catch as my mind recalls that particular scene in vivid detail.

"What about 'Ms. New Booty'?" I suggest, adjusting myself in his lap so the robe I'm wearing falls out of the way. My decoy works like a charm because Walker hisses with arousal as his eyes travel down my spine and land on my ass.

I've been teasing him with new lingerie for the past few days, and I saved the best set for last. It's a white lace robe and corseted bodysuit with detailing so intricate that has to be handmade. And considering Claire got it for me as a wedding present, it probably is.

As soon as I came out of the bathroom wearing the outfit after dinner, Walker tried to pounce. While I was right there with him because all he put on today was a tight pair of boxer briefs that sit low on his hips and show off his swimmer's body, I enjoy making him work for his dessert. I told him that I had a surprise if he could restrain himself for an hour and sit with me by the fire. But he only made it a total of maybe ten minutes before he started trying to seduce me again.

It's been a humorous game of self-control for the two of us, with his hands slowly wandering and my gentle, though lackluster, nudges to keep him at bay. Walker is totally losing though, and if he knew about the surprise I have for him, his crumbling restraint wouldn't last a second longer.

I jiggle my ass a little bit to test the waters, and a thrill races down my spine as his cock jerks beneath me.

"Morgan," he warns, forcing his attention from my body and onto my face. His unshaven jaw is tight and his lips are thin as they roll together.

"Uh, oh," I giggle, sensing that he's nearing his breaking point. "I know what happens when you call me that."

"And yet you have a huge smile on your face."

A ripple of excitement pulses through my core. I love it when he uses his dominant voice—it's so damn hot.

"I sure do." I push myself into a kneeling position in between his legs, resting my hands on his upper thighs. "It means you want to play."

Chapter 41

Walker

Each step I take on my way down from the loft triggers a dramatic creak from the old wooden boards. While I didn't intend for it to be that way, I like that the sound is only heightening my wife's excitement for what's about to happen. It's become one of my favorite parts of our dynamic—the anticipation.

I've made her wait in all sorts of positions—sometimes in restraints, and other times simply on her knees. No matter what I do though, I always find her soaking wet and needy when I finally decide to touch her. I fucking love it, and even though she's notoriously impatient, I think she loves it too.

Tonight I intended to hold out for longer after tying her to the kitchen chair, but her bridal lingerie has been testing my limits—I can't wait a second longer to do this.

"I got you a present," I say, positioning myself behind her perfect body.

I removed the robe before tying her up but opted to leave the corset on because the fabric tapers into a thin strip at the base of her spine, giving me plenty of room to work with.

Morgan tries to turn her head to see what I'm holding, but her shoulders are flush with the back of the chair, arms straight and bound to the legs with a simple column tie. Her hips are pulled to the edge of the seat, ankles secured to her wrists—it's the perfect position for a good spanking.

I trace my fingers up her arm, watching the way her chest rises and falls beneath my touch. She's so damn responsive to me, it's incredible. I could play with her for hours, studying the way her body adjusts to each tease and toy.

"Want to know what it is?" I bend down, dusting my lips against her neck to taste her.

She swallows, arching her head into me. "Yes, Sir."

God—the formal responses never get old.

I cherish making slow, sweet love to my wife like newlyweds. I crave our rough, primal fucks like two lovers who have finally given in to each other. But this, right here, is something I fucking worship.

"Remember how you forgot to wear your wedding ring to work a few times this month?"

If we weren't in a scene, I know my wife would immediately bite back with a sassy response because that's just her nature. And while I love that side of her, I also love this side of her too—the one that makes the willing choice to submit.

"Yes. I remember, Sir."

I grin, crouching down to her eye level so that she can watch me open the custom necklace from the black velvet box.

"You won't have to worry about that anymore because I'll have the key."

Her green eyes go wide with understanding as they take in the gold choker. She dips her head in acknowledgment, and for some reason, I feel my heart swell with pride.

I pull her hair to the side, threading the metal around her neck before I clasp it in the back. The jewelry maker specializes in kink, and while these types of discrete collars are usually simple chains, I had them add a small circle the size of her wedding band to the center.

I actually didn't know much about the whole collar thing until I started diving into my kink research. It didn't seem like my thing so I didn't think twice about it, but when we started playing around with our dynamic a little more, I reached out to a guy I knew in med school hoping to get some advice.

Worth and I were about as friendly as I was with anyone back then, and he was always pretty vocal about his involvement in a local club, so I figured he might still be into it. And even though he practices in Houston now, he was more than willing to chat.

It turns out that while there are universally accepted guidelines related to safety, there's more diversity in kink than I originally thought. Hearing him explain the significance of a collar in a dominant and submissive relationship helped reframe my perspective. Yes, it's a symbol of submission and ownership, but to many people within the community, it holds the same value as a wedding band.

And just like with every scene, we'll talk about this later. If she hates it, we can figure something else out. Because although nothing about our relationship has been traditional, the commitment between us has been and always will be there.

Morgan swallows as I secure the choker with a tiny hex-screw key. "Thank you for the collar, Sir."

I sweep her hair back in place. "You're welcome. I was going to spank your ass for being so bratty earlier but I'm suddenly feeling generous. Does my wife want to come?"

"Yes, Sir."

She bites her lip hesitantly as I'm about to stand, and I furrow my brow because I notice a glimmer of mischief in her eyes. When we're in a scene, we negotiated that she would only respond to questions directly, but I can tell that she's dying to say something.

"Where are you, little devil? Do you want to keep going?"

"Green, Sir."

My brows knit. "Then what is it?"

Morgan smirks at me. Her voice is like hot honey, sweet at first but filled with a kick. "I got you something too, Sir."

My lips twitch with amusement. "You did, did you?"

She nods like she's proud of herself. "I put a plug in for you, Sir."

I cock my head—it takes a lot to surprise me, but my wife continually does it time and time again. The last thing I would have expected was for her to try this on her own.

I stand and circle her without saying anything, needing to see it for myself. I bought her an anal training kit as something to work up to once she got comfortable with my fingers, but we haven't tried it yet. Sure, we also used the hook once, but it's still much thinner than those plugs.

Without much pretense, I sink to my knees behind her and unsnap the delicate fabric between her legs that was concealing the toy. My fingers glide through her soaking pussy to her back entrance, finding the plug that she promised.

I tug on the rubber and we both groan in unison, barely able to contain our mutual arousal. I twist the outer head of the toy, watching her tight muscles grip it like a vice.

I'm about to start playing with her ass like a kid on Christmas morning when something strikes me as odd. This is definitely not the smallest size—if it was, it would have easily come out by now.

"Do you want to tell me why you have such a big plug inside of you?"

I adjust my position, reaching around her torso to press her clit with my thumb while my other hand rests protectively on the toy.

Morgan whimpers, her voice soft but still confident. "I worked up to the biggest size for you, Sir."

Fuck.

I have to bite the inside of my lip to stifle my excitement because this is the best damn present I've ever received. "And why would you do that?"

I slide two fingers inside her cunt, feeling the plug press against her inner walls. She's not lying—this is definitely the biggest size. While it's not as girthy as my cock, it's much less malleable. If she wanted to take me back there, I have no doubt that we could make it work. And honestly, given how her pussy is weeping onto my hand, we might not even need lube.

"So that we could make it fit," she answers, though the last word comes out as a cry because my fingers curl to that spot I know she loves so much.

I start circling her clit in reward, and her pussy flutters around my fingers, like it's already close to coming hard for me.

"You want me to fuck your ass tonight? You want me to finally own all of your holes so badly that you prepared the best one for me as a present, didn't you?"

Her body tries to buck as her orgasm crests but the ropes I tied to her thighs hold her in place. I slow my fingers, feeling her muscles contract around them as her screams of pleasure echo through the silent cabin. She shudders as she rides out her release, and I glide my hand over her spine to soothe her.

"Good girl," I coo, rubbing her through it.

All I can think about is how incredible it's going to feel when she comes like that with my cock in her ass.

I pull back and drop my briefs to my knees, letting my aching length fall free. I settle one hand on her hip for leverage as the other goes to my shaft, pumping a few times to alleviate the pressure before I tilt my hips. My jaw clenches as her warm pussy coats me with her cum, drenching my cock in her own natural lube. I honestly don't think she's ever been this wet for me before—my girl really does love ass play.

I notch my tip at her entrance, holding it steady as my hand goes to the plug.

"God, you're soaking me," I groan, feeling her greedy pussy trying to pull me in. "I'm going to work this out of you and then replace it with my cock. We'll go slow, I promise."

Morgan pants, her chest heaving as I grab the base of the plug.

I jiggle it slightly before slowly twisting it in a clockwise motion. The widest part starts to peek through the tight ring of muscles opening for me, and I watch in rapt amazement, surprised that her petite body can handle something so large.

I continue twisting until the toy begins to taper, making it easier to slide out of her tight ass. A gush of arousal slides down my shaft when the plug springs free, like her pussy was jealous of the attention her other hole was getting and wanted to show off.

"Turn your head to the side," I grunt, sliding my tip to her now empty back entrance. "I want to watch your pretty face twist in pleasure when you take my cock up your ass the first time."

She follows my instructions and lets out a blissful moan as my free hand reaches for her swollen clit. No matter how much she prepped for this, it's not going to be as easy as she thinks—I need her to be as relaxed as possible.

"Give me a color," I rasp, jaw clenched tight as I feed my cock into her puckered hole. I push forward half an inch. There's resistance, but not nearly as much as I was expecting.

Morgan's face screws up like it's in pain, but almost instantly relaxes like she thought it would be worse than it actually is. "Green, Sir."

"Atta girl," I praise, pressing further into her ass.

Holy fuck.

She's gripping me so tight that I almost blackout. When I make it past the first group of tight muscles, I pause to let her adjust to the sensation. Her eyes close, mouth dropping open with a whimper as my fingers rub her through it.

I widen my knees, feeling pressure start to build at the base of my spine. Once I'm all of the way in, there's no way in hell I'm going to last—this feels too damn good. But she comes first, and she always will.

I move my hand from my shaft to her chest, tugging away the lingerie to free her gorgeous tits. I don't bother with teasing. I pinch her nipple hard, rolling it between my thumb and forefinger while doing the same thing to her clit.

She cries out, her eyes flying open to meet mine as she erupts in pleasure. Her inner muscles spasm, squeezing my cock in a way that nearly makes me come on the spot.

It takes all of my control to wait until her orgasm dulls before I press forward again. Both of my hands settle on her hips for leverage, and I dig my fingers into the skin at the crease as I watch her come down from her high.

"Ready?"

Morgan's lips tilt into a satiated smile. "Ready for you to fuck my ass, Sir."

Satisfaction swirls through me as I give her a crisp nod and press forward. My grip tightens on her hips as I impale her with my cock, feeling her open for me fully. I let out a noise that sounds somewhere between a growl and a purr as I feel her tight muscles clamp down.

"Fuck," I groan, not daring to move. "Are you trying to come again for me? Does simply having my cock in your ass push you over the edge?"

Her eyes fall to the floor and she nods, dragging her lower lip through her teeth like she's embarrassed by the truth.

I lean forward and cover her back with my chest, pressing my forehead to the side of her face as a sudden rush of sentimentality hits me.

"I can't believe I ever thought you were my nightmare, little devil. You are the best goddamn dream that I've ever had."

Sliding out of her halfway, I hammer back in until we both find our release. As I'm holding my wife tight, I know one thing without a doubt—this is a dream that I never want to wake up from.

Epilogue

Morgan

> Want to go to the Braves game this weekend?

I laugh, checking my phone as I search the supply room for a pair of XXL grippy socks. The space is well organized, but I swear the people who stock it change the layout every day.

Walker started his sports medicine fellowship two weeks ago, and I've already gotten far too many texts like this. I have no idea what he's doing all day since he doesn't have a call requirement, but it's safe to say that it's way less stressful than residency.

> Who are they playing?

He immediately responds back.

> The Dodgers.

I literally squeal to myself.

> Hell yeah. Fuck the Dodgers.
>
> We want Freddie back.

Walker isn't as big of a baseball fan as I am, but he's started to pay more attention to it because of his new job. His hospital is officially contracted with most of the professional leagues in Atlanta, so they handle anything surgical that comes up like Tommy John surgery or . . . other orthopedic things. He's tried to educate me on the nuances of his role, but it usually goes in one ear and out the other. I love him, but you can only listen to someone drone on about fractures for so long before you tune them out.

> I have no idea who that is.

I finally find the socks on the top shelf and have to jump to grab them. I type out a reply before leaving the supply room.

> Psh—and you call yourself a fan.
>
> I'll educate you tonight on the lore of the 2021 postseason.

As I'm closing the door, Marisa calls to me from across the hallway. "Morg—I've got an admission for you."

She looks suspiciously hesitant, and I pinch the bridge of my nose. Today has been such a good day. Why do I have a feeling that it's about to get a lot worse?

"Nice necklace, by the way," she says, greeting me with a nervous smile. "I've never noticed it, but I love it."

"Thanks." I try to look annoyed even though I'm a compliment hoe and appreciate the sentiment.

I think Walker expected me to hate the collar because he's asked me about it multiple times since the honeymoon. But I keep telling him that it's perfect.

Jewelry has never been my thing, so when he first showed it to me, I was confused. The delicate gold chain and simple ring at the center didn't seem like something I would wear, but as soon as he locked it onto my neck and kept the key, everything made sense.

I actually prefer it to my wedding ring now because the cool metal sits flush against my neck, and I know that I won't lose it if I have to scrub my body after a long shift. I don't even notice it anymore, but I love that it's become a part of me and serves as a constant reminder of our dedication to one another.

Marisa pulls me into the quiet corner where we keep our rolling equipment. "So this patient . . ."

I groan dramatically. "Please don't tell me that you're giving them to me because nobody else can handle it. You do remember what happened last time, right?"

Just because a nurse *can* handle something, doesn't mean they *should* always—I don't know how many times I have to tell our managers that.

"This patient specifically asked for you, actually. Can you, uh, go now?" she asks, voice going up an octave.

The fuck?

I feel the wheels in my head start to turn as I try to determine who the hell knows me well enough to ask for me by name. I don't usually take the frequent flyers, mostly because my tolerance for their bullshit is slim, and I always get *"fired."*

I glance over at an open workstation across from us. "What room? I'll pull up the chart and then go."

Her eyes dart around quickly, looking anywhere but at me. "They're not in the system but they're in eight."

"Okay, weirdo," I reply with a concerned laugh. "Well, can you please give these socks to Cass? She asked for them, like, ten minutes ago."

My bestie was busy running around in search of the vein finder and caught me while I was charting. Since we match our schedules to work the same days, we've gotten good at reading each other. I could tell she was stressed, so I asked what I could do to help. Even though grabbing socks for a patient is pretty much the easiest thing, little assists like that help you focus on the bigger stuff.

I hand the socks to our charge nurse and make my way to the room, not entirely sure how to prepare for what I'm about to walk into. It could be anything from a lady with a potato stuck inside her pussy, to a dude about to code from septic shock—you never know what you're going to get in this place.

My mouth falls open when I slip into the small room, because what I actually see stuns me into silence.

Weston Southerland is sitting in a chair across the room with a baby in his arms—a real-life baby that looks almost identical to Cassidy with white blonde hair and hazel eyes. I don't know much about childhood development, but the little dude isn't a newborn and he isn't a toddler.

What in the actual fuck?

"Morgan," he says my name with a calm, relaxed tone that instantly pulls me out of my daze. "I need you to do a few things for me. Starting with keeping this quiet."

"Sorry," I reply, though I'm not sure why I'm apologizing. "What, uh, whose baby is that?"

I can't take my eyes off the child. He's like a miniature version of my best friend. My mind feels like it's going ninety miles an hour down the freeway, and before Weston can respond, I blurt, "It's not Cassidy's, is it?"

He legitimately laughs, though it's tinged with tangible stress. "No, he isn't Cassidy's baby. He's mine."

Duh, you dumbass. Don't you think you would have noticed if she was pregnant?

My heart slows slightly in relief as I step forward and crouch in front of the kid.

"What happened?"

"I was changing him and walked across the room for a second to get a new packet of wipes. He's a stubborn little man, and I think he wanted to see what I was doing. When I turned back around he had fallen off the table. I feel like a piece of shit and have no fucking clue what I'm doing, but I'm pretty sure he broke his clavicle."

I know he and Cass have a complicated history, and there was all that stuff with Parker, but it's hard to dislike this guy. His hazel eyes are soft and warm, and I can tell he's terrified inside, but he's schooled at controlling his emotions like all surgeons are. I would have helped him regardless, but now I genuinely want to.

I reach out and stroke the baby's soft forehead. He doesn't look distressed—not the way I would be if I had a broken bone.

"Did you check his vitals?"

"They're normal."

"Why not take him to the children's hospital?"

I'm not trying to be judgmental, I'm just genuinely confused because I'm not sure why he would come here when we have several pediatric hospitals in Atlanta. Technically, we're all certified in pediatric advanced cardiac life support, but I can't tell you the last time I saw a baby here. I also have no idea why he would ask for me. Not only is my best friend way better with kids than I am, but she's the one with a relationship to him... well, an ex-relationship.

"My parents were worried that it would get out that their disappointment of a son had a child out of wedlock. Nobody knows."

I blink a few times, trying to understand but coming up with nothing. Why would a thirty-something-year-old guy give a shit what his parents think?

Swallowing back the words I want to say, I ask, "What do you need from me? Do you want me to call Cass? She's here today."

"No, she's made it more than clear that she's not interested in talking to me anymore. We just need to get a scan. Can you call Walker? I know general bone shit but need him to take a look."

I wince, wishing this had happened a month earlier. "He already started his fellowship at UH. Do you want me to page whoever's on call for ortho?"

"No. It has to be someone who will keep things under the radar." His tone is more curt now as he purses his lips, thinking through what he wants to do. "Page Parker."

"I don't—"

His face is tight with worry but his words are steady. "Page Parker."

I nod, squeezing the baby's tiny fingers in mine. Fortunately, there's a computer in the room, so I stand and quickly log in.

For a second I wonder why Wes doesn't just send him a page directly, but then I realize that he clearly wasn't working today because he's in running shorts and a lightweight T-shirt.

Less than a minute after I send the message, I get a call to my work phone. "This is Morgan."

"What's going on? I'm on my way."

I can feel my stomach twist. Glancing over at Wes, he simply nods like he's giving me the go-ahead to explain the situation to Parker.

The problem is . . . I'm not entirely sure he's going to come if I tell him the truth. We squashed our own beef, but he's still Parker Winters—the man isn't exactly known to be the most emotionally intelligent and forgiving person in the world.

I chew on my lip, trying to come up with an angle.

"Hello?" Parker's tone isn't harsh, but it isn't exactly pleasant either.

"Sorry," I reply, hoping what I'm about to say works. "Remember everything we talked about in Vegas? How you love Cass, and how you'd do anything for her, and how she's made you a better person?"

I don't look over at Wes, but I can feel his eyes boring into me because he knows exactly what I'm doing. They both love her, and there's no doubt that she loves both of them. If anyone can bridge the gap, it's Cassidy. Well, her, and a cute-ass baby.

"What?" A sound pings over the phone as Parker asks, "Is everything okay? I'm about to get on the elevator."

"I'll see you in a second." I hang up, cutting him off from asking any additional questions.

DR. FELLOW

I glance at Wes. "You're sure?"

He dips his chin, staring past me like he's preparing for battle. Dread pools in my body as we wait in uncomfortable silence.

Less than a minute later, Parker slides open the door. His midnight-blue eyes find mine first before they scan the room and land on Weston. I watch him, trying to discern his expression but nothing changes, not even a tick of his jaw or a pulse of that throbbing vein Claire is always talking about.

It's so quiet that you can hear the hum of the air conditioner above us, and my sweaty palms reach up to fiddle with my necklace, nervously waiting for the bomb that I dropped to explode.

Only it doesn't.

Parker slides his hands into his navy scrub pockets and calmly turns to face me. I swallow, preparing to be chewed out.

"I—"

"Morgan, can you please give us a moment?"

I cock my head to make sure I heard him correctly. When the fuck have I ever heard this man say please?

"Uh—"

"Morgan."

"Fine," I concede. My eyes pinball between the two of them to make sure they understand that I'm not joking when I say, "But don't kill each other, or I'm going to be seriously pissed."

I glare at Parker to make sure he knows that my threat is mostly directed at him, but he's already crossing the room.

Shutting the sliding door behind me, I press my back against the glass, wishing that it was thinner so that I could eavesdrop on their conversation. I close my eyes for a moment, my breaths coming easier now that the air isn't swirling with tension.

Cassidy startles me, bumping my hip like she always does. "Hey, Boo. Thanks for the socks."

I let out a nervous giggle. "No problem."

Her head cocks suspiciously. "You good?"

"Yep." I look down at my Hokas, knowing that if I meet her eyes there's going to be a problem. Not only do I suck at controlling my facial expressions, but Cass can read me like a damn book. "Never better."

I shift my feet and wait for her to walk away, but her black Danskos remain planted next to mine.

"Have you seen Parker? I noticed him speed by, and he looked off."

"Nope." I roll my lips to stop my mouth from saying anything else.

"Is this your new patient? Marisa said you were busy in here. Do you need help?"

What I need is for my best friend to walk away so that I don't spill the fucking beans.

"I'm good."

She doesn't move, so I give her my best fake smile.

It doesn't work.

Her arms cross as she glances at the room number. "Why is there no name on the door?"

This bitch should work for the FBI.

When a patient is admitted, the first thing we do is put their name on the door because it's something the administration audits. I've gotten a stern talking to by managers once or twice for not following the ridiculous policy. But seriously, in what world does it make sense to take the time to find an Expo marker when a patient is in distress?

"I don't know, Cass, chill. It's fine. Everything is fine in there."

The faint sound of a baby crying interrupts me, and I see my best friend's hazel eyes go wide. "Was that—"

All of the blood in my body rushes to the surface, prickling my skin with tension. "Nope."

I sidestep to protect the entrance to the room.

Cass is only four inches taller than me, but it feels like she's towering over me and shooting daggers into my soul. The saying *"God gives his toughest battles to his strongest soldiers,"* is bullshit because I'm definitely the weakest link here, and we both know it.

I don't wait for our war of wills to continue—I wave the white flag.

"Weston and Parker are in there," I state simply, hoping she'll understand and let them handle their shit.

And under normal circumstances, she probably would have. But I forgot about one tiny little thing—she heard a baby cry.

She pushes past me and into the room, stopping abruptly just inside the door.

I swear to God, everything feels like it happens in slow motion.

Parker is standing next to the hospital bed with his hand resting on the baby's back. The tiniest hint of a smile crosses his face as Weston finishes saying something, though it grows even wider when he realizes that we're in the room.

His midnight-blue eyes land on Cassidy, brimming with love and adoration.

"His name is Carter."

Bonus Scene

Morgan

"You know when I said that I would be your sex slave for the weekend, it was a joke right?"

Walker glances over at me with a look that's anything but funny. "Was it? Too bad."

I bite the inside of my cheek as a wave of anticipation washes over me. After Vegas, I would have offered anything to convince him to divorce me, including this particular sexual scenario. But now that we've been happily married for a month, I see no reason to revisit past promises that I made . . . especially not when I've been abnormally sassy toward my husband today, and I can tell he's itching to punish me for it.

"What if we just enjoyed our time at the cabin?" I suggest, staring out the window of Walker's Jeep Grand Cherokee as we drive up the dark gravel road. "You know, read some books. Relax."

He chuckles darkly. "It will be relaxing. For me."

I roll my eyes even though he can't see it because the space between us is pitch black. "Sounds like a blast."

Walker's voice drops low, seamlessly transitioning into the dominant man that makes my body sing with pleasure. "Keep up the attitude, little devil. You won't like what happens next."

"I feel like I'm already not going to like what happens next." I swallow as he parks the car in front of our mountain house.

He turns to look over at me, his stern face illuminated by the porch lights. "Traffic system still applies this weekend. I'll check in occasionally, but if the dynamic gets to be too much, use red and we'll come out of it completely. Are you ready to play?"

My core clenches involuntarily at his question.

"Yes, Sir."

His pupils flare at my response, and he nods once. "Grab the black bag in the trunk and change into the outfit I packed for you. Don't touch the other toys inside. I'm going to have a soak in the hot tub, but I expect to find you kneeling for me in front of the fireplace when I'm done."

I bite back a sassy response about how I'm not surprised that he wants me to wait for him. "Whatever you want, Sir."

A slight smile cracks on his lips as he jerks his chin to the door, indicating that I should get my ass moving.

When Walker left for the hospital this morning, he told me that he would pick me up on his way home. I never got a good look at what he was bringing, but when I loaded my tote into the car this evening there were several bags already taking up half the trunk. I assumed that they were to stock the house since he hasn't been up here much since he inherited it from his grandfather. But given the contents of the small duffel when I open it, I'm now slightly suspicious that my husband is planning on turning this cabin into our personal sex retreat.

Along with the black bra and panty set that I place on the bathroom counter, there are a slew of unopened toys tossed into the bottom of the bag. I like to think that I'm pretty aware of kink, but there are some toys in here that I've never even heard of.

Like what the hell is a nipple sucker? And why does it look like a torture device?

Zipping the duffel back up, I decide to let the rest of the toys be a surprise and toss the bag on the tile floor. I shrug out of my oversized T-shirt and running shorts, run my fingers through my hair, and blow myself a kiss in the mirror before I begin to figure out how to put the lingerie set on.

The black underwear looks simple enough, though once I hike it up my legs, I realize that it is both crotchless and assless. The only part of me that's actually covered by the thin leather is my waist—the rest is a complex contraption of thin strips that cross through my legs and outline my ass. I can understand why he bought the panties—they match the bra I'm about to put on—but it would honestly make more sense to stay naked because there's nothing left to the imagination here.

My eyes go wide as I unfold the bra because tiny silver tacks line the inside of the fabric. They're not as pointed as a pushpin, but they're definitely not soft and fluffy either.

I briefly consider claiming that it doesn't fit me properly, but then I remember that Walker had my measurements taken for my wedding dress only a few months ago—he would know I'm full of shit.

I slide the straps up my arms and press the bra against my chest to test it before I fasten the band. The metal tacks dig into my breasts, but surprisingly, none of them break the skin. They provide a tolerable thorn of pain that goes straight to my low belly, similar to the sensation of nipple clamps.

When I secure the leather lingerie to my chest, I look in the mirror. You would never know that this set was modified to be a kinky torment device. It makes me look sexy and would probably be something I wear under an outfit for a night out if it weren't for the sting of discomfort that prickles my tits with every breath.

Sometimes I wonder where the hell he finds this stuff. Does he have some sort of personal BDSM shopper who orders things for him? Does he spend his free time scouring the internet for toys that will torture me? If so, I need to tell him to redirect his focus to something more productive—like cleaning the house.

I walk out of the bathroom and into the living room, noticing that the fire is already on and blazing. Our bags are lined up on the stairs to the loft, so Walker must already be out by the hot tub. Considering it's August, I doubt he's going to stay out there for long, which is good because I get bored incredibly easily when he makes me sit around like this.

My least favorite part of our dynamic is the waiting. There are just too many things going on in my mind to be able to remain still for more than a few minutes. The only way that I'm able to stay in place for longer than that is if he physically restrains me. Which he didn't.

Too bad.

After five minutes of boredom, I begin to get antsy. The pricks of pain against my chest are heightening my anticipation, but I need something to occupy my mind while I wait.

I jump to my feet and grab my phone from the counter, deciding to read while he finishes his soak.

Is this technically against the rules we've negotiated?

Yes—I'm supposed to kneel quietly without any distractions.

But the fireplace has a direct view of the back door, so I'll be able to tell when he's coming and slide my phone beneath the cowhide rug like nothing ever happened.

Work smarter, not harder.

I'm halfway through a spicy chapter in a secret society romance when I hear the doorknob jingle. My heart nearly jumps through my throat as I fumble to conceal my phone and assume the proper position.

I keep my eyes glued to the flickering flames like a good little submissive as Walker closes the door with a thud. He slowly pads across the wooden floor, the deliberate nature of his steps sending shivers down my spine.

His bare feet stop directly in front of me, and I can feel the heat of his gaze scorching my skin. I inhale sharply, wincing from the spikes prodding against my sensitive nipples.

"Looking a little flushed there. Something got you worked up?"

I don't dare look up at him, though I want to more than anything. I'm dying to take in my husband and his deliciously chiseled body. Not that he wasn't fit before . . . but with the extra time from his fellowship, the man has become toned as hell. It's nearly impossible to stop myself from hopping on him every chance I get.

"The outfit, Sir."

That's partially true—I am squirming with need from the custom lingerie. But I also just read a wild scene that involved a forced enema, and now I'm wondering if I've unlocked a new kink because I can feel some serious wetness pooling between my thighs.

Walker tuts his tongue like I'm in trouble and moves out of my view.

I can feel my heart beat a little faster, wondering what he has planned.

"Brats get punished," he muses from behind me. "But liars get tortured."

There's no way he knows . . .

His warm chest presses against my back, almost like he's assumed the same position as me with his thighs caging mine in. His fingers dust my collarbone and pull my hair back to expose my neck.

Hot breath simmers against my jaw as he leans closer.

"So which one are you, little devil? A brat, or a liar?"

I swallow nervously but decide to hedge my bet. "I think you know the answer to that question, Sir."

Walker chuckles darkly in my ear. "I want to hear you say it."

I bite back the urge to roll my eyes. "A brat, Sir."

"Interesting," he muses thoughtfully. "Kneel up."

Without thinking, I rise from my heels so that I'm standing on my knees. We've worked on submissive positions over the past few weeks, and I immediately knew what he was referring to when he gave the command. Though, the only time we've used this one is during training, so I have no idea what he intends to do with me now that I'm in it.

He taps the inside of my thigh, indicating that I should widen my legs. I shift, opening myself up for him as his touch skates across my skin and toward my exposed pussy.

I nearly moan and drop my head back when he slides a single finger inside of me. I didn't realize how needy I was feeling until I finally got a little bit of relief.

"You're telling me that my wife's cunt is this wet from just a little pain? From waiting for me like a good girl and nothing else?"

My breath catches as his finger presses into the spot at the front of my sex that I love, holding it steady as he waits for me to respond.

"Yes, Sir."

As soon as the words are out of my mouth, he slips out of me and steps back. The sudden movement forces me off balance. I have to catch myself with my hands to avoid falling on my face and impaling myself with my lingerie.

"Don't move," Walker growls as I attempt to return to my knees. "Actually... kneel down."

I hesitate, remembering that the position he's requesting is only used for one thing—punishment.

"Now." His voice is low and stern, vibrating through me with tense anticipation.

I cross my wrists and slowly slide my arms forward until my chest touches the smooth wooden floor. The only difference between this and child's pose is that my ass is up in the air and not pressed against my feet.

Because my forehead is pressed against the ground, I can't see what's about to happen. But if I had to guess, he's going to pretend to be intimidating and dominant for a while before ultimately giving in and making me come—the man just can't help himself.

I smile as I hear him walk away, dig through something, and then return. I wonder which toy from the duffel bag he chose to grab—hopefully something that vibrates.

"That won't do," he mutters to himself like he's not happy with my position.

A heavy weight falls on my upper back and pins me to the floor. I cry out as the sharp points of my bra dig into my sensitive flesh, shooting bullets of pain through my body.

"Better."

If I had to guess, I'd assume that he's holding me in place with his foot. There's no use trying to fight him—not only is he overpowering in sheer size, but I know he won't let up.

"Now tell me," he rasps, dragging something hard down my spine. "Why did you lie to me?"

"I didn't—" I start, arguing on instinct because the added pressure on my tits is distracting as hell.

A sharp sting lands across the center of my ass and explodes through my lower half. Instead of the sensation transforming to arousal like anything he's used with me before, it's more intense. I normally look forward to his spankings, but I can already tell that this is different—it's going to hurt.

"Try that again, little devil. I already know that you're lying, so I suggest you tell the truth from now on to make this punishment better for you. Otherwise, there's no way in hell you'll be able to sit for the rest of the weekend."

I don't ask how he found out what I was doing because it doesn't really matter. He knows, and I'm about to be reminded of what happens when I play around with my husband in dominant form.

"I got bored, Sir," I answer. "I didn't know how long you would be, so I occupied my time with a book."

Walker snarls and digs the pointed end of whatever he used to mark me into my skin. "Was that what I asked you to do?"

I swallow, attempting to focus as he gently rubs the area that he prodded. "No, Sir."

"What did I ask you to do?"

His foot pushes me further into the ground, and I honestly don't know what's worse—the sharp stab of the metal on my chest or the searing sting of the toy on my ass.

"Kneel by the fire and wait for you, Sir."

"Hmmm." He trails the device down my thigh and back up, resting it at the crease of my ass. "I think my cane needs to remind you what this weekend is about."

Before I can respond, he swats me hard across both cheeks.

"You're my slave."

Swat.

"You don't get bored."

Swat.

"You exist purely for my pleasure."

Swat.

"Do you understand me?"

I can feel tears spilling from my eyes. The pain isn't bad enough to force me to use our safeword, but it's definitely enough to make me rethink doing this again.

I tend to test my husband's limits when we go into our dynamic—I like to get a rise out of his practiced patience, to remind him that he has to earn my submission. But he's become more and more creative with his punishments, and I think he might have just found the thing that will earn my compliance.

"Yes, Sir," I whimper, hearing the cane drop to the floor with a clatter.

Walker steps off my back, giving me a moment of relief. I take a heavy breath which quickly transforms into a needy sigh when he slides a finger through my wetness.

"Still so fucking drenched after that punishment. I thought it was effective, but maybe I was wrong. What do you think, little devil? I'm open to feedback."

"I didn't like it, Sir."

He moves to my clit and begins to slowly circle the bundle of nerves. I squirm beneath his touch because despite the pain still radiating from the spanking, I need him more than ever.

"I didn't either," he says, almost low enough that I can't hear him. "I much prefer giving you pleasure, but you like to test me, don't you?"

"Yes, Sir," I reply, though I definitely won't be testing him as often now that I know he owns a goddamn cane.

Walker starts stroking the spot that always sends me over the edge, and I feel my body instinctively arch into him.

"Do you think you deserve to come?"

The answer is obviously yes, but I know that's not what he wants to hear—he wants to hear that I learned my lesson.

"No, Sir."

"No, you don't," he tuts. "But I do."

In one swift movement, Walker picks me up and tosses me over his shoulder. He takes a few long strides before gently lowering me to my back on the wooden kitchen table. His grip hooks beneath my arms and he pulls me toward him with so much force that my head falls off the edge.

I try to adjust my body positioning to support my neck, but he holds me in place with one hand as the other reaches for the towel wrapped around his waist.

His hard cock springs free, falling directly in front of my mouth. Walker steps forward and paints my pursed lips with his glistening precum before he pauses.

"Grab my legs and open those pretty little lips," he pants, reminding me of our nonverbal safeword. "I'm about to fuck your face. Hard."

Because of the angle of my neck, my mouth automatically falls open as I reach back to rest my hands on his upper thighs. My eyes have a direct view of his heavy balls as he slides his shaft across my tongue.

I open my throat, breathing through my nose to take him as deep as I can. He makes it halfway before he pauses like he's waiting for me to protest. I close my lips around his length, feeling my arousal surge at his possession.

"Atta girl," he coos, pulling back slightly before pushing further into me. "You take my cock so well, little devil."

A rush of pride flows through me, and I do my best to avoid gagging as he increases his pace, pumping shallow thrusts down my throat. Because of the slight curve in his shaft and the angle of my head, I could probably handle it if he wanted to slide deeper, but he restrains himself.

His fingers wrap around my throat and create just enough pressure to make me squirm while his other hand trails down my belly toward my pussy. When he reaches my clit, he doesn't rub. He simply keeps a tormenting pressure on the sensitive spot while he begins to fuck my face.

I buck my hips to get some friction which only makes him slide further inside me. This time I gag at the intrusion, trying to catch my breath around his cock.

"Behave," he warns.

I attempt to respond with a garbled insult, but he distracts me by pinching my clit between two fingers. A wave of pleasure shoots through me, redirecting my natural deviance to desperate compliance. All I want in this moment is to come, and I'd do just about anything to get that sweet release.

Walker's fingers slip inside me and pump at the same pace as his cock, owning my body. I can feel myself climbing, coming dangerously close to my own orgasm despite this being just for him.

He groans and slows his tempo. "That's it. Take all of my cum like a good little fuck slave."

His fingers curl into my G-spot almost instinctively as he spurts warm liquid down my throat.

I swallow him down, trying to arch my hips to get some relief. If he had lasted only a few seconds longer, I would have exploded along with him. But instead, I'm frustrated and needier than ever.

He strokes the line of my jaw tenderly before he pulls out of my mouth and spins me to a seated position.

"You didn't come, did you?" His eyes are swirling with a dark hunger that looks like it hasn't been remotely satiated.

I blink up at him, confused by the question. "No, Sir."

"Good." He smirks, clearly pleased with my answer for some reason. "Because I'm going to edge the fuck out of you all weekend, little devil. Welcome to your own delicious hell."

Acknowledgments

To my readers – It baffles me every single day that you have stuck around to make it to this one. Thank you for seeing my potential. Thank you for encouraging my love of kink. And thank you for supporting the stories of healthcare workers. This is such a special community and the only reason that this isn't goodbye is because of you. I've had the time of my life, and I can't wait to keep making memories with you.

To Mallory, Katie, and Taylor – Thank you for drudging through the trenches with me on this one. You made this book into something that I am immensely proud of. I know it wasn't always comfortable for you (particularly chapter 34), but I am truly grateful for your time and input. Wanna do it again in a few months?

To my beta team – Allanah, Dani, Sabra, Sacha, Alli, Morgan, Haley, and Andrea – Thank you for picking me up from the floor when I debated throwing away this manuscript. Your enthusiasm and excitement for this release have made the sleepless nights worth it.

To Sadie – This book would not exist without you, not just because you forced me to write Walker and Morgan's story, but because you talked me off the ledge weekly. You are so much more than my editor—you're my sounding board, my hype queen, and one of my favorite people in the world. One day we'll go to that conference together (even if we keep it a secret from Parker . . . because we know how much he loves that).

To Team Daddies – May you be immortalized in a book that tens of people read. I am so thankful for our friendship and for being your kink club leader.

To Lemmy – I would fall apart without you. You make my life a thousand times easier, and I am so grateful for your perspective, humor, and friendship. Keep dreaming those big dreams, little devil—I have no doubt that you can achieve them.

To Andy – Once again, all of the best parts of Walker come from you. Thank you for sharing your failures, your successes, and your stories with me. You are what every physician, husband, and friend should aspire to be—a role model.

To Brad and Blair – Thank you for loving me since I was eighteen and running around your fraternity house with a Franzia bag. I could not have written this book without your vulnerability, and I feel so thankful that our friendship always picks up where it left off. I know that these past few years haven't been easy, but I truly believe that there are better things ahead for both of you. (Ladies – Brad is single and lives in NYC. Hit him up!!)

To Rachel – Thank you for keeping Lexie a secret from our parents. Thank you for inspiring me to become a nurse. And thank you for helping me with this book. I'm so proud of you and could not be more excited about your new love story—you deserve it.

To Emily – You are an incredible mom, but an even more incredible friend. When I think of ride-or-die people in my life, you are one of the first people that comes to mind. I'm so glad that we met. H-Town forever!

To my husband – There are several days when I wonder if you truly are a fictional man because you have inspired my favorite parts of each of my characters—the deliberate control of Parker, the golden retriever likability of Beau, and the practiced patience of Walker. Thank you for supporting my dreams, and for shouldering all of the burdens that come along with it. I love you endlessly.

To Walker and Morgan – You challenged me. You irritated me. You broke me down more times than I would like to admit. But you also rebuilt me. Because for the first time in my writing career, I had fun. Morg, thank you for allowing me to put a completely unrestricted version of myself into a character. It was a damn blast. Walkie, thank you for giving me a platform to talk about divorce in healthcare, but also for surprising me with the depth of your character. You still intimidate the hell out of me, but you'll forever hold a special place in my heart because I finally felt like a writer when I was putting you onto paper. I'll see the two of you soon.

About the Author

Lexie Woods is a registered nurse who writes steamy medical romance novels from the comfort of her air conditioned home in Texas. With approximately 20 failed ADHD hobbies sitting in the graveyard of her attic, her husband is hopeful this might finally stick. When she's not questioning her friends about their most unhinged fantasies, she can be found floating in her backyard pool with a margarita in hand.

Connect with me on Social Media:
Instagram – @lexiewoods_author
Facebook Reader Group – Pages from LexieLand

Made in the USA
Middletown, DE
30 January 2025

70534557R00229